INTO THE DARK

R.D. BRADY

vinci
BOOKS

BY R.D. BRADY

The A.L.I.V.E. Series
A.L.I.V.E.
D.E.A.D.
R.I.S.E.
S.A.V.E.
Into the Cage
Into the Dark

The Nola James Series
Surrender the Fear
Escape the Fear
Tackle the Fear
Return the Fear

The Belial Series
The Belial Stone
The Belial Library
The Belial Ring
The Belial Recruit
The Belial Children
The Belial Origins
The Belial Search
The Belial Guard
The Belial Warrior
The Belial Plan
The Belial Witches
The Belial War
The Belial Fall
The Belial Sacrifice

Vinci Books

vinci-books.com

Published by Vinci Books Ltd in 2024

1

Copyright © R.D. Brady 2022

The author has asserted their moral right to be identified as the author of this work in accordance with the Copyright, Designs and Patents Act 1988
This work is a work of fiction. Names, characters, places and incidents are the product of the author's imagination or are used fictitiously. Any resemblance to actual persons, living or dead, places and incidents is entirely coincidental.
All rights reserved. No part of this publication may be copied, reproduced, distributed, stored in any retrieval system, or transmitted in any form or by any means, including photocopying, recording, or other electronic or mechanical methods, nor used as a source for any form of machine learning including AI datasets, without the prior written permission of the publisher.
The publisher and the author have made every effort to obtain permissions for any third party material used in this book and to comply with copyright law. Any queries in this respect should be brought to the attention of the publisher and any omissions will be corrected in future editions.
A CIP catalogue record for this book is available from the British Library.
Paperback ISBN: 9781036700331

Printed and bound in Great Britain by Clays Ltd, Elcograf S.p.A.

PROLOGUE

CLEARWATER, FLORIDA

JUNE 20, 1997

The laughter of Shelly Crumb's children drifted through the kitchen door as she placed the frying pan back in the lower cabinet. Straightening, she leaned against the countertop as she finished drying the last mug.

With a happy sigh that the chore was done, she placed the now-dry mug on the countertop and filled it with coffee. More laughter slipped in through the kitchen doorway. Her heart lifting, she smiled. She'd worried they were growing apart, but these last twenty-four hours had changed all of that.

Her coffee mug warm in her hand, she headed to the living room. As she stopped in the doorway, she leaned against the doorframe. Sipping her coffee with a smile, she watched the miracle unfold: Her eight-year-old son, Luke, and her twelve-year-old daughter, Sandy, played happily together on the living room rug. There was no arguing. No one yelled at the other to go away, though in fairness that was usually Sandy's request, not Luke's. Luke still adored his big sister. Sandy, however, was fast approaching the dreaded teenage years.

But today, she still looked like Shelly's little girl as she rolled the strange silver ball toward her brother. Luke stopped it with a grin before rolling it back to his sister. They'd found the sphere in the woods just yesterday and had come running back to the house all excited. Shelly had trekked into the woods with them to look at it. It was perfectly round, like a bowling ball, and about the same size.

A tree had uprooted, revealing the sphere, which meant it had been there for a while. Shelly thought it might actually be a cannonball from Renaissance-era Spanish colonizers. She had taken pictures of the object and dropped them off at the university's history department to see if anyone had any answers. She hadn't heard anything yet, so she supposed it was possible it was nothing. Even so, she knew this was definitely not a normal cannonball.

Sandy, who had her father's brown hair while Luke shared Shelly's pale blonde, stood up. "Let's see if it follows us again."

Luke jumped to his feet and hurried to Sandy's side. The two of them walked toward the front door.

The silver ball, which had been rolling in the opposite direction, slowed and then switched directions on its own, following them.

The kids burst into laughter. "It worked. It worked!" Luke cried, clapping his hands.

It was an odd trick of the ball, and probably the reason the history department hadn't called her back. Shelly wasn't sure exactly why it did the things it did, but it must be some sort of new technology or kids' toy or something. If this was going to be on the shelves at Christmastime, they were lucky to have gotten one early.

But how it ended up in the woods near her house, she had

no idea. Maybe it was dropped by someone engaged in corporate espionage. She nearly laughed out loud at the idea, her imagination spinning away from her.

A knock sounded at the door. Shelly looked up. Sandy was closest to the door and hurried over to it. Peaking through the glass panel next to it, she said, "Mom, it's a guy in a uniform."

Placing her mug on the dining table, Shelly frowned as she hurried across the room. "A uniform?"

"There's a cable truck out there too," Sandy said.

Had she gotten a notice about a visit? She couldn't remember seeing one. Maybe her husband arranged it and forgot to mention it? That would be just like him. She shooed the kids back as she stepped to the door.

Sandy grinned as she squatted down and, with a grunt, picked up the silver ball to cart it back to the other side of the room.

Shelly opened the door as the kids sat back down.

A tall African American young man in a dark-blue cable uniform stood there.

"Can I help you?" Shelly asked.

"Mrs. Crumb?" he asked.

"Yes?"

"Morning, ma'am. I'm Carl from the cable company. We've had a number of outages in the neighborhood, and they sent us out to make sure that your system is all right."

Shelly glanced over her shoulder at the kids, who had once again resumed their game with the ball. "I think we're okay."

"Have you tried your TV recently?"

She shook her head. "No, actually, we haven't."

"Well, do you mind if I just check it out and make sure? It'll save me having to come back later if there's a problem."

"Sure, yeah, come on in." Shelly stepped back.

Across the room, the kids barely looked up from their rolling game.

Carl chuckled. "I wish I could get my kids to be that focused on a game and not on the TV. Is that a bowling ball?"

"We're really not sure what it is. We found it in the woods yesterday. It's ... I don't know, maybe some kind of new toy or something."

The man knelt down in front of the TV and turned it on. "Toy?" He asked.

"Mommy, let me show him what it does," Sandy said.

Shelly nodded with a smile. "They're very excited about it."

The man turned around to watch as the ball followed the two kids around the room.

His eyebrows rose. "How does it do that?"

Shelly shrugged. "We have no idea. But it seems to just kind of switch direction if people try to leave it behind. We actually had to lock it in the bathroom when we went to the store this morning."

"Well, don't that beat all," he said. He flipped through a bunch of the channels on the TV. "And you just found it in the woods?"

Shelly shook her head. "Yeah. It was just sitting out there. The kids found it. At first, I thought it might be a cannonball left over from Spanish colonizers. I even brought some photos over to the university, but now, honestly, I'm not sure what it is."

"Does it do anything else?" Carl asked as he stood.

"It hums a little bit sometimes," Shelly said with a shrug, "and other times it kind of vibrates. It's actually kind of cool. And the kids really like it, as you can tell."

"I can see why. I'll have to see if I can find one for my kids." He reached down and turned off the set. "Well, it looks like this is all fine. Whatever is happening with your neighbors doesn't seem to be affecting you."

"Well, that's good to hear," Shelly said. "Can I get you some lemonade?"

"I would love that. Thank you very much," he replied.

Shelly disappeared into the kitchen and returned with a glass of lemonade. The man now sat with the kids, rolling the ball back and forth. He grinned up at her. "I can see why you guys like this so much. It's pretty cool."

She handed over the lemonade as the man stood. "Yeah, it really is. I mean, we all saw *Star Wars*. It kind of reminds the kids of R2-D2."

The man took a long drink. "I can see that. I really can."

The small two-story home sat on the edge of the Everglades. From the van, Matilda Watson watched as her young agent was welcomed inside.

She didn't doubt that Jasper Jenkins would get the information that they needed. Even though he'd only been with R.I.S.E. for a short time, he seemed to have a way about him. He was very good at charming people. He quickly got them to believe that he was harmless while he sucked them dry of all the information he needed. He was going to be an excellent addition to their ranks.

The sun was hot up ahead. Tilda had cracked the windows, although she wasn't sure if that helped or hurt as the humid Florida air rolled over her.

Time was ticking away. She glanced again at her watch. He'd been inside for a good fifteen minutes now. With any other agent, she might become worried, but Jasper was probably just having a good yarn, as her grandmother used to say. The man could get people to talk like no one she'd ever seen. Within minutes, he could have someone spilling their guts as if Jasper were their long-lost best friend.

The front door opened, and he finally appeared. The homeowner had followed him to the door and stood smiling and chatting with him. Jasper took his leave, giving her a friendly wave. Mrs. Crumb waved in return, a smile still on her face.

He really did have a way with people. He walked down the sidewalk and then crossed the street, sliding into the passenger seat of the van.

"Well?" Matilda asked.

Jasper blew out a breath. "It's the strangest thing. It's about the size of a bowling ball, and it's silver. It follows them around, like a little, I don't know, ball dog. They said that when they had to go out, they actually had to lock it in a room so that it wouldn't try to follow them. They kept trying to close the door, but it kept attempting to slide through."

"What do they think it is?" She asked.

"At first, they thought it was an artifact left over by Spanish colonizers."

Tilda grunted. Not a bad guess, given where they were. In fact, it was because of that guess that they had found out about it. Tilda had a contact at the university. She had a contact at most universities, and they'd reached out to her. That and the meteor shower the other night in the area had piqued her interest.

"And now?" Tilda asked.

Jasper stretched out his legs. "Now they think it's some sort of high-tech kids' toy."

"They think that a high-tech kids' toy was just lost in the Everglades?" She asked with raised eyebrows.

He shrugged. "It's a nice family. I don't think they really think too much about conspiracies or UFOs."

That must be nice, Tilda thought. Conspiracies and UFOs were pretty much all she thought about.

In fact, it was UFOs that had brought them to this little slice of Florida. There had been a meteor shower the night before.

That wasn't unusual. The earth was actually bombarded by meteors every day, but the atmosphere kept them from getting through.

It would be impossible to check each time a meteor hit even just the United States. They'd spend all their time doing nothing else.

But this meteor shower had been different than the others. In a typical meteor shower, small pieces of rock managed to get through the atmosphere and land on the earth. This time, though, something bigger got through, something the size of a bowling ball.

Even that wasn't enough to attract the attention of R.I.S.E. They had more than enough things to keep them busy. But this particular piece of meteor was giving off a radio frequency, and it had slowed down shortly before it made impact.

Meteors didn't do that.

So, they needed to find out why this one did. And the Crumbs had very helpfully sent those photos to the university, making it easy to track the object down.

"So what do you suggest?" Tilda asked, wanting to see what the new recruit was made of.

Leaning back in his seat, he studied the house. "They let slip that they were going to a friend's for dinner tonight. Shelly joked about getting a babysitter for the orb. I suggest we break in, take it, and replace it with the lookalike. They'll assume that the batteries that were in it stopped working."

She had been thinking the same thing. "Will the sphere we brought work?"

Shelly Crumb had kindly included the dimensions of the sphere in her email to the university, along with a guess as to its weight. Prior to making the trip down, they'd recreated a sphere from steel in case it turned out to be something. And it looked like they would be needing it.

"The size is right, but the weight's a little off, and the finish. But if we shine it up, it should work," Jasper said.

Tilda nodded, looking at the home. "Okay, we'll go pick up some spray paint and then we'll get back here and stake out the Crumbs. When they leave, we'll replace it."

Although he nodded, Jasper asked, ""But what exactly is that thing? I mean, it's certainly not some high-tech toy."

Tilda started the car. "It *might* be a high-tech toy. It's just not one humans created."

CHAPTER 1

PRESENT DAY

CLAY, NEW YORK

The gymnasium/training area was located in the basement of the Department of Extraterrestrial and Alien Defense (D.E.A.D.) headquarters in upstate New York. It was set up like an extraterrestrial version of Hogan's Alley that police academies used to train officers. But instead of criminals with guns jumping out at people, it was aliens that jumped out at you—and criminals with guns.

As the simulations began, the lights were dimmed to represent early evening or midnight. Right now, the lights were still bright as Dr. Greg Schorn stood at the beginning of the obstacle course in his combat suit, ready to begin. Next to him stood his partner/pet, Pugsley.

Standing at two feet tall, Pugsley was a pale blue, slightly transparent creature that resembled a gumdrop with eyes. He had little arms that could extend out of his body but generally stayed within his Jell-O-like form.

Pugsley was one of the projects from A.L.I.V.E. (Alien Life In Vitro Experiments) although Greg had been unable to find his files on Martin Drummond's database. Of course, the former head of the D.E.A.D had tried to erase all of the files from that same database, so that wasn't really a shock. Gigabytes of data had been lost.

When it came to Pugsley, they'd had to learn as they went. Greg had been on the mission that had first located him in Detroit. Pugsley had been staying in an abandoned home, looking after an injured pit bull and her pups. Greg had protected Pugsley from getting shot, and Pugsley had bonded to Greg in that moment.

Or at least, that's what everyone was assuming. Pugsley wasn't exactly talking. In fact, he made no vocal noises at all, save a little chirp and hum. But from the moment they captured him, he had made it clear that Greg was his chosen person. Wherever Greg went in the D.E.A.D. facility, Pugsley would appear. They still hadn't figured out a containment unit that would hold him.

That bond was so strong that he'd even unofficially gone on a D.E.A.D. mission to find Greg when he'd been kidnapped. To avoid that in the future, or at least to make sure Pugsley didn't get himself or anyone else hurt, Norah Tidwell, the director of the D.E.A.D., approved the training of Pugsley for missions.

And left it to Greg to do the training.

Now Pugsley looked up at Greg and blinked. Greg smiled down at him. When he'd first met Pugsley, he had not been enamored. The little guy had been cute—sort of—but at that point, he hadn't been Alvie or Iggy cute. He'd been really translucent, and it was hard to get a good look at him.

The slime that Pugsley left everywhere didn't exactly help. Nor did the early wart stage of his development that coincided with the slime stage. Pugsley, though, hadn't been put off by Greg's resistance to his presence at all.

Luckily, the slime had all but disappeared, and the warts were completely gone. Greg and the other scientists believe the slime might have been part of some form of alien puberty. And the warts? Alien acne.

One attribute that had remained, however, was Pugsley's ability to expand outward and encapsulate someone or something in a protective gel. Basically, his body just inflated until it wrapped entirely around either the person or the subject, completely immobilizing the target.

And it could happen fast. That ability had saved Greg's life not that long ago.

"Okay, little buddy. Now, remember, you need to focus on grabbing the bad guys but leaving the good guys alone, okay?"

Pugsley didn't answer, but his whole body vibrated.

Greg was making a little headway in understanding the small alien. He'd begun to notice a slight difference in the tone of the vibrations. The one he'd just emitted was a little higher pitched. Those vibrations seemed to indicate agreement.

And while they were all kind of guessing as to what Pugsley was saying, he seemed to understand them just fine . . . suggesting that Pugsley might be the smarter of the species.

Grabbing his M4, Greg pulled it up to his shoulder. There were no live rounds in it, but he wanted Pugsley to get used to the weapons being around. The hope was that maybe they could take Pugsley out into the field. So far, the trainings hadn't exactly gone great.

But Greg had made it his mission to make sure that Pugsley at least got a shot. He tapped the mic at his throat. "You got us, Kal?"

Kal was Kal El Haddid, Greg's nephew through his oldest sister Martha. Greg had never intended to introduce Kal to his work but life happened. His nephew sat up in the observation booth that overlooked the training field. Through the massive glass window above the starting point of the simulation, he gave Greg a big thumbs-up.

Kal had just finished his first year at MIT. He was doing really well, and his mother had actually agreed to allow Kal to stay with Greg for the summer for his internship with the D.E.A.D.

Of course, his mother didn't know the internship was with a sub-agency of the Department of Defense. She thought Greg worked for the Department of Agriculture. But this was the second summer Kal would be spending with Greg, and Greg had found himself really looking forward to his nephew's arrival.

"I got you, Greg," Kal said over the earpiece.

"Then let's begin."

The lights dimmed. Next to him, Pugsley took on a faint turquoise glow. That was another trait that had developed lately. Apparently, his little buddy came with a glow-in-the-dark setting.

"Turn down the glow," Greg whispered.

Next to him, Pugsley's light dimmed.

The two of them started forward. The cardboard cutout of a woman holding a small chihuahua burst out from the alley to the left.

Turning his weapon, Greg aimed at the woman, but he didn't pull the trigger. Next to him, Pugsley expanded but didn't unleash himself at the woman or Greg.

Greg nodded. "Good."

They made it through the next four surprise individuals without any problems. And Pugsley even managed to expand himself around a mean-looking Kecksburg that startled him from the right.

Greg grinned. *This is actually going pretty well. Maybe I can—*

INTO THE DARK

The door to the back of the gym opened just as a cardboard cutout burst out from Greg's left.

Pugsley's light exploded as he expanded out.

"No, Pugs—" Greg slammed his mouth shut as Pugsley's goo wrapped around him and the offending cardboard cutout of a grinning Labrador retriever. Unable to move, Greg simply closed his eyes. *So close.*

Footsteps approached as Greg looked up.

Mitch Haldron smiled as he stepped into the alley. "So I take it training's not going well."

You think? Greg thought as he glared at Mitch. But he didn't even attempt to speak. He couldn't. Pugsley's goo worked as a paralytic. It had an immediate effect but thankfully wore off just as quickly.

"You can release him now, Pugsley," Mitch said.

The goo slid away from Greg's body but left a cold trail over his skin. Shuddering, Greg shook out his hands and sent goo flying across the space. The smiling Labrador tilted over on its side and crashed to the ground.

Greg sighed while Mitch chuckled.

"We were doing so well. But then you opened the door, the dog popped out and …" Greg shook his head with another sigh.

Pugsley scooted forward and leaned against Greg's leg, looking up at him with big eyes.

Even as slime slipped down Greg's forehead and off his nose, he leaned down and patted Pugsley. "It's okay, buddy. I know you were just trying to keep me safe. We'll try again later. Why don't you go see if Kal has some cookies?"

At the mention of cookies, Pugsley's glow brightened before he scooted across the floor and disappeared up the stairs.

Mitch chucked a towel at Greg. Snatching it from the air, Greg started to wipe some of the goo off his face, knowing he needed a shower before this stuff dried. The goo was like beach sand: It got in everywhere. "He's actually getting better. We made it through four separate obstacles before he slimed me. That's a record," Greg said.

Watching Pugsley disappear, Mitch said, "You know you could just take him along as your own personal protection bubble. He won't let anything happen to you."

Greg grimaced. "Yeah, but I'm afraid that I might be in the middle of something completely innocuous, and he'll slime me anyway. So I'm hoping we can get him trained a little bit better before we do that."

"Well, I'm afraid training is over for today."

"Why? What's up?" Greg asked as he ran the towel over his hair. A large piece of goo slipped down the back of his head and under the collar of his jacket. He squirmed as it slid down his back.

"The boss wants to see us," Mitch explained.

Wiping the back of his neck, Greg flung some of the goo that slipped onto his hand away. "Do I have time for a shower?"

With a curled lip, Mitch took a step back, eyeing him. "Normally, I would say no. But for all our sakes, yes, definitely yes."

CHAPTER 2

Five minutes. That was all Greg needed for showers these days. With the amount of times he'd been slimed by Pugsley, he'd gotten it down to an art form. Wasting no time, he zipped into the locker room next to the training area. He was back out the door in fresh clothes in four and a half minutes, a new personal record.

He'd left his mic and earpiece in the locker, so he pulled out his phone to call up to the observation booth. "Hey, Kal, I need to go see Norah. Can you keep an eye on Pugsley for me?"

"Sure thing. I'll take him down to the cafeteria. I'm meeting Alvie there in a few minutes for lunch."

"Okay, sounds good." Greg disconnected the call, then smiled, imagining the lunch scene. Kal now stood six feet, four inches tall with a slim muscular build and dark wire-rimmed glasses. He looked like a younger, better-looking version of Greg.

And his two best friends at the D.E.A.D. were both aliens: Alvie and Iggy. Well, aliens and Greg.

Alvie was in town this week working on some top-secret project for Tilda. But after the workday was done, he and Kal spent most of their nights playing video games. Iggy would often just hang out with them, not playing but just kind of enjoying the company. Pugsley would sometimes wander down too, especially when there were snacks.

Greg shook his head as he hurried out of the training area and down the hall. What a strange world he lived in. The D.E.A.D. facility was a completely secure building. Everyone here had top-secret clearance, which meant that Alvie, Iggy, and Pugsley could walk around freely without having to worry about being seen.

Greg wouldn't trade it for anything in the world. This was where he was meant to be. He loved what he did and the people that it had brought into his life.

And in a weird sort of way, it had actually brought him closer to his family. Before he had joined the D.E.A.D., he hadn't spoken with his family in years, in part because, well, he, along with Maeve and the others, had been hiding from the world.

Even before that, though, his relationship with them, would have been best described as strained. For some reason, getting a doctorate from MIT and working on top-secret projects for the government was not viewed nearly as prestigiously as working for an accounting firm, the family business.

Reconnecting with Kal and bringing him into the D.E.A.D. had actually resulted in Greg seeing his family more often than he used to before he joined the D.E.A.D.

Not that that was always great. His sisters were still super judgmental of him, and now their latest thing seemed to be focusing on when Greg was going to get married. His mother had also joined in talking about her needing grandchildren from him every chance she got. The fact that she already had a bunch from his sisters hadn't swayed her from her argument.

His father, at least, wasn't giving him any grief about getting married or providing him grandkids. In fact, like normal, his father was barely talking to him at all, and Greg was fine with that. He'd accepted long ago that that was how his father and his relationship was going to go.

But the best thing about all of it was getting to spend time with Kal. He saw a lot of himself in his nephew, a young smart kid who didn't quite fit in with his peers. But Kal, too, had found a place where he belonged amongst the eccentric halls of the D.E.A.D.

Not everyone adjusted so easily. Every once in a while, a new individual was added to the staff, and their eyes nearly bugged out of their head when they saw Iggy taking a hopping jump into the cafeteria or Alvie scrolling through a tablet as he walked down a hall.

Speaking of which, a young woman in a white lab coat, her dark hair pulled back in her usual French braid, walked down the hall toward him at a fast pace. Her head was down, her glasses reflecting the glow from the tablet in her hands.

Greg had to sidestep quickly to avoid getting run over. "Hey, Hannah."

Dr. Hannah Eldridge's head jolted up, her eyes widening behind her glasses. "Oh, Dr. Schorn, I'm so sorry. I didn't see you."

"It's okay, and I told you to call me Greg."

Her cheeks flushed bright red. "Yes, sorry, Greg. And I'm sorry I'm running late. We had a situation in the lab."

"What happened?"

"One of the new techs didn't have his filtration suit connected properly, and he inhaled some noxious fumes from a sample. We had to rush him down to the med bay."

"Is he okay?"

"He's fine, or at least he will be."

"Was Dr. Kerwin on duty?" Greg asked

"Um, yeah. She took care of him."

Dr. Cheryl Kerwin had been brought in nearly a year ago,

and Greg had been working up the courage to ask her out. His track record with women wasn't exactly great. In fact, it wasn't much of a record at all. It was really more of a Post-it note. But Cheryl, she'd been really friendly and open with him when she first arrived. He just couldn't tell if that was who she was or because she was actually interested in him.

Buoyed by her friendliness, about two months ago, he'd finally decided he was going to try. But before he could, he felt this shift in her interactions with him. She was less friendly, more professional. It wasn't a radical change, but it was enough that it got him second-guessing himself.

But hope sprung eternal, and he found himself looking for little nuggets of information on her. He also found himself in the cafeteria when she usually took lunch. Not that he was a stalker. And with all the MeToo stuff out there, he definitely didn't intend to cross any lines. But good old-fashioned pining was still all right, wasn't it?

"How did Pugsley do this morning?" Hannah asked. "Are you guys finished already?"

Greg pulled himself back from his thoughts and focused on Hannah. It wasn't just idle curiosity on her part. She was leading the team overseeing Pugsley's development. She normally attended the training sessions, a small quiet specter up in the observation room.

"He did well until Mitch opened the door during a run."

Hannah winced. "You got slimed again?"

"Yup."

Her hands flew over the tablet. "What was the subject this time?"

"A Labrador retriever."

Her gaze met his. "The smiling yellow one?"

"That's the one."

With a shake of her head, Hannah turned her attention

back to the tablet, her lips a tight line as she jotted down some notes.

"What are you thinking?" Greg asked.

Hannah looked up, her gaze unfocused before it cleared. Greg tried not to smile. He knew that look. That was the *getting lost in your thoughts and being surprised that there was a world outside of those thoughts* look. "Oh, well, I'm wondering if maybe Pugsley has difficulty telling the difference between animal silhouettes in Hogan's Alley."

Greg was floored. She was right. Almost all of Pugsley's mistakes involved animals. "Why do you think that is?"

"I'm beginning to think scent plays a large role in how he distinguishes between people."

"You think he has bad vision?" Greg immediately pictured Pugsley wearing glasses.

"Not necessarily. I'm wondering if he simply doesn't process stimuli that way. We humans process with all of our senses, but vision is probably the top sense. But there's no reason to believe that that's the case for all creatures. So perhaps wherever Pugsley is from, vision is less critical or less able to discern differences."

It was an intriguing thought. If Pugsley came from a dark world, vision would be difficult to rely upon to make distinctions. It would still play a role, but other senses would take the forefront.

"I think I'm going to see if we can add scents to Hogan's Alley. I'll have to figure out how to do it so they don't release until just when we want Pugsley to sense them. But it would be a way to see if he is relying more on scent to make distinctions between good and bad. Of course, getting the scents right won't be easy."

He knew what she meant. It wasn't just the scent of a Labrador that they could put in. All animals gave off different pheromones when they were angry, stressed, sad. They'd need to find the right combinations to make it work.

"You're going to need some help."

"Yes, I could definitely use some help." She looked up at Greg.

Greg nodded, agreeing. "It's a big project. I'll speak with Norah about getting you more people and diverting some resources."

Hannah's smile fell before she nodded. "Uh, great. That would be great."

Greg smiled. "I'm going to see Norah now, in fact. I'll mention it to her. And the training session was recorded. Kal should have sent it to you along with the data."

"Good. I'll check it out," she said.

"Catch you later," Greg said, hurrying past her and ducking into the stairwell.

He jogged up the two flights to Norah's office and smiled at the fact that he wasn't even slightly out of breath. Years ago, he would have been hanging on to the railing by the time he crested the second floor.

But once you'd been chased down by multiple aliens on multiple occasions, it really inspired you to get in shape. So, Greg had become a bit of a fitness fanatic, and he'd even turned Kal into one. Now they started their days with a three- or five-mile run, depending on how much time they had before they had to get to the office, plus weights three or four times a week. And then on the weekends, when they could, they took some seriously long bike rides.

Yeah, the guy Greg was now was nothing like the guy he'd been years ago. Part of him kind of missed that old guy, but at the same time, he liked the more confident guy that had stepped into his shoes.

Up ahead, he nodded at Norah's assistant, Brie. Brie was petite, age thirty-two, and looked completely wholesome and unassuming. But she was a highly trained operative that Norah had brought over from the DoD. She was the last line of defense if someone was trying to get the head of the D.E.A.D. And being that Greg had seen her in action down in the training rooms, he was always very respectful.

She smiled as he approached. "Hey, Greg, go on in. She's waiting for you."

"Thanks, Brie," he said as he slipped past her and opened the door, letting himself in.

Norah Tidwell, the director of the D.E.A.D. and one of Greg's closest friends, looked up from behind the desk. A former Marine, Norah sometimes joined Greg and Kal for their morning runs, although Greg knew she was holding herself back for their sake. Her brown hair was pulled back into a ponytail, making her look young, and she was already young for running such an important government agency. But she had earned the position.

After leaving the military, she had joined up with the D.E.A.D. under Martin Drummond. She had gone on dozens of retrieval cases that always turned into destroy cases. She'd thought she was keeping Americans safe. But after meeting Iggy, she knew she couldn't go along with the planned objective of the D.E.A.D., which was to kill all of the creatures that escaped from Area 51. And she began to question whether all of her previous kills had been necessary.

Greg knew Norah was still wracked with guilt over some of those cases. It wasn't that the creatures that escaped Area 51 weren't dangerous. Most of them were. But some, like Iggy and Pugsley and the triplets, were peaceful and deserved a chance to live. After all, they hadn't chosen to join this world. The US government had forced them to.

So when faced with Iggy, a Maldek who actually could be quite lethal when the situation called for it, she had hesitated, and then she went on the run with him against the agency she now ran. She had linked up with Maeve and the others, and now she'd been made head of the D.E.A.D. She was a good boss—smart, efficient, and completely thorough.

And right now, she looked stressed.

"What's going on?" Greg asked. He nodded at Mitch, who sat in one of the chairs in front of Norah's desk as he slipped into the other one.

Norah ran a hand over her hair. "We are starting to get some pressure from the White House."

Greg raised his eyebrows. He didn't think the White House played much of a role in their activities. He always figured they knew they were around but tried to pretend they weren't. "What kind of pressure?"

"The President's got a good friend," Norah said as she sat back.

Mitch coughed. "Donor."

She rolled her eyes before nodding. "Yes, actually, that's probably more accurate: a big donor who contacted the White House. Apparently, the son of the donor was abducted by aliens."

Greg went still, looking between the two of them. "He's missing?"

Norah shook her head. "No. It happened years ago."

Well, that was a relief. He wasn't sure exactly who they would complain to about an abducted human. The first stop would probably be the Council. And Greg really didn't want to talk to them. In fact, he tried to avoid even thinking about them. The Council had made it clear that humans were on a short leash. A very short leash that had nearly been snapped recently. It was only through the actions of Greg, Maeve, and the others that they had, not that long ago, avoided a world-ending catastrophe started by Martin Drummond's actions.

Just thinking about it caused Greg's pulse begin to race. He took some slow breaths. Nope, he was not going to think about that. He shoved those fears aside in his mind and instead focused on what he knew about the Council and alien abductions.

According to Agaren, the Gray who acted as a sort of spokesperson for the Council, abductions were no longer allowed. Decades ago, it had been normal for aliens to basically do a flyby of Earth and grab humans as specimens, do some tests, and then send them back. But it was not supposed to be happening anymore.

"So, if it happened years ago, why is it an issue now?" Mitch asked.

Leaning forward on her desk, Norah clasped her hands in front of her. "Apparently, he's lost time again."

Losing time was a hallmark of an alien abduction. People would find themselves driving on a road only to realize that four hours were gone without any memory of what had happened. It was theorized that the aliens did something to their subjects to make them forget, although sometimes memories bled through.

Norah continued. "They don't know where he's been, and neither does he. The donor's worried, and he made his fears known to the White House. Years ago, the President would have thought the donor was crazy, but you know what it's like in the media these days."

Unfortunately, Greg did. As much as they tried to tamp the lid down on the escape of creatures from Area 51, the information had made it into the news. Usually, it was just the tabloid rags that people weren't paying too much attention to. However more recently there were more and more suggestions in the mainstream media that something was going on and that the government was covering it up.

"On top of that, more former abductees have reported losing time. The President has assured his donor that he'll have his top people look into it." Norah looked across the desk at Mitch and Greg.

As Greg straightened up in his chair, he grinned. "And we're your top people?"

Norah nodded. "That you are. So, I'm going to need you to go run out and see what's going on with this guy. To be honest, he's probably got a drug problem, or maybe he's having an affair, I don't know. But you need to just run out there, talk to him, write up a report, and that'll make the President happy."

"Do you think there's anything behind this?" Greg asked.

Norah shook her head. "No. I think this is the President just trying to appease a guy with deep pockets. So go out there, make the President happy, and let's close the book on this."

"When do we leave?" Greg asked.

Norah smiled at him. "Five minutes ago. The plane is idling on the runway. Apparently, you needed a shower."

Greg grimaced. "Pugsley's getting better. I swear."

"I'm sure he is. I'll make sure he and Kal get home if you don't get back in time," Norah said.

"Where are we going?" Mitch asked.

"You're heading down to DC." Norah paused. "Is that a problem?"

Greg shook his head, wiping away his frown. "No, I was just supposed to have a video meeting with Maeve. But I'll call her to reschedule." He pulled out his phone.

"That won't be necessary. Tilda reached out to say she has Maeve working on something right now that will be fully occupying her attention for the day."

Greg stood, stretching his back. "Probably burying her in paperwork. Maeve is definitely leading the quiet life these days."

CHAPTER 3

DJADO PLATEAU, NIGER

A hot wind blew across the Ténéré. Beads of sweat rolled down Dr. Maeve Leander's back as she walked across the packed earth. Above her, a sonic boom rang out. Covering her eyes from the sun with her hand, she glanced up at the now-empty sky.

Mere seconds ago, she had been in Svente, Norway. Svente was a small island closer to the Arctic than Europe. She'd been dressed in a parka with a hat and gloves. She'd pulled them off just before Sammy transported her here.

The radical temperature change was causing more than a little sensory overload. She took some deep breaths, letting her new, warmer environment seep into her.

Her shock wasn't relegated to just the temperature issue. It was still a bit of a mind warp to realize that Sammy could not only cross time and space in seconds but that he could carry along a companion for the trip. Sammy was a Seti, the code name for the subjects that had been created from A.L.I.V.E. projects under the Department of Defense.

Sammy had just dropped her off in the middle of the desert. Normally that would be the beginning of some sort of horrific punishment, but here, a tingle of excitement rolled through Maeve. When Tilda had approached her about going on this mission earlier, Maeve had jumped at the chance.

In what she considered her previous life, Maeve had been a scientist at Wright-Patterson Air Force Base, overseeing the first subject of the A.L.I.V.E. projects, Alvie. Now she lived in Svente with her love, Chris Garrigan, and her four kids: Alvie and the triplets, Alvie's clones, who were only a few years old. They had been created in a separate project twenty-eight years after Alvie was created.

Of course, Alvie and the triplets weren't normal children. They were half human, half Gray. And she loved absolutely everything about them.

But domesticity, that she wasn't as keen on. They had added a lab to the back of their home so that she could do research there, but she found herself itching to get out of the confines of the small little town.

During all the craziness of the last few years, she had longed for a quiet life. But as people always say: Be careful what you wish for. You just might get it.

So this morning when Tilda had come to her saying that there had been a reading that she needed a scientist to go check out, Maeve had volunteered automatically. She wasn't even sure if Tilda was coming to her to see if she wanted to do it or if she was just looking for a recommendation for someone who could get out there.

But knowing Tilda, Maeve was pretty sure it was the former. Tilda no doubt knew that Maeve was itching to do something beyond the four walls of her little home and the confines of their little Arctic town.

Tilda didn't miss very much. As the former head of R.I.S.E., that was a very good quality. Tilda was supposed to be retired now, but she tended to keep one toe in the game. Or, actually, she may be up to her thighs by now. Tilda wasn't very good at domesticity either.

Up ahead, the mud-brick citadel stood, beckoning Maeve forward. The area surrounding her was such a stark difference from where she lived, it was breathtaking.

Once Tilda had given her the location, Maeve spent a little time researching it. There was scant information. Niger was a country rich with prehistoric art that dated back 8,000 years. The landlocked north African country, though, had received little archaeological attention and was a country rich in history just waiting to be discovered. In the distant past, Niger's cities had been huge for the ancient world, and their technology had rivaled Mesopotamia's. Who knew what was locked beneath these desert surfaces just waiting to be found?

From what she'd read, she knew the mud-brick citadel was actually the remains of the ancient city of Djado. It was somewhere between 800 and a thousand years old, a city made entirely of mud and stone.

Twilight glinted along the edge of the horizon as Maeve stepped past a shallow pool of brackish water. The ancient city was an incredible undertaking but also one that was steeped in mystery. It was located hundreds of miles from the nearest city, leading scholars to wonder why it had been located way out here. It sat in the middle of the Sahara on the route to Libya. But it still was a tough location to eke out a living.

There was even a mysterious group of individuals in Niger's past that raised Maeve's alien connection antenna. According to the legends, this mysterious group of people had incredibly round heads, leading some scholars to wonder where exactly they had come from and where they had disappeared to.

A chill had crawled up Maeve's spine at the description. She couldn't help but picture Alvie, the triplets, and Agaren.

While Alvie and the triplets were half human, their humanness was not at all apparent in their appearance. They each had extremely round, disproportionately large heads that almost came to a point at their chin. They looked like smaller versions of Agaren, the seven-foot-tall full Gray who was a member of the Council. Had these mysterious people also been part of the Gray race? Or had they been some sort of community of half-Gray, half-human hybrids?

Movement over by the citadel pulled Maeve's attention from her ruminations and got her head back in the game. An older Black man with white just beginning to salt his hair stepped out of the warren of alleys that made up Djado. He placed a hand above his eyes to shadow them from the sun.

Maeve picked up her pace and smile. "Hey, Jasper."

Surprise flitted across Jasper's face. "Maeve? Tilda roped you into this one?"

She shrugged. "I volunteered. I was looking forward to getting out into the field again."

Chuckling, he grinned. "I knew you'd get there someday. Once you get a taste for adventure, it's hard to step away, isn't it?"

Jasper would know. He'd been with R.I.S.E. for over thirty years now. In his late fifties, he easily could have shifted to more desk-centric activities. But Jasper was someone suited for the field. He loved going to different sites and locations all over the globe. Maeve worried a little about his home life since he didn't have any family. But then she realized that the people at R.I.S.E. were his family. And they would always be there when he got back from one of his missions.

A tall, slim individual younger than Jasper by two decades appeared on the path behind him. Mike Bileris walked up and gave Maeve a nod. Mike had always been the more serious of the two. Even when Maeve had known him as a Secret Service agent, Mike had been extremely focused on his duty. "So Tilda roped you into this as well?" He asked.

Maeve laughed. "Jasper just said the same thing."

Mike shook his head good-naturedly. "We had a bet on how long it would take you to get back in the field. It looks like I won."

She arched an eyebrow. "How long did you say it would take me?"

"I said a year," Mike replied. He tilted his head toward Jasper. "This one gave you two months."

"Two months?" She asked incredulously.

Jasper shrugged. "Well, you'd been doing a lot of running around, and from what I understand, taking care of kids nonstop is its own kind of difficulty. I thought you'd be jonesing to get out in the field months ago."

Although Maeve stayed silent, inside she recognized that she actually had been. But she'd known that she needed to give staying in one place her all for a little while, at least until the kids were settled into their routine.

And they were settled. Alvie now worked for R.I.S.E. and actually shifted back and forth between their base in Svente and the base in upstate New York, where Greg and Norah were. Alvie had really come into his own and taken huge steps toward being independent. Due to his appearance, he would never be able to have a normal human life that involved restaurants and movie theaters and those kinds of things. But she was thrilled that he had created his own set of friends outside of Maeve's connections.

In fact, Greg's nephew Kal and Alvie had become really close in the last few months. And Maeve was eternally grateful for it.

The triplets were also doing well. The town that they lived in had a rather unusual history. The people were well versed in alien mythology, and not a tinfoil-hat type of alien mythology.

They had actual experience with beings from different worlds. One, Claude, was another Maldek like Iggy. And there was Draco blood in some townspeople's veins, although a few generations removed.

As a result of their exposure, the small number of townspeople were accepting of the triplets. The triplets even managed to go to a regular school. Granted, there were only about a dozen kids in their entire grade, but it was more than the triplets ever had before. They now had actual friends. Maeve wasn't sure what it meant for their future because they couldn't count on that kind of reception from the rest of the world, but it was nice to see them doing normal kid things like having play dates or having friends over for sleepovers.

So now that all of them were settled, that just left her and Chris. Chris had started on the security detail over at the R.I.S.E. base, but then he started going off on missions here and there a few months back. Nothing dangerous because they both had an agreement on that one, but just something that allowed him to get out into the world a little bit more.

This mission was Maeve's first one off of the base. But this one wasn't supposed to be dangerous either. It was a simple check on an unusual meteorite that was reported to have landed somewhere within the citadel. It was giving off some strange radiation. Nothing that was dangerous, but Tilda didn't take chances when it came to things from space, so she was sending out a team to collect it.

Maeve nodded toward the citadel. "Any luck?"

Jasper shook his head. "No, but we weren't really looking for the meteor, just making sure it was quiet. And the place is empty. There's no one around."

Maeve frowned. "Shouldn't there be?"

"Not really. It's too hot out here for most people. And there are rumors and legends about this citadel that tend to keep people away."

"What kind of rumors?" Maeve asked as she stared up at a ten-foot-tall mud wall, and beyond, where there was a warren of passages.

"It's supposed to be haunted by the ghosts of those that lived here before," Jasper said.

A hot wind blew across Maeve's face. A few strands of hair shifted across her cheeks, and she quickly tucked them back behind her ears. "So, any ghost sightings by you two?"

Jasper chuckled again. "A ghost knows better than to come after us."

Maeve shook her head.

Mike glanced around the empty desert. "And while things are quiet now, we should probably take advantage of it, because we can't count on it. Plus we're going to lose the light soon. And while I don't believe in ghosts, I'm not keen on wandering through here in the dark."

At that thought, a chill ran over Maeve's skin, despite the heat. She completely agreed. While in the daylight this place was captivating, at night it would undeniably be something out of a horror film.

She slipped the backpack off of her shoulders and unzipped it, then pulled out the radiation trackers that she'd brought with her from the base. They weren't Geiger counters exactly. They had to be modified for this particular type of radiation. They were slim and about the size of an Amazon Fire Stick. Maeve handed them over. "These have been tuned to the frequency we're looking for. Like a Geiger counter, they'll click louder when you're getting closer."

Mike nodded to the backpack as Maeve slipped it back on to her shoulders. "You want me to take that?"

Maeve shook her head. "No, I'm good. It's the containment unit for whatever we find. But it's pretty lightweight. It's a creation from Agaren."

Agaren had been held by the US government, or more

accurately, Martin Drummond, for years before Maeve and the others freed him. If he had been a human, he would have been left bitter by the experience. But as far as Maeve could tell, he wasn't. And he had been sharing his intellect and technology with the R.I.S.E. base for years, including before he was grabbed.

In fact, the lightweight material of the containment unit had also been used to help create the R.I.S.E. base back on Svente. Besides being lightweight, it could withstand a direct hit from certain low-yield warheads.

He'd also been checking in on Alvie and the triplets and seemed to be pretty happy with what he was seeing. Or at least, that was what Maeve assumed. Agaren wasn't exactly expressive with his emotions.

"Well, let's get to it," Jasper said. "Because I do believe in ghosts, and I'm not interested in running into any. So let's make it quick."

She followed Jasper and Mike through the entrance, and then at the first cavern, they split up with promises to keep in touch by radio.

Maeve took the passage to the left. As she walked along, she couldn't help but wonder who else had walked these same paths. What had their lives been like? Had they been happy? Had their focus been on their family and the people in their lives? Or had their lives been full of strife and difficulty?

The truth was that before her little research this morning, she hadn't known much about the history of the country of Niger. It was a sad fact that the American education system tended not to focus much on the histories of other countries. The greatest attention was paid to those of Europe, and even then, it was pretty cursory.

And what a shame, Maeve thought as she walked along. The citadel must have been amazing in its day. And the determination to create it was awe inspiring.

In fact, Africa had a rich history that was completely overlooked in the history books, even though the genetic origins of all humanity could be traced back to Africa and to seven mothers. There were seven lines that led to every single person in the world and all of those lines began in Africa. But the continent received scant archaeological research compared to other locations.

Maeve would like to think that that was for some valid academic reason, but in her gut, she knew that racism and classism played a huge role in the determination of what was important for the world's understanding of humanity.

The radiation tracker beeped softly next to her. She stopped as she reached a cross passage. The walls here had crumbled and the roof was long gone.

But the tracker indicated the signal was somewhere off to her right. It was faint but there. She tapped the mic at her throat. "Guys? I've got a signal. It's to the east of my location."

"We're heading back to you now. Wait for us," Jasper responded.

Maeve rolled her eyes. "I'm good, Jasper. Just keep following that trail I went down. And then the tracker will lead you to me."

She turned to the right and had to clamber over a recent fall of rocks. Studying the debris, she wondered if it had something to do with the meteor shower, but she was getting no radiation readings from it.

As she continued on her way, the beeping grew louder. She turned left at the next dead end and had to wind her way through more than a few passageways with the tracker leading her on.

A trickle of worry rolled through her as she took turn after turn. Her route had been rather twisty and turny. She was a little worried that Jasper and Mike would have a tough time finding her. Not to mention, finding their way out would be difficult.

But all worries and concerns disappeared as she came around a corner into an area that opened up at the far end of the citadel. Ahead, the wall had given way, and she could see the desert out beyond it.

But that wasn't her focus, even though part of her recognized that now they had an easy exit from the citadel. No, all that she noted in a quick glance. Her focus was entirely on the silver orb sitting in the center of the room.

Maeve walked toward it slowly as the tracker started to beep louder.

She checked the readings to assure herself that the radiation it was emitting wasn't dangerous. And sure enough, it wasn't. She was well in the alpha particle zone. Nevertheless, she slipped her mask over her mouth. Alpha particles couldn't penetrate skin or clothing. But if you inhaled enough, they could get into your lungs and cause all sorts of problems.

After shutting the tracker off, she slipped it into her pocket and tapped the mic at her throat. "I've found it, guys."

"How are the radiation levels?" Mike asked.

"Good. Alpha particles only, so wear your masks. I'm going to inspect the meteor."

"Be careful, Maeve," Jasper warned.

"Will do," she said before she walked closer to the sphere.

It was about the size of a bowling ball. Even in the dim light the silver color was clear. She frowned as its pristine appearance. It should have been dented or scratched. Or at the very least, it should have some sand and dust covering it. But this thing looked perfectly unsullied. How was that possible? It almost looked like it had been placed in the debris.

Plus it appeared to be a perfect sphere. That shouldn't have been possible either. It was highly unlikely for a naturally created object, unless it came from somewhere that had a lot of water.

Where are you from, little guy? Maeve asked silently as she knelt down in front of the orb. It rolled slightly toward her, and she went still, staring at it.

No, that couldn't have happened.

Then she let out a nervous laugh. There must be some sort of depression. She must have dislodged some of the debris underneath it, or maybe the ground she was standing on wasn't quite as solid as she thought and caused it to roll forward.

Up close, the orb was even more pristine than it had looked from across the room. There wasn't a single mark on it. It looked brand new, like it had just come off the manufacturing floor. Who had manufactured it, though, that was the question.

But Maeve knew someone had. This was not a piece of universe rock. Tilda had been quiet with her details, as she often was, but she had most definitely said that it was a meteor.

Well, if this was a meteor, it wasn't a natural one. Someone had made the sphere in front of her. The hairs on the back of Maeve's neck rose. She let out a breath as she scanned the area around her.

"Maeve, everything okay?" Jasper's voice burst through her earpiece.

Jolting back, Maeve's hand flew to her chest, her heart pounding. Her breath came out in pants. She shook herself at how she was letting herself get worked up. Apparently, not being in the field for a while had some negative effects, like being scared easily. She tapped her mic. "Yeah. I'm good. I'm collecting it now."

"We got a little turned around in all these passages," Mike said.

Maeve flicked a glance at the hole in the wall. "There's a

way out here. Once I collect the meteor, I'm going to head outside."

"Okay, we've actually got an exit route here. We'll circle around the exterior and meet you," Mike said.

"Sounds good," Maeve said before she returned her attention to the meteor and frowned. Had it moved closer?

She shook her head at the direction her thoughts were taking. But a niggling thought in the back of her mind wondered if perhaps there was some AI involved in the object in front of her.

Carefully, she reached out for the orb, surprised to find that it was cool to the touch. It had to be 105 degrees today. It shouldn't be so cool.

She supposed the building might perhaps offer it some respite from the beating sun, although right now it wasn't doing anything to help Maeve in that regard. Her shirt was stuck to her back. It was strange, but she had seen stranger in her life. And once she got it back to the base, she'd run some tests and see what the deal was. She was no doubt letting her imagination run away with her.

Unzipping her pack, she carefully reached out and placed the orb inside it, grunting as she picked it up. It was heavier than she'd expected. She adjusted the cushioning around it to make sure that the orb was snug, and then zipped it back up.

As she stood, she picked up the bag and stumbled a little at the weight. It really was a lot heavier than it looked. It had to be at least twenty pounds.

She slipped it onto her back and adjusted the straps. Mission accomplished. Turning toward the hole in the wall, she took a step forward just as the ground underneath her gave way.

CHAPTER 4

WASHINGTON D.C.

Ninety minutes after leaving upstate New York, the landing gear lowered, jolting Greg awake. He reached over and tapped Mitch on the shoulder. "Wake up. Almost there."

Mitch's eyes slowly opened, and he stretched in his chair. "Ah, that was good."

Greg had napped as well, but he never felt as refreshed by them as Mitch did.

His partner flicked a glance over at him. "What do you think happened with Pugsley earlier? I thought he was getting better."

"He was, but—" An image of Hannah flew through his mind. "Oh, shoot." He pulled out his phone and shot off a text to Norah.

"What's going on?" Mitch asked.

"I ran into Hannah on the way to Norah's office. She had an idea of why Pugsley might be having trouble." He quickly explained about Hannah's scent theory as the plane started to taxi down the runway.

Norah sent him back a quick text: *I'll see to it.*

Slipping his phone back into his pocket, he paused, his mind turning over Hannah's theory. "Actually, that could also explain Pugsley's success in the trials."

"How so?"

"I tend to tense up when it's a Kecksburg or a guy with a gun. Maybe Pugsley is reading a change in my scent."

"And the Labrador?"

"I didn't see it coming. It was a bit of a jump scare." He sat back, trying to recall the other trials and times when Pugsley had reacted. "You know, I really think she might be onto something."

"She's pretty smart. She went to MIT too, right?" Mitch asked.

"Actually, she went to Berkeley," Greg said.

"Still a good school," Mitch said his gaze on Greg.

It was a very good school, and probably a little better as far as the biological sciences were concerned, Greg thought although loyalty to his alma mater kept him silent.

"She's also not that bad looking," Mitch said, still not looking away from Greg.

"What?" Greg did a double take of his partner. Mitch was a happily married man. Greg had never heard him utter a comment on any woman's appearance. He couldn't possibly be thinking of stepping out on his wife, could he?

Settling back in his seat, Mitch shrugged. "I'm just saying, she's smart, not bad looking, lives in the area. You could do worse, much worse."

Oh, he wasn't interested in Hannah. Thank God. Greg was not ready to have his world blown apart that way. So why would ... Mitch's meaning hit him like a ton of bricks. "What? No. Hannah? It's not like that."

"Are you sure?" Mitch asked.

"I'm sure," Greg said confidently. Hannah? That was crazy.

He could feel Mitch's heavy gaze on him. "Greg, you are an extremely smart man, and yet sometimes I wonder how you manage to make your way through this world."

Frowning, Greg asked, "What do you mean?"

Closing his eyes, Mitch sighed. "If you haven't figured it out, I'm not telling you."

Greg wanted to follow up, but the plane touched down, and he shifted his attention to the task at hand. There was an SUV waiting for them at Lee Airport in Annapolis, and they quickly got on the road, heading for Nathan Prower's home in Alexandria, Virginia.

Mitch pulled over to the curb on what Greg considered a pretty nice-looking block. Which, given DC prices, meant that each brownstone had to be in excess of a million bucks.

"How much you think a place like this runs?"

"Two million, easy," Mitch said.

Greg shook his head. He had a little two-bedroom apartment in a complex on the base. He didn't pay any rent, but it certainly wasn't anything to write home about.

But this block just screamed money. Cars were parked along the street, but all of them were luxury brands—BMW, Mercedes, Lexus, and a few brands that he didn't even recognize, although from the look of them, he knew they were expensive.

Greg shook his head again as he stepped out of the car. Two million bucks. Greg had yet to earn two million bucks with all of his years of government service. Maybe in twenty years he might hit the mark, but it meant a place like this was way out of his reach.

And he wasn't too big a person to feel the unfairness of that. After all, he had helped save the world. A bump in pay seemed the least he deserved. He sighed as he joined Mitch on the sidewalk.

"What's wrong?" Mitch asked.

"I'm just thinking that Prower here and his wife are trust fund babies who've been given every advantage. What a cushy life. Meanwhile, Maeve, me, and the others had to go into hiding, staying one step ahead of the insane Martin Drummond and killer aliens. Even with all of that, we managed to save the world, and I still can't even conceive of affording a place like this one day."

"Is that what you want? A place like this?"

"No, but I'd like it to be an option."

Mitch was quiet for a moment. "You done with the pity party, or you want me to give you a few more minutes?"

"Hold on a sec." Greg stared at the well-maintained homes across the street, envisioning living in one of them, complete with the beautiful wife, two adoring kids, and a well-behaved dog. Then he shook his head. "Okay. I'm done. Let's get to work."

He started to cross the road after waiting for a Bentley, an actual Bentley, to roll by. "What does Prower do again?" he asked. He'd barely paid attention to the file after seeing the trust fund details. He figured the guy was some spoiled brat whose daddy went running to the President when he had a problem.

"Nothing," Mitch said. "He's a stay-at-home dad to his two kids. His wife works, though. She's a lawyer for legal aid."

Greg frowned as he stared up at the red brick building with the crisp white woodwork around the windows and large black door with a brass knocker. "So I guess his family is paying the bills?"

Mitch shrugged. "His or hers. They both come from money."

Greg grimaced, not looking forward to the conversation

ahead. He'd grown up in a pretty well-to-do area of Connecticut. His family wasn't rich, not trust fund rich, but they were comfortable. But he'd gone to school with kids who were trust fund rich, and they hadn't exactly been his favorite people.

Glancing up at the staircase leading to the Prower doorway, Greg hunched his shoulders after a Lamborghini roared down the road behind them. "All right, well, let's go get this over with."

CHAPTER 5

DJADO PLATEAU, NIGER

With a scream, Maeve plunged through the floor of the citadel. Dirt and debris rained down on her as she crashed into the ground. She managed to roll to her side, but her back still ached from where she hit. She landed at an angle, part of her back hitting the pack. It dug into her side painfully.

Heart pounding, she lay on her side for a few precious seconds, trying to calm down.

I'm okay. I'm okay, she repeated to herself, not sure if it was because that was true or because she hoped that was the case.

Opening eyes that she hadn't even realized she'd closed, she took stock. Nothing felt broken, and she sat up gingerly after slipping her arms from the pack. Once fully upright, she winced. Her hip twinged painfully. The fall was definitely going to leave a mark, but that seemed to be the worst of her injuries. Nothing seemed to be broken or sprained, although she was sure she was in for a mess of bruises.

The hole in the citadel floor was above her by about ten

feet. She looked around the area and realized she was in some sort of natural cavern.

Reaching into the side of the pack, she pulled out a flashlight and scanned the area. There were a few passages that led out of the cavern. She wasn't sure where they went, and she definitely did not want to find out.

She tapped the mic on her throat. "Jasper, Mike, I have a problem here."

"What's going on, Maeve?" Mike asked.

"I fell through the floor. It just opened up underneath me. It must have been weakened when the meteor hit. I'm about ten feet below the citadel, and there's no way I'm going to be able to climb out on my own."

"Hold on, Maeve. We'll come to you," Jasper said.

"There was an opening in the wall of the room that I fell through," Maeve replied.

"Set off your emergency beacon," Mike ordered.

Right. She should have thought of that. Maeve pulled out the beacon and activated it. Then she grabbed one of the flares. She uncapped the end and then tossed it through the hole above.

"I set off a flare too. It'll lead you to me."

"We'll find it. Sit tight," Mike said.

Maeve looked around. *That's pretty much all I can do*, she thought. Stretching her back with a grimace, she walked in a slow circle around the cavern.

Making her way over to one of the dark passageways that led out of the cavern, she noted that it seemed to be man-made. The edges were too regular. Had the residents of the citadel created this eons ago?

The thought brought out a rash of imaginings. Why had they done that? What were they trying to do down here? Perhaps it was a temple of some sort. Or maybe some sort of escape route if the citadel were attacked?

The cavern itself was a good size, and there did seem to be some sort of altar created on the far side of the room.

Maeve started toward it. She had the time. She might as well see what—

The sound of rocks falling in the distance caused her to go still. She turned slowly toward one of the other passageways.

Tilting her head, she frowned. No, it wasn't falling rocks. It sounded more like something was scrabbling over them. Something that was moving fast. She could hear it moving toward her at a run. Backing away, she tapped the mic at her throat again. "Jasper? Mike? Are you down in these tunnels? Do we have any people down in these tunnels?"

"What tunnels?" Jasper asked.

Alarm roared through Maeve. "There's something down here with me."

CHAPTER 6

Alexandria, Virginia

Quickly climbing the stairs, Mitch rang the doorbell. He and Greg waited as the gong rang inside.

The first floor windows were covered with a pale white, filmy curtain. Greg didn't have any curtains on his windows, just the blinds that had been hanging there when he'd moved in.

The curtain slipped to the side, and a face quickly peeked out at them. A few seconds later the door unlocked before a man pulled it back with the chain still attached.

"Can I help you?" he asked, although his tone suggested he would like very much if they went away.

Mitch slipped his badge from the inside pocket of his jacket. "I'm Agent Mitch Haldron and this is Dr. Gregory Schorn from the DoD. The President asked if we would come and speak with you about your recent loss of time."

Relief flooded the man's face. "Oh, good. My father said you'd be coming. Hold on a second."

He closed the door, and they heard the rattle of a chain before it swung wide. Nathan Prower stood in the doorway looking at them nervously.

He was a good-looking guy, although right now he definitely wasn't looking his best. There were dark circles under his eyes, and he looked like he was desperately in need of some sleep. There was a red stain on his blue Henley that Greg knew from experience was either ketchup or pizza sauce.

Nathan's blond hair was combed back from his forehead and came just to his chin. He stepped back and waved them in. "Come in, come in. Sorry about the mess."

Mitch and Greg stepped inside to a wide front hall that had a long thick, plush dark carpet on it. Kids' toys were scattered about.

A bark came from the back of the house, before an old dog that looked like a mix between a Saint Bernard and a golden retriever slowly padded forward, barking every few feet.

"That's Bear," Nathan explained. "He can't really see or hear very well, so it takes him a while to figure out if people are actually here. But he's friendly. Just, well, loud. I think he's kind of barking just to check his own hearing."

The ancient dog walked up to them and then sniffed Mitch, licking him on the hand before shifting over to Greg and doing the same.

"How old is he?" Mitch asked, rubbing the dog's head.

"About fourteen. We're not really sure. We adopted him four years ago."

Greg grunted. Okay, the guy adopted a geriatric dog. That was pretty decent.

Assured that the new guests were not a danger, Bear padded into the living room and flopped down on a dog bed underneath one of the windows.

Nathan led them into the same room. He quickly gathered a bunch of clothes off of the couch and dropped them into a laundry basket. Then he grabbed the neatly folded clothes off of the coffee table and placed them on top of the other clothes before quickly moving the whole basket over to the corner of the room. "Sorry. You caught me in the middle of laundry day. It never seems to end."

This was not what Greg had expected. Nathan seemed, well, normal. And kind of nice.

He gestured toward the couch. "Please, take a seat."

Above the fireplace was a picture of a colonial-era ship. Greg glanced up at it as he sat down. "Is that the *Mayflower*?"

A quick grimace flickered across Nate's face before he nodded. "Yes, my family had a relative who came over on it. Apparently, we date back all the way to Plymouth Rock. My father, this is his brownstone, and he puts one of those in every single building he owns to make sure that people know about it."

From Nate's tone, it was clear he didn't think too highly of that particular heritage. Nate, who'd moved toward one of the chairs, stopped still, his eyes widening. "I'm sorry. Where are my manners? Can I get you something? Maybe some coffee?"

"No, we're good, Mr. Prower," Mitch said as he took a seat.

"Nate, call me Nate. Mr. Prower is my father," Nate said as he sat down on the overstuffed chair next to the couch.

Mitch nodded, giving Nate an easy smile. "Okay, Nate. Maybe you could tell us a little bit about why we're here. Your father told the President that you've been missing time."

Running a hand through his hair, Nate nodded, leaning forward. "Yeah, it was, uh, last week. I was home with the kids. I take care of the kids. My wife, she's a lawyer, and so we decided that I'd do this until they're old enough to go to school, and then I might go back into law as well."

"How old are your kids?" Mitch asked.

"One and three. My wife, she had the day off and took them to their play group. It's actually been a good morning. I got them down for a nap earlier without any problems. I consider that my miracle for the year."

Mitch smiled. "My kids are about the same age. It's a trial."

Nate grinned. "It is, but I don't regret it. I promised myself that if I ever had kids, I'd be there for them."

Greg remembered reading in Nate's file that he had gone to boarding school when he was young. Obviously, he didn't intend on doing the same with his own kids.

"So, what happened with the missing time?" Mitch prodded.

Nate rubbed his mouth as if trying to get rid of the words. "Like I said, I'm in charge of the kids. And, uh, you know, everything was fine. It was a normal morning. I got up. I fed the kids breakfast. We went to the park to play for a little bit. When we came home, I put them down for a nap, and then I started making them lunch. The next thing I know, I'm standing in the middle of a street."

"And where was this?" Greg asked.

"I was in Maryland," Nate said. "I didn't even know where I was. I mean, I ran to the side of the road so I didn't get hit by a car, and I looked at my watch, and it was four o'clock in the afternoon. I'd lost four hours somehow."

Standing up, Nate started pacing. "I just, I mean, I froze. I couldn't understand what had happened. My first thoughts were of my kids. I called home, and Maria, our house cleaner, she was there. She'd come that morning, thank God. She said she'd seen me making lunch for the kids, and then I just disappeared on her. I had been there one minute, and then I just walked out the door. She heard the door close behind me. She tried to call me, but I didn't pick up. I looked at my phone, and I had dozens of calls from her and from my wife. But I didn't answer any of them."

"That sounds pretty bad, but I'm not sure why your father called the DoD or contacted the White House," Mitch said, his tone sympathetic.

Nate took a deep breath. "When I was a kid, I went to boarding school from third grade to senior year of high school, Cushing Academy."

"Good school," Greg said.

Nate shrugged. "Yeah, I guess if you like to send your kids away and never see them except maybe twice a year, then yeah, it's a great school."

Yikes, tell me how you really feel, Greg thought.

Nate continued. "But anyway, it was there that I had an incident." Nate fell silent.

"The report says you were abducted," Mitch prodded.

Flicking a glance between the two of them, Nate retook his seat. "Yeah. I know that sounds crazy. I know that there's no chance that that happened, but I mean, *it happened*. I remember being paralyzed and then being in this room, and then there were these beings that were around me, and then I would be back on Earth.

"Each time, I would end up somewhere other than where I started. I'd be in the forest or a different part of town or something. I didn't tell anyone at first because, well, honestly, I thought I was crazy. Finally, I broke down during Christmas break and told my mom. She told my father, and he contacted a psychiatrist to find out what was going on, why I was losing time."

"How old were you?" Greg asked.

His eyes trouble, Nate gave them nervous smile. "It happened twice when I was twelve and once when I was thirteen. It was terrifying. I thought I was going crazy."

Sympathy welled up inside of Greg. He couldn't imagine being that young and experiencing something so traumatic.

Blowing out a breath, Nate spoke with a shaky voice.

"Then the other day when it happened, it was the same thing. I lost time. I don't know if I was grabbed or if I just had some sort of fugue incident, but I can't take the chance of that happening again. I can't."

The man looked at them with big eyes. "I need help. And I don't know who else to ask. My father, he said that your agency, they know stuff about these kinds of things. And I just ... I need to know what's happening to me, what *happened* to me."

"I'm sure you've had someone try and look into where you went?" Greg asked.

Nate nodded. "Yeah, but I mean, I couldn't find anything. I just ... I walked into the subway, and I just disappeared. They couldn't find me on any of the cameras. They said it looked like I knew where the cameras were."

"And did you?" Mitch asked.

Shaking his head, Nate said, "I've never even been on that subway before in my life. I mean, we just moved to DC not that long ago. It's just ... it doesn't make any sense. And the only thing I can think is that I was grabbed again. But I don't have any memories this time. When it happened before, I'd have these little flashes of images from the time when I was taken, but I have none of that now."

Meeting each of their gazes, Nate continued, his tone desperate. "I can't let this happen again. I have two kids that depend on me. I have a wife. I can't just lose time like I used to. I need to know what is happening."

Greg's heart went out to the guy. He looked over at Mitch, who nodded back at him. They'd already discussed the possibilities of what they would do if it turned out that Nate's case was legitimate.

"Mr. Prower," Greg began, "I'm not sure what happened to you, but I'd like you to come back to our base with us. I'd like to run some tests on you and see what we can find out. I'd also like to keep an eye on you for a little bit just to see if we can figure out what's going on."

His eyes intense, Nate nodded, even as his hand trembled. "Yes, anything. In fact, I already packed a bag because I was hoping you'd say something like that. My wife, she'll be home in a little bit with the kids, and we've talked about this possibility. We agree that this is the best thing for all of us. Um, would it be okay, though, if we waited until my wife came back? It shouldn't be long. I just want to say goodbye."

Mitch answered for both of them. "That will be fine. We'll leave after your family returns home."

CHAPTER 7

DJADO PLATEAU, NIGER

Tapping the mic at her throat, Maeve sprinted back to her pack. She threw it onto her shoulders as she headed for the other side of the cavern, the opposite direction from where the noise had come from. "I can't stay here. I've got to move."

"Do you have a weapon?" Jasper asked, his voice coming out in a pant, telling her that he was running.

"No. I don't have anything like that."

"Okay, you need to run. You run fast. Block the passageway if you can," Mike said.

Already sprinting forward, she dove into the tunnel, the flashlight bouncing erratically off the ground. Blocking the passageway was a good idea, but there was absolutely nothing here to do that.

The straps of the backpack cut into her shoulders. It bounced heavily against her back with each stride. The footsteps that she had heard stopped, and Maeve pictured someone reaching the cavern.

She sprinted forward and prayed that whoever or whatever was pursuing her didn't realize which tunnel she'd taken. She tapped her mic, speaking quietly. "I'm heading east."

She tore down the passageway, wondering why on earth she'd thought going out in the field was a good idea. She should be home, safely locked away in her lab or picking up the kids from school. She'd been doing good research there. But she had been going stir crazy.

This, though, was definitely not what she had in mind when she said she needed to get out. This was supposed to be an easy grab.

At the same time, her mind whirled, trying to figure out who or what could possibly be chasing her. It sounded like an animal of some sort. But she had absolutely no idea what kind of an animal would live in these tunnels. What she did know was that whatever it was, she certainly didn't want to meet it, especially since it sounded large.

The scrambling of nails on rock sounded behind her. Her heart jumped into her throat. She tapped the mic again. "It's in the tunnel with me."

"Maeve, you need to run. Run as fast as you can," Mike said, his voice tense.

The weight of the backpack was slowing her down. Without a thought, she slipped it from her shoulders, letting it crash to the ground as she continued forward. Without the added weight, she felt like she was flying. Up ahead, she could see brightness. "I can see light. The tunnel ends."

"Move, Maeve, move," Jasper ordered.

But Maeve didn't need the encouragement. Moving was all she was thinking of doing.

She burst forward, even as she realized that the sounds behind her had multiplied. There wasn't just one animal coming after her. There were at least two.

And from the sound of them, they were big, really big.

Oh God, oh God, oh God.

She sprinted forward, the muscles in her thighs protesting, but she didn't slow. Part of her desperately wanted to look back and see what was following her. But the more rational side of her knew that in order to do that, she would have to slow and turn the flashlight on the creatures.

And she certainly didn't want to do either of those things.

Besides, she doubted seeing a creature bearing down on her in the dark was going to do anything but add to her already high level of terror. So she tucked her shoulders and lengthened her stride.

She burst out of the tunnel exit without even looking at where she would be running into. Her feet touched down on hard-packed sand. Without slowing, she took stock.

The citadel was about four hundred yards behind her. But between here and there, there was absolutely nothing. She veered toward it. "I'm out. I'm out. Where are you guys?"

"We see you. We're coming," Jasper said.

In the distance, two figures sprinted toward her. But they were too far away.

Maeve's heart clenched as she realized she wasn't going to be able to outrun the creatures behind her, not in time.

The ground around her was completely barren.

She ran over to an old tree and grabbed one of the sticks along the ground. But it was so lightweight that she knew it would break as soon as she used it.

Dark shadows crossed the sun above her. Her head whipped up as Sammy, beautiful, gorgeous Sammy, swooped down and grabbed her.

Holding on to his hands, Maeve's gaze shot back to the entrance of the cavern. Two talons appeared, gripping the edge of the tunnel. Two eyes stared up out of the dark at her.

Maeve stared back down into those eyes as a sense of

recognition rolled through her. And the terror inside of her increased. *No. It's not possible.*

CHAPTER 8

ALEXANDRIA, VIRGINIA

After Nate's text, his wife immediately replied to say she was on her way home. Greg and Mitch stepped outside, heading back to their SUV to give them some privacy.

Not five minutes later, a woman with long brown hair came hurrying down the sidewalk pushing a double stroller. Her eyes were wide with concern, her face pale as she rushed down the street.

"Here she is," Mitch said.

Greg looked up from his phone where he'd been looking into Cushing Academy.

Nate stepped out of the brownstone's entrance and hurried down the stairs toward them. With the windows rolled up, Greg couldn't hear their conversation, but he could imagine what it was from the expressions on both of their faces. Nate was telling his wife that he needed to go away for a little while to figure out what was going on. And she was asking why it was necessary and couldn't he just stay here and have them figure it out together.

Eventually they took the kids out of the stroller and carried the stroller and their children up to the brownstone and disappeared inside.

"That can't be easy," Greg said, watching the door close.

Mitch shook his head. "Especially when there are kids involved."

"I have to admit, Nate Prower isn't what I expected. You hear that you need to talk to some guy whose dad has connections to the President, and you're not thinking he's going to be a nice guy."

"People can surprise you. Good people come in all walks of life, rich, poor, tall, short."

"True," Greg said.

"What do you think of his story?" Mitch asked.

"Actually, I was just checking into that. I was trying to remember where Cushing Academy was. All I could remember was that was where John Cena and John Kerry went to school."

"Find anything?"

"Yeah, actually. Cushing is in the town of Ashburnham, Massachusetts. There was a famous UFO abduction case in 1967 in Ashburnham, resulting in a best-selling book, *The Andreasson Affair*. Betty Andreasson had been home with her family when she noticed red lights in the backyard and a ship. Her husband went out to investigate as little men appeared and headed to the house. The small aliens entered the house and communicated with Betty telepathically. They assured her no one would be harmed and took her to their ship to be examined.

"She believes she was with the aliens for four hours before she was returned to her home, her family unharmed. She did not fully recall what had happened to her until years later in therapy."

"So you think he's telling the truth?" Mitch asked.

Greg shrugged. "I think he thinks he is. But there's been some research done on abductions that suggests it might all be manifestations within a person's mind."

"So then how did he end up in Maryland?"

Greg sighed. "I don't know. But I guess that's what we're going to have to find out."

Across the street, the door opened again, and Nate stepped back outside. He stood on the stoop for a second and glanced back over his shoulder once before slowly making his way down the stairs with a small duffel bag in his hand.

At the base of the stairs, he stopped again, looking around. Greg rolled down his window. Catching sight of the movement, Nate waited until a water truck passed and then crossed the street.

Mitch had already stepped outside and opened the back door of the SUV. Nate slid in with a nod. "Thanks."

Greg handed Nate a hood.

Nate took it with a frown. "What's this for?"

"I'm afraid you don't have clearance for where we're heading. I'm going to need you to put that on."

Nate raised his eyebrows. "Uh, for how long?"

"Until we're settled on the plane. And then I'll need you to put it on when we're getting ready to land. Once we're in the facility, you can take it off again."

"Is all of this really necessary?" Nate asked.

"You tell us, Mr. Power. You're the one who wants answers," Mitch replied.

Waiting a beat, Nate finally nodded and slipped the black hood over his head.

Mitch started the car and pulled away from the curb. Greg

flicked another glance back at the man sitting in the back seat of their SUV. He wasn't sure if they were going to be able to find Nate some answers, but for his and his family's sake, he sure hoped they could.

CHAPTER 9

SVENTE, NORWAY

Maeve sat in her office on the base with a blanket wrapped around her, taking stock and trying to wrap her head around the fact that the first time she had gone into the field in months had been a disaster. After Sammy grabbed Maeve, he took her directly home, and she had never been so happy to see the tiny cold snow-covered town.

She sipped hot cocoa as the door burst open and Tilda hustled in. "Are you all right?" Tilda demanded.

Maeve nodded slowly. She'd been checked out by the base's doctor even though she had assured her that she was fine. "It didn't get near me or at least near enough to do any damage."

Tilda pulled up a chair to sit across from her. "Did you get a look at it?"

The face in the darkness swam through Maeve's mind. "Yes," she said, but then went silent.

Tilda looked at her expectedly. "Well? Are you planning on

sharing?"

Maeve blew out a breath. "To be perfectly honest, I'd rather not, because as soon as I say it, then it becomes real."

A crease appeared between Tilda's eyebrows as she leaned forward. "What did you see, Maeve?"

Maeve looked up into Tilda's eyes, eyes that had seen more than Maeve could imagine. "It was a Kecksburg, a Hank."

A Kecksburg was one of the A.L.I.V.E. projects, and in Maeve's opinion the absolute worst one. Kecksburgs were a cross between alligators and Draco blood. Maeve had been up close and personal with the Draco race not that long ago and still had nightmares about it. The Hanks stood six feet tall with razor-sharp talons, a face like an alligator, and skin that was incredibly difficult to penetrate, just like a Draco.

Tilda's mouth fell open, and she sat back hard. She stared at Maeve for a long moment before shaking her head. "But that's not possible."

Weariness settled over Maeve as she placed her mug on the desk next to her. She slumped in her chair, pulling the blanket tighter around her. "I know. That's why I didn't want to say anything. I must have seen it wrong."

Tilda's hand went to her mouth, her eyes shifting back and forth as if sorting through data in her mind. Tilda's eyes widened for a moment, and then they narrowed just as quickly. "That bastard."

Maeve didn't need to ask who she was talking about. There could only be one person who would somehow have a hand in this.

Martin Drummond had been an absolute horror of a human being. He had been a CIA agent who'd ended up as the head of BOSAC, the Bureau of Scientific Advancement and Cooperation, which put him in charge of the A.L.I.V.E. projects. Then he had created his own little research experiment, wanting to see how the creatures reacted in real-world situations.

And those real-world situations had nearly killed Maeve and her family and countless others. In fact, many had lost their lives back at Area 51. And the D.E.A.D. had been created to track down the creatures that had escaped the base and Martin's nightmare experiment.

And in a twist that could only be created by a government bureaucracy, Martin had been put in charge of the D.E.A.D. He was deceased now, thank God, but it seemed his treacherous tentacles had stretched farther than they realized.

Maeve wouldn't put it past him to have a secret lab somewhere else across the globe. Or maybe even a few. When it came to strategy, he tended to have backups upon backups, so the idea that he might have moved some of his acquisitions across the ocean wasn't exactly crazy.

Even knowing all that, Maeve struggled to believe that Martin could be behind this. "But even if that's true, how on earth did they end up there? I mean, I could see him starting something up in Europe or even Asia, but Niger? Why would they be in Niger? And more importantly, are we really supposed to believe that it's a coincidence that he set up shop somewhere that one of these things arrived?"

"No, that can't be a coincidence. And there has been an uptick in reported animal attacks in the area."

"Is it possible there have been attacks and we just haven't recognized them? Animal attacks still happen in Niger. Could someone have mistaken a Kecksburg attack for a lion or a crocodile attack?"

A troubled expression flicked across Tilda's face. "I suppose it's possible, but it just doesn't feel right."

Maeve took another sip of her cocoa, enjoying the heat. "And I lost the meteor. But at the same time, I don't think it was a meteor."

"What do you mean?"

"It was perfectly round. There wasn't a single imperfection on its surface. That thing wasn't natural. That was man-made—or made by someone's hands."

Tilda watched her carefully. "Are you sure about that?"

"Yes. That I have no doubt about. And it was the strangest thing. I knelt down to put it into the containment case, and I could have sworn it rolled toward me." Maeve shook her head. "That was probably just the ground underneath me sinking. It should have been a warning sign."

Tilda eyebrows dipped, the crease between them growing deeper. "Was it silver and about the size of a bowling ball?"

Maeve nodded slowly. "Yes. That's what I thought when I first saw it: that it was some sort of silver bowling ball. How did you know that? Did you guys get a visual on it?"

Tilda shook her head. "I need you to come with me." She turned and headed for the door.

Slipping the blanket from her shoulders, Maeve stood up to follow her, pausing for a moment to grab her hot cocoa. She still wanted that warmth. She followed Tilda out of her office and down the long gray hallway.

The R.I.S.E. facility had been built a few years ago when they had decided to make this their home base. It had been erected in record time.

Maeve always liked the building. It looked like something out of a Star Wars or Star Trek movie, as if the designer had modeled the structure after Starfleet Command headquarters.

It always made her feel a little more important, walking along these halls. It felt as if she was part of something epic. And she supposed she was.

Tilda marched ahead of her with no evidence of the knee injury that she had suffered not that long ago. Tilda was truly a force of nature. Maeve wasn't sure how old she was, but she had to be getting close to seventy, if not eighty, but her energy could rival just about anyone's.

And right now, her energy was double what Maeve's was. Maeve wanted nothing more than to crawl into her bed and pull the blankets up over her head. That was her plan for when she got done here. In fact, maybe she'd get the triplets, Alvie, and Chris to join her and they could watch a movie together all snuggled up together. That sounded like perfection. She needed that reminder of home life after her scare.

At the same time, she knew her mind had to be playing tricks on her. There was no way that creature had been a Kecksburg. Like Tilda said, they hadn't made it across the ocean at all. All the attacks had been in the United States, and even those had been few and far between. The D.E.A.D. had done a great job of rounding up all of the escapees from Area 51.

In fact, her last conversation with Greg made it sound like he was getting a little bored. He hadn't been going out on nearly as many missions as he was months ago.

She knew that trauma could sometimes make people see things inaccurately. And she definitely had been through enough trauma in her life, so it would make sense that after all she had been through, when she was being chased yet again, she pictured one of the creatures that starred in her nightmares.

At the same time, it was so hard for her to believe that her mind would betray her that way. Maeve had had a rather unusual upbringing, and the last couple of years had been decidedly difficult. But through it all, the one thing that she could count on was her mind. The idea that it would now be working against her did not sit well with her.

Up ahead, Tilda eschewed the elevator for the stairs.

Maeve tried not to groan. Her thighs were still unhappy with her after her earlier sprint. As the two of them crested the landing, she spotted Jasper and Mike making their way down the hall toward them.

"Maeve! You okay?" Jasper hurried over and hugged her tight.

Maeve nodded. "Yeah, I'm fine. Did you find the creature?"

Jasper shook his head. "No. We searched the tunnels, but we never found it."

Tilda opened the door to her office and stepped inside. The rest of them followed her in.

"I need to show you something," Tilda said. She walked across the room and placed her hand on a scanner next to a large armoire.

A green light rolled over her hand, and then she looked into the same scanner, and that same green light scanned her eyes. Biometric sensors were everywhere within the R.I.S.E. facility.

The doors to the cabinet popped open, and Tilda pulled them back. She reached in and grabbed a large metal box.

Mike hurried across the room. "Let me get that for you."

He picked it up, his eyes widening at the weight as he made his way over to Tilda's desk.

Tilda placed her hand on the scanner on the box, and the top of it popped open. She flipped it back and then waved the others forward.

Maeve peered into the box and then frowned up at Mike and Jasper. "You were able to get the artifact back?"

Mike shook his head. "When we went through the tunnels, we couldn't find it."

Maeve turned to Tilda. "Then where did this come from?"

Tilda sank into the chair behind her desk. "Jasper and I retrieved this one in Clearwater, Florida, nearly thirty years ago."

CHAPTER 10

The silver orb was identical to the one that Maeve had seen in the tunnels in the citadel in Niger. Tilda had another one. Before Maeve could ask a question, Tilda spoke. "Have you gotten any reports back from the teams?"

"They're scouring the passageways, but there's no sign of the containment unit."

Maeve winced. "I shouldn't have dropped it."

Tilda stared straight into her eyes. "You left it behind to save your life. You are more important than that orb." Tilda turned her attention back to the two men. "What about the creatures that chased Maeve?"

Jasper and Mike exchanged a glance before Jasper answered. "They're still looking for them as well," Jasper said carefully.

Something about his tone set off warning bells through Maeve's mind. "What aren't you telling me?"

"Nothing. Like I said, we weren't able to find a creature," Jasper said, averting his gaze.

"Jasper," Maeve said with a warning in her tone.

INTO THE DARK

Tilda waved everyone toward the chairs. "Everybody, just sit down. We are well beyond secrets within this group."

Maeve took a seat while Mike went and grabbed a seat from over in the sitting area and pulled it up to her other side. Jasper sat down at the other chair with a sigh that matched the one Tilda had given earlier. "I think I might be getting too old for this," he mumbled.

"What did you find?" Maeve asked.

In answer, Tilda grabbed a remote off her desk, and a screen appeared from the ceiling behind her. She hit a couple of buttons on a console on her desk, and an image appeared.

Maeve frowned, staring at it. "What am I looking at?"

"These are tracks left by the creatures in the tunnel," Tilda said as she magnified the image. "Look familiar?"

The print on the screen was long and definitely not human. Nor did it look like any sort of mammal that Maeve had ever seen. She didn't specialize in animal anatomy, but this print was too long, too narrow.

"Let me help you." Tilda hit another couple of buttons on the console, and the image turned into a split screen. She rotated the one from the tunnel so that it matched the second one that she had placed on the screen. Maeve suddenly wished that she hadn't left her blanket back in her office. "Please tell me that's not what I think it is."

Tilda nodded slowly. "It *was* a Kecksburg down in the tunnels, probably two."

Maeve sat back hard in her chair. She hadn't been seeing things. Oh, how she wished she had been seeing things. "But how is that possible?"

The words were out of her mouth before she could think about it.

"We already know how it's possible: Martin Drummond. I have people searching the area for a possible secret base."

"The man had bases everywhere," Jasper growled. "We found half a dozen of them across the globe, but we know that there are more."

Maeve wasn't sure whether or not she was glad they had kept that knowledge from her. "And were there any signs of his experiments?"

"No live subjects, no, but the research was there. We managed to collect dozens of samples of DNA," Tilda said.

Now instead of just feeling cold, Maeve felt sick as well. Unbeknownst to most of the employees of the US government, even the ones overseeing the Department of Defense, Martin had started creating a repertoire of alien–animal hybrids. He had mixed and matched different strains of DNA to create creatures out of a horror story.

"I never did learn why Martin started all of this," Maeve said.

"Martin was highly paranoid. His greatest fear was an alien invasion," Tilda said.

It seemed a rather random event for someone to be paranoid about. Heights, horses, water, sure. But aliens? "Why?" Maeve asked.

Tilda leaned forward, lacing her hands in front of her on the desk. "Because he was once an alien abductee."

Maeve's mouth fell open as she stared at Tilda. "What?"

Tilda nodded. "Martin grew up in a small town in Arizona. His mother was, well, let's just call her neglectful. They struggled to get by. The two of them lived in a little trailer set out on an old piece of land. Martin was reported to have been abducted at least twice during his teenage years.

"As a result, he had a deep paranoia about what would happen if the aliens returned to Earth, and he made it his life's goal to make sure that he was not caught unaware again."

Sympathy rolled through Maeve at a child having to go

through that kind of experience. But it didn't justify the man Martin had turned into. He had created these horrific creatures and then set them loose on innocent humans just to see how the creatures would react so that he could have more information in preparation for some future theoretical attack.

"That's crazy," she said.

Tilda shrugged. "Maybe not. Not all alien creatures are friendly. The Draco have made that clear."

Unlike most of the alien DNA used in the A.L.I.V.E. projects, the Draco race still existed on Earth. The more evolved of the species could easily pass for human. In their natural form, they were a lizard-type humanoid that had been on the planet for decades, though most of them had been killed in a recent attack.

But there were a few that still existed. And even amongst the Draco, not all of them were cruel and violent. In fact, Maeve considered one Draco that she knew a very good friend, and he happened to be married to Tilda.

Tilda continued. "As a result of that paranoia and his distrust of the American government, Martin created satellite labs all over the world. We're working under the assumption that these creatures were released from one of those satellite labs, at least in the US. It's possible the same happened overseas."

Maeve frowned. "Released?"

"The belief is that Martin, being the absolute horrendous human being that he was, set up all of the creatures to be released upon his death," Jasper said.

"It would be consistent with Martin's personality for him to have set up something like that. The idea of him messing with everyone after he died would appeal to him and his sick ego."

Maeve grunted. She didn't have the long history with Martin that Tilda did, but from what she knew of the man, that did sound like something that he would do. Sort of like a zookeeper opening all of the cages before leaving.

"How can this man still be causing us problems even when he's gone?" Maeve asked.

"He's just talented that way," Tilda said, bitterness tainting her words.

"Have there been more sightings of other creatures outside of the US? There's no way with a release like that that there wouldn't be signs," Mike said.

Tilda shook her head. "There haven't been any other sightings. All sightings have been restricted to within US boundaries."

"So then, were these Martin's only subjects in landlocked Africa?" Maeve asked, the skepticism clear in her tone.

Tilda inclined her head, making it clear she was skeptical as well. "We're still trying to parse it out. In fact, we haven't even found the base in Niger. It seems an unlikely location for him to have chosen. There was, however, a base over in Morocco."

That made more sense to Maeve. There was no strategic point of creating one in Niger. Picturing the creature in the opening of that tunnel, though, she knew there was one other topic that needed to be proffered. "There's another possibility we should consider."

Three sets of eyes turned to her, waiting. Maeve took a deep breath. "Instead of the animals escaping, what if someone is controlling them?"

Tilda narrowed her eyes.

Maeve continued. "We know that Martin had been working on devices that were able to control the A.L.I.V.E. projects, the Kecksburgs in particular. And those creatures that were following me in the tunnel, they didn't burst out of the tunnel after me. They should have done that. Kecksburgs, when they hone in on a kill, do not stop. There's no chance that they would have broken off a chase of their own free will.

"Yet they let me get away. And they could have gotten me. Even with Sammy, they should have darted out of the tunnel toward me and made the attempt. With their speed and leaping ability, they would have been able to do a lot of damage before he arrived and even after."

"And we didn't find your pack," Mike said, meeting her gaze.

Maeve nodded. "What if they took the pack with them? That would totally be uncharacteristic of them to do naturally, but what if someone sent them to get that orb?"

Everyone's gaze shifted back to the metal box that held the orb that Tilda had held for decades.

"What does that orb do?" Maeve asked.

Tilda shook her head. "Nothing. It's been sitting quietly for decades in that container."

"But before that?" Maeve asked.

Jasper cleared his throat, and Tilda looked over at him, giving him a nod. "We retrieved the orb from a family in Florida. They found it in the woods after a meteor shower. They brought it back to their home, and their kids were playing with it."

The idea sent a chill through Maeve.

Jasper continued. "They reached out to the closest university to them, thinking it might be a relic of the Spanish colonists, maybe a cannonball because of how it looked."

Maeve could understand that. Even to an untrained eye, it was clear that this thing was made by someone.

"But the Crumb family also reported that the orb engaged in some strange behaviors," Jasper said.

"Strange how?" Maeve asked.

This time, Tilda answered. "The orb was reported to have followed the kids around the room. It would roll across a perfectly flat surface, even when it wasn't touched."

"But that's ... I mean, there has to be some logical explanation for that." Even as Maeve said it, she pictured the orb she'd found and how she'd thought it moved toward her.

Tilda shrugged. "We were never able to replicate those responses. The orb, as far as our people can tell, has been completely dormant since we got it."

"What's it made of?" Maeve asked.

"We're not even sure about that. We've been unable to break off a slice of it in order to analyze it. The surface is simply too hard. We have no tools that can even make a dent in it. But we do know that it is incredibly strong, that it can survive fire, ice, bullets. I mean, honestly, at one point we even shot a missile at the thing."

Jasper grinned. "That was a fun day."

Even the idea of taking such a risk with an artifact made Maeve shiver. But she knew that in the early days of the space program, there was a lot of cowboying. In fact, the race to the moon against the Russians got so heated that there were plans conceived to send an American astronaut to the moon … without any plan for how to get him back. They even had a plan to set off an atomic bomb on the moon just to see what would happen. Thank God cooler heads prevailed. "So you don't know anything about it?"

"We know it's incredibly dense, and we know it's not from this planet. But that's about it," Tilda said.

Mike leaned forward. "You said that's been dormant almost the entire time that you had it. What does that mean?"

As if in response to Mike's question, a rumble came from the box where the orb lay.

Tilda nodded toward it. "That's been happening on and off for the last year. The orb vibrates. Our scientists have tried to figure out what's going on, but they don't have a clue either. And when we heard about the meteor shower and the fact that it was giving off the same radiation that this thing does, we knew we had to get out there as fast as possible to grab it."

Tilda met Maeve's gaze. "We had no idea that anyone else would be interested in it."

Maeve accepted the apology with a nod of her head. "But someone obviously was. And now the question is: Who exactly is it?"

"And what do they know that we don't?" Tilda asked.

CHAPTER 11

CLAY, NEW YORK

The trip back to the D.E.A.D. base was uneventful. Nate sat nervously in his seat the whole way, looking out the window once his hood had been removed.

He didn't ask any questions, which Greg admitted was pretty impressive. If it had been him, questions would have been rolling out of his mouth like machine-gun fire.

But Nate seemed to just have this nervous energy around him.

They placed the bag back over his head before they started their descent. The D.E.A.D. facility was top secret. Most people in the area thought that it was a Department of Agriculture site.

But being that Nate would be going into the interior of the site, the secrecy was necessary. He'd be restricted to the medical wing and Alvie, Iggy, and Pugsley had been warned to stay away from it.

Now Greg stepped through the front door of D.E.A.D. main headquarters. Glass lined the front of the building, although anyone outside would not be able to see in. The large foyer was rimmed in white metal with a pale-gray-tiled floor. Elevators were straight ahead just past the reception desk, with hallways spanning off each side.

He smiled at the familiar surroundings. He'd been here for two years now, and he had to say that he really enjoyed working here. Before this, he'd worked at Wright-Patterson Air Force Base. But there, everything had been so cloaked in secrecy that he didn't know what anyone was working on. Here, he was so high up in the chain of command that he knew all the projects happening on the campus.

Plus, he had some good colleagues like Mitch and Norah. He was also excited by the work—and only occasionally terrified by it. All in all, it was pretty good.

Ahead, standing by the reception desk, which was flanked by security personnel, were two members of the scientific staff: Hannah and Dr. Cheryl Kerwin. Slim, with light-brown hair and dark-green eyes, she rarely wore makeup and didn't need to. Once again, Greg felt tongue-tied around her. "Uh, hi," he said.

"Dr. Schorn," Cheryl said before heading down the hall with a clipboard, as if expecting the others to follow.

Greg frowned, watching her. *Well, that was rude.*

"Where is he heading?" Mitch asked as he joined them, directing his question at Hannah.

"We're, um, set up in Suite 8G," Hannah said, shooting a glance at Nate.

Greg turned to Nate. "This is where we leave you, Nate."

Nate startled, turning his head toward Greg's voice. "You're leaving me?"

"Just for a little bit. But in front of you is Dr. Eldridge. She, along with Dr. Kerwin"—Greg shot a glance at her back as it disappeared down the hallway—"are going to take real good care of you. They'll get you situated in your room, and once they do, they'll take the covering off. They're going to observe you tonight just to see if there's anything of note happening, and then tomorrow we'll start with a series of tests to figure out what's going on."

Nate nodded his head. "Thank you. I really appreciate this," he said, his voice muffled through the bag.

"We'll see you tomorrow," Greg said with a nod at Hannah, his gaze lingering on the hallway where Cheryl had disappeared. Two of the guards stepped forward, and each one took one of Nate's arms and gently led him down the hall.

Watching Nate go, Greg hoped once again that they would figure out what was going on with the man. It was entirely possible it had nothing to do with his earlier experiences. Reported UFO abductions weren't all UFO abductions. Sometimes they were just hallucinations, which meant it was possible that the answers Nate was seeking wouldn't make him any happier.

It was possible he was having some sort of psychotic break. And there was no guarantee there would be a solution. It might be something that he and his family had to deal with for the rest of his life.

Mitch tapped him on the shoulder. "You okay there, Greg?"

Greg shook himself from his thoughts. "Yeah, just hoping we can figure something out for him."

"It's not on you if the answers aren't what you're hoping for. You can't control everything."

"I know that. But he just seems like a nice guy. I hate for a nice guy to get caught up in something like this. I think I prefer the stuff that we do normally to this."

"You really think that's what this is? An alien abduction?"

Greg turned and started walking down the hall at Mitch's side. "It's strange that after everything we've seen, an experience like an alien abduction still makes me roll my eyes, as if it's something only meant for the tabloids."

INTO THE DARK

Mitch chuckled. "I guess it's not crazy. With everything we know, sometimes it's hard not to hope that that's the extent of what's out there that we need to worry about."

"Yeah, that's definitely true. And what I know is out there is terrifying enough without worrying about what's hiding in the dark." Greg glanced at his watch. "Hey, it's not that late. You want to come get something to eat with me and Kal?"

Mitch shook his head. "I would love to, but I need to get home to the kids and Maya."

Greg nodded. "Of course. Tell them I said hi."

"Will do."

They had just reached Greg's office door when their phones beeped.

Greg groaned. A simultaneous text definitely was not a good sign. He pulled out his phone and groaned again. "Norah wants to see us."

Mitch's eyebrows rose as he stared at his text. "This doesn't look like a mission."

As he turned for the stairs leading toward Norah's office, Greg sighed, placing his phone in his back pocket. "Well, it might not look like it, but you and I both know that's exactly what it's going to turn out to be."

CHAPTER 12

Brie was not sitting at her desk as Greg and Mitch made their way up to Norah's office. But Norah's door was ajar, so Greg and Mitch headed toward it. Mitch knocked twice.

Norah looked up from behind her desk. "Good, you guys are back. Come in, come in."

Mitch stepped inside, and Greg followed, closing the door behind him. He didn't ask if that was what Norah wanted, because from experience, most of their conversations were not meant to be overheard. In fact, that could kind of be the motto for the D.E.A.D.: mind your own business.

Greg slumped onto the couch on the side of Norah's office, eschewing the chairs in front of her desk. After sitting on the plane for a couple hours, his back was stiff, and he was not interested in sitting in one of those executive chairs.

Mitch hesitated for a moment and then joined Greg on the couch as well.

Greg grinned at him. "Your back bugging you too?"

"Of course not," Mitch said, grimacing a little as he leaned back.

Greg chuckled as Norah headed over to them with a tablet in her hand and took a seat across from them. "How'd it go with Nate Prower? He all settled in?"

"We handed him off to Cheryl and Hannah," Greg said. "They'll observe him tonight, and I'll start working up some ideas for what we need to do after I get home tonight."

"Any ideas on what might be behind his blackouts?" Norah asked.

"Alien abduction," Greg said with a wince.

Norah stared at him. "Please tell me you're kidding."

Greg shook his head. "He had some incidents when he was younger. I mean, it's entirely possible this is psychological rather than physical. People can go into a fugue state and not remember what they've been through. So if that's the case, then we're looking for a psychological cause to Nate's behaviors.

"And to be honest, I think I would prefer it if that were the case. Not for him because, well, it's going to be a little tougher for him to lead a normal life, but for me and my ability to sleep at night? Yeah, I'm definitely pulling for the answer that does not involve little green men stealing people out of their beds."

Her forehead scrunched up, Norah rubbed the bridge of her nose. "I'll see if we can reach out to Agaren to see if he knows anything about any recent abductions. If it turns out to be the case, we're going to need some information, and hopefully the Council will be able to put a stop to it."

Greg made a noncommittal noise to that statement because the Council themselves could be behind the abductions—if that was what had happened to Nate. Or they could have sanctioned it. Greg was pretty sure keeping humans in the loop wasn't high on their list of priorities.

Even if they weren't behind it, whether or not they would actually intervene on behalf of humanity was a question. Humanity was in a bit of a holding pattern as far as the

Council was concerned. They were still waiting to see whether or not humans deserved to be saved.

It was not a comforting position to be in.

And Greg would prefer if the Council wasn't involved in any way, shape, or form unless it was absolutely necessary. If humans were indeed being tested, complaining or looking for answers from them would probably be seen as being a little whiny. And he didn't want to do anything that might make the chances of humanity's survival any harder. "Maybe we should hold off on that until we see what's going on with the tests."

Norah met his gaze, and he could see his concerns flash across her eyes. She nodded. "Yeah, that's probably a good idea."

"So what's going on? Did you just want a debrief on the Prower case?" Mitch asked.

Norah shook her head. "Unfortunately, no, although I look forward to your detailed written report." She flashed a grin at Greg, who struggled not to groan. Paperwork, when it came to government bureaucracy, never seemed to end.

"A situation may have come up," Norah said.

Greg frowned. "*May* have come up?"

Norah nodded. "There was a meteor shower over northern Africa two days ago. A team from the R.I.S.E. base went out to retrieve one of the meteors."

"Why would they go out to retrieve a meteor?" Greg asked.

"Because the meteor looks like this." Norah flipped the tablet around so both of them could see.

On screen was what looked like a silver bowling ball. From what Greg could tell, it was a perfect sphere without any blemishes. He stared hard at it for a moment and then looked at Norah. "That's not a naturally occurring object."

Norah sighed. "No, it's not. And while they found it, they lost it again when what looked like a Kecksburg appeared in the same location."

Greg sucked in a breath, picturing the Hank that he'd first been studying back at Wright-Pat before all of this had begun. Despite all the Setis he'd come across, none terrified him more than a Hank.

"In Africa? How?" Mitch asked.

Greg looked over at him sharply. Mitch's whole body was tense. He frowned. Mitch had been with the D.E.A.D. for years. And he was the most unflappable individual that Greg had ever come across. But right now, he looked stressed. And this was a guy who didn't look stressed while facing an acid-spitting alien. So what about this silver orb would cause him to be so concerned?

"That's what we're trying to figure out." Norah paused. "Maeve was on the team that went to go retrieve the orbs. She fell through a floor in an ancient citadel."

Alarm flashed through Greg, and he sat forward quickly. "Is she okay? Was she hurt?"

Norah put up her hand. "She's fine, she's fine. She wasn't hurt. She found the orb and placed it in a containment unit, and then she fell through the floor and landed in some underground tunnels. That was when she realized she wasn't in the tunnels alone."

Greg's heart pounded. He knew how it felt to be stalked by a Kecksburg. The nightmare of that experience had kept him awake for months. It still caused him to wake up in a cold sweat a few nights a month.

"How did she get away from it? Did the team find her? Do they have the Kecksburg in custody, or better yet, did they kill it?" Greg asked.

Giving him a grim smile, Norah said, "No. Maeve dropped the containment unit in her mad dash to escape. She burst out of the tunnel into the desert sands, and the Kecksburg didn't follow."

Greg stared at her and then sat back, relieved. "Then it's not a Kecksburg."

"They're sure it is," Norah said.

Greg shook his head again. "No, that's not possible. If a Kecksburg is on the hunt, if it gets its bloodlust up, there's no way it cuts off in the middle of a chase. It's not going to just stop when its prey is so close. It won't even matter what's arrayed against it. It will track down its prey."

"We know, Greg. And that's the problem. We've been trying to figure out what would cause a Kecksburg to cut off a chase, and only one possibility comes to mind."

The realization of where Norah was heading with that statement rolled over Greg. He shook his head. "No. No. Martin's alive?"

Her eyes widening, Norah put up a hand. "No, he is most definitely dead. We made sure to do every test on that body to make sure that he wasn't going to pull a Dracula on us and come back to life. But the other possibility that I was hinting at was not Martin coming back, but that someone has gotten ahold of the technology that he used to control the Kecksburgs."

The cold sweat that had broken out along Greg's back at the idea of Martin returning cooled. Not that someone having access to Martin's technology wasn't bad, but at least it wasn't Martin. That was never-sleep-again terrifying.

"I thought we had all of that technology in our possession?" Mitch asked.

"So did we," Norah said. "Martin was fastidious when it came to his technology, as indicated by his well-documented records. We managed to grab all of his stashes that we know of, but you know Martin: his hidey holes had hidey holes. It's possible that there's another stash out there somewhere that we know nothing about."

"But someone else does," Greg said.

She nodded. "Exactly. According to our records, all of the remotes that we found are still in our possession. But I need to have eyes on them to make sure they're actually there. That's where you two come in."

Greg groaned. "I take it we're taking another little trip?"

"I'm afraid so. I need people I can trust and this can't wait. Because if the technology has been taken, that means we've got another mole inside the D.E.A.D. I thought we'd flushed out all of Martin's people, but if someone has actually falsified computer records, then we haven't. We've still got the same problem."

Norah's concern was easy to understand and complete realistic. When Martin had been in charge of the D.E.A.D., he'd put a lot of his people in place. They'd remained loyal to him even after Martin had been booted from his position.

Norah had taken great pains to make sure that none of them were in any positions where they could cause any problems. But she was right. If there were still a few out there, they could be working on Martin's behalf or whoever it was that knew about the Kecksburg controllers.

The thought made Greg frown.

"What is it?" Norah asked.

"Martin wasn't exactly the sharing type. He didn't have a partner. In fact, the closest partner he had, he killed years ago."

"Robert Buckley," Norah said, mentioning the former head of the A.L.I.V.E. projects.

"Right, exactly," Greg said. "So who would know enough about Martin's stash houses that they would be able to access them? And that they'd be able to find the exact location where the Kecksburg controllers were?"

Norah met his gaze. "We're going through all of Martin's close contacts. Everyone that we have in custody and those that we don't." She paused for a second. "And that includes his family."

Greg jolted. "You can't think that Ariana would have anything to do with this."

"No, I don't think that's the case. But I need to make sure. She's being brought to a R.I.S.E. facility tomorrow for questioning," Norah said.

Greg's jaw fell open. "For questioning? Like she's a criminal? He threw her in a cell. He was planning on experimenting on her for the rest of her natural-born life."

A sigh escaped Norah's lips and she rubbed the bridge of her nose. "I know. But it's entirely possible she knows something. Maybe she overheard something, or maybe when she was growing up, her father took her somewhere. I don't think Ariana's *part* of this. But she may have some information that could help figure out what's going on."

Greg wanted to deny that that was possible. Ariana had been through enough. But Norah was right. And besides, Ariana was tough, and she had made it clear that she really didn't want anything from Greg. So he shut his mouth and nodded. "Okay."

"And I'm afraid I need you guys to get on this immediately. The warehouse is down in Jersey, so it's only about thirty minutes by air," Norah said.

Groaning, the hopes of a pizza-and-video-game-filled evening with Kal disappeared. He stood. "Well, might as well get to it. The sooner we leave, the sooner we can come back."

Norah stood as well. "Thanks. I appreciate it, guys."

Greg looked back at Mitch, who was still sitting on the couch. "Mitch?"

The big man blinked, his head jerking over toward Greg before he stood. "Yeah. We'll head there right now. I just need to make a call." Mitch strode toward the office door.

Watching him go, Greg frowned.

"Is he all right?" Norah asked.

Greg shrugged. "I don't know. He said he needed to get home and talk to Maya, so I'm guessing maybe he's just figuring out a way to tell her he won't be home just yet."

CHAPTER 13

Leaving Norah's office, Mitch made his way down the hall, trying not to draw attention to himself. It took all his focus to keep his steps even. He slipped into the stairwell at the end of the hall and then hurried down to the first floor. He stepped out into the main foyer.

"Hey, Mitch," O'Grady from the security staff called as Mitch passed by.

Mitch forced a smile to his face. "Hey, O'Grady. How you doing?"

"Good, good. Yourself?"

"Can't complain," he replied.

O'Grady grinned at him. "Who'd listen anyway?"

Mitch chuckled. "Exactly."

As soon as O'Grady turned away, the smile slipped from Mitch's face, and he pushed through the main doors of the D.E.A.D. entrance. He turned to the left and headed toward a copse of trees situated a hundred yards from the building. As he walked, he pictured the silver orb in the image that Norah had shown them.

He wanted to believe that it wasn't possible. That the orbs weren't being called into play. But he'd known that they were. His own orb's behaviors in the last couple of weeks had made it clear that they were being activated.

He had lived in a small little delusion that perhaps it would be all right, that perhaps they would be activated, and then once the process was completed, they would quiet down and things would go back to normal. That was how it had been in the past.

But this time, the orb had continued to hum for weeks and months on end. In his gut, Mitch knew something had changed.

But he'd still hoped, and shoved the concerns from his mind. A stupid human attribute to deny the evidence that was right in front of you when it was something that you wanted to not be true.

He pulled out his phone as he slipped into the woods and then hit the button to encrypt the call. He quickly dialed his mother.

She answered on the third ring. "Mitch, I was just thinking about you. I was thinking if maybe you and Maya wanted to go out for a nice dinner just the two of you, I could watch the kids and—"

"Another orb was found in Africa."

The other side of the phone was quiet for a long moment. "Who has it now?"

"I don't know. A team from R.I.S.E. went out to retrieve it, but they were thwarted."

"Thwarted? How?"

Mitch quickly explained about Maeve and the Kecksburg in the tunnels beneath the citadel.

His mother was quiet for a long moment again. "Then it's time."

Mitch closed his eyes, his chest practically caving in on itself at her words. He pictured his family: his son, who was just starting to figure out the world. His daughter, who was so full of fire and passion, just like her mother.

And Maya. His beautiful, smart, loving wife.

"I'm sorry, Mitch. But we knew this time would come eventually."

"I know. But the kids are so young. I had hoped I would have more time."

His mother's voice was insistent. "There is no more time. If the orbs are being activated, and if more are appearing, you know what that means. You need to send your family away. You need to send them as far away from you as possible until this is done."

The words were heartbreaking to hear, but his mother was right. He'd known it was possible that this moment would come. But when he'd met Maya, he'd been pulled toward her like a moth to a flame. There was no denying their feelings. And he'd shoved the possible ramifications away. After all, it had never been a problem before.

He gripped the phone tightly. "How did this happen? I thought that we had safeguards in place to prevent this."

"The how doesn't matter. We'll figure that out. Right now, we need to track him down. Right now, we need to prevent the damage that he could unleash on this world."

Mitch pulled back his fear, his rage. It would do him no good. He needed to think clearly. "I'm on my way to a warehouse in New Jersey. That's where the control units for the Kecksburg are stored. Hopefully we'll figure out if he's been there and retrieved them."

"He won't go himself. He can't. He'll send someone else in his place."

"I know, but we need to start somewhere."

"I'll head over to your home and help Maya pack up the kids." His mother paused. "Do you know what you're going to tell her?"

Mitch let out a bitter laugh. "Anything but the truth."

CHAPTER 14

After Mitch left, Greg chatted with Norah about the situation with Nate and Hannah's theory about Pugsley's ability to identify by scent. It was only a short conversation, but by the time he stepped outside, he didn't see Mitch anywhere.

He figured he was probably off calling Maya to let her know that he'd be home later. And Greg needed to do the same.

But Norah had told him that Kal was still on the base, so he headed down to the second floor where Kal was situated with the other interns. He walked down the long gray hall to a door just down from the lab.

He peered inside and saw three of their interns. All of them were from prestigious schools: Harvard, Cal Tech, and Stanford.

The intern closest to the door, Frank Leibowitz, looked up. Eyes widening as he caught sight of Greg, he stood up quickly from his desk. Frank was short and slim with thick curly hair. And he seemed to be perpetually nervous. "Dr. Schorn, sir. Um, hi."

Greg stepped into the room. "Hey, Frank. How you doing?"

"Good, good. Are you looking for Kal?"

Greg nodded. "Yeah, have you seen him?"

"He's down in the Secured Wing. He's working with Alvie."

"Okay, thanks," Greg said as he turned to leave.

"Sure, anytime, Dr. Schorn. And anything you need, just let me know," Frank said with a hopeful note in his voice.

Straightening his spine, Greg gave him another nod over his shoulder as he stepped outside. There was a little hero worship amongst the interns for Greg. He was one of them, a geek turned action star as far as they were concerned. And Greg had to admit, it did wonders for his ego when they jumped to attention when he swung by.

He hurried down to the special section, which required three security checkpoints to get through. This was where Alvie worked and where they kept their most secret projects.

Alvie's office was here just as an extra layer of protection, in case anything happened on the base. He had free run of the base, but when he was working, his projects tended to be top secret, and he was as well. Occasionally, when they had VIPs on base, Alvie was restricted to this area. He had no doubt been restricted here when Nate first arrived too.

Being that he occasionally was put on lockdown, it was agreed that it would be best if, when he was on base, he spent most of his time in the most secure wing of the building.

Greg nodded at the guard as he slipped through the doorway of the last checkpoint. He peered into one of the rooms and saw the containment units and gear that were used for their A.L.I.V.E. retrievals.

Two doors down from that was Alvie's office. The door was open, and he could hear Kal talking. "That's so cool! You really were able to get an image of the rings of Saturn?"

There was no verbal reply from Alvie. He wasn't capable of speech, but he could communicate telepathically.

Greg stepped in the doorway. The two of them sat over on the couch. In appearance, they were as different as night and day. Although today they were both dressed alike in boots, jeans, and dark long-sleeved T-shirts: navy blue for Kal and forest green for Alvie. But that was where the similarities ended. Alvie was only four feet tall with a disproportionately large and round skull. He had two extremely large black eyes, two holes for a nose, and a small mouth. His head came to a small rounded point just underneath his lips.

And, of course, instead of being one of the varieties of color for human skin, he was a pale gray. Alvie was the first hybrid between a human and the species of aliens known as the Grays.

But he wasn't exactly a creation of the A.L.I.V.E. project. In fact, Alvie's DNA had been found in a cave in Mexico over a hundred years ago. There had been a few attempts to grow Alvie from that DNA sample, and Alvie was the first successful long-term creation. There had been one attempt successful in bringing a being into life before him. He had been called Ben, but he'd only lived for a few months.

It had been Maeve's mother who'd developed the technology to create Alvie. Like Maeve, her mother had had a world-class mind for science. And Greg wished he'd been able to get to know her better. She passed away from cancer a few years after he and Maeve graduated college.

Alvie, despite the fact that he was half human, looked entirely like a Gray. Greg always thought that was so unfair. Greg had met one Gray, Agaren, and he seemed like a decent guy, although he was less emotional than humans. Alvie, on the other hand, had the full range of human emotions. He also had the biggest heart of anyone Greg had ever met. Alvie seemed to somehow be a perfect mix of all the good that was human and all the good that was Gray. Maeve's mother really knew what she was doing.

Now he sat with Kal on the couch in Alvie's office. The two of them had forged a really close friendship. Both Greg and Maeve were happy to see it. A box of pizza with most of the slices gone sat on the coffee table next to them with a bag of potato chips and some cans of soda.

As Greg caught sight of the pizza, his stomach growled in response. It drew him into the room, sniffing the air like a bloodhound. Pepperoni. "Hey, guys."

Kal looked over with a grin. "Hey. We were just wondering when you would get back. You want some?"

That was all Greg needed to hear. He hustled over and grabbed a slice of pizza, taking a bite and moaning. "Oh, I needed that."

Taking two more bites, he grabbed a napkin and wiped his mouth before speaking. "And I'm afraid I'm only back for a little bit. I've got to head out again, but it should be a short mission. I'll be back in three hours, hopefully. If all goes well."

Kal nodded. "Okay. I'll hang around on base with Alvie until you get back."

Alvie had a small apartment that had been created at headquarters within the secure wing. He usually stayed with Greg when he came into town, but when Greg was out on a mission, he stayed on the base. Kal had taken to staying with Alvie whenever Greg was on a mission as well.

"Do you want me to get Pugsley?" Kal asked.

"Um, yeah. That would be good. Where is he?" Greg asked, looking around.

"He's with Hannah."

He should have guessed. Pugsley really seemed to like the quiet scientist. Greg finished his slice of pizza and looked at the last slice in the box. "You guys mind if I take this last slice? I haven't eaten much today."

Kal nodded. "We're good. You want some chips too?"

Greg glanced at the bag and then shook his head. "No, the pizza is good. Like I said, I'll be home in a couple hours. I'll let you guys know."

"Okay. Be safe."

Greg tried not to wince. Would he be jinxing himself if he said he would be? "I'll try. You know I don't control that."

Kal's face fell, and this time Greg couldn't keep back the wince. While Kal might be used to the strangeness of the D.E.A.D. base, he was still getting used to the danger that Greg found himself in on a regular basis. Like others who were in dangerous occupations, Greg had taken to joking about it because sometimes the only other options were crying or curling up in the fetal position, not moving.

But Kal had seen Greg in a life-or-death situation not that long ago, and while he was normally okay with it, it looked like right now he wasn't.

Greg held up his hands. "Just kidding. Seriously, it's like an inventory thing we're doing. The biggest danger I face is a paper cut."

Skepticism was still clear on Kal's face as he eyed Greg. "Well, be careful nonetheless. Paper cuts can get infected, lead to gangrene, and then before you know it, you've lost an arm."

Greg huffed out a laugh. "Thank you. That's very comforting."

The tension finally eased from his nephew's shoulders as Kal smiled back at him. "You should probably wear gloves."

"I'll do that. Now, you two don't eat too much junk food. I'll see you later."

Later.

The word appeared in Greg's mind, and he smiled at Alvie before disappearing out the door. Retracing his steps, Greg made his way back to the front foyer. That was normally where he and Mitch met when they were heading out on a mission and were both on the base already.

He looked around but didn't spy his tall athletic friend anywhere. He frowned.

"Something wrong, Dr. Schorn?" O'Grady asked from the security desk.

Greg turned to the desk and then leaned on the top. "Yeah, I'm looking for Mitch. Have you seen him?"

"He was here a little while ago. He headed outside and to the left."

Greg frowned. Mitch went outside? That was odd.

Then he shrugged. Maybe he wanted some privacy for his conversation with Maya. Greg wasn't sure, but he suspected that all conversations within the D.E.A.D. were recorded. He had a feeling that there was probably a program set up to identify certain keywords, and then when those keywords were heard, the conversation would be reviewed.

Greg often forgot about that when he had his conversations inside the building. He felt more than a little uncomfortable at the idea of someone overhearing some of them. But higher scrutiny was just part of the gig. And he wasn't going to live his life watching every single word he uttered.

He thanked O'Grady and headed outside. He turned to the left when Mitch appeared, just coming out of the trees.

Greg frowned. What on earth was he up to? He waited at the edge of the sidewalk as Mitch caught sight of him and veered in his direction.

"Hey, everything okay?" Greg asked, nodding toward the woods.

Mitch nodded. "Yeah, fine. Just, after being in that plane, I wanted to stretch my legs a little bit before we got into another one."

Greg frowned again, looking Mitch over. He had his smile in place, but there were wrinkles at the edge of his eyes, suggesting he was stressed. "You know, if you need to get home and talk to Maya, I can find someone else to go with me. I mean, maybe even Norah would be up for going."

Mitch shook his head. "No, no, really, it's okay, Greg. I already spoke with Maya. She and the kids have actually decided to go visit her folks back in Georgia for a little while."

Greg knew that Maya's family lived down south, but her parents had just been up two weeks ago. It seemed odd that they would be going to visit them again so soon.

Mitch started to walk toward the parking lot.

Greg put out a hand to stop him. "Mitch, you know you can tell me if there's something wrong, right?"

Mitch stared down at him for a long moment before some of the tension seemed to ease out of his shoulders. "I know that, Greg. And I appreciate it. I'm glad you're the one I got assigned to. I have to say, you've made working at the D.E.A.D. a lot more enjoyable."

"Well, I am an affable fellow."

Mitch chuckled. "That you are. Plus, watching you figure out which end of the gun to fire when we first started was awfully entertaining."

Greg fell in step next to him. "Hey, I wasn't *that* bad."

Mitch raised an eyebrow.

Greg rolled his eyes. "Okay, okay. But some of that new tech that came out was really confusing."

Mitch patted him on the shoulder. "Sure thing, buddy. We should get to the airfield."

He headed toward their SUV.

Greg followed him but cast a quick glance at the woods behind them. Something was up with Mitch. Greg just hoped it wasn't anything serious.

CHAPTER 15

The dropping of the landing gear shook Greg awake. He was surprised he'd dozed off. It really wasn't a long flight, but he supposed he'd finally gotten into that habit of taking his sleep where he could get it. When he'd first joined the D.E.A.D., he'd been surprised at how easily the members of the task force could fall asleep when traveling. It seemed like they would barely sit down before they conked out.

He'd envied that ability to automatically shut everything off and just sleep. Greg would think about the op that was coming up, what he would face, what he would do, and in most cases, what he would fail to do. That would inevitably lead to him worrying about all of his inefficiencies, how he wouldn't measure up, and basically send him into a spiral of worry and fear.

Now, as he stretched in his chair and let out a yawn, he realized he hadn't done that in a long time. Not that he didn't still have insecurities. He and his insecurities were his most committed long-term relationship to date. But he supposed somewhere along the way, he'd made peace with them.

A glance over at Mitch showed that he was awake as well. He sat staring out the window, a brooding expression on his face.

"You get any sleep?" Greg asked.

Mitch turned to him and shook his head. "Nah. I'm good."

Greg seriously doubted that was true. The words were right, but the tone was all wrong. He wasn't sure what was up with Mitch, but he most definitely was not good.

After they'd left the D.E.A.D. headquarters and headed to the tarmac, Mitch had been unusually quiet. Normally he was the most easygoing individual Greg had ever met. Nothing fazed the guy. It wasn't that he didn't take anything seriously. It was just that he didn't really worry about things the way most people did. Things just seemed to roll off him. Greg really envied his ability to let things go.

But something was obviously weighing heavily on his partner's mind. He hoped that whatever it was, it wasn't too serious. But since Mitch didn't normally worry, Greg knew it had to be. Maybe it had to do with his family's impromptu trip to Georgia. Was one of the kids sick? Maybe Maya? He supposed it was possible that it was Maya's parents who were sick, although they'd looked fine when Greg saw them.

And if someone was sick, why wouldn't Mitch ask for his opinion? He wasn't a medical doctor, but he was pretty close. And besides, Mitch knew that Greg had connections. If someone needed medical care, Greg should be the first person Mitch went to for advice.

Even if it wasn't a medical issue, Greg hoped that Mitch would confide in him. He liked Mitch. He liked his whole family. If something was wrong, he wanted to help. Besides, Greg had found over the years that sometimes just sharing the burden with someone else, even just by telling them, somehow made problems a little easier to bear.

The plane taxied to a stop. Greg quickly unbuckled his seat

belt and stood up. Grabbing his pack, he headed for the door right after the still-silent Mitch. After opening the plane door, Mitch unrolled the steps. The two of them hustled down and made their way to the small hangar.

A man dressed in black fatigues and built like a linebacker appeared out of the hangar door and smiled at them with a wave. Greg grinned. Max Schmidt was a member of the strike force that Mitch and Greg normally ran with. And he was one of the members that Greg rather liked.

"Hey, guys. How was the flight?" Max asked.

Greg shrugged. "I don't know. I slept for most of it."

"No problems," Mitch said. "How are things here?"

"Good. Quiet," Max replied.

"What are you guys doing here? Did Norah send you to back us up?" Greg asked.

Max shook his head. "Nah. We had a retrieval over in Trenton. So being that you guys are bringing over the plane, we hustled over here to catch a ride back with you. The office says that your trip shouldn't be very long."

Shifting his backpack a little higher up on his shoulder, Greg nodded. "Yeah, it should probably only be thirty or forty minutes if we're lucky, and then we'll be back in the air."

"Perfect. Just enough time for us to go on a food run," Max said.

Despite the two slices of pizza he'd had earlier, Greg's stomach growled. He really should have taken that bag of chips Kal had offered. "What are you guys thinking?"

"We took a vote, and it looks like Middle Eastern is winning."

"Can you pick me up something?" Shifting his bag around to his chest, Greg unzipped it to find his wallet.

Max held up his hand. "I got you. You got me when we were in Chicago a few weeks back."

Greg had forgotten about that. He looked around the

hangar and spied the rest of the force lounging along the back, although two members stood by a small crate. Greg nudged his chin toward it. "What have you got?"

Grimacing, Max shook his head. "Damned if I know. The thing looks like some sort of mix between a bunny rabbit and one of those oozy slime monsters."

Intrigued, Greg studied the box. He hadn't seen that before. "Can I take a look?" He asked.

"If you want, but I would advise against it. I'm pretty sure I'm not going to be able to get its face out of my head for a while, and it's going to be starring in a lot of my nightmares."

Debating the pros and cons as he stared at the small crate, Greg finally shook his head. "You know what? I think I've got enough fodder for my nightmares as is."

"Good call," Max said with a shudder. "I wish I had had that option."

Mitch nudged his chin toward one of the black SUVs. "One of those ours?"

Pulling a set of keys from his pocket, Max tossed them at Mitch, who caught them in midair. "Yeah. The one on the left. Happy hunting."

All of Martin Drummond's old records were stored in DoD warehouses spread across the United States. Greg was just grateful that what they were looking for was so close to New York. And he was even happier that there would be falafel to chow down on for the flight back home.

The DoD facility was located only ten miles from the airfield. It was set in a business park and looked like any of the other buildings that surrounded them. In fact, Mitch and Greg had trouble finding the building they were looking for because the numbers of the building were so small next to the front door, and all of the buildings in the area were identical. There was no sign indicating what businesses were inside any of them either.

Frowning, Greg looked around. "Is this whole area government?"

Mitch nodded. "Yeah, this is actually a storage area for a couple of different agencies."

"Shouldn't there be more security?" Greg asked.

"Oh, it's here. You just can't see it. There are drones up above. Cameras on each of the buildings. The car that we're driving right now has a transponder in it that lets them know whether or not we're allowed to be here."

"What?" Greg asked.

"When we stopped at the gate, one was placed on our car," Mitch said. "You didn't notice?"

Surprise flashed through Greg. The guard had seemed so nice and easygoing. He hadn't noticed a thing.

"Everybody has to be okayed into the area," Mitch said. "If anyone were to try and enter without authorization, a security force would meet them."

Frowning again as she scanned the sky, trying to catch sight of the drone, Greg said, "Well, that sounds like it would make it awfully difficult for someone to steal anything from inside."

The security actually made him feel better. He knew that Norah needed to check and make sure that the tech was still here, but with this kind of security, he couldn't imagine how someone could slip in without being noticed.

"And we're sure there's been no unofficial attempt to break in?" Greg asked.

"I checked the security logs again when we were on the flight. There's been nothing. Everybody who's been in and out of the park has had the authorization to be here. Hopefully this will just be a quick trip in and out." Mitch pulled into one of the stalls at the back of the parking lot, and the two of them cut through the three lines of cars to head inside.

The parking lot was half full. "This seems like a lot of cars for this kind of operation."

"Most of them are dummies," Mitch said as he nodded to the silver Honda Civic they were passing.

Peering at the car, Greg couldn't see anything different about it. "Dummies?" He asked.

"They don't belong to employees but to the government. They put them here to make sure that anybody who happens to fly or drive by will just see a normal business park with lots of cars. Most of them actually have cameras on them as well that allow them to feed information to security. Security comes out and moves them a few times a day."

Greg grunted. He didn't know why he was always surprised by the security that was put in place by the government, but each time he learned about a new layer, he was.

They stepped into the foyer of the drab gray building to find a drab beige interior. The walls were a pale beige. The floor was covered in a dull ivory tile with flecks of brown. The reception desk was even a slightly darker beige. Greg wasn't even sure where you would find a dark beige desk. The whole place looked like it hadn't been updated since the seventies.

Seemingly unbothered by her lackluster surroundings, the woman behind the desk looked up with a smile. "Dr. Schorn, Agent Haldron. I'm glad you were able to find us."

She hadn't waited for them to announce who they were. So apparently Mitch had been right. They knew everybody who came in and out of the industrial park.

She placed a scanner on the desk in front of her from a drawer out of Greg's sight. "If you will each please place your hand on the scanner."

Mitch stepped up and placed his large palm on the scanner. A green light flowed over his hand before the scanner beeped.

The woman nodded. "Thank you, Agent Haldron. Dr. Schorn?"

Greg stepped up and did the same.

A small tingle rolled over his hand as the light outlined it. Once the scanner beeped, he pulled his hand back, opening and closing his fingers a few times.

"Thank you, Dr. Schorn. Sorry about the slight shock. We've been updating our security protocols."

"It's fine. No problem."

She stood and gestured to the hallway to her left. "If you two will follow me."

As they walked down the hall, Greg scanned the area around him, but there was really nothing to see. All of the dark brown doors were closed without a window in them, and there weren't even any numbers or placards to indicate what or who was behind them.

At the end of the hall, the woman from the front desk, who hadn't introduced herself, headed to the right. Once again, they made their way down the hall, but this time they stopped at the third door on the right.

She knocked sharply on the door, and a few moments later it was pulled open.

A woman with pale brown hair graying at the temples and pulled back into a bun stood there. She wore a maroon turtleneck and matching maroon pants. Glasses attached with a chain hung around her neck. She smiled at the other woman. "Cecilia, thank you."

Cecilia nodded, and without a word to Mitch or Greg, she headed back the way they had come.

"Dr. Schorn, Agent Haldron, I'm Agnes Fielding. I was told to expect you." She stepped back and allowed them entrance to her office.

Greg stepped in first and looked around. The room was only about ten by ten. And it continued the drab beige from the hall and front foyer. The one benefit of the office was a window that overlooked the grassy area along the back of the industrial park. There was a bookcase to the left of the desk that had a few books and half a dozen pictures. In them was Agnes standing with various members of her family, including what looked like two grandkids.

Stepping back behind the desk with the large monitor on it, Agnes indicated the two chairs in front of her desk. "Please take a seat."

"So, Agnes, what is it exactly that you do here?" Greg asked as he sat in the dark brown and incredibly uncomfortable chair. Either Agnes didn't like having company or she rarely did.

Agnes smiled. "I am the keeper of the files."

Greg raised an eyebrow.

She chuckled. "It sounds much better that way. Basically, I just keep track of all of the specimens in our warehouse. So I'm constantly updating and adding to the database to make sure that we don't lose track of anything."

Reaching into his pocket, Mitch pulled out a sheet of paper. He quickly wrote down a number and slid it across the table toward Agnes. "We need to check on the items associated with this file."

Agnes slid on her glasses as she pulled the slip of paper over and glanced at it. "Hmm, this is one of the newer ones. Hold on a second."

She turned to her keyboard, and her hands flew across it as she entered a variety of codes and numbers. After two minutes, she stopped and nodded. "Okay. What exactly are you looking for?"

Greg leaned forward. "We need to know if anyone has been in that particular box any time recently."

She shook her head. "No one. In fact, no one's asked about it or looked at it since it was placed on the shelf months ago."

"Is there any chance that anyone could get into the facility and grab the box without you knowing about it?" Mitch asked.

The question caused Agnes to laugh again. But then her laughter died as she looked at Mitch, her eyebrows raising. "You're serious?"

Mitch nodded.

"Oh, well, no. That's not possible. Each box has a sensor attached to it. Even if someone has permission to get into the box, the sensor would go off, and a report would be sent to my office. Plus, everyone who is allowed into the warehouse, and even on the base, has to be authorized. No one who isn't authorized is allowed in here."

That sounded good to Greg. He was already thinking about what food Max and the others might be picking up from the Middle Eastern restaurant. He'd changed his mind about the falafel. Now he was hoping for tabouleh, maybe with a little baklava for dessert.

"We're going to need to see the contents of the box and make sure that everything's still there," Mitch said leaning forward..

The keeper of the files frowned. "I assure you, there's no way someone would be able to access it without my knowledge."

"Nevertheless, I'm going to have to insist," Mitch said.

With a weary sigh, she nodded. "Very well."

Grabbing the phone on her desk, she dialed. "Hey, Kyle. Yes, it's Agnes." She paused for a minute and then chuckled. "Hey, I didn't say you had to eat all of the cookies."

Casting a glance at Mitch, the smile slipped from her face. She cleared her throat. "Hey, listen, I'm going to be bringing two guests down to see box 278-A-K-32-19. We'll be there in about five minutes. Can you have an escort meet us?" She paused for a moment and then nodded. "Thanks. See you soon."

She hung up the phone and then turned toward the door. "Well, are you two up for a little ride?"

―――

Instead of going through the front foyer, Agnes led them around the back of the building. A row of golf carts sat there, and Agnes climbed into one. Greg climbed into the seat next to her while Mitch took the seat behind them.

As soon as they were all situated, Agnes pulled away. "We use these golf carts to get around the park. It's easier than everybody trying to maneuver in and out of their cars all the time. Plus, we have these paths that cut between the buildings, which makes it quicker to take the carts."

She turned away from the parking lot and headed onto one of those paths, heading toward a deeper section of the business park. The buildings here at first looked the same as the ones that they had seen before, but then they shifted to being larger and wider.

"These are the warehouses," Agnes nodded toward them as they passed. "The facade looks like a regular office building, but inside they're almost entirely open in order to hold all of the government's property."

Greg eyed the buildings as they passed, wondering what could possibly be inside. He couldn't help but think about the last scene from *Raiders of the Lost Ark* and wondered if the Ark of the Covenant was buried somewhere deep within one of them.

Agnes pulled up to one of the buildings and parked the golf cart next to a series of three other golf carts. Stepping out of the cart, she nodded toward a ramp that led to a large door next to a massive garage door. "This way."

Before she'd reached the door, it was pushed open. A man

INTO THE DARK

about Greg's age stood there with dark hair and dark skin. He smiled at Agnes. "Afternoon, Agnes."

"Pete, I didn't know you were working today."

"Yeah, my cousins had a soccer game, so my uncle Franklin's off watching them. I told him I'd cover his shift," he said.

"That was nice of you," Agnes said as she stepped inside and held the door open for the other two. Greg grabbed it, waving Mitch in before following him.

Pete shrugged. "Not really. He's taking my Saturday shift so I can go play paintball with some friends from college. My first time."

Agnes chuckled. "Well, wear some layers because those paintballs really pack a punch."

"You played paintball?" Pete's eyebrows rose.

"I haven't always been this old, Pete," she said before she placed her hand on the scanner next to the door. Once the light on the screen flashed, she turned to both Mitch and Greg. "Gentlemen."

Each of them stepped up and went through the process. Once they were cleared, Pete stepped up and placed his hand on the scanner and then opened the door.

Once inside, Pete and Agnes led the way, chatting with one another about one of Pete's friends from school that Agnes apparently knew. Pete grabbed one of the rolling tables that was sitting with six others just inside the door and rolled it with them as they talked.

Greg tuned out their conversation, focusing on all of the crates stored in the warehouse. The warehouse was massive. It soared up three stories, but the first level was two stories tall.

There were rows upon rows of crates of varying sizes. The only indication of their contents were the codes on the labels on the exterior of the boxes. Greg itched to find out what was inside of them.

"Don't even think it," Mitch whispered next to him.

Greg looked over at him in surprise. "Don't even think what?"

"Of trying to open one of these other boxes. Did you read the waiver you signed on the plane?"

Greg shook his head. "No. I mean, I'm getting so used to signing those things that I just kind of sign them and trust I'm not donating my organs and body to the government."

"If you look at anything other than the box we're here to examine, you will be locked up for the rest of your foreseeable life."

Wincing, Greg's shoulder dropped. "Right. Well, I guess I'll just tuck my curiosity in the back of my mind and slam a lid on it."

"Do that. Because I'm really not interested in trying to break you out of some maximum-security prison."

"Aw, you'd break me out?" Greg grinned.

Mitch rolled his eyes and was about to answer when Agnes and Pete stopped. Agnes inspected the shelving in front of them and then nodded to a crate that was only about two feet by three. "That's it."

The guard reached up and pulled it off the shelf, placing it on the rolling cart. Agnes nodded at Pete, and he started to walk back down the row.

Watching the retreating figure of the security officer, Greg asked "Why is he heading out?"

"Because he doesn't have clearance to see what's inside these boxes. His job is to keep the warehouse secure and to escort anyone who needs to be escorted to the correct location within it. But once a box is pulled, he is not allowed to see its contents."

Agnes nodded toward a break in the row up above. "We'll take it down there to one of the examination rooms."

Mitch grabbed the handles on the table and started to push it.

INTO THE DARK

Once again Agnes led the way, a confident clip of her black heels echoing through the warehouse. Greg trailed behind the two of them, looking around. There didn't seem to be anyone else in the warehouse. A glance up at the roof showed that there were cameras positioned every five feet.

Bio-scanners, human security, access codes, top-secret clearances: This place looked like it would be tough to steal from. He was pretty sure that wherever the tech had come from for those creatures in Niger, it wasn't this particular warehouse.

She turned down an aisle between the crates. Up ahead was a row of doors. She placed her hand on one of the control panels next to the first door. After it slid open, she stepped through. Mitch rolled the crate in after her.

Once Greg was through, Agnes placed her hand on the control panel inside the room. The door slid shut.

The room was eight by ten and held only a steel table. There was a camera in the corner of the room and nothing else.

"Agent Haldon, if you don't mind moving the crate to the table?" Agnes asked.

Mitch did as she asked and then stepped back.

Using a code from her phone, Agnes unlocked the crate. The lock snapped open. She flipped open the top and then pulled out the sheets of paper inside. Placing her glasses back on, she glanced down at the paperwork. "Okay, according to this, we should have three headsets and one control unit."

She placed the papers next to the crate and then pulled out the top tray before glancing inside. Her mouth dropped open, and her eyes widened.

Oh no. Greg stepped forward, already knowing what he was going to see.

He peered into the box and groaned. Yup. It was empty.

CHAPTER 16

Agnes stepped away from the box, shaking her head. "This isn't possible. This just isn't possible."

"Who else has access to this crate?" Greg asked.

Quickly replacing the tray and the papers, she closed the case. "It's not a question of access. It's a question of notification. I have to clear people through in order for them to have access to this crate. Then, like I said before, even if they have access, I would be notified. There's no notification of anyone going into this crate."

Hurrying over to the door, Agnes placed her hand on the security plate next to it. As soon as the door slid open, she hurried out into the hall.

With a quick look at each other, Mitch and Greg followed her.

"Where are we going?" Mitch asked.

Agnes didn't slow as she answered. "The control room. They'll have the video of the crate. We'll be able to see who last viewed its contents."

None of them spoke as Agnes turned at the end of the hall

and then hurried up a set of metal stairs. Up above, a large window overlooked the entire warehouse.

She placed her hand on the palm plate next to the door. As it beeped, she pushed against the door and hustled inside. Pete stood there with an older woman who sat at a long console.

"Agnes? Everything okay?" the woman asked.

"No, most definitely not. I need security footage for section 2a for the last …" She glanced over at Greg and Mitch.

Mitch stepped forward. "Let's start with the last week."

Agnes nodded. "For the last week."

The woman quickly turned her attention back to the console and input a series of commands. She nodded to a door in the back of the room. "I sent it to the private monitor. You can access it through there."

Nodding her thanks, Agnes hurried to the door and pushed it open. A single computer monitor sat on a long conference table. Greg and Mitch stepped in behind her as Agnes settled herself behind the monitor.

As Greg closed the door, he asked, "Is it at all possible that the crate was empty when it arrived here? Is it possible that the items had been moved before you took possession of it?"

Agnes shook her head, not taking her eyes from the monitor. "No. I personally verify each and every piece that comes into this warehouse. If I signed off on it, then it was here."

"Do you remember seeing the items that were in the crate?" Mitch asked.

"I have a vague recollection of them. But you have to understand, I see thousands and thousands of objects. They all kind of blur together after a while unless there's something particularly special about them. Those, though, I do remember because they reminded me a bit of one of the remote controls that my grandson has for one of his race cars."

She punched a button on the keyboard and then nodded. "Okay, I'm going to fast-forward through the security footage.

This is going to take a while. You guys might want to pull up some chairs."

It took two hours before they saw anything even remotely interesting.

Greg's eyes were bugging out of his head as he sat staring at the same spot on the screen. Pete had shown up and brought in some food and drinks, for which Greg was incredibly thankful. It was hard to just stare at a box on a screen and keep your attention.

In fact, Greg's attention had wandered more than once. He kept trying to figure out who else would know about these particular devices.

Martin had to have had someone create them for him. As intelligent as Martin was, he wasn't an engineer or a manufacturer. He wouldn't be able to simply put these together on his own, or at least, Greg didn't think he would, which meant he had to have someone else create them for him. Maybe whoever had created them had created a second set for themselves.

But that didn't sit right with Greg. Martin was scary paranoid. Greg was pretty sure whoever he'd had create the controllers for him was firmly under his thumb or if not, they were firmly under the earth by six feet at this point. Martin wouldn't leave such a loose end out there.

But someone had to have known about these and somehow accessed them. That idea was terrifying.

The death of Martin Drummond was something that Greg was very grateful for. Greg was not bloodthirsty by nature, but he'd wished Martin Drummond dead more than a dozen times over the course of his life. That man was the personification of evil. And if somebody was trying to step into his evil shoes, well, that didn't exactly sit well with Greg.

It was true that Martin did have a family of a sort. In fact, he had two children and—well, Greg wasn't sure what to characterize her as, but "baby mama" was the most accurate term, if way too informal, for Ethera.

Martin had been married at one point, but he had used the eggs from Ethera in order to create his daughter, Ariana, who was a half-alien, half-human hybrid. Luckily, Ariana seemed to be absolutely nothing like her father. In fact, Martin had been the definition of an absentee father for her entire life.

And even with that, Greg had to think that Ariana had been the lucky one of Martin's two offspring. Sammy was also Martin's son, although he'd been created through Martin's and Ethera's DNA along with a third set that had been spliced in.

Sammy hadn't been raised in a home as a human child. He'd been held in a cell for most of his life. The fact that Sammy was a decent person was honestly a miracle.

He now lived in Svente with Maeve and the others, working in a warehouse operating a forklift. Greg and Maeve had created a serum that allowed him to appear as a normal human, if a rather large one.

Neither sibling had any love lost for their biological father. He couldn't imagine that either of them would be interested in utilizing his tech for any reason.

And the idea that Ethera would be interested in it was downright laughable. She was the one who'd actually killed Martin. And as a member of the Council, she had more than enough power at her fingertips. She didn't need to play around with headsets and remote-control aliens. He was pretty sure that if she wanted to, she could just call up an actual army of aliens.

But that still meant that there was someone out there that they didn't know about who had information about Martin's technology and who was also still plugged into the government, *well* plugged in if they were able to find the tech and overcome this security.

And Greg was worried about what that would mean.

A glance at his watch showed that they had been sitting here for 124 minutes. And during that time, nothing on the screen had changed. He stifled a yawn, wondering when they were going to call it. They were already nearing the three-week point.

But Greg jerked upright as he finally saw movement. "Hold on," he called out.

Agnes immediately tapped on the screen, and the recordings slowed down.

A woman with shoulder-length hair stepped into the frame with her back to the camera. She walked over to the shelf where the crate was and picked it up off the shelf, placing it on one of the carts. At no point did she expose her face to the camera.

"She knows where the camera is," Mitch muttered.

She had a bag that she slipped off her shoulder and placed on the cart next to the crate. Then she unlocked the cart by placing her hand on top of it.

Agnes sucked in a breath. "That shouldn't be possible. No one else should have access to that crate."

The woman on the screen unlocked the crate and then removed the tray from the top. She wasted no time taking the items out of the crate and placing them into the bag she brought with her.

Greg frowned as he watched the scene. "Does something look weird about her movements?" He asked.

Leaning forward as well, Mitch nodded. "Yeah. They're jerky. Kind of unnatural."

Mitch was right. There was an ease to most people's movements, but this woman, she looked stiff.

The woman on screen zipped up the bag she'd brought with her and then placed the tray back in the crate, locked it back up, and placed it on the shelving unit. Slipping the bag back onto her shoulder, she turned, and they caught their first glimpse of her face.

Agnes gasped as she froze the screen, her mouth falling open. Greg knew that his face held the same exact expression as the one on Agnes.

The DoD representative shook her head, not able to pull her gaze away when she spoke with a tremble in her voice. "That's me."

CHAPTER 17

The image on screen was very clearly the woman sitting next to them, Agnes Fielding. A visible tremor ran through Agnes's body and then she wrapped her arms around herself. "I don't understand what's happening right now," she whispered.

"When was this?" Mitch asked.

Her mouth partially open, Agnes simply continued to stare at the screen.

"Agnes?" Mitch prodded.

Agnes gave herself a shake and reached out for the mouse. She quickly brought up the date. "It was two weeks ago, on Tuesday. It was the twelfth." Her hand froze above the mouse.

"What is it?" Greg asked.

A sigh of relief escaped Agnes as her shoulders slumped. "It can't be me. I wasn't even here on the twelfth. I was sick in bed all day."

"Sick with what?" Greg asked.

Agnes shook her head. "I don't really know. I woke up that morning and I was fine, but as I was getting ready for work, I started to feel really dizzy. I called in and told them that I was going to take the morning off because I wasn't feeling right. I remember lying down on my couch, and then the next thing I knew, it was four o'clock in the afternoon. I'd slept the entire day."

"Do you remember anything about the intervening hours?" Greg asked.

Agnes shook her head. "No, nothing. But I'd been out of the house, or at least, I must have gotten up at some point because my car keys had been moved and my shoes were over by the kitchen."

Mitch stood up, heading to the door. "I'm going to have to call this in."

Agnes made a small distressed sound.

"We'll figure out what's going on, Agnes," Greg said to the distraught woman in front of him. But he couldn't help but remember what Nate had said about missing hours.

Mitch let himself out of the room, the murmur of his voice drifted through the ajar door. Greg turned back to Agnes.

She stared at him now with a cold look on her face. "You have no idea what you're in for."

Then she reached out and slammed her fist into his cheek.

CHAPTER 18

Pain exploded across Greg's cheek as he hit the floor. His hand flew to his throbbing face. "What the hell, Agnes?" he yelled.

But Agnes had already bolted for the door. She flung the door wide as she burst into the hallway. Scrambling to his feet, Greg sprinted out behind her.

Mitch whirled around from where he stood a few feet down from the doorway.

But Agnes ignored him and sprinted for the stairwell. Without a word, Mitch tore after her after pausing for a second to raise his eyebrows at Greg.

"She hit me," Greg growled as he rushed after her.

Up ahead, Agnes darted to the right, heading away from the rows of objects but toward the front door. And she was moving awfully fast. Greg lengthened his stride but was still struggling to shorten the distance between them. Was Agnes running Ironmans on the weekends?

Up ahead, Pete appeared, putting out his hands. "Agnes? Agnes, what's wrong?"

Agnes sprinted toward him and shot the side of her palm

out into his neck. Pete's eyes bulged as he grabbed for his throat.

Jesus, Greg thought as the guy dropped to his knees. Agnes hadn't even paused. She'd talked to Pete just minutes ago like he was one of her grandkids, and now she'd just clotheslined him. That was seriously cold.

Next to him, Mitch put on a burst of speed. He blew past Greg and tackled Agnes. She slammed into the ground painfully, her glasses breaking against the hard floor.

Mitch wrenched one of her arms behind her back and then the other one. He straddled her, using his weight to keep her down.

Squirming underneath him, Agnes tried to dislodge him, but she had no purchase on the slick concrete floor, and Mitch wasn't going anywhere.

Greg slid to a halt next to the two of them and stared down at Agnes as she went still. He moved to the front so he could see her face. Her eyes were unfocused, and then she blinked once, then twice. Her face seemed to fill with emotion. She looked up at Greg, her eyes wild and full of fear. "What just happened? What's going on?"

"Agnes, do you know where you are?" Greg asked.

Her mouth still partly open, her eyes watering, Agnes started to shake. "I'm at the warehouse. But why am I on the floor, and why is he on me? Can you let me up?"

If she was an actress, she was a very good one because right now, Agnes sounded terrified.

Greg looked over at Mitch, who frowned down at the woman underneath him. "What's the last thing you remember?" Mitch asked as he stepped off Agnes and helped her sit up.

Agnes took a shuddering breath, her eyes crinkling with worry. "We were in the room looking at the footage. And then we saw ... we saw my face." Tears appeared in Agnes's eyes, and one rolled down her cheek. "But how did I get down here? What is going on?"

Mitch met Greg's gaze, his eyes full of questions. But Greg had no answers for him. And he certainly didn't have any answers for Agnes. Because right now, he had absolutely no idea what was going on.

CHAPTER 19

A medical unit arrived and quickly got Pete onto a stretcher. He was taken to the hospital with a bruised trachea, but he would be all right.

A medic examined Agnes as well, and while he worried that she was showing signs of shock, he gave her the all-clear. Now she sat with a blanket over her shoulders in one of the security offices in restraints. Greg sat in a conference room a few doors down from her with an ice pack to his cheek.

Mitch walked in and nodded at it. "You're going to have a pretty good bruise from that."

Greg winced. "Great. Sucker punched by a nice little grandma. Awesome."

Mitch pulled out a chair and sat down across from him, handing him a bottle of water and a bottle of aspirin. "Well, that 'nice little grandma' used to be in the CIA. She worked with them for about a decade before moving over to the DoD."

"Sweet little Agnes was a CIA agent?" Greg asked, although that would explain why she was so fast. Apparently she hadn't lost all her skills. He quickly downed two pills followed by some water.

"Yep, and a pretty good one from all reports."

"Why'd she move over to the DoD?"

"Because she started a family. She wanted to be home for them, so she gave up the CIA and took a desk job."

Greg shook his head and then winced. As soon as her winced, he regretted it and tried not to move his cheek again, as the pain from the wince was worse than then one from shaking his head.

He was a mess.

But he did feel a little better about the hit he took. When he told the tale, he could say it was from a well-trained CIA agent and leave out her age. "So what's the story? Do we think she was on the take?"

Mitch blew out a breath. "If she was, then it would be the first time in a lifetime dedicated to working for the United States government. There's never been even a hint of scandal around her. In fact, she's turned in people that were betraying their country. From all reports, she's a complete and total straight arrow."

"Then what? Is she some sort of sleeper agent that was finally activated? Does she have ties to Russia, China, Iran, or anyone else?"

Mitch shook his head. "Not that we can see so far. She was born and raised in Illinois. Her family's been here for at least three generations, and they come from England. Her husband's family is from Mexico, but even that was a couple of generations ago. There's nothing about this woman that would suggest that she would betray her country."

"And yet ..."

Mitch sighed. "And yet," he agreed.

Greg sat back, picturing the scene in that small room. Prior to going all super spy, Agnes had been fine. Shocked at what they had discovered, but still fine, still Agnes. But then once Mitch left, it was like she was an entirely different person.

There'd been no emotion on her face. She had been cold, and even her voice had been different.

And that hit she'd given to Pete, she hadn't hesitated or shown any remorse. Yet when she saw him and the aftermath of what she had done, she had crumpled. Mitch had had to catch her.

"What about the day that she was supposed to have been sick? Is there any more information on that?" Greg asked.

Mitch nodded. "Yeah. She did call in to work sick that morning. But according to the GPS on her car and gate security, she actually came to work that day. But she was only here for about thirty minutes."

"Just enough time to get into the crate and get out again," Greg said.

Mitch nodded. "Exactly."

It all fit, and yet at the same time it didn't. It was obvious that Agnes was the one who had taken the tech from the site, but the reason as to why was completely eluding Greg.

"We've got to be missing something. I mean, she does not strike me as the type who would turn her back on everything for, what, a payday? For loyalty to Martin? Is there even any connection between her and Drummond?"

"From what we can tell, their paths never crossed at the CIA. But that doesn't mean they didn't."

That was possible, Greg supposed. It wasn't like the CIA were dedicated note takers. And the fact that Agnes had been in the CIA at the same time as Martin was a link, despite the fact that his gut was telling him there was more at play here. He kept picturing Agnes's look of confusion. Agnes betraying her country is what the evidence indicated. But it didn't feel right. "It just doesn't make any sense, and where is the tech, anyway?"

"Not on her," Mitch said. "The GPS on her car indicates that after she came to the business park, she went to a UPS store. She was inside for about twenty minutes, and then she went right back home."

"She mailed it to someone?" Greg asked.

"That's what we're assuming. I sent Max and the others to see what they could find out. They should be getting back to us soon."

That was good but also another concern. Greg frowned and tried not to wince at the pain that it caused. "Shouldn't she have covered her tracks better? I mean, she knows about the security protocols here. She had to know they would lead back to her. And then leaving a trail at a UPS store? Was she a very bad CIA agent?"

"No. Norah spoke with her former supervisor, and he was sad to see her go. He tried to talk her into staying," Mitch explained.

His gaze darting around, Greg mulled it all over. "So she was a good spy, but she left a trail a blind man could follow?"

Mitch shrugged. "It doesn't make any sense, but that's what the evidence is saying."

Once again, Greg pictured the devastated look on Agnes's face when she saw Pete. She'd truly been shattered at what she'd done. "And what about Agnes? What's going to happen to her now?"

Sighing, Mitch met Greg's gaze for only a moment before he looked away. "There's not a lot of ambiguity here. I'm afraid Agnes is going to be locked up for quite a while."

That didn't sit right with Greg either. He glanced toward the door. "There has to be a better way to handle this. We're missing something. We need to know why she took the tech. There has to be a reason."

"Are you looking for a reason to keep her out of prison? Because I don't think you're going to find one," Mitch said. "You need to accept that."

Greg knew that was true. And being that Agnes had tried

to hurt him, he shouldn't feel sorry for her, but he did. She'd just looked so lost after Mitch tackled her to the ground. It was like she was a completely different person at that moment.

And he really didn't like the idea of putting a grandmother who apparently baked cookies for the rest of the staff in prison. At the same time, he had to admit that a cookie-baking grandmother was an excellent cover for a foreign spy.

"The ice pack helping?" Mitch nodded to Greg's cheek.

"Yeah, now it's kind of numb." He grimaced and it only caused a little pain. That was an improvement. "Besides, I've had worse."

Chuckling, Mitch smiled. "Yes, but have you had worse from a grandmother?"

"No, I definitely can't say that." Greg grumbled. Standing he winced as he turned his head to the right. The wince was followed by a groan at the pain the wince caused.

Over the years, he'd sustained a lot of bruises and injuries, even before joining the D.E.A.D. As a kid, he'd been clumsy. Actually, he'd been more than clumsy, but getting glasses had definitely helped a little with that problem, although not entirely. He always seemed to be banging his knees into the edge of tables or tripping through doorways.

His grandmother had assured him that he would grow out of it when he was older. And while he didn't bump into things nearly as much as when he was younger, the injuries seemed to be growing up too.

"Think they'll let us talk to her?" Greg asked.

"Can't hurt to try," Mitch said as he stepped out of the office. They'd just turned to make their way to the room that held Agnes when a call from behind them stopped them.

"Agent Haldron? Dr. Schorn?" Cecilia hustled toward them from the front office.

Mitch stepped forward. "Yes?"

"Agnes's daughter. She's at the front gate of the complex.

They're not letting her in, but she wants to know what's going on with her mother. And we're not really sure what to say."

"Don't tell her anything. How'd she find out anyway?" Mitch asked.

"She was supposed to meet her mother to go shopping today," Cecilia said. "She came here looking for her when she didn't answer her phone, and one of the guards let slip that she was being detained. Now she's demanding to see her mother."

Mitch shook his head. "Send her home. That's not going to happen."

"Actually, hold on a minute," Greg said as Cecelia turned to follow Mitch's order. "I think maybe I'd like to chat with Agnes's daughter."

CHAPTER 20

From the file Greg read on the ride over to the main headquarters, he managed to pull together a quick snapshot of Agnes's daughter. Her name was Melody Summers, she was thirty-two years old and had two kids: a four-year-old and a two-year-old. She was an elementary school teacher, and her husband was a firefighter. On paper, they were the quintessential American family.

After Greg said he wanted to speak with Melody, she had been escorted into a conference room at one of the first buildings in the industrial park.

He grunted when he got to the part of her file which said she ran track in high school and college. Apparently, she got her speed from her mother.

She also got pretty good grades in college and then decided to go work at an inner-city school for a few years. Once she got married, she moved out to the suburbs with her husband.

"Listen to this," he said to Mitch. "Melody Summers worked in the inner city before moving to the suburbs but still donates her free time to tutoring once a month for the kids at her old school and spends some of her other time working with an adult literacy program. She is known for her bake sale cupcakes."

"You get the feeling none of this is fitting the profile of an international spy family?" Mitch asked with a raised eyebrow.

Greg sighed, shutting off the tablet. "I don't know. Espionage is not exactly my area. But yeah, this doesn't seem to be the right background. I mean, I suppose if Agnes was some sort of sleeper agent, she could have encouraged her daughter to be the all-American woman in order to throw off any suspicion."

"That's cold."

Greg nodded. And that was the problem. Agnes wasn't cold. It was possible that she was an Oscar-worthy actress, but to fool everyone for decades? Raise her daughter to be an all-American, free-time volunteering, cupcake-baking elementary school teacher just for a cover?

"Or maybe her daughter's also an agent?" Greg murmured.

"And the grandkids too?" Mitch asked, raising an eyebrow.

Greg grinned. "Not yet. Maybe they're grooming them?"

"How about we go and talk to the daughter before we send the whole family off to the gulag?"

Mitch pulled into a parking space around the side of building one. Two members from the D.E.A.D. stood there waiting. One was Max and the other was Kaylee Hughes, the team medic. With freckled tan skin and curly hair she always kept back in a bun, she was one of the most steadfast members of the force.

Greg nodded at her. "How is she?

"She keeps vacillating between being pissed off and extremely concerned for her mother. She doesn't know what's going on, but she knows her mother is in the middle of it. She doesn't seem to know how to process that."

"Does her reaction strike you as genuine?" Mitch asked.

Kaylee nodded. "Yeah. She seems confused more than anything else."

Leaving Max outside, Kaylee led Greg and Mitch inside and down a short hallway to a room two doors in on the right. This building wasn't the same one they had been in earlier, but it still had the same beige color scheme.

Another member of their task force was standing guard at the door. He gave them a nod before he opened the door.

Melody Summers stood pacing along the back wall of the conference room. Her face was pale, her eyes red. She looked like a younger version of her mother with a slightly wider nose.

She came to an abrupt stop as the door opened. Her eyes widened as Greg and Mitch stepped inside. She looked between the two of them, her hand coming to rest on her chest.

Mitch took a step forward. "Mrs. Summers, my name is Agent Haldron, and this is Dr. Schorn."

The woman's gaze immediately flew to Greg. "Doctor? Is my mother all right?"

"She's fine. She's not injured. I'm not that kind of doctor," Greg said as he gestured to a chair near her. "Why don't you take a seat?"

Indecision flashed across Melody's face before she finally gave an abrupt nod. She pulled out a chair and took a seat, sitting right on the edge of it.

Mitch and Greg took seats across from her, and before either of them could speak, Melody did. "Where is my mother? I want to see her."

"I'm afraid that's not possible. She's in custody right now," Mitch said as he shifted his chair closer to the table.

Looking completely bewildered, Melody looked between the two of them. "Custody? Why? What on earth do you think she's done?"

Mitch pointed to Greg's face. "Well, we're starting with assault on a federal agent."

Melody reared back. "You're kidding. She wouldn't hit anyone."

"I'm afraid she did. She punched my partner square in the cheek," Mitch said.

Glaring at Greg, Melody crossed her arms over her chest. "Why? What did you do to her?"

With a shake of his head, Greg put up both hands. "Nothing. Absolutely nothing. We were having a nice conversation. I turned around, and it was like she was a different person."

Melody stilled for just a moment, her hand halfway to her hair before she continued the movement.

Narrowing his eyes, Mitch said, "That's not the first time this has happened."

She shook her head. "I'm not helping you guys lock up my mother."

Greg leaned forward. "Then help us keep her from getting locked up. We do not want your mother to be locked away. But we do need to understand what happened. It was like a switch went off, and she was someone different. And I have a feeling you've seen that before."

"No," she said, not meeting their gaze, but there was a nervous twitch to her hands.

Now Mitch leaned forward, his voice taking on an edge. "We're not playing around here, Melody. Your mother is in a lot of trouble. If you know something that can help her, you need to tell us. We don't want to lock her up, but we will if we don't have a better explanation. Prison won't be easy for a woman her age."

All of the anger seemed to roll out of Melanie at the end of Mitch's speech as the true predicament of her mother hit her. She slumped in the chair, tears cresting in her eyes. "She's really going to prison?"

"I'm afraid there's no way around it unless you can help us figure out what's going on. We don't know your mother very well, but this behavior seems really out of character for her," Greg said, his tone softer than Mitch's had been.

The room was silent for a long moment. Greg felt like he should say something, maybe push Melody a little more to help them. He started to open his mouth, but Mitch grabbed his arm, giving him an almost imperceptible shake of the head. So Greg sat back and waited.

And it worked. When Melody spoke, her voice was quiet. "It's just, it was tough after my father died."

"How long ago was that?" Mitch asked, his voice decidedly softer than it had been previously.

A tear slid down Melody's cheek, and she wiped it away quickly. "Ten years ago. Cancer. It wasn't a very long illness. Pancreatic. They only caught it three months before he passed. Mom, she took off from work and took care of him. She was by his side the entire time. It took a toll on her. It took a toll on all of us."

Melody took a deep breath. "And she was just lost after he died. It was almost as if, when he was sick, she had something to focus on. So she didn't really think about the fact that he was dying. Or at least, she could shove it to the back of her mind and distract herself with just taking care of him. But once he was gone, that distraction was gone, and it was really rough for a little while."

"Rough how?" Greg asked.

Continuing with a tremor in her voice, she said, "At first it was just the normal stuff. You know, we got through the funeral and the first few weeks. And Mom went back to work after a month. But she was tired a lot, and she was just down and sad, you know?

"So, I thought maybe a little getaway might be good. I booked us in this little mountain retreat area for a weekend, just the two of us. They were having some sort of craft weekend."

Smiling, even as another tear rolled down her cheek, Melody said, "My mom loves crafts, so when I read about it, I thought it would be perfect. We'd be able to do all of these crafts and walk around in the woods and have nice dinners. I just thought it might be a nice way for her to, you know, enjoy herself."

"What happened?" Greg asked after Melody fell silent.

It took the woman a moment to answer. "She disappeared. I'd gone for a nap that Saturday afternoon because it's the kind of place where you can take a nap and not feel guilty about it. And my mom left me a note saying she was going for a walk. When I woke up, I wasn't concerned right away because I wasn't exactly sure when she had gone for the walk. I'd only napped for about thirty minutes, so she couldn't have been gone that long. But an hour later, she still wasn't back. So I went out and walked around, trying to find her. But I couldn't, and it was getting dark. I notified the resort people, and they sent out some people to look for her. But nobody could find her."

"Where was she?" Mitch asked.

"Not where she should have been," Melody said, staring out the window before turning back to them. "We got a call around nine o'clock. It was my mom. She was a hundred miles away."

"How'd she get there?" Greg asked.

"We've never been able to figure that out," she said. "The car was still with me. But a *hundred miles*. And she couldn't remember how she'd gotten there. I thought that someone had assaulted her, grabbed her from the resort or something, but she seemed to be fine. She just had absolutely no memory of the hours in between. She didn't even remember going out for a walk. Or writing that note. As far as she was concerned, one minute, she was in the hotel room, and then the next she was standing in the middle of a busy street."

"There must have been some sort of video or surveillance that showed where she was," Mitch said.

Melody shook her head. "No. It was an area that didn't have anything like that."

"What about her cell phone?" Mitch asked.

"I contacted the company, and they weren't able to trace it while she was missing. They said she must have turned it off. But when I found her, it was back on again."

"So where was she?" Greg asked.

"We've never found that out either," Melody said confusion and fear in her voice. "But it was just on the heels of my dad passing away. We just kind of shoved it aside and didn't talk about it. But I know it worried my mom for a long time. And then she had nightmares every now and then."

"Nightmares? What kind of nightmares?" Greg asked.

"She wouldn't tell me. She'd say she didn't remember, but I always got the feeling she did and she just didn't want to tell me. She didn't want to worry me."

As he put the pieces together, Greg's mind race and a pit opened in his stomach. *Please let me be wrong*, he thought silently as he stood up. "Melody, we're going to do everything we can to help your mom. But you're not going to be able to see her for a little while."

"But she needs a lawyer."

Greg shook his head. "I don't think a lawyer is going to help her with this."

CHAPTER 21

After leaving Melody, Greg and Mitch hurried back to the other building where Agnes was being held.

"What are you thinking?" Mitch asked as he drove.

"I'm not sure," Greg murmured before he turned to his partner. "But does Melody's story about her mom strike you as similar to Nate's?"

"It does indeed," Mitch said.

Five minutes later, they strode down the hall toward the conference room where Agnes had been moved. Not sure what to expect, Greg paused at the door. Mitch gave him a nod, and Greg opened it.

Sitting with her head resting on a table, Agnes looked up when she heard them enter. The room was empty except for the table and three chairs around it. Her eyes were bloodshot, her hair coming out of her bun. She looked devastated and confused.

Even though there was a chance that she was fooling them, Greg's heart went out to the woman. She just looked so lost.

"Hi, Agnes," Greg said as he stepped inside.

Her eyes locked on Greg's face, Agnes gasped. "Did I do that?"

Greg's hand went to the bruise on his cheek. "I'm afraid so. You pack a mean right hook."

"I'm so sorry. I don't know why I did that. I don't know why any of this is happening." Agnes's whole body started to tremble.

Keeping his voice calm, Greg spoke softly as he slipped into the chair across from her. "Well, that's why we're here, to try and figure that out."

As Mitch took the seat next to him, he pulled a handkerchief from his pocket and slipped it across the table toward Agnes.

Agnes took it with a grateful smile and wiped at the tears on her cheeks.

And Greg yet again was impressed by Mitch. The man had handkerchiefs for crying women. That was a seriously smooth move.

"Agnes, we need to talk to you about what happened at the mountain resort ten years ago," Greg said.

Agnes frowned. "The resort? Why?"

"It might be related," Greg said.

"I don't see how. I mean, I just, I guess I just wandered off."

"Your daughter said that you were found a hundred miles from the resort," Mitch said.

She shifted her gaze away from them. "Yes, I know."

"Do you remember driving there?" Mitch asked.

Still not meeting their gaze, Agnes shook her head. "No, I don't remember driving there at all."

She was lying. Greg knew it in his gut. He leaned forward. "That's not true, Agnes. Or at least not entirely true. You remember some of what happened to you while you were missing, don't you?"

She rolled her hand into a fist around the handkerchief. "I, I don't …"

The woman still looked devastated, but Greg pushed his compassion aside. He needed these answers, and so did she. "Agnes, you're in a lot of trouble right now. Not just for assaulting me but also for the theft of government property. And that property is really dangerous. We need to know why you did it."

"I don't know," she murmured.

"Well, we think it might be related to why you disappeared ten years ago," Greg said.

Pressing her back into the chair, Agnes shook her head, terror flashing across her face. "No, it can't. They're not related. They can't be."

"Why not?" Mitch asked.

She looked up, first at him and then at Greg. She dropped her voice to barely above a whisper. "Because I think I was abducted by aliens."

CHAPTER 22

After questioning Agnes for another fifteen minutes, Greg and Mitch stepped out of the room convinced she was finally telling them the truth. She'd never told anyone about what she believed had happened to her because she knew that she would lose her government clearance if she did.

After her husband died, she said she needed her job to keep herself sane. And there was no way the government was going to allow her to keep that job if she cried aliens.

Greg shut the door, and they walked a little farther down the hall before Greg stopped, leaning back against the wall. "What do you think?"

"I think that she definitely believes it was aliens," Mitch said.

"You don't?" Greg asked, noting the skepticism on his partner's face.

Mitch shrugged. "Even after all we've seen, I'm still looking for the human angle."

Greg nodded. "Yeah, I get that. But she seems to be

convinced. And that's the second abductee we've come across in regard to this case in the last twenty-four hours."

"To be fair, Nate has nothing to do with this case," Mitch said.

Raising his hands, Greg nodded. "Okay, technically that's true. But in all the time I've been involved with these cases, I've never come across an abductee. And now, we've come across two in a very short time period. That can't be a coincidence."

Mitch shrugged. "It could be you just don't want it to be."

"What does that mean?" Greg asked.

"You're looking for a way to help Agnes because you feel sorry for her."

"Don't you?"

"Of course. She's been through a lot. And I don't know what happened earlier today, but I don't think she's a sleeper agent. I think she may just be a disturbed woman."

Sighing, Greg ran a hand through his hair. Was Mitch right? Was he grasping at straws? Was he linking two things completely unconnected? It was possible. But he'd been at this too long to not at least investigate the possibility that these two were somehow connected.

He pushed off from the wall. "Maybe I am. Maybe I'm being pulled in by a sweet older woman. But I'm not ready to hand her over to the feds to be criminally sentenced without making sure that I'm wrong. We're bringing her back to the base. I'm going to put her through the same analysis that Nate Prower is going to go through."

"And if at the end of it, we don't find anything?" Mitch asked.

Glancing back at the closed door behind which Agnes sat, Greg swallowed. "Then I guess I turn her over to the feds."

CHAPTER 23

After deciding on a course of action, Greg and Mitch wasted no time getting Agnes loaded up onto the plane and taken back to the D.E.A.D.

Agnes looked completely bewildered by the whole experience. And Greg felt more than a little guilty when he handed her over to the medical staff at the facility.

But this was her best shot at not being locked up for the rest of her life. At the same time, he couldn't help but wonder if Mitch was right and he was just trying to save a woman who he just genuinely liked.

He wrote off a quick report to Norah, promising to give her a more detailed one in the morning. He sent a text to Kal telling him he was heading back to the apartment. Kal texted back that he was staying with Alvie for the night.

For once, Greg was glad because he really needed to sleep. When he arrived at the apartment, he wolfed down some old Chinese food and then crashed hard.

The next morning, when a knock came at his bedroom door, he was still face down on his bed in the exact same position.

"Greg? You awake?" Kal's voice called through the door.

Groaning, Greg blinked, raising his head slowly. It took him a minute to get his brain to catch up. He stared over at the clock. It was nearly nine. Shock jolted through him. Damn it. He scrambled off the bed quickly and hustled across the room, pulling open the door.

Kal stood there shifting from foot to foot. "You okay? I called, but there was no answer."

Greg ran a hand through his hair. "I don't even know where my phone is."

"I found it in the kitchen. Why don't I make you a quick breakfast while you shower, and we can head over to the base?"

"Maybe I'll just work from home today," Greg said, not really wanting to jump right back into things despite his initial leap from the bed. He could probably go over the lab work for Nate and Agnes from here. Part of him wanted to hide out in case the lab work turned up nothing. He really didn't want to face either of them to say they still didn't have any answers.

But he was also feeling awfully tired. Maybe it was because he hadn't gone to bed till four a.m.

Kal shook his head, destroying Greg's hope of a more relaxed workday. "I'm afraid that's not going to happen. Maeve's coming in today. In fact, she should already be there. She wants your help on something."

Greg's spirits lifted. Maeve was in town? That was great. He'd missed working with her. And maybe she could give her opinion on Nate and Agnes. "Okay, yeah, I'll grab a shower. Can you just make me an egg sandwich or something?

"Consider it done," Kal said before heading to the kitchen.

Flinging off his shirt, Greg hustled into the bathroom, his mind full of what he needed to do today. He was feeling a little more energized at the prospect of being able to bounce ideas off of Maeve. Last night on the plane, he'd drafted a preliminary list of testing that he wanted done on Agnes and Nate. Since he was running late, they already should have done most of that this morning. He would review those results and then hopefully go over them with Maeve, who might have a better idea of what the next step should be.

As he jumped in the shower, he wondered what had brought Maeve out. Then he remembered the silver orb. Did it have something to do with that? He was intrigued by the idea of them.

Greg let his mind wander through his case and through the possible sources of the silver orb as he got ready. Fifteen minutes later, he and Kal were driving to headquarters.

When Greg finished off the egg sandwich in the passenger seat of his car as Kal drove, he was still hungry. He drank down some water to rinse out his mouth, but he really could have used some caffeine. Unfortunately, the apartment hadn't had any. He hadn't had a chance to go grocery shopping lately.

Kal pulled into Greg's spot at the facility. "I'll go track you down some coffee."

"Have I told you what a godsend you are?"

"All in an intern's description."

"I don't think waking me up, making me breakfast, and finding me coffee is part of the intern description." Greg paused. "Okay, maybe the finding me coffee part is."

Kal chuckled. "Hey, I'm happy to not do those things if it's outside of my job description."

"It might be outside of your job description, but it's definitely in the nephew requirements."

Pushing through the main doors of the facility, Kal held it open. "There's always an angle with you. Anyway, I'll be back in a little bit. I'll just run down to the cafeteria."

"Thanks," Greg called after him.

His nephew gave him a wave without looking back.

Greg's stomach rumbled. He needed more food. But first

things first. He turned toward the medical wing. He stopped after only two steps and turned toward his office. They would send the test results to his terminal, so he wanted to go through those before he spoke with Maeve about them.

At his office, he booted up his computer and went through the laborious process of logging into the system. Headquarters had a lot of security, which, of course, made him think about the DoD facility. It had a lot of security too, but someone had figured a way around it.

He frowned at the thought. But maybe he was onto something. Had someone made Agnes steal those controllers? Was that even possible?

A few minutes later, he scrolled through and saw that only some of the test results had been inputted into the system. But the results so far showed nothing unusual in either Nate or Agnes's biology. Nate had slept well last night. Agnes hadn't slept as well, but that was completely understandable given the situation and the fact that she'd only been on the base for a few hours.

Greg frowned as he pushed away from the desk. His phone beeped, and he pulled it out. It was a text from Norah. *Meet with me and Maeve in my office in 15.*

He stood up and headed to the door. He had fifteen minutes, which meant he would have time to stop by and see both Nate and Agnes and see how the tests were coming along.

Two minutes later, he was striding down the hall of the medical wing. He stopped at Agnes's room first. There was no one inside, so he made his way down to the examination room.

Agnes, in pale blue scrubs, was walking on a treadmill with a cardiac monitor attached to her. Hannah was with her, observing the monitor. She nodded and reached over and hit a button on the treadmill's console. "That's good, Agnes."

Agnes gave her a nervous smile as she stepped off the

machine. There were two guards along the back wall keeping an eye on her. They gave Greg a nod as he stepped inside.

Hannah looked up. "Dr. Schorn. Good morning."

"Morning, Hannah." He turned to Agnes. "How are you feeling today?"

"Good. Oh, but your eye."

Greg had taken a look at it this morning in the mirror and had blanched. It was already swelling and half closed. But he waved Agnes's concern away. "I've had worse. So, anything new come back to you?"

The woman shook her head. "No, not really. But I wrote everything down like you asked me to. I gave it to one of the medical staff this morning."

He looked over at Hannah, who nodded. "When I left, Cheryl was scanning it into her file. It should be in there momentarily."

"How far have you gotten in the testing protocol?" Greg asked.

"We've got a couple more tests to do, and then we'll get you those results. They should all be completed within an hour. I think Nate's might already be done."

"Good. I'm going to go check in on him now. Agnes, I'll see you later, okay?"

She just gave him a small miserable nod. The woman was eaten up with guilt. For attacking Greg, for attacking Pete, and for stealing government property. She had a lot weighing on her, so Greg couldn't fault her for the response.

As he walked down the hall, he wondered if he was being played, but she seemed so genuine. And if she was genuine, having no memory of what she had done, then someone had abused her horribly, and that did not sit well with Greg at all.

He could also admit that Mitch was right: A big part of him hoped that was the case. He hoped that Agnes was as nice a person as she appeared to be.

Nate's room was two doors down. Greg stopped outside as his phone beeped.

He scrolled through and saw that the report that Agnes had written was now attached to her file. He quickly scanned it as he leaned back against the wall. It was almost identical to what she'd told them yesterday. She didn't remember everything about her lost time, but she had these flashes of memory. They all seemed to involve being in a room of some sort with figures hovering over her and Agnes being unable to move.

It must have been terrifying. And it had all the hallmarks of a classic alien abduction report.

As Greg finished reading it, he returned his phone to his pocket. Even if Agnes had suffered some sort of delusion, the delusion itself must have been pretty traumatic. Her report only confirmed that she was a woman who needed help, and help would not come in the form of a prison sentence.

He was about to open the door to Nate's room when it opened from the other side.

Cheryl looked up. Coming in at only about five foot two, she had long light-brown hair that she always wore pulled back in a ponytail. "Greg, hey, how are you?"

Greg fumbled for something to say.

She had been nothing but friendly and funny in his interactions with her, except for the other day when she'd been uncharacteristically abrupt. But maybe she'd just been having a bad day. He struggled to find something to say that wasn't about work. Then he remembered the conversation they'd had last month. "Cheryl, hey. Oh, how did it go with your parents this past weekend?

"What?" She frowned. "Oh, we had to reschedule. I got too busy."

That was odd. When he'd first met her, she had mentioned how much she missed her parents. But maybe that's why she was so short the other day. Maybe work was getting in the way of her relationship with them. "Oh, I'm sorry."

She shrugged. "It's okay. Part of the—"

A scream from inside Nate's room swallowed the rest of her statement. Cheryl went flying forward as Nate bulldozed past her and out into the hallway. Greg caught Cheryl before she could hit the floor.

Dressed in a hospital gown, Nate stopped in the middle of the hallway, his chest heaving, looking around before he bolted toward the front of the building.

Pushing Cheryl against the wall, Greg made sure she could stand before he went after him. "Call security!" he yelled.

Up ahead, Nate sprinted, moving incredibly fast. But as Greg watched him, he couldn't help but notice that his movements appeared jerky, not smooth. Now that he thought about it, there had been a stiffness to Agnes's run yesterday as well.

Even as he analyzed Nate's movements, Greg raced after him, trying to figure out what the heck had happened. Nate had been perfectly behaved the entire time he'd been here. He'd acquiesced to every single test without complaint according to the report. So what had just set him off?

"Nate! Nate, stop!" Greg yelled as he tore down the hall after the fleeing man.

But Nate wasn't listening. He barreled around the corner, taking out a security guard coming from the other direction. The man went flying back, his head slamming into the wall with a thud.

Greg winced at the sound. That was definitely going to leave a mark.

Leaping over the downed security guard as he rounded the corner, Greg was happy to hear more running feet behind him. A quick glance showed that three more security guards had joined the chase. But unfortunately, none were ahead of Nate, and they were heading to the front foyer. Was he trying to leave?

Nate burst into the wide-open front foyer. Three security guards sprinted toward him from the front door. But Nate, with moves that would make any football player proud, managed to dodge around them.

The group that had been walking at the other side of the foyer toward the stairs turned around. And standing in the middle of them was Maeve. Her eyes grew wide as she looked at Nate. Norah was with her, as well as Alvie and two guards.

Oh crap. Alvie. Nate wasn't supposed to see Alvie.

The two guards rushed to intercept Nate, but Nate yanked one forward, dropping him in the other's path before he leaped over the two of them. It was an impressive move, and nothing in Nate's background suggested he had that kind of training.

Norah moved to intercept, but Nate grabbed hold of her and flung her toward the two security guards behind him.

Nate charged Maeve, and Greg held his breath. There was no one who could reach him in time.

CHAPTER 24

Eyes wide, Maeve backed up, a large case in her hand as Nate charged toward her.

Reaching for her, Greg's heart dropped. "Maeve!" He yelled.

Then Alvie slid to the side and slammed a side kick into Nate's knee. It buckled. Alvie jumped onto the bent leg, crawled up his side, wrapped an arm around his neck, and leaped to the side, slinging Nate over his shoulder.

Mouth open, Nate lay stunned on the ground long enough for the security to reach him and get cuffs on him.

Greg hurried up to them. "You need to sedate him *now*," he ordered.

All of the security guards in the D.E.A.D. facility carried tranquilizer guns on them. With the type of cases that the D.E.A.D. dealt with, it was an absolute necessity. Without questioning the order, one of the guards pulled out his gun and shot Nate in the arm.

Nate's eyelids fluttered and then closed. Greg let out a breath, his chest heaving.

Kal walked up slowly, two coffees in his hands. He looked from Greg to the downed Nate, whose butt was showing through the back of his hospital gown. "Uh, Greg, you still need that coffee?"

CHAPTER 25

Greg did indeed need the coffee. Standing in the lobby, he downed the hot beverage, finishing nearly half of it in one gulp. Kal simply handed him his coffee as well, no doubt figuring that Greg was going to finish his off faster than Kal would be able to get down to the cafeteria and replenish it.

Greg took both cups and walked over to Maeve. "You okay?"

Maeve nodded shakily. "Yeah. Who is that?"

"I would say he's this really nice guy that Mitch and I met yesterday, but I don't know who the guy who just tried to attack you was." Greg turned to Alvie. "Nice moves, Alvie."

Alvie nodded at him but looked back at Nate, who was loaded onto a stretcher before they started to wheel him down the hall. Then he turned back to Greg and spoke through his mind. *Not him. Being controlled.*

The nearly identical thought Greg had about Agnes came back to him at Alvie's words. "He's being controlled? You're sure?" Greg asked.

Yes, Alvie said before walking off with Kal.

His mind spinning, Greg watched him go. He'd thought that Agnes had been acting completely out of character. What if the same thing had happened to Nate? What if they were both being controlled?

Norah walked up, her hands on her hips. "How did that just happen?"

Greg shook his head. "Cheryl stepped out of Nate's room as I was arriving. Nate burst out behind her. But it doesn't make any sense. Nate's been completely docile ever since he's been here. There's no hint of violence in his history at all. Yet he just bolted from his room and headed straight here." Greg pictured the scene in his head before turning to Maeve. "He headed for you."

Maeve shook her head. "I don't think he was heading for me. I don't know him, and there was no way for him to know I was here. I think I was just in the way."

Although she was probably right, Greg couldn't help but look over his shoulder at where Nate was being wheeled down the hall. Turning back, he eyed the large container she was holding. "What's that?" He asked.

"This is what I came to get your help with," Maeve said.

Taking a breath, Norah nodded at both of them. "Okay, Greg, Maeve, we're heading to my office." Scanning the foyer, she called out. "Mitch."

Mitch, who Greg hadn't realized was here, strode over. His partner stared hard at the case that Maeve held before returning his attention to Norah. "What do you need?"

Norah nodded toward the quickly disappearing stretcher. "I need you to go keep an eye on Nate. Make sure that he's secured and have them run tests immediately to see what accounts for this change in behavior."

"On it." Mitch nodded before he hustled down the hall.

Then Norah turned to Greg and Maeve. "Okay, now let's go figure out this new mystery that Maeve's brought us."

CHAPTER 26

Instead of meeting in Norah's office, they decided to meet in the dining room next to Norah's office. Norah called down and had some food brought up. Maeve hadn't had much to eat that morning, and Greg was pretty sure he burned up that egg sandwich in the sprint after Nate.

He gratefully helped himself to the croissant sandwiches that were brought up from the cafeteria. On the walk up, he'd finished the first coffee that Kal had brought him and was now working his way through the second. The caffeine was helping clear his mind, although it wasn't providing him with any insights. That behavior had been completely uncharacteristic of Nate. Just as Agnes's behavior had been. The one thing the two had in common was uncharacteristic behavior.

Well, that and that they had both been abducted by aliens.

But how did those two link up? Had the aliens done something to them that allowed them to be controlled like Alvie suggested? Was that even possible? He knew suggestible people could be hypnotized to engage in certain behaviors, but Agnes had driven a car, gotten into the warehouse file, taken what she needed, and then shipped the headset and controllers through UPS. That seemed way too complicated a series of actions for a simple hypnotist.

And with Nate, they still didn't know what, if anything, he'd done when he lost time. In his gut, though, Greg knew they were connected. He just needed to figure out how.

Across from him, Maeve sat quietly eating her sandwich, looking a little pale.

"You sure you're all right, Maeve?" Norah asked before Greg could.

She nodded. "Yeah. I just haven't been around that kind of activity for a while. I forgot about the adrenaline high and then the crash afterwards."

Greg chuckled. "Oh, I'm getting used to those periods."

She gave him a small smile, looking a little more like her old self. "I bet. So what's the story with those two?"

Norah gave an abbreviated version of the situation with Agnes and Nate.

"They were both abducted?" Maeve asked.

Greg shrugged. "That seems to be the common denominator. But as to what any of that means, we're still not clear. So what did you bring with you today for show-and-tell?"

Maeve nudged her chin toward the container that she'd carried up and placed in the chair next to her. "It's one of those silver orbs that I'm sure Tilda told you guys about."

Greg leaned forward eagerly. He had to admit he was intrigued by it. It obviously was crafted by alien hands. "Can we see it?"

Standing, Maeve unsnapped the bag and pulled out a box. She placed it on the table. Then she unsnapped the cover and pulled it back. Sitting inside was what looked like a pristine silver bowling ball without any holes.

Except this bowling ball was vibrating.

Greg leaned closer and felt the hair on his arms lift. He raised his eyebrows.

Maeve frowned, looking from Greg to the ball. "It's been emitting some sort of energy since it was found, but these vibrations are new. According to Tilda, they started within the last few months. Right now, though, it's vibrating a lot more than I've seen before."

"Is it dangerous?" Norah asked.

Maeve shook her head. "We don't think so. Tilda has actually had this one for over thirty years and hasn't had a problem with it."

"But that was before it woke up," Norah said.

"That's true," Maeve conceded. "But it has no seams, no identifiable power source, and the energy is very low and is harmless to humans. We simply don't know what it's doing."

"And this is the same thing you saw in the tunnels in northern Africa?" Norah asked.

"Identical. But like I said, Tilda's had this one for two decades. And it, just for lack of a better term, came to life recently."

Greg frowned, staring at it. "Well, that can't be good."

"My thoughts exactly," Maeve said. "I was hoping you and I could run some tests on it and see what we could find out because I'm just running into brick walls doing this on my own."

Greg was definitely intrigued. "I'd be happy to. I was actually hoping you could look over the research on Agnes and Nate as well."

Maeve grinned. "Looks like we're back in business."

Greg stared at the silver orb, feeling a tingle of excitement followed almost immediately by worry as he remembered all the other times he and Maeve had worked together. "Yeah. I just hope this business isn't as dangerous as our previous collaborations."

CHAPTER 27

Although Greg was intrigued by the silver orb, it was not the primary focus of his thoughts. Those still belonged to Nate and Agnes. Right now, though, the incident with Nate was taking up the most mental energy. Greg just couldn't get it out of his mind. It was so completely out of character for him.

And that strange run of his. After the meeting, Maeve went to get set up in one of the labs. Greg swung by his office to compare the video of both Agnes and Nate running. He placed them side by side on a split screen, his gaze dancing between them. They weren't identical, but they were incredibly similar. And both were not natural.

He supposed it was possible they were both just horrible runners, at least in terms of form. But he looked in her file, and Agnes had been a runner for years. She still ran a half marathon with her daughter every Thanksgiving. She had to have better form than what he was seeing here. So what did that mean?

He watched the video half a dozen more times, but it still wasn't providing him with any answers. So he pushed back from the desk and headed down to the medical suite. He wanted to ask Nate if he was much of a runner. Apparently he'd been in crew in college. Greg wasn't really sure what that involved. But for training, they must have run a little bit, right?

As he rounded the corner and pushed through the doors of the medical suite, he caught sight of Hannah. She stood in the hall looking through an observation window with her tablet in front of her.

Greg walked up and stood next to her without saying a word. On the other side of the glass, Nate lay inside on a bed with restraints around his wrists and ankles. He was quiet, his eyes closed, his chest moving up and down slowly.

"How is he?" Greg asked.

Hannah shook her head. "He's fine. There's residual adrenaline from his activities, but otherwise, nothing is different. He's the same as he was yesterday."

"Has he come to yet?"

Hannah shook her head. "Not yet. The tranquilizer will keep him out for at least another hour or so. I just don't understand what happened. He's not a violent guy. In fact, he's been nothing but pleasant to everyone since he got here. He just seems like a guy desperately in need of answers."

"I think he still is. And maybe this incident will lead to those answers," Greg said, not sure if he believed what he was saying or just hoped he was right.

Hannah crushed her tablet against her chest as she looked through the window. "I just can't figure out what's going on with him. If you had asked me before this morning, I would have said that there was nothing wrong with him. That he was perfectly fine and that whatever had happened to him was all in his mind. That maybe we needed to bring in a psych consult."

"Maybe you should. Just to cover all bases," Greg murmured, his chest heavy at the thought. He pictured Nate's wife and their two kids. Schizophrenia didn't show up until adulthood, so it was possible symptoms were appearing now. He just didn't have enough of a background in psychology to know what that could be.

"I've already put in the call," Hannah said. "They'll be here probably at about the same time that Nate wakes up."

Struggling to figure out what was going on, Greg stared through the glass at Nate. Two individuals who behaved in ways that were simply out of character for both of them. There must be a link.

But maybe Hannah was right. Maybe it wasn't biological, or at least not their type of biology. It could be psychological. Or maybe they both had some sort of virus or parasite or …

He stopped still, his eyes narrowing. "Have you checked for parasites?"

"We've run all the normal tests and haven't seen anything that indicates that."

An idea forming at the back of his mind, Greg spoke quickly. "I know, but we're talking about, or *maybe* talking about, alien abductions. If that's the case, parasites that they might have been exposed to wouldn't show up on a normal scan. We'd have to look for something that may be different from anything that normal humans would be exposed to."

"You're right." Hannah tucked her head down. Her hands flew over her tablet. "I've got some ideas on how we could do that, but those tests are going to take a couple of hours."

Greg stared through the window one last time. "That's okay. Neither of them is going anywhere until we figure this out."

CHAPTER 28

After leaving Hannah to start the tests, Greg headed back up to the lab to meet with Maeve. When he walked in, she had the silver orb sitting on a stand in the middle of one of the lab tables. It had electrodes attached to it, and she was running diagnostics.

Greg walked in, nodding to her laptop. "Anything?"

Maeve shook her head. "No. In fact, the energy that I detected yesterday is no longer registering. And you can feel that the thing's gone dormant."

Greg leaned forward and didn't feel that same energy coming off the orb he had felt earlier. He sat back. "So what's the story on this one?"

She quickly explained about how Tilda had gotten the orb from the Crumb family in Florida back in the late nineties.

Greg stared at it. It was completely quiet now. "It really followed the family?"

Maeve shrugged. "That's what they said. But they weren't able to duplicate any of that activity at the R.I.S.E. facility, even though Jasper observed some of that activity in the Crumb home. So I don't know how much stock to put in that. Maybe one of the kids was playing a trick on the other and pushing it, or maybe they, I don't know, somehow attached magnets to it so that thing would follow them around."

Maeve blew out a breath. "In fact, right now the list of I-don't-knows is a heck of a lot longer than the list of things that I've figured out."

Greg frowned, staring at his friend. "What's going on?"

Pushing back from the table, Maeve ran a hand through her hair. "I don't know. I mean, I wanted to get back out in the field at least a little bit. I was feeling cooped up in the house and just kind of going a little stir crazy. But the first time I go out in the field, I nearly get killed. *And* I lose the artifact that I'm supposed to be bringing back.

"Now I've got an artifact that's identical to it, and I can't seem to figure out a single thing about it. I mean, obviously this thing wasn't created by nature. Someone made this. And we need to find out who."

"Well, have you asked for any help?" Greg asked.

"That's what I'm doing here."

Greg grinned. "And I appreciate the confidence that you have in me. However, I was thinking of a more celestial version of help," he said, pointing to the ceiling.

"No, I haven't asked the Council. I don't know why. I guess I'm trying to stay off their radar as much as possible."

Greg grunted, understanding the feeling. It was exactly what he had said to Norah not that long ago. "How about just asking Agaren? He might be willing to keep this secret. And he might be able to shed some light on it."

"I have been thinking about that."

"Well, being that you're running into walls and I'm running into walls with my own investigation, maybe we both need to start looking for some doors. I think you should contact Agaren and see if he can tell you anything. He seems like he's on humanity's side, so I don't think he'll be reporting back to the Council."

Maeve nodded. "Yeah, you're probably right."

There was a knock at the door, and Mitch stepped inside. "Hey, sorry to interrupt, but, Greg, I found ..." His words dwindled off as he spotted the silver orb propped up on the table.

Greg looked over at Maeve, who looked back at him with a questioning expression on her face.

"Mitch?" Greg asked.

Mitch seemed to give himself a shake as he pulled his attention away from the orb. "Right, um, they found out where Agnes sent that box. It's not far from here, just up in Niagara Falls. I was going to go check it out. Want to join me?"

Greg looked back at Maeve, who waved him on. "Go on. I might take up that suggestion you made."

Greg knew it would be hours before he got the new test results back from Nate and Agnes, and he honestly was looking to get out of this place for a little while.

Maybe a trip to Niagara Falls would clear his head and give him a chance to look at the whole situation with fresh eyes. Plus, who knew, maybe this was the lead that would break the whole thing open. "Okay, I'm in."

"Great," Mitch said, his gaze once again returning to the silver orb.

Greg stood up and walked toward him. "You ready now?"

Another flick of a glance at the orb, and Mitch nodded. "Yeah. Let's go."

Greg followed him out the door, noting that Mitch seemed a little more stiff than usual in his response. Greg found himself looking over his shoulder back at the orb. Mitch had seemed rather focused on it. But he supposed it was rather unusual looking.

He shook the thought from his head. *He's probably just curi-*

ous. There were so many things going on in this building, it was hard not to be curious about everything that was happening.

And besides, who was more down to earth than Mitch?

CHAPTER 29

NIAGARA FALLS, NEW YORK

The trip to Niagara Falls was incredibly short. By car, the trip from the D.E.A.D. facility would take three hours, but by plane, it was less than thirty minutes.

They touched down just outside Niagara Falls at Buffalo Niagara International Airport. They were unfortunately heading to the New York side of the falls. Not to be unpatriotic, but Greg preferred the Canadian side. It was much more built up, with more attractions. The Canadian side honestly put the New York side to shame.

The New York side, though, did have a few things going for it. There was, of course, the Maid of the Mist boat trips and a great view of the falls along with an aquarium that despite its small size actually wasn't too bad.

And there was the hurricane deck, which was apparently where they were heading right now. The hurricane deck sat only twenty feet from Bridal Veil Falls. Standing on it, tourists were pelted with rain and wind from the rushing water. The name of the deck came from the fact that if you stood on it, it sometimes felt like you were in the middle of a hurricane.

The individual who had received the package was named Justin Moore. Moore was a former police officer who now ran security for the Niagara Falls tourist area. He was fifty-two years old. A call into the security office indicated that he was doing his rounds this morning and could be found on the hurricane deck.

Greg and Mitch stepped into the elevator. Mitch hit the button to send them down 175 feet. As he did, Greg unrolled the yellow poncho he'd been given and slipped it over his head. Both he and Mitch already had the plastic shoe coverings over their shoes.

"You're going to make sure I don't fall over the side, right?" Greg asked as he wrestled his head through the opening in the poncho.

Mitch chuckled as he slipped his own poncho over his head. "I got you. Don't worry. But are you sure we couldn't have waited until he came *up* from the deck?"

"We could have," Greg hedged, "but I've never been to the hurricane deck. And now we have a chance to have it to ourselves."

Mitch shook his head. "You know we're going to get soaked, right?"

"That's the fun part," Greg said.

Mitch just sighed deeply ins response.

The elevator doors chimed before sliding open. Greg stepped out onto the deck as a strong wind blew at him, bringing with it a spray of water.

Greg grinned. As a kid, he'd always loved the water rides at amusement parks. This was, as far as he was concerned, just another version.

Next to him, Mitch seemed decidedly less enthusiastic about this adventure. And Greg knew it wasn't just because of the location. Mitch had been off for the last few days. And he still hadn't talked to Greg about Maya and the kids leaving town. When they were on the plane back, Greg was going to bring it up. But it was obviously weighing on Mitch, and if it wasn't that, then it was something else. His partner needed to spill.

The platform was empty as Greg and Mitch made their way along it. The tourist attraction wouldn't be open for at least another two hours, but there had been a report about some trespassers last night, so Moore had been dispatched to make sure that nothing had been tampered with or left behind.

A huge spray of water blew over the wooden railing, pelting Greg. The bottom half of his pants were already soaked. As they continued to walk, the air was full of moisture and the wind yanked and pushed at his poncho. Greg loved it.

He laughed as another huge spray fell over them. Grinning from ear to ear, he glanced up at Mitch. There was no smile on his face. He hadn't said a word since the elevator.

While it was true that on a good day, Mitch didn't say a lot, today he was exceptionally quiet. He'd barely said two words to Greg on the flight over and hadn't said a thing on the drive over from the airfield.

Screw this. He wasn't waiting for the plane to speak with him. "Are you sure that everything's all right?"

Not meeting his gaze, Mitch merely nodded.

Greg wasn't buying it. "What about Maya and the kids? Is everything good there? Everybody healthy?'"

Mitch flicked a frown at him. "Healthy? Yeah, they're all good. Why would you ask that?"

"Because they're visiting your in-laws, who were just in town. I thought maybe they were going to a doctor over there and you didn't want to say anything."

"What? No, it's nothing like that. Maya just wanted some

help with the kids, and I've been busy lately, so she went to her parents."

It had a ring of truth to it, but Greg still wasn't buying it. Something else was going on. He wanted to push Mitch a little on the topic, but the water from the falls was getting a little ferocious. A spray hit him full in the face, and he turned his head, slamming his eyes shut.

When he opened them, he saw a man in a dark-green slicker walking along the deck, paying special attention to all of the posts and garbage cans.

"That's our guy," Mitch said, picking up his pace.

Greg hustled after him and reached Mitch's side when he was only about five feet away from the officer. "Officer Moore?" Mitch called out.

Moore turned around. He had wrinkles at the corners of his blue eyes and a curious though not alarmed expression on his face. "Yes?"

As Mitch pulled out his ID from his back pocket, he said, "Agents Haldron and Schorn from the DoD. We were hoping we could speak with you for a few minutes."

Frowning, Moore took a step closer. "DoD? What are you guys doing over here? Have we got another terrorist threat?"

Shaking his head, Mitch had to raise his voice to be heard over the wind and the sound of the falls. "No, it's nothing like that. We just need to ask you some questions about a package that was sent to you about two weeks ago."

Moore frowned. "A package?"

A huge gust of wind blew heavily against them, sending with it another huge spray of water, though this one felt more like a wave of water. Both Mitch and Greg stumbled back from the onslaught.

Greg turned his head to the side, slamming his eyes shut. Water rolled down his face and into the collar of his poncho.

Okay, maybe Mitch was right and they should have waited until Moore came up from the deck.

"That was—" The words died on his lips as he turned back to Moore. Mitch had shifted so he was half in front of him. But even with that, Greg could clearly see the gun that Moore had pointed at the two of them.

Greg blinked hard, trying to keep his eyes on Moore even as the wind and water conspired to make it nearly impossible. Greg backed up with his hands up. "Hey, hey. There's no need for that."

Curling his lip, Moore met his gaze. "Greg Schorn. Always causing trouble, aren't you? I think I'm done dealing with you."

Greg frowned. Mitch hadn't told Moore his first name, so how did he know it?

He opened his mouth to ask when Moore pulled the trigger.

CHAPTER 30

There was no time for Greg to get out of the way. He had the railing next to him and a garbage can to the side of him.

A dark shape darted in front of Greg while simultaneously pushing him back. Greg rolled over the garbage can, tipping it on its side.

"No!" Greg yelled, reaching forward to yank Mitch away.

But he wasn't fast enough. Mitch grunted as the bullet tore into his gut.

"Mitch!"

Moore stepped forward, pulling the trigger over and over again. Mitch reached out and grabbed the hand that held the gun. The two men wrestled over the weapon as Greg scrambled to his feet, trying to figure out a way to get in.

Mitch managed to yank the gun away from Moore just as a huge wall of water crashed over the side of the decking. Mitch, unstable from pulling the gun away, teetered for a moment against the edge of the deck before Moore shoved him hard.

Mitch pitched to the side and plunged over the metal railing.

INTO THE DARK

Time slowed. Greg felt all the air get sucked from his lungs. Then he snapped forward again. He sprinted for the railing. "Mitch!"

With horror, he watched Mitch fall and plunge into the turbulent water below. Water splashed up high as he entered. Greg scanned the waters waiting for Mitch to pop back up.

He never did.

Greg's whole body went numb. It felt like his organs had been carved out of his chest. He continued to watch the waters, looking for any sign of his partner.

But he didn't resurface.

Stumbling back from the railing, Greg's stomach heaved. Movement to his right caused him to look over. Justin Moore sat on the ground, looking around in confusion. His gaze finally focused on Greg. He frowned. "Who are you?"

CHAPTER 31

The next hour was a blur. Greg called back to the D.E.A.D. headquarters and told Norah what had happened. He didn't really remember much of the conversation.

A team had been dispatched. They had been in Buffalo and arrived in only fifteen minutes. They secured the scene.

It felt like Norah arrived almost immediately after them, but Greg knew it had been at least another fifteen minutes. But time was working weird right now for Greg. He replayed the image of Mitch falling in his mind and it seemed to take forever. But everything else around him seemed to be moving too fast.

Max and Kaylee arrived with Norah. Both of their faces were drawn as they approached. Greg had stood at the railing, his gaze locked on the waters below, looking for any sign of Mitch. Boats were already in the water searching for him. Greg convinced himself that Mitch was fine. He would just pop up and wave, even as part of his brain told him there was no way Mitch could have survived that fall, especially after being shot multiple times.

Kaylee stepped next to him and took his wrist, checking his pulse without a word. She leaned closer to his ear. "Greg, I think you're in shock. Max and I are going to take you back up top."

Greg gripped the railing. "No, I need to watch for Mitch."

"Hey, buddy," Max said, gently pulling him from the railing. "The team's already in the water looking. They'll find him."

Greg let himself be pulled away. He didn't remember the trip back up the elevator.

The next thing he knew, he was back at the SUV that he and Mitch had ridden here in. Max pulled the tailgate open as Kaylee cut Greg's poncho off him and handed it to another force team member, who bagged it. She threw a blanket over his shoulders. It didn't help. In fact, Greg felt colder now and started to shiver.

Kaylee placed some warming packets in his hands as she sat him on the tailgate. "Greg, I need you to stay here, okay? Focus on me."

Greg nodded.

"That's good," Kaylee said as she shone a light in his eyes. "Now, can you tell me what happened?"

Once again, Greg saw Mitch's body jolt as the bullets entered and then saw him fall over the railing at Moore's push. Tears pressed against his eyes. "Mitch fell."

Max, who stood next to Kaylee, nodded. "We know that, buddy. But we need to know what happened before that."

In his mind, Mitch's body jolted again. "Mitch was shot. Moore, he shoved him, and Mitch fell over the side. He didn't come back up. Why didn't he come back up?"

After that, everything was a bit of a blur. Greg wasn't sure what else they spoke about. His mind seemed to have zoned out. The next thing he knew, Norah was in front of him. "Greg? Greg, are you all right?"

Greg felt like he was swimming up from the depths of the ocean as he looked at her. "Mitch?"

She shook her head. "We haven't found him yet."

Oh God. He pictured Maya and the kids. He sucked in a breath, feeling like he'd been stabbed in the chest. "Maya. We have to tell her that—"

Norah gripped Greg's arms. "We can't tell her anything, not yet. Not until we know exactly what happened here. We're going to have to wait on that, Greg. You know that."

Greg closed his eyes. Yes, D.E.A.D. policy: until they had a full report, they wouldn't release any information to next of kin, and even then, the information would be a believable lie. That Maya would be treated that way left a bitter taste in his mouth.

Greg had been a guest at Maya and Mitch's house on at least a dozen occasions over their time working together. He really liked Maya. She was a smart, strong woman, not that Greg was surprised by that. Of course Mitch would have someone as amazing as he was.

It hit him in the gut then. Mitch was gone. He sucked in a breath, lowering his head. He tried to get air to fill his lungs but he couldn't seem to get any.

"Kaylee!" Norah yelled.

A moment later, Kaylee was in front of him, placing an oxygen mask over his mouth. "Greg, I need you to breathe for me, okay? I need you to breathe."

Greg was trying to, but he was failing horribly. His lungs seemed to have frozen.

But slowly, the oxygen began to get through. Greg took his first deep breath, and it was painful. But he welcomed the pain. He deserved the pain, because Mitch had died saving him.

CHAPTER 32

CLAY, NEW YORK

Speaking with Agaren was not as simple as making a phone call. Agaren was at the Council's base on the moon. But Agaren had left Maeve with a way to reach out to him. She had used it only once before, and that had been when Agaren had shown her the process. He wanted to make sure she could reach him if something happened to the triplets or Alvie. Their continued existence was of critical importance to the Council.

And to the world.

Maeve locked the door to her lab, initiating the privacy protocols. She did not want anyone interrupting her. Then she walked to the couch at the back of the lab. She'd already set up the tools that she would need next to it.

Taking a seat, she pulled over the electrodes she'd placed on the cart. Positioning the electrodes along the edge of her scalp, she reached over and initiated the predetermined codes in her laptop. Then she quickly lay back on the couch, adjusting a pillow under her head.

Taking a couple of deep breaths, she counted down in her mind as she waited for the program to initiate. *Five, four, three, two, one.*

The small pulses sounded deep within her mind. Maeve settled back into the pillow and didn't fight the process. Keeping her mind blank, she focused solely on the pulses, shutting out all other sounds and thoughts.

Slowly she felt her link to this plane of existence slip away.

Maeve's eyes opened, and she found herself in the void that she had visited before with Agaren. There was nothing but space around her, pure white space.

"Agaren?" she called, not sure if he was already here or exactly how he would know she had arrived.

Slowly, a form began to materialize in front of her. Covered in a white tunic and pants, the being was tall, nearly seven feet, and humanoid in shape. But this was no human.

The head was disproportionately large, the eyes pure black above two air holes and a chin that came to a rounded point, much more narrow than a human chin. The small mouth curved up at the sides as Agaren's gaze fell on Maeve. "Maeve. It is good to see you."

"And you as well." The statement wasn't a lie. A peace filled Maeve whenever she was around Agaren. He was an ancient Gray. She wasn't sure exactly how old he was, but with that age came a great deal of wisdom. And he was sympathetic to the plight of humans.

"The triplets and Alvie are well," Agaren said, and it was not a question.

"Yes, they are."

Frown lines appeared between Agaren's eyes, making him appear more human. "But you are troubled."

"I am. I was hoping you could provide me with some guidance."

"I will if I can," Agaren said, waving to his right. Out of the mist, two chairs appeared. Maeve took a seat in one while Agaren settled himself in the other. "Now, tell me what is on your mind," he said.

"A situation has developed on Earth, and I'm not sure what to make of it. It involves these silver orbs that have come from space."

The slightest shift in Agaren's posture was all that Maeve needed to see to know that Agaren knew what she was referring to.

"You know of these orbs," she said.

Agaren nodded.

"What can you tell me?"

"Not much, I'm afraid. They belong to an ancient race. They are called the Primevals. They are believed to be the oldest existing race in the universe."

"The oldest?" Maeve asked in surprise. "How old?"

"We believe them to be four billion years old."

Shock stole Maeve's voice for a moment. It was hard to even conceptualize that. Humans, in comparison, were less than half a million years old.

"You were not expecting that answer," Agaren said.

"No. I know the universe is billions of years old, but I never imagined a species could exist for that long. What can you tell me about them?"

"Most of what I know is from legend. The Primevals, they are what you would view on your planet as royalty. They have an exalted status amongst the beings of the universe."

"Because of their age?"

"And because of their power. They have the gift of reincarnation."

"Is that their only power?"

Agaren paused before answering. "I believe now it is. At one point, they were an extremely formidable race. But somewhere along the way, once they left their home planet, they lost those powers."

"What kind of powers?"

"According to the legends, they could move and manipulate objects with their minds."

"Telekinesis?"

"The human vision of telekinesis is a rudimentary form of what they were capable of, but yes."

It was a fascinating idea. Humans had tried over time to develop such ability, but no fully provable skills had ever developed. "You said they lost their powers, though?"

Agaren nodded. "Yes. Their home world was destroyed, and they spread out across the galaxy. A small group took up residence on Earth. The Council knows little of what they did during that time."

Maeve frowned. "How is that possible?"

"They were able to block us from seeing the Earth during that time. It was as if a mist had been placed over the world that we could not see through. It lasted for two thousand years. By the time the mist cleared, the Primevals had slipped into the shadows of the human world. We never saw any sign of them again."

"But you know they're still alive." This time Maeve was the one not asking a question.

"Yes. Their reincarnation ship continues to function. We know they continue to be reborn. The reason they slipped into the quiet belongs to them, and as they are not interfering in humanity's existence, we see no reason to go searching for them."

Maeve could feel her time ticking away. And as much as she wanted to learn more about this race, she still needed answers to the questions that had brought her here. "The silver orbs. Do you know what purpose they serve?"

Agaren shook his head. "Little is known of the Primevals' culture. I know the orbs are associated with death and rebirth, but that is all."

"There is an energy that the orbs emit."

Agaren frowned. "Even that I did not know."

"We're trying to figure out why someone would be trying to gain these orbs," Maeve said.

"I'm afraid I cannot help you, Maeve."

She sighed. "I understand."

"But I can give you a warning: the Primevals were an extremely powerful race at one point. I do not know if they have walked away from those powers or if they have been lost to them. You need to take care when dealing with them. Some are good and beneficent, but not all. And one of their worst, he settled on Earth. I have not heard rumble of him, but if he still exists, he would not like you looking into his people."

A chill cooled Maeve's skin. "I'll be careful."

"I hope so, Maeve. Because whatever is happening with these orbs, it is not your primary concern. Keeping Alvie and the triplets from harm—that is what will keep your world safe."

Maeve's eyes opened with Agaren's words rolling through her mind. He was right. Alvie and the triplets were her priority, but there was a gnawing in her gut that told her that simply keeping them safe might not be enough to also keep the world safe.

CHAPTER 33

NIAGARA, NEW YORK

The team was wrapping up the investigation, so Norah and Greg headed back to the D.E.A.D. facility. He grabbed his bag from the back of the SUV and went still as he stared at Mitch's. He pulled it over and unzipped it. Sitting on top of all his gear was his bulletproof vest. Why hadn't they worn their vests? If they had, maybe this would all have ended differently.

"You want me to grab that, Greg?" Max asked.

Clearing his throat, Greg shook his head, zipping Mitch's bag back up. "No, I've got it."

He transferred it to the other SUV and then climbed into the back, closing his eyes and leaning his head back against the seat. Mitch was dead. How was it possible Mitch was dead?

The car swayed as someone climbed into the seat next to him. More sways and the turning over of the engine indicated that there were at least three people in the car with him. He didn't open his eyes to see who they were. None were Mitch, and right now that was the only face he wanted to see.

At the airfield, he silently climbed into the plane, keeping ahold of Mitch's bag. He left his own in the SUV. He didn't care what happened to it. But Mitch's, he needed to take care of Mitch's. He placed it on the seat next to him and kept one hand on it for the entire flight.

Kaylee sat across from him, and he could feel her darting gazes aimed at him every few minutes. But he didn't assure her he was fine because he most definitely was not. Instead, he avoided her gaze and stared out the window.

When they touched down at the runway on the D.E.A.D. base, Greg slowly unbuckled his belt. He grabbed Mitch's bag and walked down the plane aisle toward the steps. One of the members of the task force already had the steps undone by the time he reached it.

Greg looked up into Shamus's face. He'd worked with him a few times. "I'm sorry, Greg," he said.

Greg nodded, a lump in his throat as he walked down the steps.

There were two cars waiting. And standing in front of one of them was Maeve. As soon as she caught sight of Greg, she hurried over and hugged him tight. "Oh, Greg, I'm so sorry."

Greg wrapped his arms around her and finally let his tears fall.

CHAPTER 34

The car ride was silent as Maeve drove Greg back to his apartment. Maeve didn't know what to say to him. He'd never lost someone so close to him before. But Maeve had. When her mom had died, it felt like her whole world had collapsed in on itself. And Mitch, Maeve knew how much Greg had come to rely on him. And in a way, Maeve had too. Mitch was the touch of normalcy in Greg's crazy world.

At the apartment, she hurried to turn on the lights as Greg closed the door behind him. When she was done, she came back to find him in the same spot. Hesitating for a moment, she hurried into his room and ransacked his closet for some clean clothes. Placing them in the bathroom, she turned on the shower and laid out a towel.

Then she went back and steered Greg into the bathroom. "You're going to take a shower and then come back out to the living room, okay?"

Greg nodded. Maeve left him to it. Slipping out of the bedroom, she closed the door behind her and leaned against it. *Oh god Mitch.*

She wrapped her arms around her stomach, feeling Greg's

loss and revisiting the loss of her own mother. She didn't know what to do for him. When she'd been grieving, she didn't think anything made her feel better. There were just some things that you needed to go through, that you needed to feel.

She pushed off from the door and headed to the kitchen. There might not be anything she could do to make things better, but the least she could was make sure he had food when he was finally ready to eat.

CHAPTER 35

After Maeve closed the door, Greg stripped off his clothes. Leaving them where they fell, he stepped into the hot water. He'd felt so cold ever since Niagara Falls. He shut his mind down, only focusing on the heat seeping into his bones.

After a while, he had no idea how long, Maeve knocked on the door. "Greg? You okay?"

"Yeah," he mumbled, looking at his hands, which had pruned up. "I'll be out in a minute."

But he didn't move to get out of the shower just yet. He let the water fall over him for another few minutes and then stepped outside, dried off, and put on the clothes that Maeve had left out for him.

He walked into the living room to find Kal was sitting there with Alvie and Pugsley.

As Greg walked over, Kal stood up. He hurried over to Greg and hugged him tight. "It doesn't seem real," Kal said.

Hugging his nephew back, Greg didn't know what to say. He knew that he and Mitch had grown close over Kal's time at headquarters. Kal had even gone with Greg a few times to Mitch's home.

Pugsley waddled over and wrapped his little arms around Greg's calf. A lump formed in his throat at the empathy oozing from Alvie. "No, it doesn't seem real," Greg whispered.

Kal pulled back, wiping at his eyes. "I don't know what to do. I mean, do we go and talk to Mitch's family?"

As he sank onto the couch, Greg shook his head. "No, we can't. Not until the investigation's done. And besides, they're out of town."

Kal ran a hand through his hair. "God, this is just wrong. I mean, it's Mitch. He's just … I don't get how he can be gone."

Greg closed his eyes, picturing the scene again. But he didn't say anything because Kal wasn't cleared to know what had happened to Mitch, at least not yet.

When he opened his eyes, Kal and Alvie were gone and Pugsley was sitting on his lap. He hadn't even felt him climb up there. He laid a hand on Pugsley's back. "Hey, little buddy," he whispered.

Carrying a tray in from the kitchen, Maeve placed it on the coffee table in front of him. "You need to eat something."

Greg shook his head. "I'm not hungry."

"I didn't ask if you were hungry. I told you you're going to eat." Maeve picked up a bowl and handed it to him. Greg took it. He started to spoon the chicken noodle soup into his mouth without even tasting it. In fact, he finished it without tasting a bite.

Maeve took the bowl back and placed it on the tray again. Then she went and grabbed a blanket from the basket in the corner and tucked it around Greg like he was one of her kids.

And Greg honestly enjoyed the fact that someone else was taking care of him because right now he didn't think he was capable of taking care of himself.

Sitting down next to him, Maeve took his hand. "It's okay. However you're feeling, Greg, it's okay."

He leaned over and just placed his head on her shoulder. He felt empty. Just completely and totally empty. And a world without Mitch? No, that was never going to be okay.

CHAPTER 36

The living room was dark when Greg opened his eyes. He was lying on the couch with a pillow under his head and a blanket tucked around him. That must have been Maeve's doing.

He started to move his feet but felt a weight on them. He lifted his head to see Pugsley sleeping on them, breathing softly. Carefully, he pulled his feet out from under him, wincing when Pugsley's breath hitched. But then his breathing returned to its normal rhythm. Sitting back against the couch, he still felt tired, but he wouldn't be able to go back to sleep just yet.

Across from him, there was a note on the coffee table. He reached out and pulled it over to him, squinting in the dim light to make out the writing. It was from Maeve: *I'm sleeping in Kal's room. He's staying over at Norah's tonight with Alvie. Wake me when you get up.*

Greg placed the note back on the table and sat back on the couch. Once again, he couldn't help but flash back on the events at Niagara Falls. Moore had, just like with Nate, just like with Agnes, seemed to shift in a moment from one person to another in a split second.

He knew about multiple personality disorder, or as it was called now, dissociative identity disorder or DID. An individual, in essence, had multiple personalities, with one of the personalities controlling behavior and thoughts at different times. Individuals with DID could have extreme cases where only one personality learned certain skills, such as how to drive a car. The other personalities would have no knowledge of that ability. Some could be extremely young, others extremely old.

The personalities emerged as a way to defend the original personality from some deep trauma, usually in early childhood. Memory loss was part of the symptoms, as one personality was unaware of what the others were doing.

In cases of people with the disorder, the change could happen quickly. There was one case that came to mind of a split personality named Billy Milligan. According to his doctors, Billy had twenty-four separate identities. One of his personalities was a rapist. One of his victims reported that her abductor would shift from cruel and threatening to kind and personable.

While prosecutors thought he was lying, they changed their tune once they interviewed him. They reported that everything changed when his personalities changed: voice, body language, the look in his eyes. He was found not guilty by reason of insanity and sent to a mental hospital. He was released eleven years later after doctors attested that his personalities had been fused.

But while DID was a real disorder, it was not a common one. At most, one percent of the population could be classified as having DID. So the likelihood that they had come across three cases in such a short time period completely stretched the bounds of statistical possibilities.

Which meant they needed another possibility.

For a moment, Greg wondered what the test results had revealed, but he wasn't up for looking at that. Honestly, he didn't really even care about that at this moment. Despite his momentary curiosity about Justin Moore's personality shift, right now all he cared about was the fact that Mitch was gone. Mitch was gone, and Maya and her kids didn't even know yet.

He understood the reason for secrecy when it came to most things involving the D.E.A.D. After all, it wasn't like they could announce to the world that aliens existed, and oh, by the way, they're running free in certain parts of the United States. He knew that would create a complete and total panic. But not telling Maya and the kids that didn't feel right.

Greg let out a breath, his skin feeling tight. He needed to get out of here. Quietly, he found his shoes and grabbed his keys by the front door. A small, quiet hum sounded behind him. He turned to find Pugsley slipping toward him. He thought for a moment about telling him to stay, but honestly, he wanted the company. So instead, he slipped on his shoes and then knelt down. Pugsley gave a little leap as he reached him, and Greg stood up with him in his arms.

Then Greg slipped outside, pulling the door closed behind him. Making sure Pugsley was secure, he headed over to his jeep.

Climbing in, he pulled up the basket from the floor in the back and placed it on the passenger seat and then latched it in place. Pugsley hopped into it with a happy hum. Greg backed out of the spot and headed for the base's exit.

He had no destination in mind. He just needed to get away. The guards gave him no problems as he left, merely waving him through. The roads were quiet as Greg drove along them, which wasn't surprising, being that it was close to three a.m.

But even if it had been the middle of the day, there wouldn't have been a lot of traffic around the base. In fact, they had specifically chosen this location for the base because it was so quiet. Plus, it was only a quick forty-minute flight down to New York City and a slightly longer one down to Washington DC.

But it was really the solitude of the location that made it a prime spot for the D.E.A.D. facility. Because everything they did was secret. Everything they did was cloaked in darkness.

And now Mitch's death would be one of those secrets as well. Greg wondered if they would ever even find out what exactly had caused Moore to fire.

At the time, Mitch and Greg had been no threat. And on the ride over to Niagara Falls, Greg had looked at Moore's service record. He hadn't fired his gun once in the entire time he'd been with the Niagara Falls Police Department. For twenty years, he hadn't fired a gun, and for the next ten that he had been with the Niagara Falls security department, he hadn't fired one either. So what had made him pull his gun today? After thirty years of never doing so, what had changed?

Greg hoped that they would find out. No, Greg *would* find out. He owed Mitch at least that much.

Without conscious thought, Greg drove through the empty rolling hills. There were a few houses scattered here and there, but most of them were dark.

Before Greg knew it, he found himself pulling into one of the newer subdivisions. All of the homes were two-story colonials built within the last five years. There was a uniformity to the development that had never really appealed to Greg.

But something about it must have appealed to Mitch and Maya. Maybe it was all the kids that lived in the area. It would probably be a good place to raise a family.

Of course, Greg doubted that Maya would be raising her family here alone now. The only reason they had been in upstate New York was because Mitch had been stationed here.

Now Maya would pick up her family and move somewhere else, maybe down to Georgia to be closer to her parents.

Greg made a right and drove down Mulberry Lane. Each of the roads in the subdivision were named after some type of berry. There was Black Raspberry Road, Blueberry Path, Strawberry Lane. It was pretty cute, actually.

Pulling into Mitch's driveway, he turned his headlights off. He sat there for a little while, just watching the house.

It was a pale-gray two-story colonial with black shutters. There was a porch in front of it with a swing and two chairs. He and Mitch had sat out there talking on more than a few occasions.

He felt pressure on the back of his eyes and turned his attention to Pugsley, who sat quietly next to him. Greg grabbed his messenger bag and slipped Pugsley inside. It was probably an unnecessary precaution. There was no one out. But the last thing he needed right now was some neighbor taking an early-morning stroll and freaking out at the sight of Pugsley.

Turning off the engine, Greg slipped the messenger bag over his shoulder as he climbed out of the car. Closing the door, he walked slowly toward the porch, the night air cool against his skin.

He climbed the three stairs and took a seat on the swing. His mind traveled back to the nights he'd sat here with Mitch. Their conversations had been about nothing important, nothing about work or anything like that. They'd just talked about movies or books or just life in general. It had been good. It had been really nice.

Greg didn't have a lot of guy friends. He'd always seemed to get along better with women. But there'd been something different about Mitch. He was tall and strong like all the people on the task force were. But there was some depth to Mitch that Greg didn't see in some of the others.

And he'd respected Greg's role on the task force from the

very beginning. For some of the other members, Greg had had to win their respect, and that had taken more than a little effort on his part.

But with Mitch, it had never been like that. From the get-go, he'd automatically respected Greg's spot on the team and valued him.

And in the areas where Greg was weak, like when it came to his marksmanship or fighting skills, Mitch had taken the time to help train Greg.

Greg could admit he was a better person having known him. And now Mitch was gone.

He leaned his head back on the swing as the tears once again pressed against his eyes. *Damn it, Mitch, I'm so sorry.*

In his mind, he tried to figure out a way that he could have done something different. Maybe if he had moved more to the right, Moore would have trained his gun on him, and Mitch wouldn't have been able to get in between them in time.

But Greg knew that wasn't true.

Mitch still would have jumped in front of him. It was part of what made him such a great person, that willingness to sacrifice, to do the right thing to protect others.

Greg let out a breath and closed his eyes.

When he opened them again, dawn was breaking along the skyline. A car, a Lexus, pulled into the driveway next to Greg's. Greg placed a hand on his messenger bag as Pugsley shifted inside. "Stay quiet," he whispered.

Turning his attention back to the car, Greg frowned, not recognizing it. It certainly wasn't from the base's motor pool.

The car door opened, and a tall, stately African American woman with long braids stepped out from behind the steering wheel. She looked over at Greg with a frown. "Greg?"

He straightened. "Hi, Mrs. Haldron."

She smiled as she walked up the porch toward him. "I've told you to call me Isis."

He nodded. "I know. Hi, Isis."

Mitch's mother looked toward the front door and then back at Greg. "Is Mitch here?"

Greg's mouth went dry, and his mind emptied. He wasn't supposed to say anything, but this was Mitch's mother. There was no way he could lie to her, not about something like this.

He swallowed, trying to get a little moisture back into his mouth. He hadn't planned on coming here to say anything to her. But he certainly wasn't going to lie to her now that she was staring straight at him. He swallowed again. "Maybe we should go into the house."

CHAPTER 37

While Mitch's mother gave him a strange look at the request, she simply unlocked the front door and ushered Greg in.

He stopped when he was just a few feet beyond the door. How was he going to do this? He thought of all the cop shows he saw and how they did a death notification. And then he thought about the medical shows he'd seen and how they did a notification. Could he just do that? Tell Mitch's mom that there had been an accident, and that Mitch was gone?

Before he could say anything, Isis slipped off her jacket, placing it over the back of one of the stools at the kitchen island. "Why don't you take a seat? You look like you could use some breakfast."

Greg shook his head. "No. I need to tell you something."

"It can wait. You need some breakfast. Now take a seat. Actually, you know what, why don't you unload the dishwasher? I'm pretty sure it's full."

Greg opened his mouth to insist that she stop and listen to him, but honestly, he didn't have it in him to fight her on this. Maybe it was cowardly on his part, but he wanted to give her just another few minutes of thinking that the world was okay. So after carefully placing his bag on the couch, he headed into the kitchen and pulled the dishwasher open. And she was right. It was full of clean dishes. He set about putting the dishes away while Isis cooked up some omelets for them.

A few minutes later, he had the dishwasher emptied and the counters wiped down. He placed the dishes and tools that she'd used to make the omelets back into the dishwasher.

She smiled at him as she set two omelets on the table. "You are going to make a good husband someday."

The thought of Mitch slammed into his mind. What was he doing? He was going to sit and have a nice breakfast with Mitch's mom while Mitch lay dead somewhere? They hadn't even found his body yet. He was probably stuck at the bottom of the Niagara River.

He pushed his plate away. "I'm sorry, Isis. I can't eat right now. I need to tell you something."

"Greg, it's all right," she said, looking into his eyes.

"It's not ... You don't understand. Mitch—"

"Is right here," a voice called out.

Greg's head whipped to the side as Mitch strode into the kitchen from the hallway that led to the bedrooms.

CHAPTER 38

His mouth falling open, Greg blinked hard, wondering if he had finally lost it. He slowly got to his feet, staring at the man who walked toward him. He looked exactly like Mitch.

He shifted his gaze to Isis, who settled back in her chair. Her coffee mug was nestled in both her hands as she sipped it contentedly.

Reality slammed into him as the image of Mitch's body jerking from the bullets before falling over the railing rolled through his mind. "No, no, that's not possible."

"Greg," Isis began.

Oh my God. Mitch's mom. He stepped in front of the table, blocking Isis from whoever it was that was walking toward them. He flicked a gaze at his bag, but Pugsley hadn't made a move. Of all the times for him to demonstrate self-control.

He grabbed a knife from the table and held it in front of him. "You're not Mitch. Mitch is dead. Isis, you need to get out of here. Go! Now!"

The man who looked like Mitch stopped, immediately raising his hands. "Greg, it's okay. It's me. Just let me explain."

Shaking his head, Greg could hear the hysteria in his own voice. "You got shot. You got shot four times in the chest. And then you fell from the hurricane deck. No one could survive that."

"I was wearing my vest."

"That's a *lie*. I saw your vest in your bag. We didn't wear them, remember?"

Mitch leaned to the side, looking at his mother. "I told you he wouldn't believe that."

Isis sighed. "You were right. You know him better."

Looking between the two of them, Greg took a step back. "Wait, you knew what happened to him in Niagara Falls?" he asked Isis.

"I know just about everything that happens with my son," she replied.

Greg stared at her and then at Mitch, a sense of unease rolling over him. "What's going on here? Who are you two?"

"Now that is a very good question and a very long story." Isis pushed the omelet closer toward him. "And we will be happy to explain, but your omelet is getting cold. So why don't you eat, and then we'll all have ourselves a nice long talk?"

Eat? Was she nuts? "I am *not* eating. What's going on?"

Mitch took a step forward, and Greg immediately took a step back.

"Greg, it's still me. I'm still Mitch."

Everything in Greg wanted to believe him. He wanted to believe it was his friend standing in front of him. But how could he? Sixteen people had gone over the falls in a barrel in the Niagara River. Five died, and they all had some sort of protection. One seven-year-old child actually survived going over in just a life jacket, but Greg attributed that to pure dumb luck.

Mitch had plummeted into the choppy water after being

shot. There was no way he was as lucky as that kid. "No, Mitch is dead. I don't know who you are."

Mitch sighed. "Look, I will explain everything. I promise. But I just need you to listen with an open mind for a little while, okay?"

It sounded like Mitch. It looked like Mitch. He flicked another glance at his bag. Was Pugsley sleeping? Why wasn't he out here protecting him? "*How* open a mind?" Greg demanded.

Mitch winced. "Actually, pretty open. But you do work at the D.E.A.D., so that shouldn't be too much of a stretch, right?"

A glance back at Isis revealed a woman who didn't look even slightly alarmed. In fact, she'd finished about half of her omelet in the time he and Mitch had been speaking. His stomach growled as he stared at his. But now was not the time for eating. Pulling out a chair, he sat down, pushing his plate away from him. Then he adjusted his chair so he could keep an eye on both Mitch and his mother. The knife he kept in his hand. "Okay. I'm listening. So what is all this about?"

Mitch took a seat across the table from him. "Greg, how much do you know about Egyptian mythology?"

Egyptian mythology? Was he kidding? Greg stared at him. "I can honestly say I know little to nothing."

Isis snorted. "The American school system is an embarrassment. They do nothing but focus on American history."

"Mother, you're not helping," Mitch said through tight lips.

Isis threw up her hands. "What? The system is not well crafted. I told you we should have lived in Finland. Now *they* know how to educate their children."

This was insane. His formerly deceased partner was sitting in front of him debating the merits of global education systems with his mother? Maybe he was still sleeping. He pinched himself. Nope. He was awake. "*What* are you two talking about?"

INTO THE DARK

"He's getting worked up," Isis said, her gaze on Mitch.

"He's fine," Mitch said.

"I am *not* fine. What the hell is going on?" Greg said as he stood up.

"I told you. He's hysterical," Isis said, pushing her plate away and standing herself.

Greg pulled out his phone. "I need to call base. They need to know what's going on."

He brought up his contacts as Isis moved around the table.

"Mother, don't," Mitch warned, also standing.

Greg looked between the two of them, his attention finally fixing on Mitch. "Don't what?"

Pain exploded against the back of his head, and the world turned dark.

CHAPTER 39

Greg's head throbbed. He groaned as he slowly opened his eyes. He lay on a couch that was not his. He blinked a few times as movement to his right drew his attention.

"Hey, there you are," Mitch said with a smile.

Greg started to sit up. "Hey, Mitch. What—Mitch!" He bolted upright, staring wide-eyed at his supposedly dead partner.

"He's getting hysterical again," Isis said, moving toward him.

Mitch moved quickly to block her path. "Mother, I've got this. Leave him to me."

She stared up into his eyes, and they had a silent conversation before she took a step back. "Fine."

Greg glared at her. She was the second grandmother to cold cock him in as many days.

A small chirp sounded next to Greg, and he saw Pugsley sitting on the couch next to him. Alarm flashed through him as he quickly grabbed Pugsley and slipped him into the bag. Had Isis seen him? How much trouble would he be in if she had?

He looked up to find both Isis and fake Mitch staring at him. He gave a self-conscious laugh. "Just rearranging my bag."

Isis rolled her eyes. "We saw the Noctum," she said before she leaned back against the island, crossing her arms over her chest.

Noctum?

Turning back to Greg, Mitch gave him a smile. "Now, as I was saying, what do you know about Egyptian mythology?"

Greg's head was spinning. "What?"

"Mitch," Isis said, a warning in her tone.

Mitch turned to look at her over his shoulder. "Mother, we need his help. He's a good man."

Isis snorted. And Greg wasn't sure if it was because she didn't think they needed help or because she didn't think that Greg was a good man. After a moments reflection, he decided it was probably a little bit of both.

Mitch turned back to him. "Well? Egyptian mythology?"

"Nothing. It really wasn't covered in school."

"I repeat: what passes for education these days is absolutely shameful," Isis muttered.

"Mother, why don't you let me handle this?" Mitch said with gritted his teeth.

She sent him a baleful look before finally turning on her heel. "Fine. I'll go make something else for Greg to eat. After all, he didn't eat the last omelet that I took the time to make for him, and now it's cold."

Greg winced, at the very clear annoyance in her tone.

But then he turned back to stare at Mitch. And it *was* Mitch. He looked exactly like him. He had the same mannerisms. He had the same voice.

The only problem was he had seen Mitch die. "You can't be here. You can't have survived that fall. Even without being shot, that fall is un-survivable. Niagara Falls is kind of known for that."

"A few people have survived the fall over Niágara," Mitch said.

Narrowing his eyes, Greg felt like his losing his mind. "Yes, *very* few. And they certainly didn't survive it after being shot four times in the chest."

"I told you, I was wearing my vest."

Greg put up a hand. "Mitch, I don't know what the hell is going on, but it's not going to work if you keep lying to me."

Mitch nodded. "You're right. It's just, it's a complicated story."

"Well, I have a PhD from MIT, so I'll try and keep up," Greg responded.

Mitch grinned. "You know, back when we first met, you never would have talked back to me that way."

"Well, a lot's happened in between then and now. And right now, I'm not liking how you've been lying to me."

Mitch squirmed under Greg's gaze. "I haven't been lying, not exactly. But I haven't been telling you the truth." He paused.

"So why don't you tell me the truth. All of it," Greg said. "Is Mitch even your name?"

"No. But in my defense I've had a lot of them."

A numbness started to fall over Greg. He'd thought Mitch was the straightest of arrows. How could he have been so completely wrong?

Studying his partner, he spoke slowly. "Why did you ask about Egyptian mythology?"

Mitch gave him a sad smile. "Because my explanation goes back thousands of years, to the heart of ancient Egypt."

CHAPTER 40

Thousands of years? Now Greg was wondering if this was some sort of prank. The guys on the strike force would sometimes haze newer members. Greg wasn't new, but maybe they had finally gotten around to hazing him.

"Who put you up to this? Was it Max?" He looked around the room. "Max, are you here?"

"Max is not here. And I'm telling you the truth. Now, will you listen?"

Greg had no idea what to say to that. He wanted to know what was going on, but a story thousands of years in the making didn't sound like it would be very relevant. Nevertheless, he found himself crossing his arms over his chest and giving Mitch a nod.

Relief flashed across Mitch's face as he sank back in his chair across from Greg before his gaze turned serious. "I know you said you don't know much about Egyptian mythology, but have you heard about the Egyptian god Osiris?"

The name sounded vaguely familiar, but Greg couldn't really recall much about him, although he did remember a little bit. "A little. He was an ancient god, and I think he was well liked if I remember correctly. He was kind of the god of earth, wasn't he?"

"Something like that. He was one of the nine primeval gods of the ancient world. These days, we tend to think of Osiris and his compatriots as being the gods of Egypt, but it really was a fourth of the entire world. Osiris, he was a good god, beloved by the people of Earth. But he had a brother, a brother named Set, who was jealous of how respected Osiris was because Set was not nearly as respected or beloved."

Mitch took a deep breath. "In a jealous rage, Set killed Osiris. He dismembered his brother and then scattered his pieces across the earth."

"That's … brutal," Greg said with a wince. Ancient stories always seem to have an incredible level of violence to them, and apparently this one was no different, but the image it conjured up in Greg's mind made him more than a little queasy. At the same time, he always thought of ancient myths as giant games of telephone. By the time the story trickled down to the modern world, it probably bore little resemblance to the truth. And Greg still didn't understand what this could possibly have to do with Mitch.

"Osiris was married to a woman named Isis."

Greg's gaze immediately went to Mitch's mother, who had her back to them as she stood at the stove.

"She was distraught by the death of her husband. She mourned him and was inconsolable. And her anger toward Set was unrivaled. Set was actually married to Isis's sister, Nephthys, who felt for her mourning sister and joined Isis in her search for her husband's body. The legend says that together, they brought Osiris back to life."

Sitting back, Greg scoffed, . "Mitch, I don't see what this has to do with—"

Mitch held up a hand. "I know. But you will. Let me finish, okay?"

He took a deep breath before continuing. "The people of the time called it magic, but it wasn't magic. It was science. She was able to harvest sperm cells from his body, and she was able to use them to create a child, their son, Horus. Horus was raised in the swamps, hidden from Set so that the uncle who had taken over Osiris's rule of the world couldn't harm him.

"But somehow word of Horus's existence leaked out. Set went looking for him and poisoned Horus when he was just a child. Isis barely got to her son in time and saved his life. The two of them hid themselves even deeper, Isis keeping her son from Set's view.

"And so, Horus grew up, and while he grew, thought every day of the father that he never had a chance to meet. His mother kept Osiris's spirit alive and would tell Horus stories. Wonderful stories of what an incredible man his father had been."

By the stove, Isis glanced over at the two of them. The look in her eyes was undecipherable before she returned her attention back to the stove.

"And with each of those stories, Horus grew more and more angry. What right had Set to take his father away? And why, if Isis was so powerful, had she not been able to bring Osiris back?"

Mitch took a deep breath. "When Horus was old enough, he challenged Set to a fight, a fight for control of Egypt. Set accepted, and of course, he cheated at every game that was placed in front of them. And so, every game, he won.

"Finally, the judges, who were the remaining primeval gods, realized what Set had done and made him play fair.

"Horus was incensed and flew at Set in a rage. Isis intervened, saving Set's life. Horus was so angry that he lashed out at his mother, screaming and yelling at her for stopping him from killing Set.

"The judges were horrified at Horus's behavior toward his

mother, and Horus himself was horrified at his own behavior. His mother had loved him, had protected him, and had kept him safe all these years. She was the last one he should have been angry at."

Meeting Greg's gaze, Mitch continued. "By rights, the judges should have declared Horus the winner. But the judges were angry at Horus for his outburst. So they decided that instead of just declaring him the winner because Set had cheated so much, there would be one last challenge. And that Set would be able to choose what challenge it would be. He declared it would be a boat race.

"Horus crafted a boat out of wood, but he made it appear as if it were made out of stone. Set, who was no boat maker, copied what he thought was Horus's example and cleaved a rock face from the side of a mountain, declaring that it would be his boat, but as soon as he set it in the water, it sank. The other judges laughed at Set's mistake as Horus climbed into his boat and began to sail across the water.

"Incensed by the judges' laughter, Set attacked Horus, ferociously lashing out at him and nearly killing him. The other gods intervened and stopped the fight as Horus gained the upper hand. They stopped it just before Horus struck out with a killing blow. The gods decided it was a tie because they remembered Horus's anger toward his mother and were still mad at him, despite what Set had done.

"Which meant they still didn't know who was allowed to rule the world. So they contacted the spirit of Osiris, and he declared that no one should be allowed to rule if they took that position through murder. He declared that Horus, his son, was the rightful ruler of the world.

"The judges were horrified when they heard what Osiris said. They hadn't realized that he had been murdered. They enacted a horrific punishment upon Set, one that would last throughout his existence.

"And so, Horus became the ruler of ancient Egypt. Through time, he had different names, Apollo among them. Eventually, he and the rest of the primeval gods slipped out of humanity's consciousness."

A headache was beginning to build now in the front of Greg's mind, a combination of stress, worry, and the hit he'd taken from Isis. He rubbed the bridge of his nose. "Well, that's a very interesting story and all, but I don't see what that has to do with you somehow escaping death."

Mitch met his gaze. "Because I am Horus."

CHAPTER 41

Greg stared at Mitch. "You're Horus? You've been alive for thousands upon thousands of years?"

Mitch shrugged. "In a way. Our lifespan is slightly longer than a human's, but we will eventually die, just like I died in Niagara Falls."

Greg was beginning to think that he was actually still asleep. Maybe he hadn't pinched himself hard enough. Or maybe he was just hallucinating all of this. Maybe when Nate escaped from his room, Greg got knocked out. Maybe he'd dreamed everything that had happened since then, and he was actually lying passed out in a hallway back at headquarters.

Mitch leaned forward. "For years, people have wondered how the ancient ruins in Egypt were created. It was known that they could not be created by the technology available at the time. And they were right. Those sites, many of the ancient sites, were not created by humans. They were created by my race of people. We were escaping a dead planet when we found Earth. We settled here, bringing all of our technology with us. Over time, much of our technology has been lost.

Once it broke down, we had no way to replace it. But a few of our pieces still exist. And one of them is the key to our survival."

"And what's that, some sort of magic serum?"

Mitch shook his head. "No. It's our reincarnation ship."

CHAPTER 42

Pain from the back of his head flared up, telling Greg that he was very much awake. So maybe he'd been exposed to a noxious gas and was hallucinating. Or maybe his hearing was going. He'd heard of auditory hallucinations, although since he was sitting across from Mitch, he supposed this was also a visual hallucination. A combo hallucination.

He licked his lips, looking between Isis and Mitch. "Um, a reincarnation ship. Did you just say a reincarnation ship?"

Mitch nodded.

"Have you been watching too much *Battlestar Galactica*?"

Mitch smiled. "The ideas for much of your science fiction comes from reality. It's buried deep within the human consciousness, and every once in a while, someone creative taps into it. The reincarnation ship is real. It's how I'm sitting before you now."

Greg stared at him. "So you, what, just beamed up to the ship and then beamed back down?"

"Something like that. Back in the ancient days, we used stargates to travel between Earth and our ships. Over time, the ships were eventually scavenged in order to get parts to keep the reincarnation ship in good shape. We could do without the other ships, but the reincarnation ship is the key to our survival. It is the only ship of ours that still exists."

Isis stood by the island, sliding omelets onto plates.

"Uh-huh," Greg said. "So how does that even happen, you going to the reincarnation ship? I mean you're dead, so what is there to travel?"

"When our bodies die, they disintegrate and disappear. At least, my mother's and mine do. Our essence can then travel without hindrance to the ship, and a new body is created for us. Normally, we die after a long life, and we reincarnate into a new body, a new existence, and we start over again. But this time, that's not possible. This time there's too much that needs to be done, and I need to be inside the D.E.A.D. to do it, so I returned in the same body."

"Sure, that makes complete sense," Greg said, shooting a glance at the door. It was about fifteen feet away. He might be able to get to it and out the door before—

"He's going to run," Isis announced.

Greg glared at her. "I am not."

"You were thinking about it just now."

Greg paused. "Are you psychic?"

Isis rolled her eyes. "No. You're not exactly good at hiding your intentions. Honestly, how you've stayed alive up to this point is beyond me."

Greg often wondered the same thing, but he certainly wasn't going to say that out loud. "Yeah, well, two crazy people trying to convince me that they're the reincarnation of ancient gods apparently sets off the flight response in me."

"That's understandable. And I know it's a lot to take in. But you said you'd listen with an open mind," Mitch reminded him.

Actually, Greg didn't think he'd said that. In fact, he was

pretty sure Mitch had *told* him to have an open mind, but Greg didn't recall agreeing.

"Okay, so let's say I believe all of this. You said you need to do something inside the D.E.A.D. What do you need to do?" Greg asked, still not even sure why he was listening to all of this. It was absolutely insane.

"Set is returning," Mitch said, his eyes deadly serious. "I don't know how, but somehow, he is coming back. For thousands of years, he's been reborn time and time again, but he's had no knowledge of who he once was."

"Was that his punishment?" Greg asked.

Isis nodded. "Set is the only one who has ever killed a Primeval. We didn't even know it could be done. We still don't know how he did it. So we banished him from our ranks, locking up his memories of who he truly is, forcing him to be reborn from baby to old man each lifetime, hoping that he would become a better man."

"I take it that hasn't happened," Greg said.

Isis shook her head. "The other Primevals believed it was possible. I never did."

"That's why you stopped Horus from killing him. Because he would just be reborn and start right back where he left off."

She nodded. "Yes, and that was no punishment. Now Set is coming back."

"How do you know that?"

Mitch looked over his shoulder at his mother, who had just placed a stack of muffins on the kitchen island. She met his gaze for a long moment, and the two of them had another silent conversation before she slipped from the room.

Mitch turned back to Greg. "Our larger technology has been destroyed, but some smaller pieces still exist. And one of our critical pieces has sent off a warning for the last few months that Set was looking to find his way back in. I didn't think it was possible. My mother didn't either. But now I fear that it may be."

Isis reappeared with a large metal box in her hands. She placed it on the coffee table between them. Then she stepped back, looking at Mitch. "Are you sure?"

Mitch nodded, unlocking the crate. "Yes. He needs to know everything if he's going to help us."

He pulled back the lid, and Greg stared in shock at a silver orb identical to the one he had just seen at headquarters. "How did you get this?"

"It's mine. I've always had it. There are nine that exist. They are spread out across the globe and across the sky. Most of them have been hidden away. But this one, it belongs to me."

"And the one at the D.E.A.D. facility?"

"It belongs to one of the other gods. They were killed in the same way my father was, a way that prevents them from reincarnating."

"That's why you think Set is alive."

Mitch nodded. "Yes. The old gods, they walk the earth, but you'd never know who they are. They are simple, quiet people. After such long lifetimes, we've all learned to just appreciate what the world offers without looking for any recognition. We have no ambition for more than a quiet life."

"Then why did you join the D.E.A.D.?" Greg asked.

Isis sat on the edge of Mitch's chair. "That was at my encouragement. When I learned of the US government involving itself in alien experiments, I knew that we needed to keep an eye on it to see what was happening and to make sure that none of the old gods were targeted. Mitch, he was our eyes on the inside."

"And the old gods?" Greg asked.

"The D.E.A.D. is not aware of any of them. The only person

outside of the gods who's aware of them is you," Isis said. The warning and threat were clear in her voice.

"I won't tell anyone."

"I know," Mitch said. "But we need your help in finding Set. You have access to more in the D.E.A.D. than I do. I need that access."

"You just want me to help you? You realize I would be breaking, I don't know, half a dozen federal laws if I did?"

"My son says you have a good imagination. I'm sure you can come up with some sort of plausible explanation," Isis said with a wave of her hand.

Greg shook his head. "That's assuming I believe any of this."

Mitch stared into Greg's eyes, his voice confident. "You do believe it. You don't want to, and you're looking for the flaws, but somewhere deep down you believe what I'm telling you."

Greg wanted to deny that it was true. He wanted to tell this person standing in front of him to get lost, that he'd known what he saw and that he couldn't possibly be his friend Mitch.

But the other part of his brain was screaming that this *was* Mitch. It was screaming that he had seen incredible things over the past few years and was wondering whether this was simply one more stop onto the crazy train.

Greg stood up. "I'm not helping you until I've verified a few things."

"You can't tell anyone what we've revealed to you," Isis said, standing as well.

Greg took a quick step away from her, placing himself out of striking distance. A small smile appeared on Isis's face as he did so. If he didn't know any better, he'd think she liked that he was a little scared of him. He shot another glance at her: amusement in her eyes, slight smirk on her lips. Yup, she definitely liked that he was a little bit scared of her.

"I won't. But I need to check and see that what you're saying is true," Greg said.

A glance was once again exchanged between mother and son.

Keeping an eye on Isis, Greg swallowed, reaching for his bag and hoping that Pugsley would help him out if it came down to a fight. "Are you going to stop me from leaving?"

Mitch shook his head. "No. You do what you have to do. We'll be here waiting when you're done."

Greg backed away, heading toward the door. He was waiting to see if either of them attempted to stop him, but neither of them moved. So Greg let himself out and hustled down the stairs and across the driveway to his car.

He climbed in and started it. But he didn't put it in gear right away. Instead, he sat behind the steering wheel for a long moment, staring at the house. Mitch was back. He wasn't dead, or at least he was no longer dead. Giving himself a shake, Greg finally put the car into reverse, not sure what to think but knowing where he could go to get some answers.

CHAPTER 43

Keeping his head down, Greg made his way through the D.E.A.D. lobby. He focused on the tiles in front of him, not wanting to make conversation with anyone. He felt a few curious glances aimed his way, but no one called out to him.

They no doubt thought he was devastated by Mitch's death. Death often made people feel awkward, not knowing what to say to the bereaved. But Greg wasn't bereaved right now. Right now, he was just confused.

As he reached his hallway, there was someone waiting for him. Hannah was just turning from his door. She wiped at the tears on her cheeks. "Oh, Greg, hi. I was just looking for you."

"Are you okay?" Greg asked.

Hannah nodded, even as she wiped at another tear. "Yeah, it's just, I really liked Mitch."

Greg wasn't sure what to say to that, so he simply unlocked his door, picking up the basket that sat in front of it as he let himself in. Holding the door open with his foot, he nodded at Hannah. "Do you want to come in?"

"Uh, yeah, thanks," she said, scooting in after him.

He let the door close and then placed the basket on the desk. He glanced at the card and saw Hannah's name. He turned back to her. "You brought me muffins?"

"Yeah. I remember you saying once how much you like pumpkin spice muffins. And I wanted to do something when I heard about Mitch, so food always seems a good thing at a time like this."

Greg unwrapped the cellophane from the basket and pulled one out. Pulling off the wrapper, he took a bite, and his eyes widened. He finished the muffin in three more bites and then grabbed another. And he realized that, twice now, he hadn't eaten Isis's omelet. He really hoped the Egyptian goddess let that slide.

He took a bite of the second muffin before nodding at Hannah. "These are delicious. Where'd you get them?"

Pugsley slipped out of his messenger bag and climbed up onto the desk. Greg broke one of the muffins in half and handed it to him.

"Oh, um, I made them. It's my grandmother's recipe," Hannah said.

Now Greg was really touched. "That was really nice of you. Thank you."

"I know how it is to lose someone close to you, and I just wanted to do something. But I should let you go. I'm sure you've got stuff to do."

He did, but he also had a question. "Hey, were you able to do any work on that pheromone theory about Pugsley? I know it hasn't been that long, but—"

"Actually, yes. I ran some preliminary tests. It was only with samples in the lab, but the initial results are promising. Pugsley reacted negatively to known aggressive Seti, neutrally to most animals, and warmly to well-known stimuli."

"Well-known stimuli?"

"It was only a basic test, so I just grabbed some samples of blood from people that Pugsley knows and likes."

"Was Mitch's blood one of those samples?"

Hannah's face fell, her chin trembling. "Yes, of course. Pugsley always really liked him."

So that meant that at Mitch's house, he would know the difference between Mitch and someone posing as Mitch.

"Um, I really should go. But I'll send you those results." Hannah moved to the door.

"Okay, thanks. And thanks again for the muffins. They really are delicious."

She gave him a smile before slipping out the door.

Taking a seat at his desk, Greg opened up the bottom drawer. Pugsley hopped inside and curled up on the cushion in there before giving a contented sigh. Greg dropped another muffin down then stared down at him. Pugsley had recognized Mitch. Or at least hadn't been bothered by the sight of him.

But could he trust Pugsley's sense? He really didn't know what type of creature Pugsley was. Isis's words floated through his mind. *We saw the Noctum*.

He hadn't followed up on that statement because there was so much else happening. But was Pugsley a Noctum? Noctum in Latin meant night. And they had theorized that Pugsley might come from a dark planet. But how would she know that?

Because she's the ancient goddess Isis, a voice whispered from the corner of his mind.

He leaned his head in his hands. He didn't know what to think about any of this. Which was why he needed some answers.

He stared at the phone on his desk, playing with his bottom lip as he did so. He knew exactly who he needed to call.

But at the same time, it was difficult to make himself actu-

INTO THE DARK

ally pick up the receiver. Tilda wasn't exactly a warm and fuzzy individual. And he wasn't sure how successful he'd be at keeping her from figuring out what he was up to. He wasn't very good at lying. And Tilda, well, she was very good at sniffing out the truth.

But he needed answers, and she was the only one he could think of to get them from.

Worst-case scenario, I'll just burst into tears and make her feel guilty for upsetting me, he thought. With a nod of his head, he grabbed the receiver and dialed.

Tilda's assistant answered. "Director Watson's office."

Greg cleared his throat. "Hi, this is Dr. Greg Shorn. I need to speak with Tilda , um, if she's available."

"Hold, Dr. Schorn," the receptionist said.

An instrumental version of "The Girl from Ipanema" played across the receiver as Greg waited. He found himself humming along with the tune before Tilda joined him. "Greg?"

"Tilda, hi," Greg said, sitting up straight in his chair as if she could see him. "I was hoping I could talk to you."

"I was actually going to call you. I'm so sorry about Mitch. If there's anything we can do to help, please let us know."

Greg paused for a moment, scrambling for what to say. "It's a tough blow," he finally said. "Mitch is a good man."

"Yes, he was. Now, what can I do for you?"

Once again, Greg felt tongue-tied. How exactly did he suddenly work questions about ancient primeval gods into the conversation?

And the answer was, there was no way to subtly work this into a conversation. He had to just come straight out and ask. "Well, with Mitch's death, I've decided I'm just going to focus on work, and so I've been trying to figure some things out with a case I've got here. I was wondering—and I know this sounds kind of crazy—but is there any chance that there's a spaceship orbiting Earth, and maybe has been for a long time, that doesn't belong to any humans?"

As soon as the words were out, Greg winced and slammed his palm into his forehead multiple times. That was horrible.

Tilda didn't answer for a long moment. Greg was preparing to apologize for disturbing her before hanging up when she finally spoke. "Why are you asking about that?"

Picturing Nate, Greg spoke quickly. "I have this person who's claiming to have been abducted by aliens. And so I was doing a little research online, and I came across some conspiracy theorists talking about a spaceship that's been orbiting Earth. So I was just figuring, rather than scrambling for hours and hours through files and trying to figure out if it was true, I would go straight to the source."

"You're talking about the Black Knight satellite. Conspiracy theorists have been talking about it for decades."

Greg sat in his chair, stunned. "So there's actually a spaceship out there? The Black Knight satellite is an actual spaceship? The conspiracy theorists are right?"

"Oh, no, they're completely wrong. They're looking at a thermal blanket that came off of the space shuttle during mission STS-88 back in 1998. It's been floating out in space for decades now. But because of its shape, when people catch a glimpse of it, they make the argument that it's a spaceship. There's really no point of reference out there to determine size in space."

Greg slumped in his chair. So Mitch was what, crazy? Was that better than being a reincarnated alien? It still didn't explain how he was alive. "Seriously? They're basing all of this on a space blanket?"

"Well, not just on that. They will actually argue that Tesla was the first one to have uncovered the spaceship's existence."

"Nikola Tesla?" Greg asked.

"The one and the same."

Nikola Tesla had been a Serbian scientist who'd come to the United States back in 1884. Greg didn't know a lot about him except that he was a huge fan of electricity and that he and Edison had been going back and forth with their inventions in trying to get electricity to the masses.

Edison had won, but Tesla's invention would have provided free electricity to the world. It also would have been a lot less polluting than what the world currently used. In fact, Tesla's inventions had received a lot more attention recently, as people were looking for more sustainable ways of delivering energy.

Tesla himself had never been interested in money and had actually died penniless in a hotel in New York City. Of course, government agents had then shown up and taken possession of his papers and personal property. Tesla's nephew had to sue to get them back. But when the government delivered Tesla's effects, they were twenty trunks short.

"So how is Tesla related?" Greg asked, his mind scrambling to find some sort of link to a satellite. And that made absolutely no sense because the first manned mission to space wasn't until the 1960s. Tesla had died back in 1937.

"Back in 1899, Tesla claimed to have received a radio signal from outer space," Tilda said.

Greg's eyes widened. Radio signals had often been detected from deeper in space. The fast radio bursts, or FRBs, seemed to be coming from multiple directions, but due to the briefness of the signals, they'd proven hard to investigate, even with all of today's technology. And the first FRB was only discovered back in 2007.

But back in 1899? He couldn't imagine how Tesla could possibly have detected one. "Did he actually receive one?"

"It's highly unlikely. It was probably some sort of radio signal bouncing off Earth that he was detecting. But the conspiracy theorists, they took Tesla's proclamation and the images of a thermal blanket that was drifting in space alone and came up with a spaceship that had been orbiting Earth for thousands of years."

Disappointment rolled through Greg. He didn't know why. Tilda's explanation made a lot more sense than the idea that Mitch was somehow an ancient god reincarnated in a spaceship in orbit.

Nonetheless, a large part of Greg had hoped that Mitch had been telling him the truth. Because what was the alternative? That his friend was simply crazy? Both him and his mother? That was no less daunting than the idea that he was dead.

Because if that were true, then the Mitch that he had met, the Mitch that Maya and her kids knew, had just been some sort of mirage.

At the same time, it didn't explain how Mitch was alive. It did however mean that he needed another explanation for how Mitch had survived being shot and falling into the Niagara Falls.

And Greg simply didn't know how to explain that. Maybe Mitch had been wearing a second bulletproof vest, and maybe he had somehow hit the water correctly so he didn't break every bone in his body?

But Greg had stared at that water long after Mitch had gone in. He hadn't seen any sign of him. And he didn't know where else to look for an explanation.

"Greg?"

He shook himself from his thoughts at Tilda's voice. "Yeah, I'm still here. I was just … the person who told me about it, they were so convinced. And with everything that's been going on, I just kind of thought maybe it was possible."

"The Black Knight satellite isn't an alien ship. I can guarantee you that."

Thinking about how Tilda and her people had been very careful about keeping any mention of aliens or extraterrestrial life out of the public sphere, Greg frowned. "Tilda, if that's true, how come you haven't tamped down on the rumors? I mean, isn't that something that you guys as the men in black do all the time?"

"Normally it is, but we have good reason for keeping the Black Knight satellite theory going."

"And what's that?" Greg asked.

"It's to keep anybody from looking for the other alien spaceship that actually *is* orbiting Earth."

CHAPTER 44

Once again, Greg sat back, stunned. "Come again?"

Tilda's sigh was clear across the phone line. "This stays between us. You have clearance to know about this, but it should not be revealed to any civilians, is that clear?"

Greg nodded and then realized that Tilda couldn't see him. "Yes, of course."

"Decades ago, an anomaly was noticed over South America and the southern Atlantic. The magnetic field of Earth was lessening. In fact, the dent in Earth's magnetic field was growing, and it was causing it to become a danger to satellites and ships. As a result, satellites and ships stay away from that part of the sky—and that part of space."

Greg stared at the wall behind his desk. Back when Norah had been asking for names for the new department, Greg had suggested calling it H.A.L.T. Help, Alien Life is Terrifying.

And right now, he was definitely feeling terrified.

"Did you ever find out what was causing the reduction in the magnetic field?" he asked.

"At first, we didn't have the technology to do so. It was

simply beyond our capabilities. But as our capabilities improved, we began to take pictures of that area of space. And an anomaly showed up."

Greg swallowed, his mouth feeling dry. "What kind of anomaly?"

"There was a ship, or at least there was an object that appeared to be part of a spaceship. It stayed on a constant trajectory orbiting around Earth but always staying at the same rotational speed as the planet, so it always stayed above that same particular spot."

"And it couldn't be an asteroid or something like that?"

"No. Its exterior is too smooth from the pictures that we've managed to get."

"Why haven't you sent something closer to check it out?"

"We've tried. Any sort of probe, manned or otherwise, that we've sent to get a closer inspection has lost all power as they approached the object. No one can get any closer than 592 miles before their power is shut off. We've managed to get some pictures of the object, but no one has been able to get close to it. The countries of the world know that that is a no-go zone."

"And the world at large has never figured this out?" Greg asked.

"They almost did," Tilda said. "Back in 2015, astronaut Scott Kelly took a picture of the spaceship. He didn't know that it was in the frame of the shot he was taking. And it was published on social media. I don't know who the numbskull was at NASA who allowed that picture to be sent out, but they were fired shortly thereafter. He nearly ruined the whole thing."

Greg remembered something about Astronaut Kelly and the uproar he caused when he had sent out that particular picture. "Didn't they say it was just some sort of space debris?"

"That was the company line. The truth is that ship has been there for a long time, and we don't know what it does."

"How long is a long time?"

"It's been there for decades at least."

"Is there a chance it's been there even longer than that?" Greg let out a breath, not sure what answer to hope for.

Tilda's voice though, held no answers. "I'm afraid we just don't know, Greg. In fact, we know nothing about it at all."

CHAPTER 45

After Greg hung up with Tilda, he brought up the information that had been published by Astronaut Scott Kelly. Kelly took a photo on his 223rd day on the International Space Station that sent UFO believers into a frenzy and even excited some not-quite believers.

The photo was of Earth at night, but it wasn't the beautiful lights of Earth glimmering in the night sky that drew people's attention. It was the lighted object floating in space in the top-right-hand corner of the frame. The object bore a striking resemblance to the cigar-shaped UFOs that individuals had reported.

Now Greg stared at the object in Kelly's photo. Was it possible? Was that the resurrection ship? Had it been orbiting Earth all this time and no one knew?

Greg ran his hands over his face. He did not know what to believe. He was at a loss. Which meant he needed more answers.

For a moment, he thought of Agaren. Maeve was supposed to have met with him about the silver orbs. He wasn't sure if she had. He grabbed his phone and quickly dialed.

Maeve answered almost immediately. "Greg, where are you?"

He winced. He hadn't left her a note. He'd only planned on going out for a little bit. "Sorry. I just went for a drive."

"It's fine. I just want to make sure you're all right. Are you?"

Was he? He wasn't sure. He was kind of in a holding pattern until he figured out what was going on. "I'm ... getting through. I'm actually at the office. I thought maybe burying myself in work might help take my mind off things."

"Are you sure that's wise? You should probably take a little time."

"And I will. I, um, was just thinking about the silver orb and was wondering if you had a chance to speak with Agaren."

"I did. He said the orbs were associated with an ancient race, almost royalty amongst aliens. The orbs are associated with death and rebirth, but he didn't know how they were created or their actual purpose."

Greg grunted. Great. Although the bare bones of that information lined up with what Mitch had told him, he needed more than that. And it looked like he wasn't going to find those answers here.

CHAPTER 46

Greg wasted no time leaving the D.E.A.D. He didn't want anyone to catch sight of him. And he needed time to think.

Luck was once again on his side, and he made it to his car without anyone bothering him. He hopped in with Pugsley once again as his sole companion. Driving off base, he only waved at Victor, who was working the gate this morning.

Once again, he had no destination in mind. He drove around the city of Clay and then out beyond it, through some of the rolling hills. Finally, he pulled over to the side of the road near a farm. Two cows stood in the distance, their tails swishing away.

Watching them, his mind whirled, trying to make sense of everything he'd learned. Was any of this possible?

Pugsley gave a little chirp from the passenger seat next to him.

Greg reached over and pulled the flap back from his messenger bag. Pugsley was very good at not escaping from things if Greg was nearby, which was why these little car rides were possible. The last thing he needed was to be driving down the road and have someone glance over and see Pugsley riding shotgun.

Pugsley blinked up at him with his big eyes. Once again, Greg was struck by how much he wished Pugsley could talk. It would be nice to get his interpretation of the current situation.

The truth was, he did seem to recognize Mitch. And Greg couldn't deny that it was Mitch. Oh, sure, originally he'd thought it was some sort of prank. Or that maybe he had finally lost it.

But in his gut, he'd known that it was Mitch. At the same time, he was struggling to accept everything else, and part of him nearly laughed at his struggle.

Reincarnation ship? When he was a kid, he'd completely believed that was possible. In fact, not only did he think it was possible, he'd hoped it was possible.

He was a true sci-fi geek that loved stuff like that. He must have watched the newer *Battlestar Galactica* series dozens of times. And not just because he had a not-so-subtle crush on Starbuck. She was the first girl he'd ever fallen in love with. But he also loved ideas like a reincarnation ship or aliens pretending to be human and living on Earth.

It was one thing though to believe and enjoy those things in the comfort of your family's basement. It was another thing altogether when those things were real, or at least someone was saying they were real. He just wasn't sure what to think.

At the same time, Mitch hadn't exactly been the one with a wild imagination. Mitch was so straightlaced that it often made Greg wonder how he'd ended up in the D.E.A.D. He'd wondered how anyone had been able to convince him that any of this was real. He'd wondered how his head hadn't split in two at being faced with the reality that humans were not alone in the universe.

But now he had his answer. Mitch's head hadn't split in two because Mitch knew better than anyone that humans weren't alone in the universe. Because Mitch had been on this planet for thousands of years.

He leaned his head on the steering wheel with a groan. But if he believed Isis about that, he had to believe Mitch and Isis about everything else. And it all just seemed so crazy. When faced with it in real life, it was actually pretty darn terrifying.

And more than that, when it turned out to be someone you thought of as a friend, the betrayal cut pretty deep.

Although he had to admit, he wasn't sure how exactly Mitch would work that into the conversation: Hi, Greg, nice to meet you. By the way, I'm a 20,000-year-old Egyptian god reincarnated as a mild-mannered soldier from Georgia.

Yeah, one didn't exactly slip that into a conversation easily.

His phone beeped. Greg pulled it out from his pocket and glanced at the screen. It was a text from Maeve. *Are you okay?*

He stared at the screen, not sure how to answer. He'd gotten off the phone with her rather abruptly after she'd relayed her conversation with Agaren. He could see why she might be worried.

Was he okay? He didn't think he was okay. Of course, not for the reason that Maeve thought. She thought he wasn't okay because one of his close friends had just died saving his life.

But the joke was on all of them because Mitch didn't actually die. Or at least, he didn't die for long.

Letting out a breath, he typed in a response. *Yeah. I just needed to get out for a little while. I'm okay, just driving around. But I've got Pugsley with me.*

Three dots appeared as Maeve typed a response. *Okay. But if you need anything, I'm going to stay at the base today.*

He smiled at her concern but also felt guilty that she was concerned about the wrong thing.

Thanks, he replied before slipping the phone back into his pocket. He leaned his head back against the headrest, staring up at the roof of his car.

He tried to imagine what the reincarnation ship would look like. Did it look like the reincarnation ship from *Battlestar*? He had to admit, he hadn't really been impressed with the set design for their ships outside of the *Galactica*.

But this reincarnation ship was sitting out there for everyone to see. As technology improved, it was only a matter of time before they found a way to get closer to it, if not actually board it. What would happen then?

Even now, all the major countries of the world knew that there was something there and that they couldn't go near it.

Greg shook his head, wondering why they hadn't just tried to blow the thing out of the sky. That seemed to be the way they handled new discoveries.

Heck, ever since he'd learned about the plan to blow up the moon, he'd lost faith in humanity's ability to handle the unknown. Humans were just a bunch of toddlers running around with explosives. Greg was shocked that anyone of any race that came across them thought that they were worth saving.

Why was he having such trouble with this? He'd accepted the Hank that he had worked with at Wright-Pat with very little difficulty. Of course, in that case, the extraterrestrial was half extraterrestrial and half earthbound crocodile.

He supposed that was what made it easier. They had created the Hanks. The Hanks hadn't already been here. In some weird sort of way, it was like the humans were still in control by creating the Hank.

And wasn't that arrogant?

But if what Mitch said was true, then he and the other Primevals had been walking around on this earth for thousands and thousands of years.

He wondered why they stayed. Hadn't they had enough of humanity? Sure, Greg liked the idea of a nice long life. But thousands of years? He wasn't sure if he would want that.

But what did he know? Maybe thousands of years stretching out in front of you would be appealing. But thousands of years stretching out in front of you where you had to hide who you were from everyone except for a select few? Greg didn't think he'd want that.

But maybe Mitch did. Maybe when you were essentially immortal, it was different. Greg wasn't sure what to think. And more importantly, he wasn't sure what Mitch wanted from him. And he was more than a little scared to find out. But he owed it to, well, the world, to find out what was going on.

And there was only one way to do that: he needed to go talk to his old, old, old friend.

CHAPTER 47

An hour after he left the base, Greg was pulling into Mitch's driveway. For the second time that day, he sat behind the steering wheel, staring at the house. Agaren's explanation, along with the information from Tilda, rolled over and over in his mind on the drive over. Then it rolled through his mind once again as he sat there.

Yet, it wasn't the same this time. He wasn't looking for the flaws in the argument. He was looking for the path forward. Somewhere along the way, he decided that he just needed to go along with the delusion to see where he ended up.

Or maybe he was the one being delusional not believing what Mitch, Tilda, and Maeve were telling him. Because added together, it all supported Mitch's explanation.

Pugsley gave a small chirp from the passenger seat. Strange as it sounded, he felt better having Pugsley with him, even though Pugsley hadn't exactly helped him out when Isis knocked him out before. Maybe he should have brought Iggy, or better yet, a gun. Why hadn't he at least stopped by the armory?

But he didn't think that Mitch would harm him. And he hoped Mitch would keep Isis from harming him again.

I'm crazy for coming back here, he thought as he lifted his head from the steering wheel and looked at Mitch's home. A quaint little house, it looked like all the other houses on the block. Yet, this little two-story home was not like the others that surrounded it. It housed an immortal being.

An image of Mitch's mother flashed through his mind. Correction: two immortal beings.

He shook his head as he stared at the small house. He should have told Norah. But Mitch had asked Greg to keep it quiet while he figured things out.

And for some stupid reason, Greg had agreed to that. *I'm that idiot in the horror movie that everybody in the movie theater is yelling at.*

Gripping the steering wheel, he turned to look at Pugsley. "Okay, buddy. We're going in, but either of them makes a weird move, you wrap them in goo while I call in the cavalry, okay?"

Pugsley chirped next to him, and Greg nodded. He'd take that as Pugsley's agreement.

A dozen memories from his times here flowed through his mind. He'd really enjoyed coming here. Mitch and his family had all seemed so normal. A thought rocketed through his brain.

Mitch's kids. They were all half gods. Did Maya know? Was she part god or one of the other Primevals? Wow, that was a little crazy to even think about. Had he been the only non-god at their barbecues?

He shook his head, knowing that if he sat here for much longer, his imagination would spin wildly out of control. Or more wildly out of control.

So he looked over at Pugsley. Pugsley blinked back at him. "Okay, little buddy, let's go see what's going on."

Gently he closed the flap over the messenger bag and then slid it over to him. After climbing out of the car, he made his way to the front door. He raised his hand to knock. But Mitch pulled it open before he could.

He wasn't sure what he expected to see. Maybe Mitch had gone back up to the reincarnation ship and switched bodies. Maybe he'd returned to his original form, whatever that might be.

But no, it was the same Mitch he'd always known standing in the doorway. Mitch slid the door fully open. "Come on in."

Nodding, Greg stepped inside and looked around. "Where's your mother?"

"She went back to her house."

Greg wasn't ashamed to admit that he felt relieved at that. There was something very intense about Isis.

Mitch closed the door behind him.

"Well?" Mitch asked, and Greg couldn't help but hear the hopeful note in his voice.

"Well, I know that there is a ship orbiting the planet. It's above—"

"South America and the South Atlantic Ocean," Mitch finished for him.

Greg nodded slowly. "Yeah."

"The ship has protection capabilities so that no one else can get too close."

Greg was quiet for a moment. "So you're telling the truth?"

Mitch nodded. "Yes. And I really need your help, Greg. In fact, I think the world needs your help."

Greg frowned, but before he could ask, Mitch nodded toward the kitchen. "I made some coffee."

"That sounds good," Greg said, following him in.

Mitch moved over to the counter and started to pour coffee into the two mugs sitting waiting.

Greg scanned the kitchen. There were a couple of Marissa's crayon drawings attached to the fridge, and the high chair was in the corner with two dog bowls next to it. It looked like such a normal kitchen.

Mitch nodded to the kitchen table. "Do you want to sit?"

Greg gave him a stiff nod and took a seat. He placed the messenger bag on the floor and opened up the flap.

Pugsley slipped out and let out a happy little cry as he slid across the floor. Two arms extended from his body, and he hugged Mitch's calf.

Mitch placed the mugs on the table, and as he sat down, he ran a hand over Pugsley. "It's nice to see you too, little guy."

Greg stared at Mitch and then down at Pugsley. "Your mother called him a Noctum."

Mitch nodded. "Yes. He's from a planet in the Proxima Centauri region. It's a planet of darkness. Your theory about his senses is accurate. He identifies by scent, although he can see. And technically, he's not a he."

"Pugsley's a girl?" Greg asked.

"No, Noctum are asexual. They have no gender distinctions."

Huh, well, that was interesting.

"And once they bond with someone, it's for life. Pugsley will always be true to you."

The words made Greg smile. He liked the idea of someone who'd always be there for him. "How long will his life be?"

"He will die when you do. It is one of the benefits and one of the downfalls of being a Noctum. Without a bonded partner, they live about twenty of your human years. With one, they live as long or as short as their bonded mate."

That statement brought up a whole new set of questions, and it was an effort to push them aside. But Greg did because Pugsley wasn't the primary topic for this conversation. He pulled the coffee over and added a huge amount of sugar before taking a sip. "Can I ask you something?"

"Sure."

"What do you really look like? I mean, do you have, like, tentacles instead of eyes? Are you more a Jabba the Hutt–style alien or …I don't know. Are you actually two inches tall?"

A deep chuckle emitted from Mitch. "No, I'm afraid nothing like that. Our original forms were, well, they were much like human forms. We were a little taller, a little thinner, but we looked human. But over time, as our planet began to die, we shifted more and more to our ethereal forms."

"Ethereal forms?"

"The forms that encapsulate all of our consciousness. It's what returns to the reincarnation ship each time and retrieves a new body."

"About that. How does that work, exactly? I mean, you came back as you, but do you come back as an adult each time? Or do you start the whole process over as a baby?"

Mitch smiled. "We come back as adults. We would struggle as babies. Imagine having your current consciousness stuck in a body that couldn't communicate, couldn't take care of itself, couldn't do anything for itself. That would be a rather torturous existence."

With a grunt, Greg acknowledged that was true. "So do you get to choose the body, or is it kind of a random lottery thing?"

"We can choose for the most part. But sometimes we like to leave it up to fate to decide who we will be."

"And you and your mother? Do you always reincarnate together?"

"Usually. Like I said, we live longer lives. But these bodies, they are human, so eventually they wear out. And then my mother and I will reincarnate with one another in a different part of the world."

"What about powers?"

"We have none beyond the ability to reincarnate."

There was something in his tone that suggested there was more to that answer. "But that wasn't always the case, was it?"

"No, it wasn't. But that is a longer story."

A picture of what looked like a walrus but was probably a dog on the refrigerator caught Greg's eye. "And what about your family? Your children?"

Gripping his mug, Mitch flicked a glance at the picture on the fridge. "I've never had a family before, at least not a biological one. Maya and the kids, they're my first."

Greg sat back, stunned. "Your first? Seriously? All this time, and you never …" He let the words drift off at the expression on Mitch's face. He looked so sad.

Taking a sip of coffee, Mitch then placed the mug back on the table, lining it up with the condensation mark already on the tabletop. "For the longest time, our principal responsibility was just surviving. And I didn't think that bringing children into this world would be wise.

"I mean, there have been people I've grown close to that have moved on. But they all died before me, so by the time my death came around, there were very few people that knew me. Usually in those cases I would slip away so that they wouldn't know what had happened to me. It would be like placing myself in an old folks' home or just taking a trip and never returning. It was sadly easy to slip out of people's lives."

A burst of compassion rolled through Greg. "That sounds lonely."

Mitch shrugged. "I suppose in some ways it was. But there are always ways to connect with people. Even if it was just the nice young man that made me coffee at the corner store every morning. There was always someone willing to give a bit of a smile to me as I made my way through this world. That's one of the great things about humanity. You have your darkness and you have your difficulties, but you're always ready to extend that friendliness to a complete stranger. It's one of the reasons that we've stayed here so long. It's one of the reasons my mother and I never gave up on humanity. We've seen what great potential you have."

It was a nice statement to hear, but it still left Greg with more questions. "So that's why you admire humanity, right?"

Mitch nodded.

"When the Council helped create humanity, were you part of that?"

Mitch shook his head. "No. We outdate almost all species. But we had not been in this part of the universe at the time the Council got together and decided to create humanity. That was on them. But we are very impressed with their creation."

"Even the Draco parts?"

A darkness settled over Mitch's expression. "That was a mistake. Or at least, allowing them to place so much of themselves within humanity was a mistake. The Draco, they are cruel and hateful individuals bent on ambition."

"Not all of them."

Mitch inclined his head. "That is also true. At first, we were aghast that they had allowed the Draco to be part of humanity's DNA. But then again, my own uncle tried to kill me and did kill my father. So I suppose no race is perfect."

Greg chuckled. "Yeah, that would kind of take the wind out of your ability to be self-righteous."

"That it would."

"So what about your kids? Are they like you? Will they reincarnate?"

Mitch shook his head. "No. The only way to reincarnate is to be born of two Primeval beings. My children will be like anyone else. They will hopefully live long, happy lives, and then they will pass away just like everyone else. That will be hard for me to watch."

"That's sad."

Mitch shrugged. "That's the human existence, isn't it? My children will be no different. But even the short time I've had with them has been life changing. I never realized how much joy could be experienced through something as simple as a laugh. When I hear my children laugh, everything else goes away. I am truly living in that moment, and it is a wonderful one.

"So yes, it will be sad when the day comes, but there will be so many good memories. There will be so many incredible highs—and I suppose lows—to sustain me through that. Even knowing what happens at the end, I'm still glad that I made the decision to experience my own family."

"Why did you choose to finally have children?"

The smile came easily to his face. "Because I met Maya. She is just an absolute force of nature. I couldn't help but fall in love with her. And to be honest, I didn't think I could have children. I haven't exactly been celibate up to this point, but children never resulted from those unions. But with Maya, I suppose it was meant to be."

A philosophical alien. That amused Greg. "You said that you were created from two Primeval beings. And that there were nine of them. If this orb exists, it means another Primeval died, right?"

Sadness entered Mitch's eyes. "Yes. The silver orbs contain our essence. When we stop reincarnating, they hurtle through space. And I suppose because the reincarnation ship is in orbit around Earth, they end up coming back down to the surface."

"So you can just choose to stop?" Greg asked.

"Not exactly."

Greg frowned. "What does that mean?"

"The first Primeval being that was unable to reincarnate was my father."

"Was that because he was killed by Set?"

"We're still not sure. We're not sure if it's because he was killed by another Primeval or the manner in which Set killed him."

"How did he kill him?"

Mitch's face darkened. "We don't know that either. Until he died, it was so rare, that it was viewed as practically an impossibility."

Frowning, Greg asked. "But others had died before?"

"There were stories of one, but it was so long ago, it was more legend than fact."

"And then your mother found your father and created you."

Mitch nodded. "She had hoped to bring him back. But the damage was too great."

Even centuries later, Greg could still see the impact of that event on Mitch. The sadness, the grief, and the anger.

But instead of the emotional aspect of the tale, Greg focused on the scientific. A comment Mitch had made earlier floated back through his mind: *The people of the time called it magic, but it wasn't magic. It was science.*

Mitch was right. Just a few decades ago, artificial insemination would have been the work of science fiction. In fact, much of early science fiction was coming to be reality, with trips to space, talk of colonizing other planets, and even some more basic technology like levitation devices. So Mitch was right: What was once magic was now science.

"So these other silver orbs that have appeared are other Primeval beings that no longer exist?"

His jaw tight, Mitch said, "Yes. And I need to find out who they are."

"Can you do that?"

Glancing down the hall, where Greg assumed the orb was, Mitch said, "Yes. If I'm near the orb, I can sense who the being was. And I'm hoping perhaps I can sense how they died."

Greg glanced over into the corner of the living room where the case that held the orb that Mitch had shown him earlier sat. "Whose orb is that?"

"That is my father's."

Surprise flashed through Greg. "Osiris's? You've had it all this time?"

Mitch shook his head. "No. My mother has. She brought it to me when it started to vibrate. My father, he can still communicate in some ways. And he was telling us that something was coming, that something was wrong." Mitch leaned forward. "I need to see the other orb, the one that Maeve brought with her."

Greg shook his head. "That's from decades ago. How will that help you?"

"I don't know. But I have to think it will. You have to understand, my father was the first orb that appeared. Then there were two more in the late twentieth century, and now there's another one. For thousands of years, the Primevals existed without a single one dying. And now, within the span of forty years, three are gone. Something is wrong. Something is happening. And I need to learn what it is."

Staring over at him, Greg asked, "You think someone is targeting them? Targeting you?"

Mitch shook his head. "I don't know what to think. I don't know if perhaps there's a time limit on Primevals, which would mean my mother …"

Breaking off, Mitch swallowed hard. "She is thousands of years older than me. Just as the other Primevals are. And if there is an end date for them, I need to know. I need to prepare myself for going through this world on my own."

The fear in Mitch's eyes was clear. But he had a feeling there was more behind that fear. "What aren't you telling me?"

"Sorry, it's an old habit that is hard to break. There is something else you need to know. Another reason why we need to find out what is happening to the Primevals." Mitch fell silent.

"And it is?" Greg prodded.

"If I die, the rest of the world will soon perish."

CHAPTER 48

The D.E.A.D. seemed quiet today. There was a large black flag draped across the main entrance, symbolizing the loss of one of their own.

Maeve walked under it with a heavy heart. She hadn't known Mitch the way that Greg had, but from the few interactions she'd had with him, she liked him. He seemed like a solid, steady guy. It had comforted her to know that he had Greg's back.

But now she was worried about Greg. Actually, she was always worried about Greg. He was kind of like a little brother and best friend all rolled into one. She worried about him being on his own, even though he was a grown-up. A man. And truth be told, he'd faced a lot of situations and come out of them relatively unscathed.

But she liked the idea of him having people around him that he could count on. And Mitch had been one of those people. Now she worried about the toll Mitch's death would have on him.

Maeve pushed through the door of her lab after keying

herself in. She reached over for the lights and flicked her hand over the sensor.

The room stayed dark.

She paused with a frown and ran her hand over the sensor again. Still nothing. *That's odd.*

She pulled out her cell phone and flicked on her flashlight. She scanned the room, but nothing was amiss. Across from her the lights blinked on the equipment, so the lab still had power.

Maybe a bulb was out. Was that possible? She'd never actually seen a R.I.S.E. facility with something as mundane as a bulb being out. Everything ran like a well-oiled machine.

Of course, this wasn't technically a R.I.S.E. facility. This was very much a US government facility.

The door closed behind her as she debated whether or not to call someone to replace the bulb. But she really didn't feel like speaking with anyone. She had too many thoughts rolling around in her mind, not the least of which was the conversation with Agaren.

She had hoped he would provide more information about the orbs, something that would help with her analysis. But he seemed to know as much as she did about them.

Which wasn't much.

Crossing the darkened room, she turned on the desk light near the safe for the orb. A warm glow suffused the room. Maeve smiled. Actually, this was better than the bright overhead lights. There was something cozy about it.

Slipping her bag off her shoulder, she placed it on the desk and stretched out her back as she pushed thoughts of Greg aside for a little bit. She wanted to run a couple more tests on the orb and see what else she could find before she packed it up and took it back home.

Greg wouldn't be any help with analyzing it for the next few days. And she really didn't want to push him on that, despite him saying he wanted the work distraction. The fact that he'd left the base so soon after their phone call made it clear that he hadn't been ready for that. He probably wouldn't be for a while.

So she'd take it home and then bring it back when he was up for it again. She walked over to the safe and placed her hand on the flat screen before punching in her code.

The door popped open with a hiss of air. She pulled it back and stared inside. It really was an incredible artifact.

Every time they learned something new, she grew more in awe of the universe around them.

This orb was something that even Agaren didn't know much about. What did that mean? Was it some sort of symbolic ceremonial object? Agaren said it had something to do with death and rebirth, but that seemed to be what everyone said about ancient religions: death and rebirth. All of them seemed to float around those two ideas.

Maeve herself wasn't sure what she thought about the whole rebirth concept.

She liked to think that when you went through this world, you did what was right as much as you possibly could, and then after your death you got to spend eternity with those you loved.

She wasn't sure if that was part of any particular religion. She'd never grown up with religion. Her mother had been so science minded that thoughts about an afterlife hadn't really played much into her upbringing.

But after her mother's death, she had wondered more than once about where her mother had gone. It seemed impossible that the woman who'd had so much energy and such a presence could simply disappear and be no more.

She liked to think that she was somewhere watching over her. But then Maeve winced, imagining if that were the case. What her mother would have seen the last few years hadn't exactly been peaceful.

But it would be nice to think that her mother had gotten a chance to see the triplets. Maeve shook her head as she started to wander down memory lane.

Now wasn't the time for that. She needed to finish these last few tests and send the orb back. She'd already contacted Sammy and asked him to come by in a few hours to pick it up.

She would stay to keep an eye on Greg and to go to Mitch's funeral. Chris was going to fly in with Sammy for that as well. Adam had agreed to watch the kids while the two of them were gone. She hadn't heard anything about the preparations yet, but she was sure that Norah would be working on that.

Pushing her melancholy and philosophical thoughts from her mind, she slid the tray out that held the orb and then carried it over to the table. Placing it on the flat surface, it sat without moving. That alone made it clear that this was not a normal orb. If she had placed a bowling ball the same way on a table, it would have rolled right off.

But the orb sat contentedly. She took a step away, and the orb emitted a small noise.

Maeve whirled back toward it as the hairs on her arm stood on end. The orb rolled toward her, letting out another small noise that almost sounded like a cry.

She stared at it, not sure what had set off that reaction, her mind racing. The orb rolled even closer toward her. Involuntarily, Maeve took a step back.

Pain bloomed across the back of her skull. Darkness swam across her vision before she sank to the floor.

CHAPTER 49

If I die, the rest of the world will soon perish. Mitch's words hung in the air over the kitchen table. Greg stared at his friend. "Um, that seems a little egotistical, don't you think?"

"I wish it was. In the ancient days, protecting the pharaoh was of primary importance. People would give their lives to keep the pharaoh safe. Do you know why?"

"Because the pharaoh was believed to be the living embodiment of a god."

Mitch nodded. "Yes, he was the living embodiment of my father, Osiris. When Osiris died, there were floods and famine. The world became unsettled."

"That's a coincidence."

"I wish that it were. My family, my father's line, are the originators of my people. We are linked into the world in a way I do not truly understand. When I said we do not have any powers, that is true. But I can feel the earth. I can feel that she is struggling. I worry that the death of the Primevals is hastening her end."

"End?"

Mitch nodded. "The climate is radically shifting. Humanity has been a scourge to this world. But the damages would be so much more without the Primevals to keep them at bay."

"So the idea of keeping the pharaoh alive at all costs comes from …" Greg wasn't sure how to finish that sentence.

Mitch did it for him. "From the need to keep the Primevals alive."

"But you think Set doesn't care about that," Greg said.

"Set is so filled with anger and ego, he does not care. He will dance over the ashes of this world and rule amongst the rubble that is left."

"I still don't understand how he can come back. You said he was punished."

"He was. The Primevals placed restraints on his consciousness that keeps him from remembering. But each time he dies, the restraints are loosened. When half are gone, he will be able to break free. He will return to full consciousness."

A chill had crept over Greg's skin. "So we need to protect the Primevals. Let's just do that."

"That will be impossible. I do not know where they are," Mitch said.

"So what can we do?"

As Mitch looked into Greg's eyes, he could see the reflection of time in them. "We must keep Set from gaining control of the orbs."

"The orbs? Why?" Greg asked.

"There is a ritual that must be completed in order for Set to return. For it, he needs four orbs."

Mind racing, Greg catalogued the three orbs they knew about. "The orb in Africa. You think Set retrieved it."

Mitch nodded. "I have no proof of that, but yes, I believe that is the case. It's why I needed to return like this. I need to make sure the other orbs are safe. I need to hide them away where Set can never find them."

"Are you sure Set is this big a threat?" Greg asked, hoping that for once Mitch was exaggerating.

His voice deadly serious, Mitch met Greg's gaze. "If I were to die, Set would be released from his punishment and the world would suffer for it. I don't know if the world's suffering from his release was meant because my death would be the catalyst, or because, as the youngest, I would be the only one alive when Set is freed to fight him. But whatever the case, finding out how the others were killed is critically important."

The chill that had crept over Greg's skin had now shifted into a tremor. He stared at Mitch, wanting to deny what he was saying.

But he couldn't. Mitch was right. They needed to know more. "So what do you want me to do?" Greg asked.

"I want you to help me get reinstated back at the D.E.A.D."

CHAPTER 50

While Greg didn't think he could be more surprised than during their conversation about reincarnation ships, the idea that he could bring his deceased partner back into the D.E.A.D. definitely topped it. He thought when Mitch mentioned getting back on base before that he meant sneaking him in somehow. But actually getting him his position back? That was nuts.

The dead man sitting across from him had to be crazy. Or Greg couldn't have heard him correctly. "I'm sorry, did you just say you want me to get you your position in the D.E.A.D. back?"

Mitch nodded.

Staring at Mitch, Greg's mind went blank for a moment. "Back in? You're *dead*. How exactly am I supposed to get you back in? You do realize they all think you're dead, right? I mean, I can't just walk a dead guy back into the offices. They've seen a lot there, but that's probably a step too far for even them."

"Not if I was never killed," Mitch said calmly.

Although Greg let out a laugh, Mitch didn't join him.

"Yeah, but you *were* killed. I saw you *get* killed. I told *everybody* about you getting killed. Unless you can time travel ... Wait, can you time travel?"

"No, Greg, I can't time travel. But what if when I was shot, I was wearing my vest?"

"But you weren't wearing your vest."

Mitch leaned forward. "But what if I was? And then I fell. I survived the fall but washed up downriver. When I pulled myself out, I called you. And you weren't sure if it was really me, so you came out to check and discovered it was, in fact, me. So then you returned to the base with me."

His mouth hanging open, Greg stared at him and then threw up his hands. "You've got to be kidding. Who's going to buy that?"

"Wouldn't you buy that? Wouldn't you be happy to hear that rather than hearing that I was dead?" Mitch pressed.

"Well, yeah, but I mean, why would I go out to get you alone? Wouldn't I take someone? And how exactly did I get back out there?"

"You didn't go out there alone. You took Pugsley as backup." Mitch nodded to Pugsley, who'd made his way over to Marissa's dollhouse in the corner and was inspecting it. He looked up at the mention of his name and chirped.

Mitch continued. "You didn't bring anyone else because you weren't sure if it was a hoax or not, and you didn't want to tell anyone until you were sure. And you got out there by chopper. We can simply falsify some records to make it appear like you took one."

"Falsify records?" Greg all but shrieked. "You do realize that people get incarcerated for that, right? And you might have multiple lifetimes, but I only have this one, and I'm not really interested in spending it locked behind bars."

"I won't let you get locked up," Mitch promised. "The one

thing I have gotten very good at is creating a paper trail. They'll never know."

Greg stared into Mitch's eyes. Mitch, who had saved his life on he didn't know how many occasions. Mitch, who had patiently trained him for hours and hours on the gun range and never made one snide comment. Mitch, who had invited Greg over weekend after weekend after things had gone sideways with Ariana.

Mitch, who had opened his home to Greg. And to Kal. He let out a breath, knowing there was no other answer. "Okay. Tell me exactly what we're going to do."

CHAPTER 51

Nerves rolled along the edges of Greg's skin as he sat in Mitch's living room. They had a plan. It wasn't a great one, and they would need Greg to sell it, but they had a plan. Mitch sat across from him and nodded.

Picking up his cellphone, Greg let out a shaky breath as he dialed. He pulled the phone to his ear.

Norah answered. "Greg? How are you doing?"

He stared over at Mitch, who nodded back at him. He cleared his throat. "Good. Actually, better than good. Do you know how Mitch kind of, well, we thought he died?"

"*Thought*?" Norah asked.

Greg gave a nervous laugh. "Yeah, turns out, not so much. He was wearing a vest when he was shot, and he went over the falls, but I don't know, I guess he must have hit the water right or something because he ended up washing up downriver. And he called me."

Norah was silent for a moment, and there was a touch of incredulity and a whole heaping of concern when she did speak. "Greg, are you feeling all right? Are you at home? Should I come by?"

Even without Mitch rolling his eyes across from him, he knew he was blowing this. He stood up and started to pace. "No, no, I'm fine. He called me, and I went out to Niagara just now. It's Mitch, Norah. I swear it is."

Silence greeted him yet again, this one a little longer than the previous silence. "Greg, I know you want Mitch to be alive, but he's not, honey. There's no way he could have—"

Okay, now he was getting a little insulted. He knew Norah was worried about him, but she was talking to him like he was a kid. "I know it sounds crazy, Norah, but I swear to God, I'm staring at him right now. We're at Mitch's house. I brought him here so he could get a change of clothes."

"He's there with you now?" Norah asked slowly.

Greg nodded. "Yeah, we're sitting having some coffee."

Norah's voice took on a serious tone. "Okay, Greg, I need you to listen to me. You keep him talking. I'm going to have a strike force out there in minutes. Do not let him know that you suspect anything, okay?"

Not sure how the Greg who had just discovered his partner was alive and well would react to that statement, he paused for a moment before he answered. "Okay. Will do."

"Just keep everything nice and normal. And we'll be there in just a few minutes, okay?" Norah said.

"Okay, sounds good. But everything really is okay," Greg said again.

She disconnected the call without replying, and Greg set the phone face down on the table.

"Well?" Mitch asked.

Greg took a sip of his coffee and placed it back on the table. "Well, they think I'm crazy and you're an imposter."

Mitch grinned with a chuckle. "Kind of figured that would happen. They're sending a strike force?"

"Yep," Greg said.

"Good. They'll run some tests. They'll see who I am, and then we'll be all good," Mitch assured him.

Greg eyed him. "Shouldn't you be bruised?"

Lifting up his shirt, Greg winced. His rib cage was a mass of dark bruises. "When did that happen?"

"I made sure that my body looked like it had fallen over the falls. So yeah, I'm a bit bruised," Mitch said.

"Does that hurt?" Greg asked, having to hold his hands back so he didn't poke at the bruises.

Lowering his shirt, Mitch nodded. "It doesn't tickle, but I figured this was the best way to get back into the D.E.A.D."

"You're sure this is all worth it?" Greg asked.

His gaze locked on Greg, there was only determination in Mitch's response. "Oh, it's definitely worth it."

The strike force arrived ten minutes later. Greg and Mitch had moved to the living room, and Greg had placed Pugsley back into the messenger bag.

They were sitting on the couch when Mitch tilted his head to the side and then nodded to the door. "They're here."

Greg's eyes widened. "Is that some sort of alien thing? Being able to hear really well? Or maybe a psychic thing?"

Placing his mug down and his hands on the sides of the chair, Mitch shook his head. "Nope. That's a special forces kind of thing. They're on the porch."

The door swung open. Members of the strike force stormed into the living room. His mug still in his hand, Greg's coffee sloshed over the sides and onto his pants as he startled. His heart pounded as guns pointed at him and Mitch.

Greg nearly groaned when he saw that Hannibal was leading the force. Although, he supposed that made sense.

With Mitch gone, Hannibal was the next in line to lead. But he was easily Greg's least favorite of all the strike force members.

"Mitch Haldon, place your hands above your head," Hannibal ordered.

Slowly, Mitch raised his hands.

Inching forward, his finger way too close to the trigger, Hannibal glared at Mitch. "Stand up," he barked.

Mitch did as he was ordered.

Kaylee, who was toward the back of the group, hurried over to Greg with Max. She grabbed Greg's arm and pulled him from the couch and away from Mitch. But she kept her gaze locked on Mitch the whole time.

With zero gentleness, Hannibal slipped his cuffs around Mitch's wrists. Mitch winced as his arms were pulled behind his back.

Greg took a step forward. "Hey, careful, he's hurt."

Hannibal glared over at him. "We've got this, Schorn." And then he grabbed Mitch by the bicep and shoved him toward the door.

Next to him, Kaylee and Max watched the whole thing. Kaylee's hand stayed on Greg's arm, keeping him back.

"It's really him, isn't it?" Max asked.

As Mitch's frame disappeared out the doorway, Greg nodded. "Yeah, it's him."

"They're going to need to make sure of that. There's too much crazy swirling around the base to simply take his word for it," Kaylee said.

"They won't hurt him, will they?" Greg asked.

She shook her head. "No. They'll run a genetic profile and make sure he is who he says he is, and then they'll question him about where he's been." She turned to Greg. "How did you end up with him?"

"He called. I went to go see for myself, to make sure it was him," Greg said, repeating the cover story. He reached down and grabbed his messenger bag. "I took Pugsley for backup." He pulled the flap back, and Pugsley's head popped out.

"Yeah, no offense to Pugsley, but next time reach out to me or Kaylee, okay?" Max said.

"Yeah, okay," Greg said.

A group of three individuals in bunny suits stepped in through the front door. Two headed down the hall toward the bedrooms while one walked toward the kitchen.

Frowning, Greg stared at the technicians. "What's going on?"

Kaylee gave him a nudge toward the door. "We need to get you back to base. They're going to search Mitch's home."

"Is this really necessary?" Greg asked.

"He just came back from the dead. Yeah, it's necessary," Max said as they stepped outside.

CHAPTER 52

It was still early as Greg stepped outside. Barely halfway through the morning, and yet Greg felt like it should be dark already.

"You want to ride with us?" asked Kaylee.

Greg shook his head, pointing at his car. "No, I'm good."

He hopped in his jeep and waited until the rest of the strike force had left except for the ones who were searching Mitch's home before he pulled out of the driveway.

He flicked a glance at the back of his car through the rearview mirror where the silver orb lay in its box covered with a blanket.

So far, Mitch had been right about everything that the D.E.A.D. had done. He'd known that they were going to take him in and then search his home. That was why they'd moved the silver orb to Greg's car to keep it safe.

Greg drove back toward the base, his mind whirling. He needed to get to Maeve and see what she thought was going on with the orbs. But first, Mitch would have to be evaluated.

As he drove, he realized that if something was up with the silver orbs and that they were critical for Set's reincarnation, then maybe the two of them could figure out a way to block the energy the orbs gave off. Maybe they could neutralize it so that even if Set got a hold of them, he wouldn't be able to use them.

The thought brought Greg up short. How exactly was Set doing all this? From what Mitch said, Set was basically just a consciousness right now. Was one of the other Primevals helping him? Or was his consciousness able to influence humans?

Immediately, he pictured Nate, Agnes, and Officer Moore. Were they somehow part of this?

He shook his head. One issue at a time. First, they needed to see if they could block or power down the orbs' energy. He wasn't going to be able to figure that out on his own.

Which meant they needed to bring Maeve in and tell her exactly what Mitch was. He knew Mitch was going to balk at the idea of revealing himself to someone else, but Maeve was pretty good at keeping secrets. She had her whole life.

It seemed no time had passed before Greg pulled onto the base. After showing his credentials at the gate, he made his way to D.E.A.D. headquarters. For a moment, he contemplated stopping by his apartment and dropping off the orb, but he didn't want to take a separate trip and maybe get people wondering what he was up to. So he continued toward headquarters and pulled into a parking spot at the back of the lot.

He flicked a glance at the orb in the back. He couldn't risk taking it into the building. There were all sorts of scans constantly happening, and it could trip one of them. But he didn't like the idea of leaving it out here.

Then again, no one knew Mitch had it, and he'd had it for thousands of years. A few hours in Greg's car should be all right.

He turned his gaze to the building. The strike force had driven a lot faster than him, so he had no doubt that Mitch was already up at the medical wing. Greg grabbed the messenger bag and looked down at Pugsley.

Preparing himself for what was to come, he let out a breath that he hoped was calming. When it wasn't, he tried five more times. Nope, still stressed. Apparently, breathing techniques did not work when you'd just learned about a serial killer immortal alien. "Okay, buddy. Let's get our game faces on. We need to convince everyone that our recently reincarnated friend is the same Mitch that we all know and love."

Pugsley chirped and blinked his eyes.

Greg nodded. "You're right. Let's just go hide in our office until all of Mitch's tests are done. That's a much better plan."

CHAPTER 53

Keeping his head down, Greg made his way through the front foyer. He felt as if everyone's eyes were on him, but when he dared to look around, no one was actually paying him any attention.

For a moment, he thought of going down to the medical wing to check on Nate, Agnes, and Officer Moore, but honestly, his nerves were strung so tight he didn't think that would be a good idea. He didn't trust himself to go and speak to anyone with the way he was feeling, so he made his way down to his office.

Letting himself in, he locked the door behind him before leaning against it. Then he walked over to the couch, placing the bag on the ground next to it. Pugsley crawled out and let out a little chirp, looking up at him expectantly.

"Oh, right, breakfast." It really was still early.

The base wouldn't be busy for another few hours.

Greg walked over to the desk and pulled out the peanuts he kept there for Pugsley, putting them on the placemat that he left on the ground for Pugsley to eat from. Pugsley let off a happy little hum as he sat down and started eating.

Eating actually sounded like a good idea. Greg hadn't eaten a meal in a while. He glanced at the basket of muffins. No, come to think of it, he had no interest in food.

Instead, he walked over to the couch and lay down, pulling the blanket from the back of it over himself. He stared up at the ceiling as thoughts raced through his mind.

Mitch was some sort of ancient god. No, not just an ancient god, an ancient alien god. And his evil crazy uncle looked like he was trying to come back into this world.

Greg closed his eyes with a groan. Why couldn't his life ever be normal?

Of course, he *had* chosen to work on alien hybrids, so normal was probably always going to be a bit of a stretch. But it seemed as if he had really jumped the shark lately on crazy.

Weariness rolled over him. *I'll just close my eyes for a few minutes, and then I'm sure the world will look much different.*

A few minutes stretched into much longer. When he opened his eyes, Mitch was sitting in the chair next to his couch. Greg scrambled up with a yelp.

But Mitch raised an eyebrow at him. "You okay there, Greg?"

Greg sat back hard against the couch, glaring at him. "No, because some crazy person was sitting next to my couch, watching me sleep."

Mitch chuckled. "I'm not a crazy person, and I wasn't watching you sleep. I was letting you sleep because it seemed like you needed it. And people keep looking at me when I walk through the halls, so I decided I would just come here and wait for you to wake up."

Greg took a closer look at Mitch and noticed that he seemed uncomfortable. He didn't think he'd ever seen Mitch look uncomfortable.

Reaching out, Mitch grabbed one of the coffees on the table in front of the couch and slid it toward Greg. "When I saw you sleeping, I went down to the cafeteria and got us both some coffee. I figured you could probably use it, and so could I."

Pulling the coffee to him greedily, Greg asked, "Ancient gods get tired?"

Adjusting his legs out in front of him, Mitch sighed. "There's nothing different about me. Physically, I'm human. I don't have any special powers or special abilities. I can't fly. I don't have laser eyes. I just have a different way of living and dying. But otherwise, I'm practically as human as you are."

Greg knew that was possible. Everyone thought that aliens from outer space would look so radically different from humans, with green skin, tentacles, and strange blob-like bodies.

And to be fair, there were some of those.

But if an alien planet was similar to Earth, the aliens would be almost identical to humans. The humanoid form was an efficient form of life. And there was no reason why Earth would be the only place where it would pop up.

Wiping at his eyes, Greg scanned the room but didn't spy Pugsley anywhere. He'd probably wandered off to see if he could find Iggy. "Okay, so what's the plan?"

"The plan is to see the orb. Do you know what lab it's in?"

Greg nodded. "Yeah, they put it in Maeve's lab." He glanced at his watch and noted that he'd been asleep for just over two hours. But it had made him a little more energized, and the world didn't seem quite so crazy.

Just the normal level of crazy he was used to. He stood up and stretched his back. "Okay, I'm ready. Let's go see Maeve."

CHAPTER 54

Sipping his coffee, Greg walked with Mitch through the halls toward Maeve's temporary lab. And as they walked, he understood what Mitch meant about people doing double takes. Everyone seemed shocked by his reappearance, not that Greg could blame them.

But it did make him feel awfully self-conscious. He leaned a little closer to Mitch and whispered, "If we're going to try and do anything under the radar, you can't be a part of it."

Mitch nodded. "Yeah, that's becoming pretty clear."

Together, the two of them eschewed the elevator and jogged up the stairs to the third floor. Turning down the hall, they headed to the last door on the right.

Greg placed his hand on the screen next to the door, and it scanned his hand before turning green. He inputted the code for the lab and let himself in. He frowned at the dark room. "What's up with the lights?"

Mitch put out a hand, holding Greg back. "Let me go first."

Greg was about to argue and then realized that if something happened to Mitch, he'd be more than okay. He could simply regrow a body. So he stepped back and let Mitch go first.

Pulling out his phone, Greg turned on the flashlight, scanning it across the room. He'd never known a room in the D.E.A.D. to be dark. This was weird.

Mitch walked forward slowly, and Greg followed him. He swung his flashlight back and forth, looking for what, he wasn't sure. Because there was no way that Maeve was—

"Maeve!" Greg pushed past Mitch as he raced to the crumpled figure on the floor.

He crouched down next to her, his hands hovering over her for a moment, not sure if he should touch her or not. He didn't want to cause her any more injury.

Maeve groaned, and relief rolled through Greg. "Maeve? Maeve, are you all right?"

She groaned again and rolled onto her back before she started to sit up. "No, I've got one hell of a headache."

Greg quickly helped her into a sitting position. "What happened?"

Shaking her head, Maeve winced, stopping the motion. "The lab was dark when I came in. Someone hit me over the back of the head."

Juggling his phone in his hand, Greg called Norah. She answered almost immediately. "Hey, Greg. Mitch is all good. I don't understand how, but—"

"Maeve's been attacked in her lab. Send security immediately."

"Got it," Norah said.

After Greg placed the phone on the ground, he turned back to his friend.

"Help me up, would you?" Maeve asked.

Greg wrapped an arm around her as Mitch did the same from the other side, and the two of them helped her to her feet.

She patted Mitch's hand. "Thanks, Mitch." Then she did a double take. "Mitch!"

Grimacing, Greg spoke quickly. "It's a long story, but he's alive."

She stared at Mitch and then smiled at him. "It's good to see you."

"It's good to be seen," he said as he helped her across the room and to a desk chair. He gently lowered her into it.

While Mitch helped Maeve, Greg scanned the room, looking for the silver orb. He frowned when he couldn't see it. "Maeve, where's the orb?"

"It's on the table." Maeve waved to one of the long silver lab tables.

All the tabletops were empty. "It's not here."

"What?" Maeve stood up and swayed for a moment. Mitch reached out and steadied her. "Did I put it back in storage?" She murmured.

"Where was it being stored?" Greg asked.

She pointed to the shelving unit at the back of the room.

Greg headed toward the back wall and started to input his security code into the plate. But as soon as he touched it, the door moved. He frowned and then gripped the handle and pulled it wide. "It's unlocked."

It took no time to check the shelves inside. On the second one, there was a glaring empty space, just the right size for the containment unit that the silver orb had been held in.

Dread settled in his gut as he stepped back. "It's gone."

CHAPTER 55

Maeve's head pounded as Greg's words registered. "What?" she said, wincing as more pain throbbed through the back of her head. Whoever had hit her had done a really good job. She felt like she'd been out for hours.

Mitch held onto her, and she stepped away once her legs felt steady. Peering into the cabinet she saw that Greg was right. The space where she'd last placed the orb was now empty.

"What do you remember?" Mitch asked.

"I, um, wait, yes. I took it out and placed it on the table. It stood perfectly still, not moving. I stepped away from it, and it almost seemed to roll after me, giving off a cry. Then someone hit me over the back of the head." Maeve reached up to touch the tender part of her head. There was a large swollen lump there now.

"They were going for the orb," Greg said, looking intently at Mitch. "They must have been in here when you entered, but they needed you to unlock the storage unit."

"But why? What are these things? What do they do?" Maeve asked.

Greg looked over at Mitch, but Mitch shook his head. And before Maeve could say anything, security burst through the door, led by Norah. "Maeve, are you all right?"

Turning, Maeve nodded. "Yeah. The lights were out when I got in here. And someone hit me over the back of the head. It looks like they took the orb."

"Somebody get these lights on," Norah ordered. "And I want all security footage for the last few hours. I want to know who was in this building. In fact, lock the building down."

Alarms went off across the building as Norah's orders were initiated.

Security was hustling around the room, and Norah had stepped back to give more orders, but Maeve kept her gaze on Mitch and Greg, who were having an intense conversation across the room.

She narrowed her eyes. What was up with those two?

CHAPTER 56

Someone hurt Maeve.

Greg's stomach bottomed out at the thought of it. She was all right, but the possibility that something more dire could have happened to her terrified Greg. She was family.

As the security team hustled into the room, Greg tilted his head to the side, waving Mitch to his side. The two of them made their way back to the couch, and Greg lowered his voice. "We've got to tell Maeve what's going on."

Mitch shook his head. "No."

Greg waited, but apparently that was all Mitch was going to say. "No? Someone just attacked her because she had that stupid silver orb. And if we're going to figure out what's going on, we're going to need more help than just the two of us. And Maeve has a way of figuring these things out."

"You are the first person I have told in a very long time. Let's just see what—"

Another thought hit Greg, and his head snapped up as he stared at Mitch. "They took the silver orb, Mitch."

"Yes, and we don't know why."

Greg grabbed his arm. "No, but we also know where there's another one, and that means—"

Mitch's eyes widened as he finally realized what Greg was getting at. Without another word, the two of them sprinted for the door.

"Greg? Mitch?" Norah called after them.

But neither of them answered as they sprinted down the hall and burst into the stairwell.

There's no way someone could know the orb was in my car. There's no way, Greg repeated over and over in his mind as he ran.

But the words didn't make him feel any better.

He burst through the first-floor landing and into the front foyer, startling two technicians walking by. Mitch outpaced him and sprinted for the front door, but it was locked. He rattled the frame as he yanked on the door handle.

"Hold on. Hold on." Reaching the doors, Greg swiped his ID over the card reader next to the door. He, Norah, and about three other people on base had the ability to override a lockdown order.

The two of them darted out into the parking lot and headed to the back row where Greg had parked while Greg berated himself the whole time. *Stupid. I should have parked in the front.*

But he thought if he parked in the back, it would be better for keeping the orb hidden. That also meant if someone was going to steal it, though, they'd have less eyes to worry about.

As he approached, he saw something glittering along the ground next to his car. *Oh no.*

Mitch came to a halt next to his car, staring with dismay at the shattered window. Greg careened to a halt next to him and stared in at the empty trunk space of his jeep.

The orb was gone.

CHAPTER 57

The glass from the back window of Greg's jeep littered the parking lot. Greg stared at it before looking around at the cars that were nearby, but nothing in the surrounding area offered any sort of clue.

Mitch nodded to the building. "We need to go look at the security footage," he said before striding across the parking lot.

Greg hustled after him, scanning the parking lot still, as if the individual would be standing nearby, holding up the box and saying, "Hey, it was me!"

Sadly, they weren't that stupid. But they were gutsy. It took a lot of balls to break a window in the parking lot of a secret government facility. So whoever they were looking for wasn't exactly a shrinking violet.

At the same time, how did they know that the orb was in his car? And how were they able to get the orb out of the parking lot without someone seeing?

One thing was clear: Someone on the base was working against them. Set had a partner. Because this was not something done by some ethereal form.

The foyer was a mass of security as Greg and Mitch

stepped back inside. The alarm had sent everybody into defensive positions.

Mitch grabbed Kaylee as she hurried past. "Where are you guys heading?"

"We've been asked to secure the western hallway. You two coming?"

Greg shook his head. "There's something we need to do first. We'll come find you guys after."

Kaylee and Max nodded as they headed off with the rest of their unit.

The security office was down the hall. Greg and Mitch hurried inside. The room was set up with a series of monitors spread along the perimeter of the room, manned by a dozen technicians.

Greg was unsurprised to see Norah and Maeve already there. Maeve looked a little pale and was sitting in one of the chairs.

Norah was standing over one of the techs. She turned as they entered and narrowed her eyes. "Where did you go? What are you two up to?"

"Uh, nothing. We just, um, wanted to check and see if you found out anything about Maeve's case," Greg said.

Norah shook her head. "No. The attacker knew where the cameras were and kept their face hidden from it. But from what we can tell, it looks like it was probably a female."

Greg frowned. For some reason, he hadn't been expecting that.

Norah's phone beeped, and she looked down at it. "Okay, I've got to go." She looked at the technician. "Keep going through the recording. See if you can see a reflection in a surface that might ID our attacker."

"Will do," the tech said, turning back to the monitor as Norah stepped away from it. She turned to Maeve. "I want you to go down to medical and get checked out, okay?"

Staring at the computer monitor, Maeve waved her off. "I'm fine."

"Nonetheless, I want you to go get checked out to make sure. In fact, why don't you come with me now?" Norah asked.

Greg knew that tone. Norah was making it sound like a request, but it was really an order.

Apparently Maeve knew that tone as well. She sighed. "Fine, fine," she said before following Norah out the door.

Greg waited until the two of them were out of earshot before he leaned toward one of the technicians sitting at a console near him. "I need you to bring up parking lot C from this morning."

One part of being in a military facility that Greg loved was that people didn't question when someone of higher authority made a request. The technician immediately started typing on the keyboard and brought up the recording.

"When do you want to start?" the tech asked.

"About two and half hours ago," Greg said.

With a nod, the tech hit a few keys. An image of the parking lot from this morning flared across the screen. Greg watched his car pull in and then saw himself get out and walk across the parking lot. "Can you fast-forward a little bit and just stop it when we see someone over by my jeep?"

"Sure," the technician said, speeding it up.

Greg watched a few cars pull in. The people got out and headed toward the main building. Nobody went near Greg's car.

And then finally, a figure appeared, coming out of the building in the opposite direction than everybody else who'd been on the screen so far had been heading. They headed to the back of the parking lot.

Greg leaned forward. "Go back to normal speed."

The action on the screen slowed. The individual weaved

between the cars and then stopped at the side of Greg's. They cast a look around and then slammed a metal baton into Greg's back window.

The picture wasn't great, and he still couldn't tell if it was a man or a woman who turned their head as glass exploded onto the parking lot ground.

Then they reached in, unlocked the back door, and pulled it open. Their head disappeared inside the car for a moment. A moment later, they reappeared holding the orb. They slipped it into the bag that they'd been carrying along their back. The bag now bulged as they made their way back to the building.

Nudging his chin toward the screen, Greg asked, "Can you zoom in on their face and clean it up a little bit?"

The technician nodded as he did as Greg asked. Greg and Mitch leaned forward. The individual had a hood up over their head.

But it looked like they were female, just like Norah had said about the person who had attacked Maeve.

Greg stared at the screen as the face came into view more clearly. He sucked in a breath. "Kaylee."

CHAPTER 58

The technician copied the recording onto a flash drive. Then Greg swore him to secrecy as Greg and Mitch tried to figure out what the next steps were going to be.

It was clear they needed to question Kaylee. But if she was in on it, then maybe other members of the strike force were as well. Plus, Kaylee had been with the rest of the strike force when Maeve was attacked, which meant there was at least one other person working with her.

At the same time, Greg's mind rebelled against the idea that Kaylee was somehow working against the United States government.

And he completely rebelled at the idea that Kaylee would be part of a plan to hurt Maeve. Kaylee was their medic, for God's sake. Yes, she was still a trained soldier, but it was completely out of character for her to sit in the dark in Maeve's office, waiting to knock her out.

The thought brought him up short: another person behaving out of character. Was it possible Kaylee was afflicted by whatever had affected Nate, Agnes, and Moore? And if so, did that mean whatever it was was contagious? Were they looking for some sort of contagion? Then he remembered that he'd asked Hannah to look for any sort of parasite. He pulled out his phone to text her. *Hey. Did you find any parasites?*

Three dots appeared before she replied. *No, no parasite. But I did find implants.*

He frowned. *What kind of implants?*

I don't know. It's not in any of their medical records, and I can't get a good handle on what they might be. I'm sending you the files.

Greg flipped to his email and quickly brought up the scans. It was hard to see on the small screen, but Hannah had circled the implants on the images. What would account for—

Greg's eyes widened. *Of course. Alien implants.* "We need to talk to Kaylee *now*," Greg said.

The halls were busy as Mitch and Greg made their way through them, everyone on a heightened state of alert, which Greg figured was actually a good thing: if he looked stressed, he could blame it on the attack on Maeve.

"I think I figured something out," Greg said.

"What?"

"The reason Agnes, Moore, and Nate are all behaving strangely. They all have alien implants," Greg asked.

Mitch frowned. "Really?"

Grunting, Greg thought over what they knew, which wasn't much. "It's such a strange phenomenon amongst alien abductees. Different parts of their bodies being tagged with small little implants that have no medical explanation. No one has been able to explain why they're there. The theory is that they've been placed there by aliens."

"Like they're being tagged," Mitch said softly.

Greg nodded. "Exactly. Is it possible that they could also be used to control them?"

Mitch frowned. "I've never heard of it. But I don't see why not."

INTO THE DARK

By now, they'd reached the front foyer. There were too many people around for their conversation to go unheard, so Greg buttoned up about the implants. Was it possible? If so, it meant that whoever was controlling them would have potentially hundreds of people at their disposal. Was that how Set was doing it?

Even as the questions swirled in Greg's mind, he knew he needed to hold off on asking them. Right now they needed to find Kaylee. But they couldn't tip her off. They needed to approach her in a nonthreatening way.

They stopped by the front foyer and checked the duty assignments. Sure enough, Kaylee and the rest of the unit was set up at the west entrance. At least she had been truthful about that.

He and Mitch hurried down the hall, seeing the concerned faces of the non-security personnel as they watched the goings-on with big eyes. Greg felt a growing sense of concern as well. Someone had stolen two critical objects from the D.E.A.D. and attacked a leading scientist. Nothing like this had ever happened in the agency before.

And if it was an inside job, Greg didn't even want to think about that possibility.

Martin, which of your little acolytes is messing with us now? Greg silently asked as he hurried down West Hallway C. Of course, this probably had nothing to do with Martin. Set was apparently the one to blame for the current goings-on, if Mitch was right. But Greg still liked to blame things on Martin. It felt good.

As they rounded the corner, Greg spied Kaylee's unit up ahead. They were standing along the hall, just waiting for action. A few leaned back against the wall. Most chatted in groups of two.

Looking over from the back of the pack, Max grinned. "About time you two showed up. Mitch, you rested from your little vacation there?"

Mitch smiled. "Well, you know, getting declared dead is the only way we get a day off around here."

Max chuckled as Kaylee grinned from her spot next to him. "Now that's the truth."

Nothing in her demeanor indicated that she was nervous. Nothing indicated subterfuge. She looked relaxed. And yet Greg had seen her on the video.

He stepped up toward her. "Kaylee, we need to speak with you for a minute."

Kaylee looked between the two of them, a furrow appearing along her brow. "Everything all right?" Even before she finished asking it, she turned to Mitch. "Are you okay? Did you get the all-clear from medical?"

Of course her mind would automatically go to some sort of health concern.

"I'm fine," Mitch assured her. "But we do need to speak with you."

Pushing off the wall, Kaylee nodded. "Okay."

Greg and Mitch led her just down the hall to the lounge area for the technicians. It was empty right now, and Greg headed over to one of the computer terminals. He quickly inserted the flash drive and brought up the video footage from the parking lot.

With a frown, Kaylee stared at it. "What am I looking at?"

"This is from earlier today. Someone broke into my car in the parking lot," Greg said.

Kaylee's eyes widened. "What? Here?"

Greg nodded. "But we found out who it was."

"Who?" she asked.

"Just watch," Greg said as the image began to move.

Kaylee leaned forward with a frown as she stared at the screen, watching the figure cut through the parking lot. No sign of recognition slipped across her face.

She sucked in a breath as the glass was smashed in on Greg's car and then turned to him. "No one heard them do that?"

Greg shook his head. "No, not a soul."

Kaylee turned back to the screen. If she was faking it, she was one heck of an actress.

Greg paused as the person turned back toward the building. He nodded toward the backpack. "They took something from my car, and it's in that pack."

Kaylee squinted toward the screen. "I can't make out their face."

Greg continued forward. "We had the technician zoom in. Hold on a sec."

He let the image play for another second before the enhanced image of Kaylee's face splashed across the screen.

Mouth falling open, Kaylee stumbled back from the terminal. She stared at the screen for a long moment before her eyes narrowed. Her mouth became a thin line. Hands on her hips, she turned to look at the two of them. "What kind of joke is this? We're in the middle of a lockdown and you guys are playing games?"

"It's not a game, Kaylee. You're the one who broke into Greg's car," Mitch said.

Kaylee shook her head. "No, I would never do that."

"Where were you this morning?" Mitch asked.

"I was on the base. I was on duty, except for when we went to go pick up Mitch."

"What about between 8:05 and 8:27 a.m.?" Greg asked.

Her mouth opened, but no words came out.

"Kaylee?" Greg asked.

"It's nothing. I was on base. I couldn't have done that, Greg." Kaylee pointed at the monitor. "I wouldn't have."

"Kaylee, what happened?" Mitch asked.

She was quiet for a few moments, and Greg worried that

she wasn't going to tell them what she was obviously concerned about. "I just, I sort of, I don't know, zoned out for a little bit this morning," she said.

"You mean you lost time?" Greg asked.

"That's one way of putting it, I suppose," she said slowly.

"Can you tell us exactly what happened?" Greg asked.

After darting a glance at the monitor, she nodded. Then she looked around as if to see if anyone else could overhear them before she spoke. "I was heading to the training room, and then the next thing I knew, I was in the front foyer. *Forty* minutes had passed. But I don't remember anything that happened during that time at all. It was like it was just gone. My memories are completely and totally gone."

CHAPTER 59

After Kaylee's revelation, she looked rattled. Now she sat on the couch staring at the monitor. Greg and Mitch had moved over to the kitchen area and were grabbing coffees for themselves and Kaylee. Neither of them really wanted coffee, but Kaylee looked like she needed one, and they needed to compare notes.

Grabbing the pot, Greg started to pour the hot liquid into the mugs Mitch had laid out. "Missing time. It's got to be some sort of abduction thing, like with Nate and Agnes."

"Which means Kaylee wasn't in control of her actions any more than the other two were."

Greg leaned against the counter as Mitch poured cream into the coffees. "Has Kaylee ever mentioned anything about an abduction?"

Mitch shook his head. "No, but I haven't exactly asked either. But we do need to ask her now."

"Okay." Greg grabbed his coffee and Kaylee's before heading back across the room. He placed the coffee on the table in front of Kaylee. She nodded her thanks as she grabbed the mug.

Mitch took a seat across from her. "Kaylee, this is going to sound a little unusual, but have you ever had an experience of losing time before?"

"No, never," she said emphatically. "I mean, I've done the automatic driving thing. You know, where you're heading to work because even though it's your day off, you weren't really thinking, you just kind of got in the car and started driving. But no, I've never lost time."

That couldn't be true. The abductions had to be the common denominator. Maybe he was being too subtle. Greg licked his lips, not sure how to phrase the next question but knowing there was no easy way to ask it. "Any chance you've ever been abducted by aliens?"

Kaylee gave him a baleful look. "Really? We're trying to have a serious conversation here, Greg."

Greg shrugged. "I know normally that would be a crazy question, but look where we work. So seriously, have you ever been abducted by aliens?"

With a sigh, she rolled her eyes. "No, nothing like that."

"You never found yourself driving on a road and then not having any memory of how you got there or losing a couple of hours of time?" Greg prodded. "Any strange dreams, feeling paralyzed at night, anything like that?"

She didn't answer right away, a crease appearing between her eyes, and then finally she shook her head. "No. I just ... I don't have anything like that in my history. Why?"

"Because we're trying to figure out why you did this," Mitch said.

She pointed at the screen. "I know that *looks* like me, but there's no way that *is* me. Greg, you know me. I wouldn't do that."

He did know her, and the behavior would be completely out of character for her.

But at the same time, that didn't explain what they were seeing on the screen. And until they had a better explanation, Kaylee being the guilty party was the best explanation they had.

CHAPTER 60

The next steps weren't so clear. Greg didn't want to bring Kaylee up to Norah until they could understand exactly what had happened. Nor could they just let her go. Luckily, Kaylee seemed to understand their dilemma, and she agreed to stay with them until they figured out what was happening.

Now Kaylee was sitting at the monitor going over her actions frame by frame. Greg figured she was trying to look for some sort of splice in the recording that showed it had been manipulated. He didn't think she was going to find it, but he understood her need to look.

So Kaylee had something to do, but Greg wasn't sure what his and Mitch's next step was. The whole point of bringing Mitch onto the base was so he could see the other orb. It made more sense, then, to focus on Kaylee.

But if Kaylee had no recollection of being abducted, was it possible she just didn't remember? That seemed possible. But at the same time, those memories seemed to slip through. Although, maybe it only slipped through in a few cases. Maybe most abductees didn't remember anything at all.

"We should head back to the security office and track Kaylee's movements this morning. Maybe we can figure out who she was working with or where she stashed the orb," Mitch said.

Greg barely heard him, his mind still trying to tie together Nate, Agnes, and Kaylee. They'd experienced lost time. But Kaylee was convinced she'd never been abducted. He needed to find Hannah. Maybe she could—

He sat upright. "The implants."

Mitch frowned. "What about them?"

"If Kaylee was abducted, and if that wasn't really her working under her own consciousness, then she would have an implant, right?"

Mitch nodded. "That is the common denominator between Nate, Agnes, and Moore."

"Okay, well, then we just need to get her scanned."

"You want to take her down to medical?" Mitch asked.

Greg hesitated. He really didn't want to let more people in to this than they had to. And if they were going to requisition testing through medical, they would have to. "The equipment we need is actually on the third floor as well. It's part of the scientific suite. But we're going to need Maeve's help."

"Greg," Mitch said with a warning in his voice.

Running a hand through his hair, Greg understood Mitch's concern. "Look, I get it. You don't want people to know your secret. I do understand that. But *you* have to understand that we can't do this with just the two of us. Maeve's kept more secrets in her life for longer than anyone. She's not going to go blabbing about who you are. She respects the need for privacy. Trust me on that. And I need her help. *You* need her help."

"Isn't there a way we could get her help without telling her the whole truth?"

Greg shook his head. "I won't lie to her or manipulate her. I want to help you, Mitch, I really do. But I won't use Maeve to do it. She doesn't deserve that. And like I said, we can't do this with just you and me. We need to let more people into the circle of trust. The next step needs to be telling Maeve."

"Fine. But telling Maeve what's going on it could place her in danger. If Set is coming back ..."

"If Set is coming back, we're all in danger anyway."

CHAPTER 61

As Norah ordered, Maeve had gone over to medical and gotten checked out. She didn't have a concussion, for which she was very glad, but they did warn her that her head was going to be pretty sore for a while. They'd given her some aspirin. It had taken the edge off some of the pain.

Now, Maeve sat up in her lab. The lights had been restored. Someone had disabled a couple of wires. A simple fix. But it also had been a simple thing to shut the lights down.

Maeve sighed as she sat down on the couch, mindlessly eating her snack. Those orbs. Someone was after them and was going to some seriously great lengths to get them.

She still didn't understand what purpose they served. She could tell that they had some sort of energy. But it was more than just an energy source.

She couldn't help but think about the orb rolling toward her just before she had been knocked out. It almost seemed as if the orb was trying to warn her about the danger with those small noises. The Crumb family did report their orb rolling after them. At the same time, she had thought that was just a fanciful notion.

The orbs weren't cognizant, or at least, she didn't think they were. But she supposed that since she had no idea what alien race had created them, she couldn't entirely rule it out.

She wiped the edges of her mouth as she finished up her apple Danish and then took a long drink of her coffee.

Now she wasn't sure what to do with herself. The whole point of her being here was so that she could work with Greg on the orb. But now they no longer had the orb. Tilda had not been happy when she learned that the orb she had kept safe for thirty-plus years had been stolen. And Maeve wasn't happy about it, either. She also felt a little guilty. She should have known something was up when the lights wouldn't turn on.

I am very rusty at this, she thought as she walked over to her workbench and pulled up a stool. She grabbed her tablet and started flicking through her notes.

The orb gave off an energy that they couldn't quite pinpoint. It was intriguing. And the orb had felt warm to the touch. That had been strange. It was different from the first orb which felt cool. They still weren't sure what kind of metal it was made of. In fact, the list of what they didn't know was much longer than the list of what they did.

She couldn't help but think back to Greg's and Mitch's appearances this morning. Mitch's, in particular, had been a huge shock.

Greg had been so devastated yesterday at Mitch's death, and for Mitch to appear unharmed today was more than a little surprising. But she supposed stranger things had happened.

The door to her lab beeped. She looked up quickly, her breath releasing as Greg and Mitch stepped in. Greg caught the look on her face and winced. "Sorry. Did we startle you?"

Maeve placed her tablet back on the table. "I'm just a little jumpy, I guess. Getting attacked will do that to you."

"Don't I know it," Greg said with a grin.

And Maeve knew he was telling the truth. They had both been through their share of violent incidents in the past.

Maeve tilted her head at the woman that entered the lab with them.

Greg nodded over at her. "This is Kaylee. She's the medic for our unit."

"Nice to meet you, Kaylee," Maeve said.

"You too, Dr. Leander."

"Call me Maeve," she immediately said before frowning. The young woman looked distraught. "Is everything all right?"

Greg shook his head. "No. There are some things we need to tell you. But first, we think that Kaylee here might have one of those implants that Nate, Moore, and Agnes have. We don't want to go through medical. We don't want to raise any flags if we don't need to. So we were hoping we could do the scan here."

"What implants?" Maeve asked with a frown.

Greg quickly explained about the implants and the belief that they might be behind the uncharacteristic behavior of the three individuals in the medical wing. No wonder Kaylee looked so distraught.

Maeve looked between the three of them and then nodded slowly. "That shouldn't be a problem. An MRI scan should pick it up. We can do a full-body scan."

"Can we do that now?" Kaylee asked.

Maeve nodded. "Yeah, the machine's just down the hall. Come on. We'll go get you set up."

Fifteen minutes later, Kaylee was in the MRI machine, and it was thumping away as Maeve sat at the console, with Greg and Mitch sitting next to her. "It'll take a little while for the readings to complete, so why don't you two tell me what's going on?"

Greg looked over at Mitch, who nodded his head before Greg spoke. "Well, it kind of starts with Mitch dying."

Then Greg told Maeve about Mitch being shot, falling into the churning water, and then reappearing at his home the next day.

Maeve sucked in a breath as she stared over at Mitch. How had he survived? How was he sitting here?

But that wasn't the most shocking part of the conversation. Greg explained how Mitch was one of the original ancient Egyptian gods and how he had been reincarnated over and over again. Greg explained about the reincarnation ship and how the orbs appeared whenever one of the Primevals died.

"The Primevals. Agaren mentioned them. And the orbs, those are their consciousnesses, aren't they?"

"How'd you know that?" Greg asked.

"Before I was attacked, it almost felt like the orb was trying to warn me. Is that possible?" Maeve asked Mitch.

Mitch nodded slowly. "After my father died, the other Primevals contacted him and asked him about who should be the ruler, myself or Set. They contacted him through the orb. It does hold their consciousness."

"Why is someone going after the orbs?" Maeve asked.

Mitch explained about how his father had been killed and then Set had been punished so that in each life, he didn't know who he had been. He was simply reborn as a child each time.

Maeve frowned. "But if he has no memory of who he was, then he couldn't be the one who started this whole process. Something must have awakened him."

Mitch's face fell. "Yes, and that could only be done by another Primeval."

"Someone's helping him," Greg said.

"And they probably still are," Maeve said.

Mitch stared at her and then nodded slowly. "You're right.

We've been working on the assumption that it was Set behind this, but it would have to be one of the other Primevals."

"Do you know where any of them are?" Maeve asked.

Mitch shook his head. "No. There's a way to tell if we are nearby one another. Just kind of a vague sense of familiarity, but you have to be very close, no farther apart than we are now. Beyond that, there's no way to track them down in any meaningful way."

"Have you ever felt that?" Greg asked.

"Only when I've been near my mother, but that could just be the closeness of a mother and son. To be honest, it's been so long since I've been around a Primeval, I'm not sure I would even remember what it feels like."

The machine beeped, and Maeve turned her attention back to it.

"Okay, we've got all of Kaylee's scans done." She leaned forward into the microphone. "Okay, Kaylee, you're done. You can get out of there now."

"I'll go help." Mitch stepped out of the control room and appeared in the other room. He pulled the stretcher out, and then she and Greg watched as he helped Kaylee sit up.

An ancient Egyptian god. She thought she'd heard everything, but apparently not. But that wasn't even what truly intrigued her. What really intrigued her was the reincarnation ship. She itched to see it and learn about its technology. The possibilities of that kind of science were mind-blowing. It could help the human condition in so many ways.

"What have we got?" Greg asked.

Shaking herself from her thoughts, Maeve turned her attention to the scans. She quickly flipped through from screen to screen, looking for any anomaly.

"Where were the implants located in the others?" she asked.

"Different places. With Nate, it was his shoulder; with Agnes, it was her hip; and with Moore, it was his back."

Maeve nodded, checking those locations, but she didn't see anything.

But it was entirely possible that the implants could be located anywhere on the body.

Mitch and Kaylee joined them in the room, with Kaylee wrapping a robe around herself. "Well?"

"Nothing yet." Greg said.

Kaylee let out a breath. "I don't know if that's good or bad."

Maeve had to admit she wasn't sure either. Then she went still as she focused on one of the screens. She zoomed in on a small anomaly in the scan and pointed to it.

"I see it," Greg said before he turned to Kaylee. "Looks like you do have an implant."

CHAPTER 62

The room was quiet as all four of them stared at the scan on the screen. The implant was clear. It was a small thin cylindrical object, obviously not a natural part of the body.

"Where is that?" Greg asked.

"It's in her armpit of all places," Maeve said.

Kaylee shook her head. "That's not an implant, or at least not an alien implant. That's my birth control."

Maeve frowned, staring at the screen. "That's not a birth control implant." She hit a few buttons on the screen. An image appeared right next to the original image. "This is Nate's implant."

Greg looked between the two of them.

Mouth falling open, Kaylee shook her head. "But, I mean, that's not possible. It's for birth control. It's not alien tech."

"When did you get the birth control implant?" Maeve asked.

"Just two weeks ago. The incision is barely healed." Kaylee slipped off her robe and pulled back the sleeve of her hospital gown to reveal the red mark along her armpit.

Greg frowned as he stared at the mark. "Where did you have that done?"

"Here on the base. I mean, this is where we get all our medical."

"Who implanted that for you?" Maeve asked.

"Cheryl. Dr. Kerwin. She's been doing all my medical stuff since she arrived."

Greg frowned, looking between the screen and Kaylee. There was no chance this was a coincidence. The alien implant was in the same location that her birth control supposedly was? And there was no way that Cheryl would have missed it when she went to go implant the birth control. And there was no actual birth control device.

Which meant that either Cheryl implanted it, or someone else removed the birth control device and implanted the alien device. And the latter possibility seemed extremely unlikely. "We need to go talk to Cheryl."

CHAPTER 63

Checking with the main desk, they found that Dr. Kerwin had been at headquarters early this morning, but she left just before the lockdown was initiated. She hadn't made it off the base entirely, however, and was believed to be back at her apartment.

There were three separate apartment complexes on the base, and Cheryl lived in one that was a short distance from Greg's. Greg and Mitch were going to head over to the doctor's apartment to see if they could get an explanation.

Even though Greg knew that the evidence was pointing to Cheryl being involved, he struggled with it. She'd always been so nice. Plus, it was more than a little disappointing to think that the woman he'd had some romantic feelings for might be involved in something so horrific as using humans as puppets.

Kaylee demanded that the implant be removed. She still had no recollection of what she had done that morning, and the idea that there was something in her that could make her do things against her will was unacceptable to her.

Maeve had gotten permission from Norah to remove the implant after explaining what they believed. Maeve would help oversee the removal, which would only be a quick procedure. The implant wasn't buried too deep, less than half an inch below the skin.

Norah also ordered that the implants be removed from Nate, Agnes, and Moore as well. They had intended on removing them at some point anyway, but with everything moving so fast, the medical staff said they hadn't scheduled it yet. They argued they needed to observe them for a little longer. And the name on the paper making that decision was Cheryl's.

Norah overruled her, arguing that the base's safety had to come before the observation benefits. Greg completely agreed. But he was also worried. If Kaylee had been implanted with the device without her knowledge, it was entirely possible that other members of the D.E.A.D. staff had been as well.

Maeve was going to start going through and reviewing all of the medical records to see if there had been any other procedures that involved cutting the skin. That was not going to be a quick process.

He turned to Mitch. "How would Set or one of the Primevals know about the implants? I mean, is it common knowledge among your people?"

Mitch shook his head. "No. In fact, I've never heard of this being used at all. I know about the implants, of course. Anyone who knows anything about abductions knows about the implants, but I was under the impression that nobody really understood what they were used for."

"But you must have some theories. After all, you're an alien too."

Mitch watched him from the side of his eyes before he returned his attention to the road. "Like I said before, I assumed they were used to keep track of subjects. You know in nature documentaries or studies where they tag animals and then release them to see what they do? I always figured it was kind of like that. That the implants were a way of tagging humans and then monitoring their behavior. I never thought that the implants could be used to control their behavior."

Greg wasn't sure that he felt more comforted by the idea that they were being tagged like animals. But someone had apparently found out an alternative use. Or maybe that was what they had been designed for initially, but it had never been used that way.

Although, he couldn't be sure that it hadn't been utilized. Maybe at some point, they had taken control of different subjects, and no one was aware of it.

Abductees reported having lost time at various points in their lives. It was always assumed that meant they were being taken up into a ship and examined. But what if that wasn't true? What if, during those lost times, they had been engaged in active behaviors here on Earth?

Greg wasn't sure what to think, but the whole topic made him uncomfortable. The fact was that the aliens they had come across were light-years ahead of them in technology. Humanity was grossly outmatched.

And that was terrifying enough. But the idea that some race was directly manipulating human behaviors took terrifying to a whole new level. Free will was the cornerstone of humanity. And the idea that not only could someone remove it, but that they already had … Yeah, that was not going to make it easy to sleep well at night.

But aliens were responsible for humans' very existence to begin with. And if that wasn't the greatest manipulation, he didn't know what was. Would it really be such a huge surprise that they would, at some point, decide to manipulate specific individuals?

At the same time, he couldn't understand why. For Agnes, it made sense because they were trying to get access to the remotes. But why go after Nate? Nate was a stay-at-home dad.

He didn't have access to any sort of technology or information that would be beneficial to anyone.

Greg grabbed his phone and called Norah. She answered quickly. "Did you find anything?"

"No, we haven't reached the apartment yet. But I'm wondering about Nate Prower. Why would they use him? I mean, he's a stay-at-home dad. He doesn't have access to anything that would be useful to anyone."

"Maybe he was a test of some sort?"

Greg shook his head. "I don't think so. I'm betting they knew the tech would work. There has to have been a reason that they chose him."

"I'll look into his background and see what we can find. And I'll talk to Nate and see if he has any ideas."

"It's got to be something related to the D.E.A.D. or R.I.S.E. There has to be something there."

"I'll look into it. But I need you to focus on the task at hand. Call me when you've spoken with Dr. Kerwin."

"Will do," Greg said before hanging up.

Up ahead, the apartment complex loomed. It was almost identical to Greg's. Each building was a pale blue with gray and white accents. There were four units in each building for a total of sixteen apartments.

Mitch pulled to a stop near one of the buildings and nodded at the small blue Honda parked in the spot next to them. "That's Kerwin's car."

Greg stepped out of the car, glancing around. It was quiet. Of course, everyone had been notified about the lockdown, and they were supposed to stay where they were.

But still, it was eerie that it was so quiet. He tried to ignore the chills rolling up his spine but didn't quite succeed. Mitch was about to get out of the car when Greg put out a hand. "Maybe you should stay here."

"What? Why?"

"Because you just came back from the dead. I'll go speak with her and see what's going on. And then we can see where we go from there. If there's a problem, you can come in. But I think it would probably be better if I speak with her without the shock of you being alive getting in the way of the conversation."

Mitch drummed his fingers along the steering wheel before he sighed. "Fine. But don't do anything stupid."

"When have I ever done anything stupid?"

Mitch grunted. "Do you really want me to answer that question?"

CHAPTER 64

As he walked to Cheryl's front door, Greg tried to tamp down his nerves. He wiped his sweaty palms on his jeans. He had imagined walking up this path many times, but never like this.

On the stoop, Greg noted that there was a flowerpot filled with dead mums. Apparently, Cheryl didn't have much of a green thumb.

Taking a deep breath, Greg knocked on the door. It took a few moments before he heard the locks disengage.

Still wearing her scrubs from the hospital, Cheryl stood with a frown on her face as she looked at him. "Greg? What's going on? Is everything all right?"

Greg peered past her to the interior of the apartment. It was quiet. "Could I speak with you for a few minutes?"

"Uh, sure," she said, her confusion obvious as she stepped back to let him in.

While the layout of Cheryl's apartment was identical to his, she had obviously taken pains to decorate hers. The walls were a pale yellow with bright framed photos of flowers lining the hall. The wood floor was covered by a heavy flowered runner.

INTO THE DARK

Stepping into the living room revealed a bright white overstuffed couch with two matching armchairs. Pillows with a floral design lay on the ground.

She gave a nervous laugh as she grabbed the pillows off the floor and tossed them on the couch before grabbing the plate and glass from the coffee table. "Sorry about the mess. I wasn't really expecting anyone."

Greg shook his head. "Oh, no, don't worry about it. Your apartment is a lot neater than mine. And nicer. I still have all the furniture that came with the place."

"You live in one of the apartments on base too, right?" Cheryl asked as she placed the plate and cup in the sink. The kitchen had a cutout, so he could see her. "Do you want anything?" She gestured to the fridge.

Greg shook his head. "No, I'm good. And yeah, I live over in Alpha neighborhood."

"That's right. You live next door to the director."

"Yeah," Greg said still feeling nervous.

Cheryl walked back into the living room, wringing her hands. "So what's happening on base? We're still on lockdown, right?"

"Yes."

"Do you know what set off the alert?" She asked.

"Just a small security incident."

Cheryl raised her eyebrows. "A small one? They tend not to lock the base down for small incidents."

He shrugged. "Well, small for us, I guess."

She gestured to the couch as she sat down. "So, what are you doing here?"

Taking a seat next to her, he said, "I needed to talk to you about Kaylee Hughes."

A furrow in her brow, Cheryl asked, "Kaylee? What about her?"

"Two weeks ago, you implanted her birth control device,

correct?"

Now she frowned at him. "Greg, I can't discuss her medical records with you. That's a complete violation of HIPAA."

Greg pulled out his phone and handed it over to her. "This is a form signed by Kaylee giving you permission to discuss her medical history with me."

Taking the phone, Cheryl quickly scanned the form and then handed it back. "Okay. Yes, I implanted it two weeks ago."

"Were there any problems with the implant? Anything unusual?" He asked.

"No. It was just standard. Everything was normal. Why?"

"Because the implant that we found in her is not birth control."

First surprise flashed across Cheryl's face. Then her eyes widened before confusion replaced it. "What? What was it?"

"Something else," He hedged. "Have you implanted that type of birth control in anyone else?"

Cheryl shook her head. "No, actually, Kaylee's the only one that uses that particular type."

"What about any other sort of implants?" Greg pressed.

"I don't know. I mean, I'd have to check my records and again, I don't know if I can tell you that."

Looking around, Greg nodded. He should have gotten that information before he left headquarters, but they had wanted to speak with Cheryl quickly. "How come you came home today? You were at headquarters and then you left again."

"Yeah, I wasn't feeling too well, so I decided to come home and just lie down for a little bit," she said.

"You could have just used one of the call rooms at HQ."

Narrowing her eyes, she studied him. "I could have, but I didn't really want to. I prefer my own surroundings. And I figured I was only a few minutes away if anybody needed me."

Greg supposed that was true, but protocol was that you stayed at headquarters.

Cheryl stood up. "I'm going to get myself something to drink. Are you sure I can't get you anything?"

"Actually, some water would be good," he said, his unease growing.

"Great," she said, looking relieved. She headed into the kitchen, and Greg watched her over the half wall.

He glanced around the apartment, noting that she liked plants but didn't seem to be able to keep them alive. "I guess you don't have much of a green thumb?"

"What?" she said and then followed Greg's gaze toward her dead plants. "Oh, yeah. I always have great intentions, but I never quite seem to remember that whole watering thing."

Greg chuckled. "Yeah, I've never been good at keeping house plants alive either."

"But you've managed to keep Pugsley alive," she said.

"Well, he's a little easier. He reminds me if I don't feed him." He looked up as she walked back into the living room.

She placed a glass on the coffee table in front of him. "Here you go," she said, her other hand behind her back.

Greg reached for the glass of water as she lunged toward him.

Volts of electricity screamed through him. He let out his own little scream as he dropped to his knees, shaking, and then fell forward onto the coffee table.

CHAPTER 65

It was not easy for Mitch to keep himself in the car. He understood Greg's reasoning. The looks he'd gotten from people had been more than a little disconcerting as he'd walked through the halls of HQ. But he didn't like the idea of Greg going in by himself.

At the same time, he struggled with the idea that Cheryl was somehow mixed up in all of this. She'd always been nice and kind whenever he had spoken with her. He'd never gotten a bad vibe from her.

Although he had to admit he hadn't interacted with her much over the last few months. Their paths just didn't seem to cross. But before that, he'd enjoyed their short interactions. She hadn't given off any red flags.

Of course, it was entirely possible that she'd been affected in the same way that Kaylee had. If that was the case, then she was someone who needed their help.

Mitch drummed his hands on the steering wheel before finally shaking his head. *This is crazy. I'm going in.*

He'd just stepped out of the car when the front door to the apartment opened. Cheryl walked out.

Mitch frowned as she walked toward him, looking behind her for Greg, but the door stayed closed. "Cheryl? Where's Greg?"

She nodded back toward the door. "He's back inside. I told him I'd come out and get you to join us."

"Everything's good, then?" Mitch asked as he moved toward her.

"Yeah, everything's good. Although I am curious as to how it was you managed to return." She stepped closer to him. A feeling of familiarity rolled over him.

She pulled a Taser from behind her back. Distracted by the sense of recognition, he was slow to respond. She jabbed the prongs into his chest. Electricity rolled through his body. Every muscle seemed to seize.

He crashed to the ground, his body shaking as the volts of electricity danced through him.

Cheryl walked closer to him and then knelt down, looking at him. "Well, I guess that answers that question, doesn't it, nephew?"

CHAPTER 66

A groan slipped through Greg's lips as he grabbed onto the edge of the couch and started to pull himself up. Cheryl had tased him ... twice.

The second time, he lost consciousness for a while. He wasn't sure how long it had been. But when he opened his eyes, Cheryl was gone.

Bracing himself on the couch and the coffee table, he pushed himself to his feet. He stumbled back for a moment as he fully gained his footing. She'd actually stunned him. Had she been implanted as well?

He did a quick scan of the apartment, just opening doors and seeing if she was around, but he was most definitely alone. He hustled to the front door and yanked it open.

Mitch was just coming up the path, looking a little unsteady himself. "Mitch."

He looked up at Greg. "You okay?"

Greg nodded. "Cheryl hit me with a Taser—twice."

"Same. I already contacted security from the base. They're going to keep an eye out for her."

Greg shook his head, trying to accept the fact that Cheryl had actually attacked both of them. "What's going on?"

"Let's go back inside," Mitch said.

Greg nodded, noting the serious look on Mitch's face. He led Mitch back inside to the living room. "What happened?"

Mitch took a breath, his gaze scanning the room. "That wasn't Cheryl."

"She was implanted as well?"

Mitch paused. "No. We need to search the apartment."

Greg frowned. "I already did. She's not here."

Mitch stared at him for a long moment. "Let's just look again, okay?"

Greg shrugged but did as Mitch asked. He started in the kitchen as Mitch started pulling open the closet by the front door. Greg frowned, looking over at him. Did Mitch honestly think Cheryl was curled up in the back of the closet hiding?

But he turned his own attention back to more realistic hiding places. Five minutes later, Mitch called out to him. "Greg, you need to come in here."

Greg headed down the hall and stopped in the doorway of Cheryl's bedroom.

Mitch was kneeling on the ground on the other side of the bed.

"What's going on?" Greg asked as he rounded the bed, and then he stopped still.

Lying on the ground next to the bed was what was clearly a body wrapped in plastic. Mitch nodded toward it. "I found this under the bed."

He pulled out a knife and quickly cut the plastic and pulled it back.

Staring out at them was the face of Dr. Cheryl Kerwin.

Greg stared down at the face of Cheryl in confusion. There was no doubt it was her. The same features, the same hair. Her eyes were closed. Greg wasn't ready to pry them open to check, but he had no doubt he'd be staring into Cheryl's blue eyes if he did. "I don't understand. We were just talking to her. This body, it's been dead for, what, weeks?"

"At least." Mitch stood up and stepped back. "You know how I told you that there is that faint sense of recognition when one of us is around another Primeval?"

A feeling a dread welled up in Greg. "Yes, why?"

"Because I felt that just before Cheryl tased me. She's been replaced."

"Then who is she?"

Mitch took a deep breath. "I think she's my aunt."

CHAPTER 67

The words were barely out of Mitch's mouth before base security arrived. Which, as far as Mitch was concerned, was good because he could see the questions in Greg's eyes. And he wasn't sure he had any answers for them.

Mitch let the security in and explained what they had found. Greg stayed with the body and looked shell-shocked. Mitch knew that Greg had been attracted to Cheryl. But even though he thought it had died down the last few months, he knew how jolting her death had to be for him.

And to think she had been replaced for months. Even Mitch was struggling to process that. He had felt that sliver of recognition when he had seen her outside, but he'd never felt that at the base. Then again, he wasn't sure when the last time was he'd actually been near Cheryl. The times he'd been in medical, she hadn't been there. Now that he thought about it, he'd only seen her from a distance these last few months. If he'd sensed her sooner, so much might have been avoided.

But even that wouldn't have saved Cheryl.

When security arrive, they politely but firmly booted Greg

and Mitch out of the apartment so they could start collecting evidence.

Mitch was more than happy to step outside. He knew he'd have to give a statement about what had happened, but he really wasn't up for doing that right now. There were too many other things they needed to do. And too many questions to answer.

So before they could get waylaid, both Greg and Mitch hopped in Mitch's car and headed back toward headquarters. Some of the shock had faded from Greg's expression. He turned to Mitch. "What do you mean she's your aunt?"

Mitch shifted his gaze to Greg before returning his attention to the road. "I can't be sure, but she called me nephew."

"Nephew? You mean Nephthys? Or do you have another aunt?"

Mitch shook his head. "Just the one. If it were Set, I don't think any of this would have been happening, and the only other person it could be is my aunt, my mother's sister."

"But she helped your mother find Osiris. Why would she do that if she still loved him?"

"I asked my mom about that once. She said Nephthys's love for her and her love for Set weren't mutually exclusive. She loved Set with all her heart, despite the cruel streak that ran through him. She never chose sides between the two of them. So when my mother needed her help, she helped."

"How did she handle Set's punishment?"

"Not well," Mitch said, his face darkening.

"When's the last time you spoke with her?"

"It's been literally eons. I don't even think that she realized it was me until just then. She looked just as surprised as I was."

"So she's behind all of this?"

"I guess so. But I don't understand why." He grabbed his phone and dialed quickly. "Mom?"

His mother's voice was calm on the other side of the phone. "Mitch? Is everything okay?"

"Yes. I mean, no."

Greg tapped him on the shoulder. "Speakerphone," he whispered.

Nodding, Mitch switched to speakerphone and took a deep breath. "I think I might have just seen Nephthys."

"What?" Shock laced his mother's voice.

Mitch quickly ran through what had happened and what they had learned at the D.E.A.D. He saw Greg flick a glance at him from the passenger seat about the fact that he was revealing highly classified information. But classified or not, his mother needed to know.

When he was done with his recitation, his mother was silent on the other side of the line. Then she spoke softly. "Oh, Neffy, what have you done?"

"You think it's her?"

His mother gave a deep sigh. "Yes. She's always been blind when it came to Set. She loved him with all of her heart and soul. His punishment ... she always felt it was too cruel. But we all agreed that Set was too ambitious, too violent to be allowed to retain his memories."

"But she helped you find Dad. Why would she do that?"

"Yes, she helped me find your father. That was because she understood what true love was. Because that was what she felt for Set. I don't think she expected the punishment on him to be so harsh. I haven't seen her in hundreds of years. We lost track of one another. You know when we reincarnate there's no guarantee that we'll find one another, except, of course, for you and I. But with Nephthys, she would be on her own. Perhaps that loneliness drove her to desperation."

"Desperate enough to kill other Primevals in order to bring her husband back?" Mitch asked.

The silence was heavy on the other side of the line before

his mother answered. "I don't know. But I suppose it's possible that over all of these years, she longed more and more for him until she could no longer stand being apart from him. And so she would do whatever was necessary to bring him back."

"But killing Primevals to do so?" He asked.

"From her perspective, she probably thinks it's fair. After all, if Set had been without his memories all these years, he would be, in her mind, as good as dead. Meanwhile, the Primevals have lived for thousands of years. From her perspective, it would only be fair for them to trade their lives for his."

"And now she has three orbs," Mitch said, fear running through him. "Mom, she needs one more orb in order to complete the process. I need you to get out of there. I need you to go somewhere safe. I need you to—"

His mother's voice was barely above a whisper. "It's too late. She's here."

The line went dead.

CHAPTER 68

She's here.

The words rolled through Greg's mind as Mitch drove like a bat out of hell toward the exit of the base. Those were words you always expected to hear in a horror film, and it never ended well.

Greg grabbed the phone and quickly dialed gate security. "This is Dr. Greg Schorn. I need the gates opened. We have an emergency off—"

"We can't do that, Dr. Schorn. We're in lockdown," came the reply.

Heart in his throat, Greg knew Mitch would not slow down. "I understand, but this is an Alpha Charlie 2-7 emergency. I need those gates open now."

A flick at the speedometer indicated they were approaching the still closed gate at sixty miles per hour. "You need to let us through now."

"Dr. Schorn, during a lockdown, you don't have authorization for that override, and without authorization—"

Next to him, Mitch simply crushed down on the accelerator even harder.

Holding on to the side of the car, Greg sucked in a breath, and closed his eyes as they barreled straight ahead. Two guards stood in front of the barrier. Greg silently prayed.

"Get down," Mitch said.

With a yell, Greg ducked low as bullets rang out against the car. But Mitch didn't slow. With his head down, Greg only heard the crash as they broke through the barrier.

Mitch didn't slow. If anything, the car seemed to pick up speed.

"You can get up now," Mitch said as he pulled a left that sent Greg flying against the side of the car.

"Are they chasing us?" Greg asked, whipping his head toward the back window.

"Probably."

Greg looked around the car in shock. It seemed to be in one piece.

Mitch grunted at him. "Bulletproof glass. I made sure this car is basically a tank."

"Because you figured this was something that might happen?"

Mitch shook his head. "Because with the kind of cases we get, I figured better safe than sorry."

Greg's phone rang, and he picked it up quickly. Norah was on the other end. "Greg, what the hell are you doing?"

"We think that Dr. Kerwin is going after Mitch's mother. We didn't have time to go through all the paperwork to get us off the base. We were on the phone with Mrs. Haldron when she said that Cheryl was there."

"Why would Cheryl be going after Mitch's mother?"

And that's when Greg realized that in all the craziness of discovering Cheryl, he hadn't told Norah about what happened at Cheryl's apartment. "Because she's not really Cheryl. Cheryl's been dead for weeks. We just found her body at her apartment. There's a team there now going over the site."

Norah was quiet for a long moment. "Fine. I'm sending a team after you. In fact, they're already trailing you because they're trying to bring you back to base. I'll change their orders so that they will be there to accompany you."

Greg nodded. "Good, thanks."

"But you will be giving me a full debrief when this is over."

"Happy to," he said before he disconnected the call and turned to Mitch. "Norah's sending a team to help us, or at least, she's telling whoever the guys are chasing us that they need to help us."

Mitch nodded, his whole body tense.

"How would Cheryl know where your mother is?"

"She must have checked my phone or my GPS to see where I had been. I led her right to her," Mitch said.

"She'll be okay. I mean, even if the worst happens and Nephthys kills her, she can just be reincarnated."

Mitch shook his head. "No. She needs one more orb to complete the ceremony. The only way for that to happen is for her to kill a Primeval—permanently. We need to get there."

CHAPTER 69

It was amazing. All the time he'd spent alive. All the people he'd loved and lost over the years. All the death he'd seen, and yet he'd never really considered the possibility of his mother being killed. He knew his father had been killed, but it had never occurred to him that the same fate could befall his mother.

They had lived for so long that it was impossible to conceptualize a world where she did not exist. Long ago, they had left the trappings of mother and son behind and become equals, best friends, although that term was too shallow for their connection. She was the constant in his life, the ultimate source of guidance and joy.

And the idea of her not being there was quite honestly not something he could wrap his head around. It would be like trying to conceptualize not having an arm. It was just something that was always there. And trying to figure out and think about what it would be like not to have one was just so difficult.

Ahead, he saw the intersection just before his mother's

street. He eased up on the gas just a smidge in order to make the turn, and then crashed down on the accelerator again.

In the passenger seat next to him, Greg sucked in a breath but didn't ask him to slow down, and Mitch appreciated that. In fact, he appreciated all of the help that Greg had given him.

Greg was a rather unusual human. When he was friends with you, he was fully on your side. A true ride-or-die kind of friend.

Mitch had never had a friend like that before. In all his life, he'd never taken the time to get to know humans the way he had in the short time that he'd been with Greg.

He'd had friends, of course, but none like the man sitting next to him right now. And he felt bad for all that Greg had gone through as a result of that friendship. But even with that, he was going to ask even more of him.

"Greg, we need to take out Nephthys. Even if she doesn't pose a threat, even if she's not holding a weapon. She cannot be allowed to escape."

"I understand," Greg said. "And I agree with you, sort of. I just don't think we should kill her."

"What?" Mitch exclaimed.

"We need to incapacitate her. Because if we kill her, she can just go up to your ship and get a new body, and this starts all over again. We need to figure out what's going on. So we need to get her alive."

He was right. Keeping her alive and finding out exactly what her plan was and everyone that she had manipulated, that needed to be the primary focus.

"You're right. We'll do it your way. But if there's no other way …" Mitch warned.

"Then we take her out," Greg said with nod. "But let's try to find another way."

Mitch slowed only enough so that he didn't flip the car as

he jumped the curb and parked on his mother's front lawn with a jolt.

Greg slammed back into his seat as the brakes engaged. "So I guess we're not going to go in quietly," he muttered as he reached for the door.

"Nope," Mitch said as he bolted from the car.

He sprinted up the stairs. The front door was already ajar. A grunt sounded from somewhere deep in the house.

He sprinted in, his gun drawn, and then stopped still as he stared at a disembodied hand that lay in the front hall.

CHAPTER 70

Greg was right behind Mitch as he bolted up the stairs and into his mom's house. Mitch seemed completely oblivious to any of the dangers that might be surrounding him. He didn't check corners. He didn't go in slow, making sure that he wasn't ambushed. In fact, he ignored absolutely every single piece of training that he'd drilled into Greg.

Which meant that Greg needed to be Mitch's eyes and ears. Which was why he sprinted in right behind Mitch and nearly collided with him as Mitch stopped still just inside the door.

Greg quickly shifted to the side, checking the corners, but saw no threats, and then his gaze fell on the object that had caused Mitch to stop in his tracks.

A hand lay in the middle of the front hall, blood pooling around it and seeping into the ivory-colored rug.

Oh God, no.

His eyes wide, Mitch stared down at it, perfectly still. And then his jaw tightened and his eyes narrowed as he strode forward, his gun raised.

He was going to kill her. Their plan to grab her and figure

out what was going on had just flown out the window. And Greg really couldn't say anything to stop Mitch.

And he wasn't sure he should.

Greg followed him and saw the other parts of what he assumed was Mitch's mother's body strewn around the kitchen. As he rounded the corner, he caught sight of the kitchen table.

And there standing over what remained of Isis's torso was Cheryl.

CHAPTER 71

Everything in Mitch had grown cold. It was as if his body temperature had just dropped ten degrees. But it wasn't just his temperature that had been affected. All sounds were muffled. His sight had been locked onto his mother's hand in the hall. Nothing else had registered. His training wasn't even a thought. Anyone could have attacked him, and he wouldn't have raised a hand to stop them. He couldn't.

His mother was dead. He knew it. He felt it in his bones. His whole world had collapsed in on him.

Then everything seemed to snap back into place in a rush. Sounds returned. His body warmed as rage like he'd never felt before rolled through him.

When he stepped into the kitchen, that rage only increased. Pieces of his mother littered the space. He stepped through her blood as he turned to face the woman who had just ripped his world apart.

She looked up with a smile. "You're too late."

Blood soaked her arms up to her elbows. His mother's

blood. She held a knife with a dark blade in her right hand, pieces of tissue still attached to it.

Mitch leveled his gun at her.

She raised her hands, seemingly oblivious to the blood now dripping onto the floor. "That won't do you any good. It won't bring her back."

She was right. But he didn't care. "It'll make me feel better."

"Mitch," Greg whispered from behind him, a warning to stick to the plan. But the rage was so great, Mitch was shaking. "Why are you doing all of this? Why did you kill her?" he demanded.

"She's lived a long life. Meanwhile, my husband has been trapped, trapped in a human body without knowing who he actually is. Do you have any idea what that is like for a man like him?"

"Do you know where he is?" Greg asked as he came up next to Mitch, his gun aimed at Cheryl.

A smile filled with insanity crossed Cheryl's face. Her eyes brightened, and what could only be described as joy filled them despite the macabre scene she had just created with her sister's blood.

"Yes. I have searched for him for so long. And then, this last lifetime, I found him. I could feel who he was, even though he didn't know who I was."

"How? Where did you find him?" Greg asked.

"It was a chance encounter. We passed on the street. I followed him, tracked him, plotted out his life. And when I spoke with him, he had no idea who I was. The love of my life didn't know me. Can you imagine how painful that was?" Tears appeared in her eyes.

"But it was a beginning and I knew what I had to do. I killed Ptah. We had found one another years earlier. It was as if everything were lining up to make my love's return possible.

"And when I had the orb, I exposed Set to it, which meant when he died, his consciousness would return. I had planned on getting all of the orbs and then killing him. But he died before I could. Now my beloved has been in an ethereal state for too long. I need to bring him home to me."

Mitch stepped forward, his voice strained. "But why did you kill my mother? She was your sister."

"Yes. And I loved her. Just as she loved me. But her time was at an end." She smiled, her eyes shining. "And now it is time for my husband to return."

CHAPTER 72

Greg stared over at the woman across from them. She was bathed in blood, and she held a strange-looking knife. It looked ancient, with a dark blade. That was not a normal blade. Keeping his gun leveled on the crazy woman across from them, Greg leaned toward Mitch. "The knife," he whispered.

Mitch's gaze rocketed to the weapon.

Cheryl held it up, turning it from side to side. "Oh, this? Yes, this is the only reason that my husband was able to kill your father. This is the only blade that can truly kill one of us. Beautiful, isn't it? When my beloved was killed, it took me forever to find another one. But then one was uncovered in a pharaoh's tomb. And I knew that it was only a matter of time before we were reunited. I spent years looking, and then a simple coffee run brought us back together." She gave a small giggle. "Life is so funny, isn't it?"

Yup, this woman was nuts. Next to him, Mitch was so tense that Greg knew it was a miracle he hadn't shot her already. It was taking everything in Greg to ignore the detritus surrounding them.

Instead, he was focusing on the fact that the strike force was just a few minutes behind them, so all they needed to do was keep Fake Cheryl talking, and then they could have the house surrounded. Hopefully that would allow them to take her alive. "Which pharaoh?" he asked.

Cheryl frowned. "What?"

Greg felt more than a little nervous with the woman's attention on him. "You said the knife was from a pharaoh's tomb. Which one?"

"King Tut."

"It's a meteor blade," Greg said.

Surprise flashed across her face. "You know it?"

Greg nodded. "Yes, I try to know just about everything that has to do with objects from beyond our world." And amazingly, the King Tut blade was one of them. The dagger, which did not rust or show any signs of age, was made from a meteorite, which the ancient Egyptians called "iron from the sky."

And Greg knew that was the weapon that had killed Osiris, or one like it. It wasn't the dismemberment that was necessary to end the circle of life, but the metal of the blade that was used. Did Nephthys not know that, or was she just enjoying herself?

Nephthys flicked a glance to her right, as if calculating whether she could make a run for it. Greg stepped forward. "How long have you been Dr. Kerwin?"

The calculation in her eyes disappeared, and Greg realized she wanted to talk. After eons of being on her own, she wanted to tell people what she had done and why.

"For about two months now. I knew I needed to find a way into the D.E.A.D. I befriended her at a flower market a few months back. We got to talking, and eventually we went out for drinks.

"I killed her at her apartment one night after she asked me

over for dinner. Then I hid her body, and I killed myself so that I could reincarnate as her. I've been her ever since."

Greg closed his eyes, picturing it. Nephthys's explanation lined up with the changes in Cheryl's behavior. Cheryl had been a good person, a kind person. "She didn't deserve that," Greg said unable to keep the anger out of his voice.

Nephthys cackled. "Didn't deserve it? She's a human. None of you matter. What matters is what we deserve."

Her gaze shot to Mitch. "We were the greatest beings this universe had ever seen. And now we're, what, walking around this earth, hidden from our former glory?"

"Our glory resulted in the destruction of our planet. And it nearly resulted in the destruction of this one," Mitch said.

"So what? That is the price that you pay for greatness."

Her words only seemed to send Mitch's anger boiling higher.

"Why did you kill Isis and not Mitch?" Greg asked. "You had him dead to rights back at the base."

"I thought about it. My fingers itched to do exactly that. But that is a privilege I will reserve for my husband. Horus is responsible for my husband's banishment. And it is only right that my husband be the one that takes his pound of flesh." Nephthys nodded to Isis's remains on the table. "And besides, isn't the pain of your mother's loss a far better punishment than anything I could give you?"

Mitch roared as he pulled the trigger. Nephthys dodged to the side, rolling and disappearing into the dining room. Mitch followed quickly.

Greg was right behind him. "Mitch, no! We need to take her alive!"

But Mitch was well past listening to anything Greg had to say. He opened fire as he stood in the dining room's doorway, unloading his weapon on the dining room table. And then he pulled the trigger again but all that was heard was a click.

He growled as he stared down at his weapon. He slid the magazine out and pulled another one out from his pocket.

Before he could slam it into place, his aunt launched herself at him from underneath the table, the knife held high.

Greg knew if Mitch was killed with that, he would be truly dead this time. Visions of Maya and the kids rolled through Greg's mind.

He couldn't let that happen. He slammed into Mitch, sending him flying as Greg turned and unloaded his own weapon into Nephthys.

Caught out in the open, the bullets sent her stumbling back. She swayed on her feet for a moment before she smiled. "We'll see you soon," she said before the light disappeared from her eyes and she crumbled to the ground.

Greg scrambled back, his heart pounding before he hurried forward and put his finger to her neck. He looked over at Mitch and then shook his head. "She's gone."

CHAPTER 73

Greg and Mitch sat out back behind his mother's house in a little gazebo. Mitch hadn't said a word since Greg had brought him out here. Greg stared at the house, replaying Nephthys's death over and over again, looking for another way he could have played it. But he simply didn't see one.

Although he supposed he should find a different word to use. She wasn't dead. She would be back. And she would start this all over again. Her body had disappeared before the strike force had even arrived. She had simply disintegrated into ash, which quickly rose up into the air and then disappeared.

The strike force burst into the room only moments later.

Greg had hurried to the door and stopped them, telling them that the threat was over but that they needed an investigative unit there. He didn't let anyone into the house.

When he returned, Mitch was sitting in the corner of the kitchen staring at what was left of his mother's body. Greg walked over and grabbed him by the shoulders and tugged him to his feet. "Come on, Mitch."

"I can't leave her."

"They'll take care of her, but this is not something you should be seeing," Greg said, his voice quiet but firm.

Mitch let Greg lead him out of the house and to the small gazebo in the back. And that was where the two of them were sitting when the investigative unit arrived with Norah.

Norah quickly made her way to the back of the house and to the two of them. Greg intercepted her halfway to the gazebo. She glanced over his shoulder at Mitch and then looked back at him. "What the hell happened here, Greg?"

Greg quickly recounted arriving and finding Mitch's mother dead, how Cheryl/ Nephthys had been standing poised over the body and then how she had attempted to kill Mitch as well, but Greg had turned and shot her.

Running a hand through her hair, Norah stared at him for a long moment before she spoke. "So where's the body Greg? And why Mitch's mother? And right after Mitch came back from the dead?"

Greg eyed her.

She nodded back at him. "Yeah, I know there's more to that story. And you're going to need to explain all of it to me."

He nodded wearily. "I know."

Blowing out a breath, she looked back to the house. "Okay, I'm going to get this scene locked down. I'll make sure that we take care of Mitch's mother's remains. Is there anything in particular I should be looking for?" Her gaze now bored into him.

"The remains will come up human, but there's a knife that's inside, the one that Nephthys used, I'd like to get a look at that as soon as possible," Greg said feeling so very tired.

"Nephthys? Is that Mitch's aunt? Where is she? Do I need to send out a BOLO?" Norah asked.

Greg shook his head. "No, we don't have to worry about her. At least not for a little while."

Norah narrowed her eyes. "What does that mean?"

He winced. He hadn't meant to say that. "It means it's a long story. But no BOLO is required. Honestly, I wouldn't even know what description to use for it."

The silence stretched between them for a long moment before Nola nodded. "Okay. I'm going to accept that for now because between this scene, Dr. Kerwin's death, Mitch's reappearance, and what's happened at HQ today, I've got enough on my plate. But soon, you and I are going to sit down, and you are going to tell me this long story."

Greg knew Norah would hold him to that. And he also knew she needed to be read in. "Okay."

Glancing once again over Greg's shoulder, Norah nodded toward Mitch. "I'm sending you two back to the base. You will both be under confinement until we sort this all out."

With a weary nod, he looked back at Mitch, who didn't look like he had any fight left in him. "Yeah, that'll be fine."

CHAPTER 74

A security unit escorted Mitch and Greg back to the base a few minutes later. Mitch still hadn't said anything, and Greg was growing more than a little worried.

When they reached the base, Maeve was at the front foyer waiting for them. She escorted Greg and Mitch back to Greg's office. A security unit also escorted them there and then took up residence outside the door.

Mitch took a seat on the couch and then just stared at nothing. Maeve pulled Greg over to the other side of the room. "How is he?"

Greg sighed. "I don't know. It's a lot. I mean, not just his mom dying but the way she was killed. I really wish he hadn't had to see that."

"It must have been terrible."

Looking for something to distract him at least for a moment, he asked, "How did it go with Kaylee?"

"Fine. The implant was removed without any problem. Hannah removed two of the other ones and was working on Moore the last I checked."

"Well, that's progress, I suppose. What about other implants in people on the base? Were you able to find any?"

"I created an algorithm to search for them. We've gotten a couple of hits, but we're in the early days yet. It's going to take a while to get them all scanned."

Greg had no doubt about that.

Maeve continued. "I've got a team on it already, though. Questionnaires are automatically sent to those who we get a bead on. A rep is sent to speak with them personally and go over their answers."

"A questionnaire?"

"Alvie created it. It tracks if anybody's lost time. Those guys will go to the head of the line when it comes to getting scanned. But, Greg, we're talking weeks of going through and finding everybody, and even then, I'm not sure we'll be able to identify all of them. It would be pretty easy to keep that kind of information out of a medical file, especially if the doctor is the one who was in on it."

Greg nodded. "Well, at least Kaylee and the others had theirs removed. We don't have to worry about them being controlled. Have you examined the implant?"

"Just a preliminary look. Unsurprisingly, we can't identify the material. And it's not possible to scan the interior. We're going to have to take it apart."

Greg's phone beeped, and he glanced at the screen. It was one of the analysts.

"What is it?" Maeve asked.

"I asked Norah to look into Nate's background to see why it was that he might be targeted. One of the analysts did a deep dive on him." The analysts had sent him a rather lengthy file. It would take time to go through, but apparently he wouldn't be going anywhere for a while, so it looked like he had the time. "You want to help me go through his background and see if anything pops?"

Maeve nodded. "Happy to."

The two of them pulled up chairs to the conference table in the corner, and Greg brought up the file. He sent it to Maeve, and she brought another copy up on her iPad.

"I'll start with Nate and his wife. You want to start with the extended family?" Greg asked.

"Sounds good," Maeve said, pulling her tablet over.

Greg flicked a glance over at Mitch, who now lay on the couch, his eyes closed.

Knowing there was nothing he could do for his friend except figure out what was going on, he turned his attention back to the file.

Thirty minutes later, he still had no clue why Nate would be beneficial to someone. His wife had a number of cases that involved the government, but there was nothing there that really stuck out to him.

Maeve grunted.

Greg looked up. "What is it?"

"Did you know Nate is a twin?"

"No, actually, I didn't."

"They're identical twins." She brought up an image. There on the screen were almost two identical Nates. The one on the right had slightly longer hair than the other one, but other than that, they were carbon copies of one another.

A tingle ran through Greg. "What does the brother do for a living?"

Maeve scanned down the file, and her eyes widened as she turned to Greg. "He works for the DoD."

"Doing what?"

"It's classified."

Greg was already reaching for his phone. He called Norah, who answered quickly. "I'm in the middle of something here. In fact, I'm in the middle of a lot of somethings here. Can this wait?"

"I don't think so. I need to get authorization to learn what Nate Prower's brother was doing for the Department of Defense."

"Nate's brother works for the DoD?" Norah asked.

"Yes."

"Okay, hold on a minute."

As silence reigned on the other side of the phone, Greg tapped his fingers along the desk.

After about two minutes, Norah came back on the line. "Okay, I put in the request. I told them it's a high priority. You should have clearance in about five minutes."

"Thanks, Norah." He disconnected the call.

"Well?" Maeve asked.

Greg explained what Norah said, and Maeve nodded. "I'm going to run down to the cafeteria and get us some drinks and some food."

"I'll go with you," Greg said, standing.

Maeve shook her head at him, nodding toward the door. "You're confined to this room, remember?"

He sank back down. "Right. Forgot about that. Grab me a sandwich and some fries, will you?"

"Sure, and I'll grab the same for Mitch," she said, glancing over at the couch at Mitch, who still looked like he was asleep, before she slipped out the door.

Greg flipped through the remaining information about Nate's brother. He'd gone to the US Naval Academy and gone on to become a Navy SEAL. Eventually, he was stationed at the DoD after being injured overseas. He was married with one child.

On a hunch, Greg checked to see if his brother worked in DC. Yep, sure enough, he did, but it looked like he'd been out of town on the day that Nate had had his lost time issue. There had been some sort of government conference on the west coast that he'd attended that day.

Sitting back, Greg frowned. Actually, that could work. If Nate was posing as his brother, he'd need him to be out of town.

Maeve returned with the food and drinks, and Greg had just taken a bite of his turkey sandwich when his phone beeped again, indicating that he'd been given clearance. He inputted the code into his computer, and then the information on Nate's brother appeared.

Greg scanned it quickly, trying to figure out what it was he was looking for.

Maeve sat next to him, reading the same information. Then she sucked in a breath.

Greg looked where her gaze was focused, and he, too, felt the air in the room shift. "Oh my God."

Nate Prower's brother had been in charge of organizing the retrieval subjects from the A.L.I.V.E. projects. He cataloged and organized them before having them shipped to containment areas across the country.

Greg met Maeve's gaze. "Nephthys used Nate to find out where the controls for the creatures were."

"But this lists more than that. This tells where the *creatures* from the projects have been sent," Maeve said.

Greg leaned forward with a frown. "We asked about this. Even Norah didn't have access to this. Someone's been hiding things." He didn't even want to contemplate who that could possibly be.

"Were there any in Africa?" Maeve asked.

Greg scanned the document and nodded. "Yes, in Morocco."

"That must be where the ones that I came across in Niger were from." She froze. "Greg," Maeve said, a warning in her tone.

Greg followed her gaze. There was another installation in the US that still had four Kecksburgs. *Oh no.*

Greg grabbed his phone. "Please don't let us be too late."

CHAPTER 75

This time, Greg didn't bother interrupting Norah. He called the containment facility directly. The individual who answered sounded stressed.

Greg immediately offered his name and his security clearance.

"Dr. Schorn, this really isn't a good time," Edgar Allen said on the other side of the line.

A quick glance at the directory for the facility showed that Edgar Allen was in charge of security. "Yeah, and I think I might know why. Did you have a security breach?"

"Yes, we did," Edgar said quickly. "But we just learned about it today. Fifteen minutes ago, in fact, when we were doing sweeps. The computer didn't register any problems, but it was when my team went through for their visual inspection that they recognized that some of the creatures were missing."

Greg rubbed the bridge of his nose. "And let me guess, they're Kecksburgs, aren't they?"

Allen was silent for a beat. "How'd you know that?"

The containment facility was located only two hours away

from the D.E.A.D. base, closer to the Ohio border. Greg felt his world tilt. That was a little too close for comfort.

"How did you know it was Kecksburgs?" Allen demanded.

"You don't want to know. Unfortunately, I think I know where they're heading. When's the last time the creatures were seen?"

"Last night, when they went for their last visual round before this one. We rely on electronic surveillance during the day. And somehow, someone managed to fool it. The creatures are automatically fed at specific intervals, and their food is laying untouched, which means that they were gone at least an hour and a half ago."

Greg nodded.

Then a thought hit him. "The monitoring system that you use for your facility. Where did you get it from?"

"From you guys. It's a D.E.A.D. program."

Greg sat back as a thought began to form, but he didn't even want to give it any sort of purchase. "Okay, thanks."

"Wait a minute. I need to know how you knew that we had a break-in."

Greg grimaced. "Because I know somebody who wants your creatures. Look, Allen, I know you're in the middle of stuff, but so am I. I promise I'll let you know everything I'm allowed to as soon as I can, okay?"

Allen was quiet for a long moment before he gruffly answered. "I'm going to hold you to that, Schorn."

"I hope you do," he said before he hung up the phone.

Maeve, who'd been sitting next to him, had heard the whole conversation. "Somebody's got Kecksburgs," she said.

"Yeah, and the controllers," Greg said, his chest all of a sudden feeling tight. "Things just went from really bad to worse."

CHAPTER 76

The idea that someone had gotten a hold of a Kecksburg struck fear through the center of Maeve. And from the terrified look on Greg's face, he was just as horrified at the idea. Both Maeve and Greg had been up close and personal with Kecksburgs before. Neither had walked away from those interactions unscathed.

"Okay, so somebody is grabbing the Kecksburgs. That must mean that they've got a plan for them," Greg said, standing up and pacing across the room.

Maeve ran a hand over her mouth, trying to figure out what the plan could possibly be, and then her head jolted up as a thought ran through her. "The last time they used Kecksburgs, it was to retrieve one of the orbs."

His mouth falling open, Greg's eyes grew large as he stared at Maeve. "Which means they're going to do the same thing this time."

He crossed the room and crouched down in front of Mitch. He hesitated for a moment and then reached out and touched the large man's shoulder. "Mitch?"

"I'm not sleeping," Mitch said, opening his eyes and sitting up.

"Hey, sorry. I know you're going through a lot right now."

Mitch dropped his head into his hands. "How am I going to tell Maya and the kids? They love my mother."

And obviously, so did Mitch. Grief was stamped across every inch of his frame.

Maeve knew that grief well. When her mother had died, she had felt completely cast adrift. But Alvie had needed her. Mitch's family needed him to but they weren't here at the moment. It was just Mitch, feeling lost.

"Did you hear what Maeve just said about the orb?" Greg asked.

Mitch shook his head. "Sorry. I wasn't really paying attention."

Maeve moved closer. "It's perfectly understandable after what you've been through."

"The orbs that appear after …" Greg hesitated. ". . . after a Primeval is killed. Is there any rhyme or reason to how they fall back to Earth?"

Mitch shook his head. "Not that I know of. In fact, I'm not even sure that they all return to Earth."

Maeve stepped forward with a frown. "What do you mean?"

Mitch sighed. "The orbs, they contain the individual's essence, that's true. But Earth isn't the only possible place that they could go. They could go anywhere, in any direction. One could be created and simply slip out into the void of space."

Greg sat back, his eyes intense. "But we know that Set is trying to reemerge, correct?"

Mitch nodded. "Yes."

"And now we know that your aunt also is in the process of reincarnating, correct?" Greg asked.

Mitch nodded again.

INTO THE DARK

Maeve knew where Greg was going with this. "Do the orbs originate on the reincarnation ship as well?"

"Yes," Mitch said slowly, a frown appearing on his face. "I never really thought about that before, but yes, that's where they originate. It's the only place they *could* originate."

"Is it possible that if Set or Nephthys is at the reincarnation ship, they could guide the orb toward Earth?"

"I suppose it's possible. I mean, I don't see why it wouldn't be."

Greg frowned before he stood up and hurried over to the desk. "There are programs that scour the sky to check for meteors that are bound for Earth. That program might be able to pick up an orb."

Maeve followed him. "Yes, but there are over 48.5 million tons of meteoric material that hit the Earth's atmosphere every day. Almost all of them are vaporized by the atmosphere. In fact, only about seventeen get through each day. But something as small as the orb, we might not even see."

"That's true," Greg said, sitting down and pulling his chair into the desk. "But we have to try."

Greg's hands flew across the keyboard as he started to make his way into the media program. A large klaxon sounded throughout the room. Maeve's head jolted up, her eyes widening. "Now what?"

A warning flashed across the screen of Greg's computer. The color drained from his face. "We're all being warned to take cover. There's an incoming missile."

Maeve glanced at the screen. "A missile? Seriously?"

Standing up from the couch, Mitch crossed the room to join them. He pulled out his phone and dialed. After a moment, someone answered. "I need a report on the incoming. What's the origin of the missile?" He nodded, listening before he disconnected the phone.

Maeve and Greg turned to him. "What is it?" Greg asked.

"It didn't originate on the planet. Whatever is coming at us, is coming from space." He paused. "And it's coming from the exact location where the reincarnation ship is located."

CHAPTER 77

Greg wasted no time bringing up the radar system to see if they could get a lock on where the object was heading.

It wasn't coming alone. It looked as if there was some space debris landing alongside it.

"Well?" Maeve asked.

"According to this, it'll be landing in the field not too far from headquarters. Some of the debris might hit the actual headquarters itself."

As if in response to Greg's statement, crashes were heard along the roof. Greg winced, staring up at the ceiling, waiting for it to cave in, but everything held.

He turned to the screen and could see from the feed of the incoming object that it was growing nearer.

"Three, two, one," Greg whispered.

A large boom sounded from the back field. The windows in the headquarters rattled. Greg grabbed onto the desk as the room swayed. When the shaking subsided, he looked at Mitch. "We need to get to that before anybody else does."

Maeve waved them on. "You guys go grab it. I'll let Norah know what's happening."

Greg yanked open the door. The two security officers stationed there turned. "Back inside, Dr. Schorn," one of them ordered.

"Um, would you guys believe me if I told you it was a matter of world security that we need to get out of here?" Greg asked,

"No," one of them replied.

Mitch pulled Greg out of the way. "Greg, they have a job to do." Mitch turned to the guards. "Sorry about that—and this." He grabbed the guard's Taser and crushed it into the man's side, pulling the trigger.

The other guard went for his gun, but Greg kicked him in the groin, wincing as he did so. The guy dropped to the ground. "I'm so sorry," Greg said as he jumped over him and sprinted down the hall with Mitch right next to him.

Without a word, they burst into the stairwell and scrambled down the steps. Greg's mind moved as fast as his feet. If the orb was here, then someone would have to come to collect it. He turned to Mitch. "How long does it take to reincarnate?"

"Anywhere between twelve and forty-eight hours."

"Then it can't be your aunt that's coming to collect this thing."

"Maybe she's going to show up in a few days once she's returned."

It was possible, Greg supposed, but in his gut, he doubted it. "Or maybe she's hijacked someone else to capture it for her. Or it could be Set's consciousness hijacking people. He would be able to take over someone else's form for short times, wouldn't he?"

Mitch nodded. "Yeah."

"What if Set is the one who's behind these retrievals? I mean, yes, he's working with Nephthys, but what if he's the one who sent the Kecksburgs to retrieve the orb in Africa? What if he's the one who took over Nate and that we spoke with when we were down at the DoD facility? What if he's the one that's going to be coming for this orb?"

By this time they had reached the main foyer and burst out into the large entryway, turning right and heading toward the back of the building. "Well, if it's Set that's coming, then we all need to be terrified."

The lockdown had been called off when Greg and Mitch were on the way back from his mother's, so the halls were empty of soldiers. Greg wasn't so sure that was a good thing. As they burst out the back doors, there were six people standing staring out into the field.

Greg and Mitch ran past them, noting the new indentation in the ground that had created mounds of dirt around it.

At the same time, Greg's phone beeped, as did Mitch's. More beeps came from the phones of the individuals standing at the parking lot.

Not slowing, Greg pulled out his phone, trying to read while he ran. Finally, he had to stop because he was bouncing too hard.

A second alarm went off from the base. The text message read: CODE 24. Greg stared at the code with dread. Code 24 meant a base incursion was imminent. Maeve must have notified Norah, who put eyes on the area around them.

His heart started to pound as he looked up and saw that Mitch had made it to the edge of the crater. He walked down the side of it and had just reached the center as Greg reached the edge. Mitch knelt down and placed one hand on the orb. He dropped his head, and his shoulders shuddered.

They needed to get moving. He kept his gaze scanning the horizon, looking for any sign of movement, but there was nothing yet.

If that orb was his mother's consciousness, then Mitch no

doubt was getting some sort of message from his mother. Greg really didn't want to interfere with that, but this was taking too long. "Mitch! We need to get going!"

Tears in his eyes, Mitch looked up and nodded. He reached down and grabbed the orb before climbing back out of the crater.

Greg cursed himself for not grabbing a containment unit of some sort to make it easier to carry. They turned back for the headquarters when Greg caught sight of movement from the corner of his eyes.

He stopped and turned to see what was there. It was a creature of some sort, running toward them. Greg's chest hollowed out as he recognized the familiar gait, even from a distance.

The group he and Mitch had passed was still huddled at the edge of the parking lot. "Get inside!" Greg screamed as he started to run. "Get inside now!" He picked up his own pace. "Mitch! It's the Kecksburgs."

Mitch glanced over his shoulder. His jaw tightened and he picked up his pace. In no time, they were flat out sprinting for the doors.

Finally catching sight of the creatures bearing down on them, the individuals in the parking lot ran for the doors as well, disappearing inside. Greg and Mitch reached it seconds after them.

Behind them, Greg could hear the scrabble of talons on cars as six Kecksburgs leapt from car to car. He sprinted to the door, holding it open for Mitch, and then slammed it behind them, engaging the emergency locks.

He stepped back as a Kecksburg threw itself at the door over and over again. He backed up, staring at the door.

Mitch grabbed him by the shoulder and dragged him away. "That door isn't going to hold. We need to move."

They sprinted down the hall. Every door they passed was

INTO THE DARK

closed and locked. They tore around the corner, and Mitch slammed into the wall. Greg crashed into him, jostling his arm.

Mitch let out a yell as the orb slipped from his hands. The two of them sprinted down the hall. Mitch managed to grab the orb, but the fumble had slowed them down.

Behind them, Greg heard the screech of metal and a crash as the doors were flung open. "They're inside!" Greg yelled.

Mitch's face was tight as he sprinted toward the main foyer. The door to the stairwell burst open.

Kaylee appeared with an M4 pulled in tight to her shoulder. "Get down!" she yelled before she let out a stream of suppressing fire.

Ducking and running, Greg and Mitch sprinted toward her. A scream came from one of the creatures behind him.

Greg darted a look over his shoulder, noting that one of them had been caught with a series of bullets in the middle of its gut.

Ahead, Mitch barreled into the stairwell, and Greg dove in after him.

Kaylee continued her onslaught and then jumped in after them, slamming the door shut behind her and engaging the locks. "Let's go!" she yelled, grabbing Greg by the shoulder and dragging him toward the stairs.

Getting his feet under him, Greg sprinted up the stairs next to her. "How'd you know we were in trouble?"

Kaylee rolled her eyes. "Greg, you're always in trouble."

Inclining his head, Greg conceded the point. "Where are we going?"

"Panic room, third floor. I figure they're after that thing?" Kaylee gestured to the orb in Mitch's hands.

Greg nodded.

"Well, then we're going to hide this thing until we've taken out those creatures," Kaylee said.

Greg sprinted up the stairs to the third floor and bolted down the hallway.

Waiting down the hall at the door at the panic room, Maeve stood wringing her hands. Finally, her shoulders dropped with relief as she caught sight of them coming down the hall toward her. "Hurry up!" she yelled.

None of them needed the extra encouragement, but they did pick up their pace. As they reached the door, they quickly dove into the room. Maeve followed them in and slammed the door shut. The locks automatically engaged.

"Thank God." Letting out a breath, Greg slumped to the floor. The panic room had been built to withstand alien attacks. There were a few of them scattered throughout the building. Norah had made sure that they were a requirement.

And there was no chance that even the Kecksburgs would be able to get into it.

The door thumped as a Kecksburg tried nonetheless.

Scrambling to his feet, Greg backed away from the door, staring at it, his heart pounding harder with each thump of a Kecksburg's body. "They can't get in here, right?"

Kaylee shook her head. "No. These things were built specifically with these guys in mind. They're not going to be able to get through."

Despite that assurance, Greg's heart raced as the Kecksburg continued its onslaught against the door. For a full five minutes, it attacked the door continuously. Then it simply stopped.

Moving to the computer monitor in the corner of the room, Maeve brought up the cameras in the hall. Onscreen, two Kecksburgs stood outside the panic room, staring at the door. Together, they tilted their heads at it. Then they turned and sprinted down the hall away from them.

Frowning, Greg leaned closer to the monitor. "Now where are they going?"

CHAPTER 78

On the monitor, Greg and the others followed the Kecksburgs progress through the hall and into the stairwell. But then they lost them. They didn't show up on the first floor. Maeve backtracked to the second floor, but there was no sign of them by the time they shifted the camera.

"Where are they?" Greg asked.

Maeve flipped through different camera sites, which showed mostly empty halls. Everyone was once again in lockdown except for the security patrols that were starting at the first floor and making their way through to flush the Kecksburgs out.

Maeve continued to cycle through images, looking for the Kecksburgs as Greg's nerves stretched thinner and thinner. There was one lying on the ground on the first floor. That was the one Kaylee had tagged. But none of the others were in evidence. Where were they? They had taken off at a run, which normally meant they had sensed another target. But there was no one nearby.

The images continued to cycle, one scene after the next,

before movement appeared on screen. "Stop!" Greg yelled. He stared at the screen, his heart pounding. "Where is that?"

"That's your office," Maeve said softly.

On screen, Kal and Pugsley stood against the back wall of Greg's office. A horrible thought crossed Greg's mind. "Bring up the camera outside my office," Greg whispered.

Maeve did as he asked, and then Greg sucked in a breath. Four Kecksburgs were heading down there, two coming from each side of the hall. His heart pounded as he stared at the monitor.

His office had windows along the back wall but the windows wouldn't be operable due to the lockdown. And the only other exit was the hallway door. And with the Kecksburgs in the hall, Kal and Pugsley wouldn't be able to get out that way.

They were trapped.

CHAPTER 79

Greg's mind reeled as he stared at the screen. "They're going after Kal and Pugsley."

"That can't be a coincidence," Kaylee said.

A feeling of ice cold fear lodged in Greg's chest. He shook his head. "It's not."

Whoever was controlling the Kecksburgs had sent them after Kal and Pugsley because they knew that would draw Greg out. There was no one else in the room with him who had someone they cared about on the base right now. It was only Greg.

His mind raced. Pugsley could incapacitate one, but no more than that. And there were no weapons in his office. Besides, Kal wasn't equipped to take on three Kecksburgs.

No one was equipped to take on three Kecksburgs. He scanned the room. *A plan. I need a plan.*

His eyes fell on a bag sitting on a shelf near Kaylee. "I need that backpack," Greg said, pointing at it.

She quickly handed it over. He turned to Mitch, who, without a word, dropped the orb inside it.

"Thank you." Greg zipped the bag up as Mitch walked

over to the armory cabinet and started pulling out weapons. He handed an M4 to Greg along with a couple of clips. Greg took them and slipped them into his pockets.

"What are you doing?" Maeve asked.

"I'm doing exactly what you would do if it were Alvie and the kids. I'm going to protect my family."

"I'm going with him," Mitch said.

"Me too," Kaylee said as she grabbed some additional magazines.

Greg wanted to tell them no, to stay back, that it was too dangerous, but with four Kecksburgs, he wasn't even sure that the three of them would be enough.

Maeve opened her mouth as if she was going to volunteer, but Greg immediately shook his head. "You are not set up for this, and you know it. Alvie and the triplets need you. And besides, if this doesn't work, we need you to tell everybody what's been going on and figure out what the next steps are. Because if Set comes back, well, that's just not going to be good for anyone."

"Set? Who's Set?" Kaylee asked.

Greg slammed a magazine into the chamber. "A really bad guy we need to make sure does not reincarnate."

Kaylee looked at the others. "He's kidding, right?"

"Unfortunately, he's not," Maeve said quietly before she hugged Greg tight. "Be careful." Then she gave a small laugh. "Well, I guess that's a really stupid thing to say right now. Because if you were being careful, you wouldn't be leaving."

"How about 'be accurate'?" he said, lifting the gun.

Maeve nodded. "Okay, be that."

"I will."

Maeve unlocked the door, waited until the three of them were outside, and then locked it behind them.

With a quick glance at his two compatriots, Greg hurried down the hall. But once they reached the doorway to the stairwell, Mitch held out a hand, indicating he would go first, with Greg in the middle, and then Kaylee would bring up the rear.

It was quiet on the stairs. Even so, Greg couldn't help but think of all the stairwells he had run through in a panic over the course of his life. It was a shockingly high number. So even without any current threat, his heart began to race and sweat broke out along his back.

God, he hated this. He was not made for these high-adrenaline situations. Yet, somehow, he always seemed to find himself in the middle of them.

This time, though, the stairwell offered no threat and no new nightmares to add to his collection. They encountered no one. They made it to the first floor. Mitch paused, looking at the other two before he opened the door.

They moved quickly down the hall and stepped into the front foyer when Greg heard the unmistakable sound of talons on tile. He turned around as a Kecksburg leaped out from behind the security desk.

"Down!" Kaylee yelled as she flung a small explosive device at the Kecksburg. It latched onto the creature's chest. Kaylee grabbed Greg and rolled him away as the bomb went off. Tissue and blood exploded across the foyer, landing along Greg's back. He winced at the thwap sound as the parts of the creature hit the tile floor.

He lifted his head and looked around. "That's disgusting," he muttered as he started to stand.

"Disgusting but effective," Kaylee said as she reached out a hand and hauled him up.

Mitch, who'd taken refuge behind one of the lobby chairs, appeared not to have gotten any Kecksburg pieces on him. Kaylee only got a little on her sleeve.

Greg, however, was soaked in the creature's innards. He must look like an extra in a horror movie.

"You two good?" Mitch asked.

Using the edge of his shirt, Greg wiped what he could from his face. "I could've done without the blood and tissue shower, but yeah, let's go."

They were around the corner from Greg's office when he heard the splinter of wood and knew it wouldn't take long for the Kecksburgs to break through. Another hit or two and they'd manage it.

Kaylee stopped at the corner. "Okay. We need to come up with a plan. How do you think we should—"

"Hey!" Greg yelled as he stepped out into the hall. "I've got what you want."

"Or we could just do it that way," Mitch muttered with a sigh.

CHAPTER 80

The Kecksburgs paused for a moment before they turned simultaneously, looking at Greg. All four of them, at the same time, tilted their heads to the left.

It was easily the eeriest thing that Greg had ever seen in his life, and that was saying something. All four went still, then they took off sprinting toward Greg. Greg turned around and ran for everything he was worth.

Mitch was right behind Greg, and Kaylee was on his side.

"Does this plan of yours involve anything other than us being bait?" Mitch yelled.

"Uh, no, not really. I just wanted to get them away from the door," Greg yelled, his thigh muscles already burning as he sprinted faster than he ever had in his life.

"The training facility in the basement. Head there," Kaylee yelled as she burst ahead and through the nearest stairwell.

She held open the door, and Mitch and Greg barreled through. She slammed it shut before sprinting after them. "That door won't hold. I didn't have time to put in the top lock."

As if the Kecksburgs heard her, the door to the first floor blew open, crashing against the back wall.

By then, they'd reached the bottom level and raced into the hallway there. Mitch pulled Greg out as Kaylee dove through, and Mitch slammed both locks into place. They hustled down the hall toward the training gym.

Greg sprinted inside as Kaylee followed, her weapon aimed at the doorway.

Mitch hustled in. Together he and Kaylee locked the double doors.

Turning around, Greg stared at the part of the gym that they had entered through. It was the Hogan's Alley replica. There were lots of obstacles and corners. Which could be good.

"Ideas?" Greg asked.

Nodding to the alley, Kaylee said, "We lead them in there and ambush them."

Mitch nodded his agreement. "We've got some flashbangs that we can use to distract them and keep them on course. How many of those explosive devices do you have?"

Kaylee reached into her jacket pocket. "Four."

"Good. We make sure that we're close enough to make sure that those stick. We'll take them down with gunfire and follow up with the IEDs. Okay?" Mitch asked.

"Got it," Greg said.

"And Greg, you need to hide farther into the alley to make sure you're not caught in the crossfire. Your job is to keep the orb away from them, okay?"

"But—" The door to the hallway outside slammed open. A terrible screech rent through the air. There was no time to argue for a bigger part in the drama to come. Greg backed up, his heart pounding. "Here they come."

"Hide," Kaylee ordered, sprinting into the alley. Greg and Mitch were right behind her.

By passing the other two, Greg headed into the farthest

parts of the alley. He hunkered down behind a couple of makeshift boxes at the far end and over to the left. Mitch and Kaylee were located somewhere up closer to the entrance.

As he heard the sound of talons along the concrete floor, he realized he was perfectly okay with Kaylee's plan. He was more than happy to stay away from the Kecksburgs.

A screech sent the hairs at the back of Greg's neck straight up. They were close.

Gunshots rang throughout the cavernous space. Greg crouched further down, his eyes scanning the area behind him to make sure no one was sneaking up on him. But from where he was at, he couldn't see anything. He wanted to peek out and check on Kaylee and Mitch, but he knew they'd have his head if he gave away his position like that. So he stayed low and prayed that Kaylee and Mitch were having some success.

CHAPTER 81

"Damn, they're fast little suckers," Kaylee said with a grunt as she unleashed another spray of gunfire.

Mitch had to agree. Greg had told him about the Kecksburg, but he hadn't yet seen one up close and personal, at least alive. They were a lot faster than he thought they would be. "I've got an idea. I'll lead one away, you take it out."

"Do you have a death wish?" Kaylee asked.

Mitch grunted. "No death wish, but we need to separate these guys out. And they're smart."

Grabbing one of the IEDs with a shake of her head, Kaylee nodded. "Go."

Bursting from his hiding spot, Mitch sprinted down the alley. He heard the talons on the concrete floor trying to find purchase.

Gunfire burst out from behind him before Kaylee yelled, "Take cover!"

Mitch dove to the left as the Kecksburg behind him exploded. Organic debris rained around him, and he had to suppress a shiver. Greg was right. That was disgusting.

And for a moment, the image he'd last seen of his mother

flashed through his mind. He shoved it aside as the wave of grief reared up inside of him. Now was not the time. But he would make the time as soon as he made sure Kaylee and Greg got out of this.

Crawling through a small hole in the wall, he ended up one room beyond where Kaylee had been. She let out a scream, and then he heard a second explosion.

He sprinted back toward where he'd found her and caught her climbing through a window. She tumbled to the ground. There was a fresh gash along her calf. "Kaylee."

She waved him off. "It's okay. I'm fine. It's not deep."

A Kecksburg burst through a wall near them. Kaylee was still on the ground, and Mitch had slipped his weapon to the side to help her up.

The two of them were caught out in the open unarmed..

The Kecksburg looked at them, tilted its head, and then turned, heading deeper into the alley.

"What the hell was that?" Kaylee asked.

"Where's the other one?" Mitch asked pulling his M4 into his shoulder. Damn it. He no longer had it in sight.

"I don't know. I don't see it," Kaylee replied.

Mitch followed the retreating Kecksburg with his eyes and yelled as loud as he could. "Greg, they're looking for you!"

CHAPTER 82

"Greg, they're looking for you!" The absolute last words that anyone wanted to hear when hiding from terrifying monsters. Greg slipped deeper into the shadows, his mind racing.

He knew that they weren't really looking for him. It was the orb that they were trying to find. He slipped the bag off his shoulders and unzipped it.

Taking a deep breath, he reached in and felt a profound sense of loss as soon as he touched the orb. An image of Isis wafted through his mind. He shook his head as the hair on his arm stood straight up. "Okay, Isis, I could use a little help here."

Spying an old crate sitting exposed in the middle of the space just beyond the Hogan's Alley replica, he darted over to it and placed the orb on the ground in front of it. Then he sprinted back to the spot where he'd been.

He leaned up against another crate and trained his weapon on the orb. "Come on, guys. Come on," he whispered.

But the sound of the Kecksburgs running had disappeared. They had gone silent.

Holding his breath, he hoped that they would make some noise to let him know where they were.

But it wasn't a sound that alerted him to their location. It was the drop of saliva on the back of his neck, as one of them stood directly over him.

CHAPTER 83

Greg dove to the ground as the Kecksburg lashed out with its talons. The creatures liked to disembowel their prey first, allowing them to then slowly devour their meal.

Rolling out of the way, Greg fired blindly behind him. From the cry, he knew he'd caught at least part of the Kecksburg with his wild shooting.

On his hands and knees, Greg scrambled along the floor. He needed a little distance. But the Kecksburg wasn't cooperating. It leapt down after him. Another one appeared ten feet behind him.

"God dammit, you guys were supposed to go after the orb!" he screamed. Scrambling to his feet, he looked between the two of them.

A hum emitted from the orb before it rolled slowly down the alley toward them. The Kecksburg who'd been injured turned its head toward it.

Greg wasted no time. Bringing his M4 up he unloaded it into the creature's chest. It screamed as its blood and tissue poured out onto the ground.

The creature to his left let out a simultaneous roar, but this one wasn't of pain. It was rage. It darted toward Greg. On hands and knees, he backtracked, tripping over an exposed wire.

Gunfire rang out from behind the creature charging him. It cut into the creature from shoulder to hip.

The creature whirled around with a vicious snarl.

Greg dove to the side as Kaylee and Mitch both threw the IEDs. The two explosive devices found their mark, attaching themselves to the creature's torso.

Scrambling behind a box, Greg covered his head with his hands as the Kecksburg exploded. Once again, blood and tissue rained down around him.

He waited until the storm of body parts ended before he got to his feet. Breathing hard, he looked around. "Was that all of them?"

"That was all of them," Kaylee said. "You all right?"

Greg nodded, his mouth dry. He had to swallow a few times before he could speak again. "Yeah. Just … yeah."

Mitch slowly walked to where the silver orb lay. "At least we still have this."

Kaylee hobbled over to Greg. He looked down at her leg in alarm. "You're hurt."

"Just a little scratch." She nodded toward where Mitch was crouched next to the orb, one hand on it. Kaylee's voice was quiet as she watch Mitch. "What's the deal with that thing? What's he doing?"

Grief was stamped on every inch of the big man's frame. "I think he's saying good-bye," he said softly.

CHAPTER 84

Half a dozen Kecksburgs had infiltrated the facility, all of the ones from the Fredonia containment area. Headquarters was still in lockdown, and extra troops were being brought in.

Greg, after taking a very long shower, met up with the others in the lounge outside Norah's office. Mitch was inside giving her a complete briefing along with Kaylee and Maeve. Greg knew that he'd have to give his own, and he didn't feel like interrupting to let everyone know what his thoughts were.

Instead, he headed down to his office, where Kal and Pugsley were still waiting. Knocking on the door, he opened it slowly. "Kal? It's me."

Kal, who stood with a baseball bat, dropped the bat and hurried across the room. "Greg."

Greg brought him in for a quick hug. "You okay?"

There was still a small tremor in Kal's hands as he answered. "Yeah, I'm good. But those things, they were right outside the door."

Fear rolled through Greg again as he pictured the Kecksburgs in the hall. He swallowed, trying to chase the image away. "Yeah, I know."

Pugsley waddled over to him and wrapped himself around Greg's legs. "I'm okay, little buddy," he said, patting Pugsley on the head.

"What was that all about? Were those Kecksburgs?" Kal asked.

Impressed he recognized them, Greg nodded. "Yeah, they were. And it's a bit of a long story."

Raising his eyebrows, Kal gave Greg a piercing look. "Does that long story include why Mitch is back?"

"Yeah, it does. But I'm not sure how much of it I can tell you."

Sighing, Kal slumped against the wall. "So what can you tell me?"

Looking at his nephew, he spoke quietly. "I can tell you that we averted something really, really horrible today."

Kal stared at him for a long moment and then nodded. "Well, I guess I'll take it, then."

CHAPTER 85

Maeve stood with Norah along the back entrance of the D.E.A.D. facility. She still couldn't believe everything that had happened.

It was insane to think that Kecksburgs had been under someone else's control. They still didn't know who it was. Norah had initiated a kill order for all Kecksburgs held by the US government, although even Norah didn't know how many there were. She'd launched an investigation, but the government's wheels moved slowly.

The base was still in an uproar over the infiltration. Four security individuals had been seriously injured in the attack, but thankfully none had been killed.

Norah glanced over at her and nodded at the containment unit at her feet. "You get that right to Tilda."

She had said the same thing at least twice so far. But Maeve couldn't blame her for repeating it. These orbs had created all sorts of drama. So she simply nodded again. "Absolutely. And you'll let me know when you figure out who was controlling them?"

"Assuming I find out, yes. I figure you deserve to know

who's out there and who's causing trouble, especially if you guys are going to be the ones holding on to the last remaining orb."

Picking up the orb, Maeve adjusted the straps on her shoulder. Once again, the orb felt heavy in her pack.

It was decided that they needed to get the orb off the D.E.A.D. base as quickly as possible. Maeve and Sammy would take it back to the R.I.S.E. facility, and it would stay there for the foreseeable future. After all, the other orb had been safely in the care of R.I.S.E. for decades. This one should be safe there as well.

A sonic boom rang out above them, and Maeve looked up as Sammy appeared in the sky. "There's my ride. Take care of yourself, Norah."

"You too, Maeve," Norah said, her eyes looking serious.

And Maeve couldn't blame her. A lot had happened in a very short time period, and if Maeve was reading the situation correctly, it looked like they had just opened up a whole new front in a whole new war.

She crossed the field to where Sammy stood with his long leathery wings spread out behind him.

In her gut, she knew the road ahead was going to be tough, even though they had more fighters this time. So maybe, just maybe, luck was on their side, and they had prevented this new front from opening up entirely.

CHAPTER 86

SVENTE, NORWAY

The sonic boom rang out across the sky. Next to Matilda, Pearl Huen raised her head to watch Sammy's progress. Pearl had been Matilda's right-hand woman for years now. Small, standing at only five feet, she was a power pack of knowledge and efficiency. Matilda cast an appraising gaze over her, glad to see the color had returned to her cheeks. She had been unwell this morning but seemed to have fully recovered.

A cool wind ruffled Matilda's hair as she stood waiting for the silver orb. To say she was worried about the events of the last few days would be an understatement. The silver orb had sat quietly in storage in her care for decades. She still did not know its purpose, but in her gut, she'd known it was important.

Then a few weeks ago, it had started to vibrate. Then a second one appeared and was grabbed. Sending the orb with Maeve to see if they could finally figure out what it was had been the most logical approach. Maeve and Greg had proven in the past to be a formidable team. Tilda was convinced they would be able to ferret out the orb's purpose.

But they had never gotten the chance. Tilda had only received a small briefing on the events that had transpired at the D.E.A.D. facility, but she knew there was more to the story. Maeve was returning with a second orb. It would never leave here again. Tilda still intended on having Greg and Maeve examine the orb. After the events of the last few days, understanding their purpose was even more critical. This time, however, Greg would have to come here to do so.

Up ahead, Sammy slowed enough that Tilda could make out Maeve in his arms. Tilda had encouraged Maeve to go out into the field again, knowing how difficult it was to sit back after years of being thrown into this world. No one was a better example of that than herself. Officially, she no longer ran R.I.S.E., but she couldn't stay away. She loved Adam, and she loved Sebastian as well. But she was not content to simply stay home and live a normal life. She never would be. Adam understood that, and he was more than happy to be the stay-at-home parent, leaving Tilda to wade once again into this world.

Extending seven feet, Sammy's strong wings cut through the sky, sending a batch of chilly air toward Tilda and Pearl before touching down ten feet away from them with a little running stop. Allowing Maeve's feet to touch down, he held on to her for a few moments until she had her balance. From what Tilda understood, Sammy's form of dimensional travel wreaked havoc on the inner ear.

Smiling up at Sammy, Maeve nodded her thanks as Sammy stepped back. With a nod at Tilda and Pearl, he took off back into the sky, heading toward the coast where his home was. Tilda watched him go, awed yet again that this was her life. Who knew the girl from Huntsville, Alabama, who worried that she'd never get out of her tiny hometown or do anything exciting, would end up in love with a being not of this earth and surrounded by others.

Maeve strode across the ground toward them, her gait confident. Tilda searched her for signs of injury, but she looked unharmed. In fact, she looked determined. Tilda had to hide her smile. Yes, she and Maeve were cut from the same cloth. The quiet life did not suit either of them.

As Maeve drew closer, Tilda narrowed her eyes. Perhaps she'd spoken too soon. There were dark circles under Maeve's eyes. When Maeve met her gaze, Tilda asked, "Are you all right?"

"I'm fine. Just annoyed that we let the other orbs get taken."

"It sounds like you had no indication the doctor was working against you."

"True, but I still don't like that we got played." Maeve slipped the backpack from her shoulders and crouched down on the ground

Tilda turned and waved a soldier who held a containment unit forward.

Unzipping the backpack, Maeve pulled out the orb as the soldier unsnapped the containment unit. Tilda stared at the object. It looked identical to the one that she'd had in her possession for so long.

Maeve handed it to Tilda, who stared at it. Shock flashed through her at the feel of it, along with a wave of sadness. "This one's warmer than the last."

"I think that's because it's newer," Maeve said with a heavy tone.

Tilda met her gaze. There was more to this story that Tilda had not been told. And that could not continue. But first things first. She placed the orb in the containment unit and snapped it shut before she turned to Pearl and the soldier. "See that it's stored safely while Maeve gives me a debriefing."

CHAPTER 87

The orb was safely in the containment unit next to her. Pearl couldn't help but dart more than a few glances at it. So close. She gripped her tablet tightly to keep from reaching for it.

Ahead, the R.I.S.E. facility stood. It was an architectural wonder. State-of-the-art security, innovation, and secrets all hidden behind bright white polymer walls.

The doors slid open as they approached, recognizing the security clearance of the implant beneath the skin at Pearl's wrist. Another security measure that similarly analyzed a number of biometrics to make sure that their people were working for them and not against them.

A necessary precaution after the actions of Martin Drummond.

The soldier started to head to the escalator, but Pearl shook her head. "This way." The soldier hesitated for a moment with a frown before following her.

Pearl moved quickly through the foyer, slipping her hand into her pocket. She hit a button as soon as she stepped into the hallway with the soldier at her side. The camera would loop the same scene unchanged in this hallway for the next five minutes.

She stopped at the first door on the right and quickly unlocked it. She swung the door open and nodded to the table in the middle of the room. "Place it up there, please."

Once again, the soldier hesitated, this time standing uncertainly at the room's threshold. "I thought we were supposed to take it down to Room 7C."

Pearl stared at him, raising an eyebrow. "Soldier, are you the second in the command of the R.I.S.E. base? Do you know more than I do?"

The man shook his head and quickly placed the containment box on the table. "No, ma'am. Sorry, ma'am."

She nodded and indicated the door. "Close the door behind you and stay outside. No one enters."

He snapped off a salute and stepped back outside, closing the door behind him.

Waiting a beat, Pearl took a breath, the hair along her arms rising. So very close. She walked over to the closet in the corner of the room and pulled out an identical containment case. She snapped it open and made sure that the replica silver orb was inside. Placing it on the table, she picked up the original and put it in the closet.

She glanced at her watch and then pulled out the encrypted phone.

I have it. I will run a view tonight at the previously discussed location, she typed before slipping it back into her pocket. She didn't need to wait for a response.

Placing the replica back in the containment case, she snapped it shut before she walked over to the door and pulled it open. "Okay, you can take the case now. Let's head down to 7C."

The soldier grabbed the case with a questioning look but didn't say anything more as he followed Pearl down the hall.

CHAPTER 88

CLAY, NEW YORK

The funeral had been lovely. Isis had had a surprising number of friends. People traveled from all over the country to attend. As Greg had stood in the church, he couldn't help but wonder if any of them were also Primevals.

He knew that Mitch would know if they were. Although, he wasn't sure at this moment he would care. Mitch sat in the front pew with his children and Maya. Marissa was curled up in his lap, leaning into him. She didn't really understand what was happening. She knew her grandmother was dead, but the permanence of that was lost on her.

And if not for that stupid blade, it wouldn't have been permanent at all.

The blade had been analyzed and found to be made of a very rare type of meteor rock, along with three strands of elements that also could not be identified. There were four more of the meteor blades in museum collections around the globe.

Or at least, there used to be. Just this morning, Greg had

received a package with one of the blades. A short note from Tilda simply stated: JUST IN CASE. Tilda had been made aware of what the blade could do, and Greg had no doubt she had collected all the blades for safekeeping.

Greg had the knife in a sheath on his belt. He would be wearing it at all times until they determined whether or not Set was truly returning. The choir broke into "The Lord Bless You and Keep You," cutting into Greg's thoughts and sending him to his feet with the rest of the people in attendance. He watched as Mitch and his family walked down the aisle behind the empty casket.

No one knew she wasn't inside. Mitch couldn't risk an undertaker looking at her body. And he needed to make sure no one dug her up in the future to examine her, should they realize she wasn't human. So Isis's remains had already been cremated, per Mitch's wish. He could not stand the idea of her being laid to rest in parts.

But he had wanted the church ceremony for his family. They needed that closure. And a burial was important to Maya, so Mitch figured one more deception would be all right. Norah had taken care of the details setting everything up. But Greg knew the weight of the deception was weighing on him.

The rest of the church filed out and waited as the casket was placed in the hearse. Then Maya turned to everyone as it drove off. "There will be some refreshments in the church basement. We hope you will all join us."

People broke off, some heading for the parking lot, but most headed toward the basement. Maeve tugged on Greg's shirt. "You want to head in?"

Greg cast a glance at Mitch, who'd walked off alone toward the small man-made lake behind the church. "I'll meet you guys inside," he said, nodding toward where Chris Garrigan stood speaking with Norah, Max, and Kaylee.

Skirting around the few people chatting in low tones, Greg

followed Mitch's hunched shape. Mitch took a seat on a bench, staring out at the water. Greg slowed his steps, not wanting to intrude, but feeling like he needed to be around if Mitch needed him. So he leaned against a tree to wait.

After a few minutes, Mitch called out. "I know you're there, Greg."

Greg winced as he stepped forward. "I wasn't trying to hide. I was just giving you your space."

"I'm okay."

Greg reached the bench and glanced at the empty spot next to Mitch. Mitch nodded, and Greg took a seat. "You're not okay. And that's okay. I just wanted you to know you're not alone."

The loss in Mitch's gaze tore at Greg's heart. "But I am. For the first time in my very long existence, alone is exactly what I am."

Greg didn't have any answer for that. Any reply would feel like it was diminishing the loss that Mitch had suffered, so he stayed silent.

Finally, Mitch let out a sigh. "Sorry. I know you mean well, but I'm not very good company right now."

Stretching out his legs, Greg crossed his feet at the ankles. "That's okay. You've never been great company."

A chuckle escaped Mitch. "Thanks."

Greg grinned. "You're welcome."

The two of them slipped into an easier, more contented silence. Greg watched as a family of ducks swam along the edge of the lake before climbing out.

"Has there been any news from R.I.S.E.?" Mitch asked.

Greg hesitated and then told Mitch about the package that had arrived this morning from Tilda.

"That's good. I'm glad you have that."

Greg slid open his suit coat and pulled out a slim leather case. He handed it over to Mitch.

Mitch took it, raising his eyebrows.

Greg shrugged. "It took me a little while to get a replica made, but I switched out the one at headquarters. I figure if anyone needs to keep one of these blades handy, it's you."

Mitch looked down at the gift in his hands and then back at Greg. "Thank you."

And Greg knew that Mitch wasn't just thanking him for this gift, but for everything. He nodded back. "You're welcome."

Mitch cleared his throat, staring out over the water. "I'm going to tell Maya everything."

"You are?"

Mitch nodded. "It's going to be tough for her to hear, but she needs to know, especially if Set is coming back."

"But we don't know that he is. Everything's been quiet since we sent your mother's orb to R.I.S.E. I think we stopped him. I think we're good."

Mitch looked over at Greg and then back out over the water. "I hope you're right. I really do."

CHAPTER 89

SEDONA, ARIZONA

TWO WEEKS LATER

The old truck was in need of some struts as it headed across the uneven ground toward the Doorway of the Gods in Sedona.

Earl Oakley pulled the truck to a stop and then leaned over to the passenger seat and pulled the small bag over. He had to use a little extra muscle to pick it up because it was awfully heavy. He slipped it over his back and staggered under the weight.

The contents of the bag weighed over one hundred pounds. Taking a deep breath, he headed toward the natural archway created by red rock.

Or at least, that was what the humans thought, that it was a natural creation.

But it wasn't.

He supposed he could give them credit for recognizing that there was something different about the location. The name,

Doorway of the Gods, indicated that they understood at some level its original purpose, once acting as stargate that allowed travel between this planet and others.

Stopping a few feet from the opening of the archway, he scanned the surrounding area. It was quiet. There wasn't a soul in sight. Convinced he was alone, he slid the bag from his shoulders and then picked up each of the silver orbs and placed them in a line along the front of the opening.

Anticipation rolled through him. So close. A hum filled the air, causing the hairs on his body to rise. An electrical current sparked to life in the first orb. It rolled around the orb in a streak of lightning before shooting toward the next. The same process happened in each of the others until the orbs were all connected by arcs of light.

Earl took another step back as the orbs began to glow a bright white. Then another arc of light burst from each of the orbs toward the opening. But instead of cutting through, they all coalesced at one point in the dead center of the archway.

The archway immediately filled with a cloudlike substance, blocking the view from the other side. Slowly, the opaque substance began to shift.

But instead of the Sedona landscape, Earl found himself looking at the inside of a ship. There was a long silver table in the center of the room with tall monitors and flashing lights beyond it. Laying on that table was a body.

He leaned forward to get a better look just as a flash of light burst from the archway. It slammed into Earl, sending him flying back. Pain radiated through his back as he crashed into the hard rocky ground and the world turned black.

———

"Sir? Sir, are you all right?"

Earl Oakley blinked staring up at the unfamiliar woman in

the park ranger uniform. Concern and apprehension were on her face as she looked down at him.

He frowned. Why was she looking down at him? He became aware of rough objects cutting into his back. He sat up slowly, and the ranger took a step back, her hand on the gun on her waist. That was when he caught sight of the other ranger.

He turned his head to take in the barren landscape. Tall red rocks surrounded him. More striking in front of him was a massive archway. Even though Earl wasn't a religious man, there was something that felt almost spiritual about this location.

Which, if he knew where he was and how he'd gotten here, he might have appreciated. He licked his lips, the first stirrings of fear starting to mix with the confusion. "What the—? Where am I?"

"You're at the Doorway of the Gods."

The name meant nothing to him. And suddenly he felt cold. He didn't recognize any of this.

"What's your name, sir?"

"Earl, Earl Oakley. You said I'm at God's Doorway? Where the heck is that?"

"Sedona."

The name was a little more familiar to him. "Sedona? I'm in Sedona?"

The rangers exchanged a look. "What's the last thing you remember, sir?" the male ranger asked.

Earl shook his head. "I don't know. I mean, I was heading to the quarry, and that's it, that's all I remember."

"What quarry?" the female ranger asked.

"Lanscombe Quarry," he said.

"And where is the quarry located?" she asked.

"Over on Broderick."

"What town?"

"Hopkinsville."

The female ranger stared at him and spoke slowly. "What state is Hopkinsville in?"

Frowning at the woman, he answered just as slowly. "New York."

Eyebrows raised, the female ranger looked at the male ranger. He nodded and stepped away, pulling out his radio.

Earl shook his head, his thoughts slow, but then he finally realized where he'd heard the name Sedona before. His sister's in-laws had retired there a few years back. "Did you say I'm in Sedona? Isn't that …" He looked around at the red rocks that dotted the desert landscape around him. There was definitely nothing like this in New York. "I'm in Arizona?"

"Yes, sir. Do you know what day it is?"

Finally, a question he could answer with faith that his answer was right. "Tuesday."

The ranger shook her head. "I'm afraid it's Friday, sir."

Earl's jaw dropped open. "No, that's not possible. I mean, I was just on my way to work. I know it's Tuesday."

"I'm sorry, sir, but it is Friday." The apprehension was gone from the female ranger's face, concern now the primary emotion being displayed.

But Earl barely registered it. "I lost three days?" he asked, but he was no longer looking at the rangers. And then his jaw slammed shut as another thought rolled through his mind.

Not again.

CHAPTER 90

THE RESURRECTION SHIP

It had been so long since Set had been free. Even now, in his ethereal state, rage poured through him. What right did they have to banish him to this impotent existence?

His memories of the glory of his first incarnation rolled through him, followed by the other ones when he'd had no memory of his legacy, of his birthright. They had kept him from remembering his past lives, but now they all returned to him in a rush.

His race was meant to rule this world. *He* was meant to rule this world. But for eons, he had been kept from the memories that would have made that possible.

Even now, he felt the need to return to a physical body. The need had been growing this last year. It had been only pure force of will that had kept him from giving in.

Because once he gave in, he would be a slave to the process. He would be reborn a child, with no memory of the glory of his true state. He would live in ignorance of his true calling, once again believing he was nothing more than a simple human being.

Anger at his Primeval brothers and sisters gave him strength. It allowed him to hold on when others would have given in.

This time, it would be different. He would make sure of it. He just needed to hold on a little bit longer, and then he would be fully restored. He could feel the weakening of the chains on his memories. His first exposure to the orb had made all of this possible. And with each death of a Primeval, those chains weakened even more. Now he could feel that he was so very close, even as the pull to the body on the table grew in intensity.

Nephthys had left just a short while ago to complete the last of their steps. She was holding off on her own reincarnation to guarantee his own. Set could not go himself. It would tax him too much, and he was just barely holding on.

It galled him to be weakened in such a way. But soon he would be free, and he would make those who had driven him to such a pitiful state pay for what they had done.

A buzzing sounded along the edge of the ship, followed by the opening of the stargate.

Finally.

Energy burst through the stargate, filling the ship, searching for Set. He welcomed it in. The last restraints around his memory slipped away.

Set surged toward the body on the table. His essence filled up every cell. Pain roared through him as the body awoke. He had forgotten about this part. The pain that came with each new awakening. But this time, he embraced it, knowing it was the birth pains to his final freedom.

Wave after wave of pain rolled through him as the memories from a lifetime of ignorance filled his mind. He gritted his teeth at the indignity of it all.

INTO THE DARK

And finally, blessedly, the pain stopped.

He opened his eyes, seeing the tall towers of the data center of the reincarnation ship. A glance to the right showed the reemergence pod where the bodies were created. For a flash of a moment, he considered destroying it so none of the other Primevals could reincarnate. But that would leave him stranded as well, so he pulled that rage back. He would make sure they couldn't reincarnate another way, and he would take his time doing so to enjoy the process as they screamed in pain.

But the Primevals were not the only ones who would pay. The memories from his latest incarnation were freshest in his mind. He sorted through them, focusing on the faces of those who had thwarted him at every turn.

They would pay as well.

He sat up, waiting a moment for the strength to return to his legs before he stepped off the table. These bodies were not that dissimilar from their original form. He walked over to the staging area and pulled on the clothes that had been manufactured for him. Then he stepped to the long mirror.

Even with the dark pants and fitted sweater, his muscle tone was clear. He reached up and pulled his long dark hair back, pulling a hair tie from a shelf next to him that had been created for him as well.

With his hair pulled back, he felt comforted at the sight of the reflection in the mirror. This was a face that he knew well. It was a face that would help him with the next stage of his plan.

It was a face that would strike terror in the heart of his enemies. And terror was exactly what he intended to unleash.

He shifted his jaw, his mouth feeling dry. He tried to speak, but it did not work right away. That was always an issue for the first few moments. Finally, the moisture returned to his mouth. He stared at his reflection in the mirror and smiled.

"Welcome back, Martin."

ENJOYED THE A.L.I.V.E. SERIES?

YOU'LL LOVE THE BELIAL SERIES

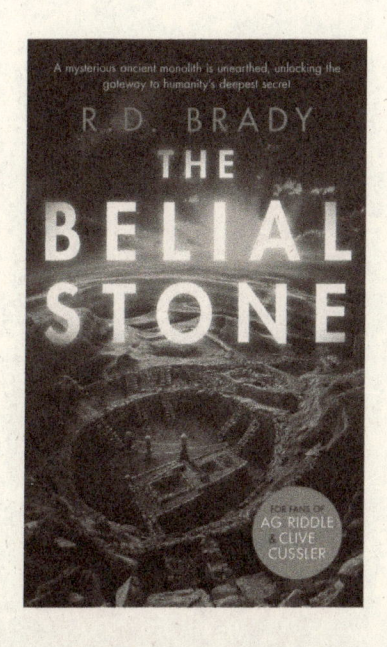

An ancient secret. A deadly pursuit. The fate of humanity hangs in the balance.

When an ancient monolith is unearthed in Montana, it unlocks a secret that could unravel human history.

Archaeologist Drew Masters' murder plunges Professor Delaney McPhearson into a dangerous quest for truth, while ex-Navy SEAL Jake Rogan investigates his brother's disappearance.

Together, they uncover a conspiracy tied to the groundbreaking work on Gobekli Tepe, revealing a hidden truth at the core of human existence.

FACT OR FICTION

Thank you for reading Into the Dark. I hope you enjoyed it.

A lot of facts went into the crafting of Into the Dark. Many of them are listed below.

The Black Knight Satellite.
   The Black Knight satellite is real . . . sort of. Or at least the rumor about their being a UFO that has been orbiting the Earth for years is real. According to NASA, the object known as the Black Knight Satellite is actually a thermal blanket that fell from the space shuttle back in 1998. Conspiracy theorists however argue that it is a UFO and that the thermal blanket argument is an attempt to keep the truth from the public.

Hurricane Deck.
   The Hurricane Deck at Niagara Falls is also real and fun. I really enjoyed my visit there. And, the Canadian side of the falls is much more built up than the US side. If you get a chance , you really should visit.

Egyptian Mythology.

The story of Set, Osiris, Horus, Isis and Nephthys is true, at least the ancient part. According to the story, Set was jealous of his brother and killed him, spreading his body parts across the globe. Devastated, Isis with the aid of her sister, reconstituted Osiris enough to allow her to get pregnant. Horus was born and hidden from his uncle. When he was of age, he challenged his uncle for the rule. Eventually he succeeded.

Silver Orbs.

Believe it or not, the silver orbs are real. For years, there have been reports of metal spheres falling from the sky. They have been reported in Peru, Great Britain, Russia, Vietnam, and even the United States. Each time they crashed to Earth, they did so as a fireball.

I have of course, made them look a lot more otherworldly than they actually are. In all likelihood, the silver orbs are space junk that has finally crashed to Earth. Although in one case, the silver orb did react a little strangely. Check the next section on the Crumb family for more information on that.

The Crumb Family.

The Crumb Family is not real . . . but the Betz family is. Back in 1974, the Betz family of Florida found a strange silver orb on their property. It was reported to be a little smaller than a bowling bowl, but heavier at 22 pounds

According to the family, the sphere acted of its own accord, moving and making noises. It would roll by itself, vibrate and hum. It reacted to sounds such as a guitar being played. When rolled it would sometimes stop halfway to the other person and return to the person who started the rolling. It was unblemished and moved more intensely in sunlight. Like the silver orbs in *Into the Dark*, it was reported to have been clean, free of corrosion, and shiny. The Navy x-rayed it but were unable to get an image. Radio waves were however recorded being emitted from the object and a magnetic field was also noted to surround it.

Tesla and UFO.

The anecdote about Tesla believing he had received a radio signal from space is actually true. The signal Tesla uncovered had a uniform pattern to it, convincing Tesla they were alien in origin. The year following the discovery when asked about man's greatest achievement he said he may have already accomplished it: making contact with another world.

Earth's Magnetic Field.

There is actually a growing dent in the Earth's magnetic field located over South America and the southern Atlantic Ocean. The dent allows solar particles through which interferes with technology, in some cases knocking it out completely. Because of the risk, satellite operators regularly shut down satellite components when they travel through the anomaly so they don't risk losing key instruments or the whole satellite.

Daily Meteors.

As Maeve mentioned, over 48.5 million tons of meteoric material that hit the Earth's atmosphere every day. Almost all of them are vaporized by our atmosphere. On average about seventeen of them get through each day.

Reincarnation Ship.

As far as I know there is no reincarnation ship orbiting the Earth.

Astronaut Scott Kelly's Photo of a UFO.

Astronaut Scott Kelly did take a photo while on the

International Space Station that sent up alarm bells across certain circles. The photo was of India at night but what captured people's attention was the cigar shaped object in the sky in the upper right corner of the image. According to the official report, it is part of the space station that Astronaut Kelly caught.

King Tut Dagger.

A dagger whose blade was crafted from a meteorite was found in King Tut's tomb.

Alien Implants.

I'm not sure what to say about this one. Reports of alien abductions also sometimes include information about unknown implants found as well. In one case, the implant was found to be made of rare earth elements and to emit an electromagnetic frequency suggesting it could be used as a tracking device.

Thank you again for reading *Into the Dark*. If you haven't done so yet, please leave a review.

Until next time,
RD

ABOUT THE AUTHOR

Author, Criminologist, Terrorism Expert, Jeet Kune Do Black Sash, Runner, Dog Lover.

Amazon best-selling author R.D. Brady writes supernatural and science fiction thrillers. Her thrillers include ancient mysteries, unusual facts, non-stop action, and fierce women with heart.

Prior to beginning her writing career, RD Brady was a criminologist who specialized in life-course criminology and international terrorism. She's lectured and written numerous academic articles on the genetic influence on criminal behavior, factors that influence terrorist ideology, and delinquent behavior formation.

After visiting counter-terrorism units in Israel, RD returned home with a sabbatical in front of her and decided to write that book she'd been thinking about. Four years later she left academia with the publication of her first book, *The Belial Stone*, and hasn't looked back.